The Relics of Errus series

THE RELICS OF ERRUS

VOLUME 2

GORDON GREENHILL

ST. ASINUS
PUBLISHING

Plight of the Rôkan Boy
Copyright © 2021 by Gordon Greenhill
Published by St. Asinus Publishing
Rockford, MI
gordongreenhill.com

ISBN 978-0-9996795-3-1 (print)
ISBN 978-0-9996795-4-8 (ebook)

Editor: David Lambert
Cover design: Jeanette Gillespie
Interior design: Beth Shagene
Cover and interior illustrations: Elisabeth De Cocker/www.liefsbeth.com

Printed in the United States of America

First printing in 2021

For Asher Gordon
My own little Opsiercom,
who continues to delight and amaze

∿

Contents

The Errusian Pantheon

♀ Merris

She who lights the heavens and is known as Echinda in Mulek, the eternal mother; to whom is entrusted the hearth, home, and all things hospitable. Protector of women in childbirth. She is present in every green tree and the fruits of the earth. The bear is her consort.

♏ Vercandrus ♏

The great father and protector of all. Sovereign of war, provision, and strength. He carries the sword, and the boar is his consort.

↗ Emerrus

The younger brother in whose care are the weak of the world. Protector of the cunning laborer and the resourceful poor; to him are entrusted all the vulcani—the fire lizard, the wyrm, and all who dwell within the living flame. He carries the hammer, and the serpent is his consort.

☿ Berdduca

Firstborn. Guide to the prosperous. Protector of merchants and all commerce. To her are given all the gnomi, such as the dwarf, the woodwoose, the giant, and all the great host who dwell below. She wears the diamond between her horns, and the badger is her consort.

♐ Thierra

She dwells upon the surf. Goddess of fortune, adventure, gladness, and all the waters of Errus. Mother to all the undini who dwell within her—the merfolk and kraken, the water sprites and the kelpie. Preserver of sailors upon the boundless sea, she lifts the goblet of cheer, and all the fish of the sea escort her.

♃ Avonia

Fairest of the daughters of Merris, she dwells in halls of air. All music, arts, youth, and innocence are hers. The sylphi are her children—the fairy, the roc, the imp, and all the creatures of the sky. She bears the harp, and the hawk is her consort.

♌ Errus

The Eldest. The World. He is common to all the longaevi and binds them together. And all justice, law, nobility and courtly grace is his. Guardian of kings and kingdoms and all official service. He wears the crown, and the panther is his consort.

From Dr. Gerundius Bask, Berd. 1ˢᵗ. *Errulogia and Astrologia Omnibus: That is, the properties of the generative elemental natures and of the heavenly emissaries and their relations as they exist in perfect order and by degree.* 4r.

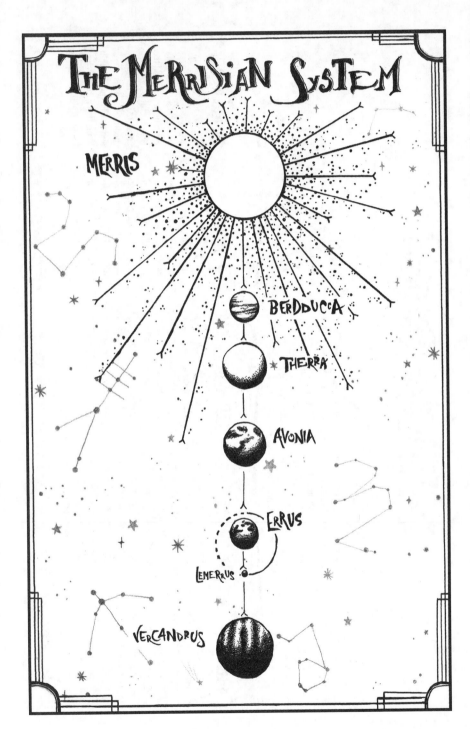

Sonji's Preface

The manner in which the Rokan people entered the saga was indicative of their social status in Garlandium. From ancient times—almost from the moment of their "late" arrival in Errus—they were an oppressed people, marginalized, without rights or representation outside their own tribal lands west of the Aracadian Mountains. Known by their hair dyed white—the albsignum, as it was called—they play an unrecorded role in Garlandian history as farmhands, foundry laborers, servants, and lower-class merchants—which is to say, they made society livable for others while receiving almost no credit for it. Even in the foundry city of Farwell, where they outnumbered Garlandian citizens three to one, they were regarded as a nuisance, despite the essential roles they filled. Thus the Rokan part of the prophecy's fulfillment was a surprise to everyone. That they even *had* a role in it may have been the greatest surprise. As I note repeatedly throughout this volume, that the vanguard of this shunned people's rise should have been an orphaned whelp from the mountains, bereft of every social grace, now seems entirely appropriate given the particular role he would one day be asked to play.

DR. SONJI RAZHAMANÌAH, *An Attempted History of the Halighyllian Prophecies and Their Fulfillment*, Vol 2: *Legends from the Dawn of Rokan*, 30r.

BOOK 1

A Host of Incredible Stories

Oh Rokan people, sore oppressed.
Undignified and dispossessed.
You must choose between two wrongs—
Subsistence in your tribal land
Or slavery at Garlandish hand.
Your only grace—your native songs.

FRANKO RAZHAMANÌAH,
"Rokan Woe" in *Songs from
the Rokan Highlands.*

Chapter 1

The ragged boy tore through the underbrush and up the hill, his heart knocking like a woodpecker on a tree.

"This just ain't fair!" Sweat dropped into his eyes and stung, but he clambered upward almost on hands and knees. His pursuer was gaining. He didn't know what it was, but it was certainly animal, not human. This was worse. Humans couldn't smell for anything. They were noisy and easy to avoid. Animals were neither.

He wouldn't have even known the thing had picked up his scent but for that chattering squirrel in the tree. He hadn't understood a thing it said—nobody ever did. Squirrels talked so fast it was hardly even speech. But its little nose had pointed frantically behind him, and he'd had the distinct impression it was telling him to run. In his wanderings, he'd learned to trust the word of wild animals.

Wild things look out for one another.

The moment he'd bolted, he'd heard a rush of cracking twigs behind him and knew the pursuit was hot. Now he heard the tinkling of the stream at the same moment he blundered into it. *Aw, man! My boots! My beautiful boots!* Most Rokan boys didn't even have shoes, and he'd been rather proud of himself for liberating these last month from the doorstep of a wealthy-looking Garlandish plantation house out west near Farwell. He was clothed more or less in rags, the boots were the nicest thing he owned. Now they'd be soaked and squishy.

No time to think about that now. He pelted across the splashing brook, hoping it would throw the brute off his scent. He thrust his way through the brambles and bracken as fast as he could for a hundred yards or so before stopping to pant and listen.

He had no idea how old he was. Eight? Nine? Maybe he was only seven. No, he just had to be eight. He couldn't bear the thought of being only seven. He'd already spent a whole year pretending he was seven. *I am eight,* he thought, realizing that if his luck failed him now, it might be as old as he ever got.

The wood was silent—not a bird singing or insect buzzing. He took the silence as good news and began picking his way forward as quietly as he could. Still no sound of pursuit. Maybe he'd lost the thing. He came out of the thick brush into a little clearing, where a large gray boulder sat.

"That'll work," he said in the slow, unsophisticated drawl of his people. Since none of the trees were climbable, he thought of trying to get on top of the rock. As he rounded it, however, he started. Maybe fate had not totally abandoned him. A small structure—like a lean-to—had been built up against that side of the boulder. Made with sticks and branches—ages ago by the looks of it—it had collapsed at one end, and the wood was rotted. But it was clearly man-made. He took this as a sign that human habitation was near. *It won't come near a farm.*

He threw himself down on the threshold and began fishing in his pocket. "Maybe I'll just sleep here and look for that blasted city tomorrow. And then—" he smiled to himself—"I'll find my mom!"

He pulled a small object out of his pocket and held it gingerly in his hand. He called it his "firebrand," the only thing he owned by right in the whole world.

Movement at the edge of the clearing caught his eye. To his horror, a large cat prowled out of the undergrowth. No house cat, this. It was a panther, black—so black it looked purple in the late afternoon light. It was looking at him as if he were a ham in a grocer's window.

It took a step toward him.

"Nice kitty. Good kitty." He knew better than to expect a reply. He had never heard of a cat speaking so much as a word. Oh, not because they were too dumb to speak, like the sheep back home. Rather, he had the impression that cats didn't think humans were worth speaking to, and he was sure *this* cat wasn't looking for conversation.

Seated as he was, running wasn't an option. So he did the only thing he could. He held out his firebrand, quieted his mind, and thought about heat . . . fire . . . smoke. It grew warm in his hand, then hot. Then a little jet of flame burst up from it and hovered an inch above his palm.

The panther stopped. It might have become stone but for the slow swish of its tail.

The boy concentrated, and the flame grew till it was like a small torch, burning away above his hand.

He stood.

The panther backed a step.

He took a step toward it, thrusting the flame forward. He hissed at the cat.

The panther shied and backed again.

"Get gone, you old tom, or by Angish, I'll set you to blaze! He*yah!*"

The panther—so black it looked purple—turned and bounded away into the brush.

The boy extinguished the flame with a thought and fell in a heap, panting again. He would light a campfire immediately, keep it going all night, and sleep with one eye open . . . if he slept at all. Sleepless nights outside were nothing new to him.

He stroked his firebrand lovingly. It was a small, flat, roughly triangular piece of gray metal, plain but for a small and meaningless etching on one side. It looked to him like a crossbow or maybe an axe, but he couldn't read, so it might be a letter of some kind. It didn't matter. This little trinket was his only clue to who he was, and—he grinned—it was the only one like it in the whole world.

Chapter 2

He was seriously reconsidering his plan. He stood looking up at the arched gates of Halighyll, while being pushed and bumped this way and that by the throng of merchants, soldiers, and travelers moving in and out of the city.

Only by luck was he here at all. He'd have wandered straight east through the forest, missing the city altogether, if that stinking cat hadn't turned up. When he'd awakened that morning, he knew better than to go back the way he'd come and risk running into the panther again, so he went the other way, north. Before long he'd stumbled out of the forest onto a bluff looking down on the old city. He'd stood there slack-jawed for several minutes. Halighyll was huge! Twice the size of his hometown of Farwell. Bigger even than the river port of Umbra, which had taken his breath away, but this . . .

Now he stood before the gates, the hood of his cloak pulled up, concealing his hair. At one time it had been dyed white, as was required of all Rokan living in Garlandium. Only the last inch or so was still a dingy gray, and he would remove that as soon as he got his hands on a pair of shears. Once the last trace of the albsignum was gone, he could pass as a Garlandish boy . . . he hoped. That was dangerous, though. A Rokan caught trying to pass himself off as Garlandish-born was guaranteed some really unpleasant consequences.

Till now this had been a straight-forward quest to find his long-lost mother. Now he felt paralyzed. Everything here was so much larger and more intimidating—the walls, the pillars, the towers. It staggered the mind. The old woman back home—a bodacha, they called her—had only said he would find answers "in the city of the holy hill," which everybody knew meant Halighyll. But she hadn't said what he should do once he got there. Did she even know how big this city was? Had she been only joking with him after all?

He hadn't really considered what he would do when he got here. Had he been expecting someone to meet him at the gate and answer all his questions as they ambled down the street together? How foolish that sounded now.

He turned around to leave just as a flock of sheep encircled him. As the bleating mass banged against his legs, he was drawn through the gates against his will. "Get on, wastrel!" shouted the shepherd behind him. He didn't know if the scruffy man with white hair was talking to him or to the sheep till he was thumped by the end of a staff. "Get a move on, you little weed, or get out the way!" The shepherd brandished his stick again. It took the boy a moment to fight his way out of the bleating flock.

Once through the gate, however, the crowd quickly dispersed in the wide streets. And before he'd gone a hundred steps, he could feel his confidence returning. He paused to breathe deeply and take stock of his surroundings. He was approaching two large hills, one on each side of the road. Above him, a great arch spanned the road like a bridge. That must be the temple. It was impressive in its own grimy way. No, not impressive. Just big. He'd seen finer workmanship on the ramparts of the great foundry in Farwell. The stone here was crumbling, and the whole thing looked ready to collapse at any moment. The thought made him quicken his pace as he passed under the arch.

He soon came to a section of the city heavily occupied by street merchants and costermongers. The wide road was crowded with carts and wagons and people rummaging through piles of fruit, leatherwork, and tools. This was encouraging. He knew what a market was good for—a square meal. He ducked behind the first set of stalls and emerged from the other end holding an orange and a meat roll. He slide immediately behind another stall to avoid two soldiers passing by.

Most of the junk was familiar to him from back west. The only difference here was that the stalls were manned by a mixture of Garlandish and Rokan merchants. In Farwell, the Garlandish merchants had shops; only the Rokan set up in the streets this way. He even saw a few Mulkadese Guild-bonded master merchants, which he recognized by their long robes and tricornered cloth hats.

He paused in a section of tickers' stalls. These were far more entertaining than anything he'd seen back home—table after table of small delicate machines that gimballed and whorled on tiny pedestals. One seller was shouting to everyone who passed by that his invention would reproduce signatures automatically. Another was wearing a piece of complicated headgear that appeared to be massaging his gums, which although clever, prevented him from saying anything intelligible to his customers. A third was energetically squeezing the bulb on the end of a long complication of copper tubing that made honking sounds, but its purpose was never quite clear. Then there were the really big noisy machines that coughed and sputtered and spat steam into the air. They did everything from split wood to shoot arrows to churn butter.

He watched several demonstrations and even got to see a steam-driven wagon blow up. He was disappointed, for although watching the great boiler explode was exciting, he'd really wanted to see the wagon move itself without a horse.

He wandered along, eating his breakfast, and before he realized it he'd passed from the industrial to the religious. Merchants were now hawking statuettes, prayer beads, and relics. This interested him far less, but what he saw in the next stall made his mouth fall open in shock. It was only a tiny ceramic figurine, maybe six inches high, but the whole universe stopped when he saw it.

It was a figure of a boy holding a tiny torch above his head. A lizard encircled his neck, and the boy wore a maroon robe as if he was a priest. But none of this really registered, because carved into the base of the figure was a tiny character. It looked like an axe or a crossbow. It was, in fact, the same mark his firebrand bore.

He didn't know what the symbol was or what it meant, but he had to have the little statue. This might be the key to his quest, the very thing he'd been sent to Halighyll to find. He gave a careful sidelong glance. The stall's purveyor was haggling over a string of beads with a dour priest in brown robes. He bit his lip. This was not like nipping fruit out of a surplus basket behind a tent. This was an open theft of a costly artifact. But it had to be done.

With the single fluid movement of one stretching, he turned round slowly, palmed the figure and drew his sticky hand back into the sleeve of his cloak. He'd done it. He smiled and took a step.

"And just where you think you're off to?" A heavy hand clamped painfully onto his shoulder. He turned and found himself staring into the grinning face of a soldier. It was not a good-humored grin. He was caught.

"Um . . . I was just—"

"Captain!" came a high voice from somewhere behind the soldier. "We really are kind of in a hurry."

"Just a minute, dollies," called the soldier over his shoulder. "I've got a wee problem to attend to a minute." The soldier looked down at him and yanked the hood back from the boy's head, exposing the gray-fringed hair.

"Thought as much, ye dirty little Rokan Opsy!" The soldier shook him violently by the shoulders. The boy lost his grip on the statuette. It fell out of his sleeve and shattered on the stones.

Now the proprietor of the stall was at his shoulder. "Thief!" he cried, giving the boy a hard cuff on the back of the head. "Dolphus, that Opsy's got to pay for that statue what he broke."

He began to struggle in the soldier's iron grip.

"Here now. Settle down," The soldier struck him full in the face with his metal-shelled hand and knocked him to the pavement. The boy sat dazed, his ears ringing with the blow and his cheek already swelling painfully.

"Captain," came the voices from behind the soldier again. "Captain, what's going on?" Into the boy's blurred vision three small figures appeared and stood beside the soldier. It was just three girls.

"He's just a kid," said the smallest of them.

"What'd he do?" said the second.

"Don't fret it, missy. Nothing but a little trash to clean up." He grabbed the boy by the cloak and hoisted him back to his feet. "Just need to see if this little Opsy's got the means to pay for what he broke." He began to paw underneath his cloak, and in a moment his hand detected the lump that was the firebrand.

This cleared the boy's mind immediately, and he began to struggle again. The soldier yanked the firebrand free from his pocket and held it up before the shopkeeper. "Lookie here what I found. Well, Rufius, looks like your stall ain't the only one he's frequented today. We've got ourselves a regular—"

The three girls had uttered a collective cry. The oldest was pointing at the firebrand.

"Don't worry, dollies. We'll make sure it gets back to—"

But the distraction was all he needed. He aimed his kick squarely at the fork of the soldier's legs, and he did it with all his strength. The soldier barely made a sound as he crumpled to the street. But before his captor had reached the pavement, the boy had wrenched the firebrand out of his hand and was running down a side street.

The sound of booted feet echoed behind him. Other soldiers had witnessed his escape. He thought only of what was in front of him. He cut across a side street, through another small stock of stalls, and then back out to the main street. The soldiers wouldn't expect him to return that way . . . he hoped. If he could get across the main street to the buildings on the other side, he would probably be in the clear.

He squatted among a collection of hawkers with blankets spread out on the paving stones. He looked back up the street toward the place he'd been caught. The proprietor was helping the captain back to his feet. The three girls were still there too. He hoisted his cloak back over his head and, trying to look nonchalant, stepped out into the thoroughfare. He walked through the bustle of the main street without looking up.

Once across the street, he paused in the shadow of an alley to collect himself. *That was close . . . a bit too close.* He turned to make his final get away down the narrow street.

Without warning, something plowed into him from behind and drove him to the ground. He'd been tackled! He began to kick and struggle, and remarkably, he found his foe giving way. He looked up and was surprised to find himself staring into the eyes of one of the girls from the street. She was just a few years older than he was. Her blond hair was nearly as ragged as his own and had a tiny streak of purple running through it.

Still holding his legs, she looked him intently in the eyes. "Where'd you get it?" she demanded in a voice just above a whisper. He didn't understand. He fought and got one leg free, but she threw herself onto his chest, pinning the hand that held the firebrand to the ground. "Where did you get it?" she asked again with an urgency he didn't understand.

"It's . . . it's mine!" He tried to wrest his arm loose, but she was in control now. He fought but could not dislodge her. She was rummaging inside her shirt now, which, despite his panic, he noticed was strange. But he forgot about her clothing the moment she produced what she'd been hunting for—a small amulet on a chain around her neck. She held it out in front of his face. He stared at it in agonized surprise.

It was... It couldn't be . . . But it was. He turned his head and looked at his firebrand, clutched so tightly in his hand, then back to her pedant-thing. There was no mistake. She had one too.

She whispered again, more fiercely now. "Where did you get it? Tell me!"

He could not speak. His head swam. It couldn't be. He only vaguely heard the approaching boots of the soldiers, only vaguely felt himself being hoisted up and bound at the wrists. His most precious possession—his only possession—was ripped from his hands.

He hardly felt it. He'd thought he was special, that he had a destiny. Was this what the bodacha had wanted to show him? That he was as common and worthless as everyone had said? In his mind, he could almost hear the old crone laughing at him.

Chapter 3

Now bound hand and foot, he was thrown into the back of a wagon. He was guilty of theft, assaulting a soldier, and worst of all, of hiding his Rokan blood. The first two would have landed him before a magistrate, but the third would put him directly in lockup without hope of release. The Rokan had no legal rights in Garlandium save those that were economically beneficial to the Garlandish. He was rolling to his death as likely as not.

As the wagon left the business district, the sounds of the city grew less. Eventually a shadow passed overhead. The wagon clattered under a great arch and then stopped. Voices began speaking in low tones.

He was dragged out of the wagon by rough hands and set upright on his bound feet. He tottered slightly between the two soldiers who held him. He was in the courtyard of what looked like another temple. Nowhere as grand as the one on the two hills, this one looked even older and more decrepit. The lofty tower that dominated the courtyard looked ready to fall down.

The captain was arguing with the three girls.

"But, Captain, you don't understand. It is absolutely vital that Whinsom see him. Please, just let us—"

"You're right, missy. I don't understand. That boy's nothing but a worthless Opsy. He has nothing of value except this here bauble." He waved the firebrand in front of them.

Rage welled up in the boy. Rage at the soldier for taking his treasure—rage at the girls who stared at it with greedy eyes.

"I tell you what—" the soldier smiled indulgently at them—"if you want this trinket, just say so. You're welcome to it. I don't have the time to find where he stole it from. But I *have* to take the little brute in to have the justice done to him."

The oldest girl was glad enough to take the firebrand from the soldier, but to the boy's surprise they didn't stop their pleading to take him before this "Whinsom." The youngest girl, who looked about his age, was the only one who didn't participate in the conversation. Rather, she looked around the courtyard aimlessly, taking in whatever was to be seen.

The captain finally threw his hands up in the air. "Fine, fine! I cannot fight the both of you at the same time. I surrender. Take the little wretch, but you make sure and tell Whin that it's on his own head if he wakes up with his throat cut." He turned to the soldiers. "Cut him loose. He's their problem now." One of the soldiers removed the ropes from his ankles, but to his frustration, his hands remained tied.

As the wagon rattled away toward the garrison, the boy was left standing by himself in its dusty wake. When he turned around, he jumped. The three girls were standing right behind him.

The oldest was looking at him with pity in her eyes. "What's your name?"

He hated her instantly. "What's it to you?" He spat on the ground in front of her. He wasn't afraid of them.

The middle one exploded. "And you're welcome! Geez, we should have left him with Dolphus. Come on, we've got to show this thing to Whinsom."

He hated her too. He would have spat again, but his mouth was so dry. He was thinking about making a break for it, but he had no idea where to run.

"Tell you what," said the oldest one. Then, realizing he wasn't really paying attention, she tapped him on the forehead. "I'll make you a deal. You promise to come with us to meet someone important—someone not like the soldiers—and I'll cut your hands loose and give this back to you." And she held out the firebrand.

"Oh lordie!" The middle one put her hand over her eyes. "Eli, I'm not tackling him again."

"Anna, will you shut up and let me handle it," Eli said through gritted teeth.

Anna shuffled her feet and mumbled, "Last time you *handled it*, we were almost murdered by a psycho dwarf."

He knew how this would go. Once he got his hands free, he'd grab the firebrand and bolt. And no way in Angish was he letting her tackle him again.

When he nodded his "agreement," the girl pulled something out of her pocket. He watched, fascinated, as she unfolded the thing. It was a knife—a folding knife. He wanted to laugh. It was both the most ingenious and the most worthless thing he'd ever seen. The blade wasn't even two inches long. Who would carry such a joke of a blade?

But he was disappointed. Before she could keep her half of the deal, he heard a gruff voice call out, "So you've decided to return at last!"

The girls spun around. Clearly they recognized the speaker, but rather than answer him, they took a collective step back, as if in surprise. The voice came from a thin, frowning, frail-looking priest in a light-blue robe, standing in a doorway with his arms crossed.

"Mr. Cholerish," said Eli, glancing sidelong at Anna.

"Took your sweet time, did you?" He approached and extended his arm. The girls hesitated a moment, and then each in turn shook the boney hand.

"Now that we've observed the niceties, follow along. We have much to discuss and precious little time." He began walking across the courtyard.

"Um . . . okay." Eli looked helplessly at Anna.

Anna shrugged. "Maybe he's inside."

They started to follow, but the youngest pointed back at the boy. "What about him?"

"Oh, Rose, I almost forgot." Eli pointed the knife at his wrists. "Do we have a deal? Remember, you have to come with us."

Anna pointed after the priest. "That man—or maybe his brother—knows what this is." She held up the firebrand. "If you come with us, you may learn something about it."

His desire to escape evaporated. This priest knew about his firebrand? Was this the one the bodacha had foreseen? He nodded again, but this time he meant it. The ropes fell to the ground, and the firebrand warmed again to his palms as if itching to start a blaze.

The priest didn't take them into the temple but along an arched portico that circled around the crumbling tower. As soon as they caught up to him, he glanced at Anna's purple hair. "What's wrong with your head? Is it some disease you have in your country?" Stroking his thinly clad scalp, he added almost wistfully, "Is it catchy?"

When Anna merely rolled her eyes, the priest looked down at the boy with narrowed eyes. "Before we get down to business, who's the little rogue of a Rokan tagging along? Can we trust him?"

The girls looked at him too. Of course, they didn't know who he was any more than the priest did. That was how he liked it. No puppet strings attached.

Anna banged him on the shoulder. "Well, what *is* your name?"

"What's it to you?"

"Look, you little blister—" began Anna, but Rose interrupted with great excitement.

"Let's call him John!" She said this with the authority of a divine decree.

Anna sighed. "Ever since Eli told you that story about the tree in Brooklyn, you want to call everyone John."

"I do not," said Rose.

"The UPS guy? Mr. Pummel in gym? You were even calling old Putterly 'John' days before you found out that was his real name."

"But it's such a pretty name."

"For a toilet, maybe."

The possibility of being christened after a toilet broke his will. "My name ain't John! It's Romul." Then he felt his face turn red, wondering if he'd just been played by the little red-haired girl.

"Like the general?" asked Eli. He stared at her blankly. He didn't know any general by any name, but the possibility was attractive to him. Anna was just as lost and said so.

"You know," said Eli. "General Rommel, the German general from, you know, World War II?"

"You think he's named after a German general from World War II . . . from earth?" said Anna with pronounced sarcasm. Eli deflated. The girls confused Romul, who had never had a sibling. They seemed stuck together by a weirdly tight bond, but they also needled each other constantly.

"Should I be comforted," the priest said, "that you have world-wide wars in your world also? Very tragic. Well, Errus, too, it would seem, is on the cusp of another worldwide war . . . thanks to you lot."

The girls bristled and started to object, but the priest silenced them with a pointing finger.

They'd been walking as they talked and now emerged on the backside of the temple which, it appeared to Romul, butted up against the northern wall of the city. And there a wonder drew him up short. In the middle of the city wall, built right into it, a great stone fish head stared back at him. A small stream of water was flowing out of its puckered mouth, falling into a great chasm encircling the temple.

"It's . . . it's . . ." Anna began, but nothing more came out.

"Yes," said the priest. "It is. The Flow of Segancurs has been restored."

Chapter 4

"Eight years!" the girls cried. Romul wondered why their faces had all gone pale.

"Yes, it has been eight long years since you left us, and I have waited far longer than a man my age should have to in order to hear your story." The priest collapsed onto a stone bench overlooking the great fish head—the Amplabium, he'd called it.

"Our story?" Anna wore a dumbfounded look.

"Confound it, young lady! What story do you think I mean? You, who braved Kavue with Lambient; you, who have beheld the courts of the Azhiona; you, who have seen stranger things in your short lives than these eyes have seen in near a century! I have endured secondhand tales until my ears droop with exhaustion. And now that I've got you here, you shan't leave until I've heard the whole of it down to the last grimy detail."

The girls looked at each other, then at the Amplabium, anywhere but into the goggling eyes of the priest.

"But where's . . ." Eli hesitated.

"Yes?" said the priest.

"Where's . . . um . . ." She tried again. "I mean, we were hoping to see . . ."

Recognition dawned on the priest's face. "Oh-ho! I see what's troubling you. You were not looking for me at all. You were expecting my portly brother." He didn't sound hurt or offended, just a little amused. "Well, you won't find him. At least not here. He's off to Garlandvale again. Hasn't been the same since your visit.

Flitting off here and there. Full of mysteries, he is. Convinced he's discovered something new in the prophecy. Rubbish! He hasn't spent half the time on it that I have—not a tenth, even. Thes only knows why, but I can't get a useful word out of him either way these days. That is, when I see him at all."

"But we've got to see him! He's got to . . ." Anna's eyes shot a sideways look at her sister that clearly meant something. Romul couldn't guess what.

"What is it with people that they will never finish their sentences when I'm around? Everyone acts as if I'm the very Legate of Hamayune! Now, you listen to me, missy." The priest waggled his finger at Anna. "It is partly out of concern for my brother that I ask you to tell me of your journey. There are certain peculiarities which only I am in a position to interpret. Now if you would like me to say *please*, I shall."

Romul, already bored, began to move restlessly around the balcony. The priest pointed to the spot on the bench next to him. "And you, my dirty little one, sit here at my right hand. I don't know how you got dragged into this by these three meddlers, but I'm sure it means no good for you!"

Over the next twenty minutes, Romul learned more about the history of his world than in his whole eight years of life. From the girls' story, Romul learned that eight hundred years ago, the desert had been a wide green prairie, and this little stream before them—then called the Flow of Segan—had been a river running from the lost well of Vizuritundu, deep in the Alappunda Mountains of Azhiona, all the way to Halighyll. Because of that flow, the city, too, had been green and fertile.

For some unknown reason, however, the flow of water had slowly dried up and the Plain of Kavue had gradually become the Flats of Kavue. A war had broken out between Azhiona and Garlandium, each blaming the other for the growing desert. The Ever-War had raged for centuries, but the desert eventually had grown too wide to cross.

On their historic flight across Kavue on a flying boat the girls and their companions had discovered that the real cause of the drought was a great dragon-creature, who had sealed Vizuritundu shut in its death throes. This was a greater mystery than the well itself, for dragons were thought to be merely mythical. Using her amulet, Anna had accidently reawakened the well. Now eight years later, they were seeing the result.

As they finished, the girls stood in awed silence for a long moment, watching the water cascade out of the fish's mouth.

"We did this." Anna wasn't asking a question. She was observing a fact.

The priest eyed her sideways. "Yes, it has come to pass, just a Dashonae predicted."

"Then . . ." Eli choked back a sob. "Then Azhwana and Garlandium are . . ."

"Don't be silly, child. The Ever-War has not been renewed. The truce holds for now. This little trickle of water is of no use to horsemen. But it grows with time and someday, perhaps . . ." He tilted his head knowingly. "But not for years to come. In fact, your old comrade Dashonae the knight has been our greatest advocate for peace."

"Then he got back okay?" asked Rose.

"Why shouldn't he have?" snapped the priest. "He is young and strong and resourceful. Upon his return from your quest, he was handsomely rewarded by the king with the position of garrison commander in Landembrost itself—perhaps the most important active command in the army. I have not seen him myself, but from what I can gather, Whinsom visits his offices not infrequently." The priest sighed.

"What about Dr. Lambient?" asked Eli.

"The crazy inventor? Oh, he also came into his own . . . in a manner of speaking. His credentials were restored to him, and he is now a senior member of the Avonian research council. No one doubts his conquering of the desert in his SkyCricket machine, but many still disbelieve what followed. Azhiona refuses to allow any further expeditions within its borders to confirm the details. He, too, is apparently in the confidences of Whinsom on a regular basis."

"Did Sazerac stay with him?" asked Eli.

"Of course. That dog is true to form and still Lambient's greatest assistant. But of Finch, the fairy who accompanied you, I have heard not a word. Just like a sylph." And he guffawed.

Then without any warning, he clapped his hands on his knees and turned to Romul. "And now, you poor little wretch of a Rokan, let's hear of your unfortunate life."

Before Romul could think of anything to say, Rose asked, "Cholerish, why don't your people like Rokan people?"

The priest was unperturbed by the question. He just looked at Romul and said in a commanding tone, "We of Rokan make our pledge . . ."

Romul responded without even thinking, "Hail, Queen of Angish, our Lady and Protec—" He caught himself. He felt ashamed. He hadn't spoken the pledge since he left the Rokan school, but years of indoctrination are not cast aside in a few months.

"You see?" said the priest to the girls. "The Rokan do not acknowledge Thes or even the celestial emissaries. They give their allegiance to their own sovereign—a queen, they say, whose kingdom is not of this world. So they are considered heretics and outcasts in Garlandium. If they would simply admit that their queen of another world is nothing more than a metaphor for Merris herself, then all would be well with them."

Despite his mixed feelings about his heritage, Romul grew hot and bothered by the priest's comments. He found himself speaking with a passion he hadn't known he felt. "And if the Garlandish would honor the Queen of Angish, too, then things wouldn't be so hard!"

"That is true, but to honor either Merris or the Queen of Angish instead of Thes would be to embrace falsehood, and only a fool embraces what he knows to be untrue."

Romul opened his mouth to say something, but Eli jumped in before he could figure out what to say. "But what queen? What other world? I don't understand." She'd directed the questions at Romul, who now realized he didn't know the answers. These were only things he'd been taught to say, not to understand.

But he tried. "She's the queen of . . . of another place. A better world than this."

"See, that's all you ever get out of them. They do not know themselves what they mean. Now, my little Opsiercom, for your story?"

Romul was so shocked by the slur that he felt a strong urge to jump up and run away. Not only had he not expected the question, but he could not remember ever having been called the full word—Opsiercom. Oh, he'd been tarred with the abbreviated Opsy at least twice a day his entire life, but never the whole word. That was an almost unthinkable insult. He trembled and stared down at the pavement, not knowing what would happen next.

"Is that the same as an Opsy?" asked Eli.

The priest drew a sharp breath. "You will watch your mouth, young lady. I do not permit such language in my presence." Eli turned pale.

"But *you* called me . . ." Romul whispered without looking up.

The priest was confused. "Yes, I called you an Opsiercom. That is what you are, is it not?"

He didn't answer.

Anna stepped up. "Dolphus called him a . . . well, the other word. The shorter one."

The priest was unmoved. "I don't doubt it. Dolphus is a good soldier and an obstinate fool. Do not worry, lad. You will not be so mistreated here."

Romul was not mollified. The priest had used the full word. No one used the full word. No one.

Eli tried once more. "But what does it mean? I don't understand."

The priest's demeanor softened. "Of course, how could you know? Opsiercom is a very old word. We do not know from where it comes, but it merely means 'latecomer,' which is what the Rokan are."

"Latecomers to what?" asked Eli.

"To Errus, of course. At least that's what we believe it means. Their coming to Errus was later than ours."

"Recently?" asked Eli.

"Oh no, no. The Rokan have been here since long before history began to be recorded. We have no record of what Errus was like before they arrived. We know only from tradition and that word that they came . . . well, later."

"But what does Ops . . . I mean, the shorter word mean?" asked Anna.

The priest's face grew red. "That is an abominable insult. They use the short word as a weapon. It is derisive, a slur."

Romul found his voice now. "But the full word's worse."

The priest was dumbfounded. "Who told you that?"

Romul realized he didn't know. He'd always believed it was, but now that it came to it, he didn't know why. The priest understood. "You are mistaken, young man. Opsiercom is not an insult. The only reason you might have thought so is that deep down you have a generous heart. I mean that, till now and without knowing it, you have given every Garlandian the benefit of doubt, disbelieving that they would be as cruel as they could. I am sorry to disabuse you of that notion, but it is true—people *are* often as cruel as they can be. Now that you know this, that generosity, which once came by nature, must now come by choice. This is harder. It is called growing up."

Romul looked up into the eyes of the priest. No gentleness or compassion was found there. The eyes were hard and piercing. In that moment, Romul knew the priest had not spoken from sentiment but out of his own painful experiences. He'd told the truth without softening it. It was this that made Romul trust him.

"Okay, um . . . my story is . . . uh . . . a bunch of months ago, I found out that the lady I always thought was my mom weren't." He hesitated as waves of shame welled up in him. "Um . . . she made like I was hers. We lived way over on the mountains, above Farwell. Leaserae—that was her name—weren't very nice, and we was real poor like everyone who's not Garlandish.

"Well, one night she got real drunk, and I came home and found her crying. I don't know why she told me. Maybe she was just so drunk she didn't know what she was saying. But she told me she was sorry for what she done to me. I thought she meant all the beatings, but then she said that I weren't really hers. She said she stole me newborn from my mom. Tried to sell me, but couldn't find a buyer, so she kept me.

"Well, I didn't know what to say. I was angry, I guess, but all I could say was, 'Well, where's my mom, then?' She started crying again. Said she didn't know, 'cause she never saw her again. But she'd stole the firebrand from her too. She pulled it out of her pocket. Well, I'd seen it a bunch of times, but never thought about it. But now I saw it was the only way of ever finding out who I really was." He paused again. His face was burning now. He didn't want to say the next part.

"Like I said, I was angry. See, she stole me, and that weren't right, and I was angry . . . so I took the firebrand from her . . . kinda hard, 'cause she didn't want to let go. But I made her . . . then I . . . hit her." He swallowed hard. "And I kicked her, and I called her awful things. Then I left, and I ain't been back." He ended with a single, shuddering sob.

The room was very still. He didn't want to look up, but when he did he saw the priest was eyeing him hard. "This firebrand you speak of. What is it?"

"Yeah, see, that's why I tackled him. I knew Whin . . . uh . . . you just had to see it."

The priest inhaled sharply as Romul produced it. He took it and turned it over gently in his hands. "Anna, this is like your Therran relic, I think?"

"Uh, yes, I think so." Anna produced her amulet and held it out. Cholerish held them next to each other. They were identical in every way, except for the symbol they bore.

Anna pointed at the crossbow-like rune on the firebrand. "What is that?"

"'Tis the smithy hammer—the sign of Lemerrus."

"That's the moon, isn't it?" asked Eli.

"Yes. And to him is entrusted labor and industry, cunning . . . and the poor." He glanced at Romul. "He is Errus's lesser brother and son of Merris and Vercandrus. And all the vulcani are in his care."

"Vulcani," said Eli thoughtfully. "That's the salamanders?"

"Yes, along with the khalkotauroi, the pyrausta, and others, but I'm guessing that our young friend has deciphered its more elemental property." He put the firebrand back in Romul's hand and motioned in a "carry on" sort of way. When Romul didn't move, the priest grew impatient. "Come on, don't be shy. Show us the power of Lemerrus."

Then he understood. He bent forward, held up the firebrand, focused on it, and thought of heat. Suddenly a small tongue of flame appeared, hovering just above the lump of metal. The girls jumped, but the priest let loose a loud, cackling whoop. "That's it! That's it! I knew it!"

Anna's face broke into a grin. "Like my amulet found the water in the desert! This one is about fire."

The priest was standing now. "Yes, yes. These relics represent one piece of the great puzzle we must unravel. The other is written on the walls of the temple below us. The prophecy! Grave things are afoot, and the time grows short. The fulfillment is nigh." The priest put his hand to his forehead, quoting, "'Creation in mourning,' 'families torn asunder,' 'murders,' 'wars,' 'time itself unmade.'

Yes, the rise of Hamayune is upon us—and with it the end of all things."

Romul and the girls sat in shocked silence before his proclamation. Romul looked up at the stone blocks of the tower, half expecting them all to come crashing down on him right then. But nothing in particular happened. Apparently the priest did not mean the world was ending at that exact moment, only sometime soon.

The reprieve gave Romul no comfort.

Chapter 5

"So this . . . um . . . prophecy? Could it be wrong?" Eli wrung her hands nervously.

The priest was aghast. "If it could be wrong, it wouldn't be much of a prophecy, now would it? But I wouldn't expect you to understand these things. Every word has many possibilities—layers upon layers of meaning. If you'd read them as carefully as I have—"

"Can we?"

"Can you what?"

"Read them."

Cholerish nearly fell off his bench. "Of course not. What good would that do you? You've no training. Thesian priests study the articles of the prophecy for years, read widely about them, and write dissertations on them. You can't just *read* them."

"But how are we to—"

"I'm telling you." The priest was frenzied now. "They speak of great war at the beginning of the world between the celestial emissaries and Hamayune—a war the emissaries won only because Thes brought men into the world, and—"

"Wait! Who had a war on their honeymoon?" Rose looked back-and-forth from Eli to Anna in confusion.

Cholerish stared at Rose as if she were a nincompoop, as if he'd forgotten that he'd just told them they wouldn't understand. "*Hah-may-YOON*. We do not know exactly what it is. The ancients surmised it was a great force that arose at the creation of the world, intent on destroying or enslaving all things—a dark and terrible power. A power now poised to return."

The girls were riveted on the lecture, but Romul wasn't all that interested in Garlandish prophecy. He just wanted the priest to talk more about his firebrand, but he didn't think he should interrupt. Before the priest was done, however, he'd learned more about it than was probably good for him.

"*That*, young ladies, is the mystery we must solve before it is too late. And it all seems to hang upon your little dragon friend up north."

Anna guffawed. "That pile of bones won't be destroying the world any time soon."

"But don't you see, my little bufflehead? It already has." The priest's quoting hand went back to his forehead. "'*In death, he takes the water from the earth.*'" Then he let loose his explosive laugh. "It's incredible to imagine! My own dissertation and that of many of my betters overturned by you three wastrels." He clapped his hands together and then spread them out toward the girls.

"What do you mean?" Anna bristled at being a wastrel.

The priest continued quoting. "'*And the lips of the great shall thirst, and everlasting war shall be his offspring.*' It was of long-standing interpretation, mine included, that this series of articles referred to Azhiona. We had always believed that our northern neighbors had destroyed Vizuritundu and brought the drought upon the southern lands. The 'lips of the great' was assumed a reference to our great fish head here, and the everlasting war a reference to the Ever-War that followed. We always thought Azhiona was responsible for it all. Now we know better."

"But what's all this got to do with your honeymoon?" said Anna, winking at Rose.

"Hamayune! Don't be blasphemous. To the point, the prophecy predicted that a legate would arise to pave the way for the return of Hamayune."

"A legate?" said Eli.

"So. Not always the sharpest arrow in the quiver, eh? Ha! Legate means a representative—*the* representative of Hamayune—one who comes to prepare the way. And now that we know the legate *has* come, the prophecy appears to be in full swing."

Anna was still feeling her oats. "Okay, fine. So this Hamayune thing is coming back, and blocking the well was the first sign of it. When's the end of the world actually going to get here?"

The priest sighed heavily, wearily, as though it took all his energy to deal with such ignorant charges. "*Four ages shall pass from the Great Procession. When the children of Merris descend, the rise of Hamayune is near.*" Then he stared at her as if his words were self-explanatory.

"Huh. Four ages," said Anna. "That sounds like a long time, so what's the big deal?"

The priest pounced. "Pah! This is no novel. You can't just read the prophecy start to finish like a book. As I said, every word has many possibilities—layers upon layers of meaning. Most authorities believe the Great Procession refers to an alignment of Merris's planetary children in the heavens—which is an unusually rare occurrence. The last time it occurred was 128 years ago."

"But that's hardly an *age*," said Anna.

The priest sniggered. "Unless it refers to the age of a man, as I believe is the case. The Garlandian generation is measured at about thirty years. Four generations of thirty years is 120 years . . ." He paused on the up-beat as if inviting someone to continue.

As Eli spoke, her face was ashen. "Plus eight years."

The priest nodded. "Yes, and exactly eight years ago, you three peripatetics blundered into the picture."

This revelation sobered Anna in a hurry. "Then . . . then *we* are the children of Merris?"

The priest was genuinely disgusted. "You? You! Of all the arrogant, self-centered, egotistical . . ." He spluttered with frustration, unable to continue. "That may be the most blasphemous thing you've said yet. No, the emissaries cannot be *people*. All the dissertations agree on this. It would be . . . profane, utterly beneath their dignity. The emissaries are the great forces put into the world by Thes to master its substances—the earth, the air, fire, and water. For eight years I have pondered, and now this little Opsiercom has shown me the way." The priest held up Romul's firebrand.

Anna gasped, producing her amulet again and staring down at it. "You mean—"

"Yes, I believe Therra herself hangs about your neck." The priest paused to let the implications sink in. "The emissaries have begun to descend. The rise of Hamayune is upon us . . . the end of the world!"

"But . . . but," cried Eli, "how do we stop it?"

"Stop it? How many ways must I say it? It's prophecy! It is in the nature of a prophecy to be fulfilled."

Eli was flustered into silence, but Romul was just starting to get the point. "But what happens next? How does this prophecy thing end?"

For the first time, the priest looked defensive. "We are not exactly sure. The final lines of the prophecy were obliterated from the stone—the Ravagement, it is called. We do not know how or when the marring occurred. Long ago, certainly. The oldest dissertation we have speaks of it as a legend even in its day. The work of a deranged priest with a chisel, it supposes."

Eli's fingers flew to her mouth. "So you don't even know how the prophecy ends?"

"We *know* that the only hope we have is the return of the emissaries, which we now know has also begun. Two of the children of Merris and Vercandrus are reunited in this very place. But what of the others—of Avonia and Berducca, and especially of Errus himself? We need information on two points."

He began ticking them off on his fingers. "First, we must learn the fate of the other emissaries. Where have they gone? Why do they not descend? Second, we must decipher the deeper meaning of your dragonish discovery at Vizuritundu. Whence came this creature, and what was its game? Unfortunately, the libraries of Halighyll were burned at the beginning of the Ever-War, and no man now possesses these answers."

Eli grimaced. "Then who are we supposed to—"

"The longaevi themselves. I deeply wish we could consult each of the four classes of longaevi. What is their status? What do they know of these things?"

Anna gave a long *oooh* as the penny dropped. "If you mean dwarves, then we found one on the last trip, and he was crazy."

"You met no dwarf. You met the wreckage of one—a gnomian carcass, mad from long isolation. Nothing more. Sadly, we must assume that dwarves are as scarce here as in the north. So, too, all the longaevi. In fact, I know of only one who can be reliably contacted—a vulcani."

An explosion went off in Romul's mind. He knew exactly what the priest wanted. "The Old One!" Four sets of eyes turned on him, and he suddenly felt very important.

"Yes," said the priest in mild surprise. "Though I must confess, I had not expected you to know of the old salamander in the Farwell foundry."

"Know of him? I seen him."

The priest's eyes went wide, then narrowed. "Come now, let us have no hyperbole. You cannot have seen the Old One. His hall is under constant—"

"Did so! Just afore I left Farwell a few months back, I decided I'd have myself a look-see."

"You did, now." The priest waved for him to continue.

"So I snuck in. There's this tunnel, see, next to the mountain. They send the hot water out of it from the meltings. If you get in there between the dumps, you can walk right in. I climbed right up on the skywalk and looked down on him as he talked to people."

"People? What sort of people?"

"I don't know. Priests and soldiers and stuff." Romul shrugged.

The event really hadn't been as exciting as he'd hoped. "Then I got caught, and they tossed me out."

"Well, now, it sounds as though we may have found you ladies a guide."

It took a moment for the implication to sink in. "Oh, no, no. Not a chance!" Romul leapt to his feet. "I just came from there. I ain't going back."

"Most certainly you are. You have got to show these young ladies to the Old One. We need answers to these pressing questions. The longaevi know things—things they would never tell me but they may tell you."

Romul was shaking his head violently. He didn't want to be mixed up in all this. He just wanted to find his mom. He said so, then added, "And the bodacha told me to come here, and I'd find answers."

"Bodacha! You mean ignorant, superstitious fool of a sorceress! Don't be daft, my little Opsiercom. Why do you think she sent you here?"

"She told me I'd find my mom."

"No!" The priest waved a finger. "You just said she told you you'd find *answers*. Well, whether she meant it or no, there they are." And he waved his hand at the three girls.

Romul was dumbfounded. His mind was in agony at the thought of a return journey. "But it took months to get here." He suddenly felt very tired. He'd thought his wanderings would end with a sweet reunion here in Halighyll, and now it was turning out to be only a moment's rest before turning around and marching back the way he'd come.

He was spared further pleading. Eli took up his cause. "Um, Cholerish, we don't have months. Based on what happened last time, a week here is a little over eight hours where we come from. Our dad thinks we're just gone to a friend's overnight, which means we only have, like, a week—ten days at most—before we're missed."

The priest rounded on her. "Then you'd best leave immediately! Farwell is not just across the street, you know." Then he put his hands to his head in thought. "I know someone who can help. It's only two days' ride by coach to Umbra, where he lives." The priest lifted his head toward the ceiling and uttered a sort of prayer. Romul didn't get all the words, but it sounded like "And may the son be of sounder mind than the father."

Romul stood frozen, consumed by his own cares. It had all been for nothing. All those nights sleeping on the ground—the rain, the cold. Now here he was turning right around and going back to the place he'd run away from. *If I've gotta go back to Farwell, I'm going to walk into that bodacha's cave and punch her right in the nose.*

He came back to the conversation just in time to hear the priest conclude his instructions with, "And this all assumes, of course, that our young Opsiercom can get you into the complex. I will arrange for passage to Umbra and a letter of introduction to your . . . uh, conductor. You three may rest in my brother's room tonight, and the boy can sleep here on the couch. You will leave on the morrow, making all haste to Farwell."

The girls looked at Romul, their eyes filled with a mixture of fear, apprehension, and even some gratitude. He began to feel a weight settling down upon him. They were all depending on him. He was unfamiliar with feelings of responsibility. They were heavy, suffocating. He didn't want to go back, and he certainly didn't want to do it with three girls in tow.

The priest stood, joints creaking and popping. "One last thing before you go, dear Opsiercom. I believe you have some business to attend to. The Rokan are not permitted to walk the streets of Umbra without papers. We must get you a pair of shears."

BOOK 2

The Crescent Sea and All It Contains

Oh you watery sprites. You, the Therran undini of Errus,
Most suspicious of man—the net-hunter, the fish-eater.
More withdrawn than all the longaevi, both in nature and in habitat.
If your ocean-dwelling cousins are aloof,
What shall be said of you, oh Undini Crescentia—
Unreached, unknown, unheard of for so long?
How shall we explain what you did in the final war?
How shall we forget?

> FRANKO RAZHAMANÌAH, "Meditations on Merfolk"
> in *Sweet Songs of the Longaevi.*

Chapter 6

Romul's head hung out the coach window like a dog's, and he inhaled the delicious air rushing past. So far the westward journey was nothing like his eastward one. Never having ridden a horse, even the lumbering gate of the coach produced in him the heady sensation of reckless speed. Since Rokan were not permitted to ride inside coaches, even that was new to him.

His head also felt absurdly light, having been freed from nearly two inches of hair by Cholerish's scissors. Despite his hair's ragged appearance, he felt less self-conscious than at any time in his life. He was no longer Rokan. He was free. He could go anywhere he wished, do anything he wanted, pass for any common Garlandish boy.

His only frustration was that the girls seemed totally unimpressed by his newfound self. They didn't treat him any differently than they had before. In fact, they treated him exactly like they treated everyone else—even the old Rokan carriage driver, whose long albsignum bounced along behind him in a thick, snow-white braid. They had thanked him when he helped them into the coach, and Rose had even asked about his family. Imagine! They talked to the old man as if he were an equal.

He had not thanked the driver. He didn't have to. He was Garlandish now—one of the ones who mattered. He was *inside* the coach, and he was not going to lose any opportunity to savor the superiority that came with his new station in life. He'd ignored the driver as was right and customary.

Yet the girls continued to gall him with their ignorance of such things. Even now Anna was hanging out the window on the other side, talking up to the man, asking him for permission to help feed the horses when they stopped. Permission? Why should she have to ask permission of a Rokan coachman? Did she not know how degrading it was? It was simply no fun coming into one's own around people who thought everyone already had it. He pulled his head inside and sat back in his seat, his mood ruined.

In an effort to memorize the questions Cholerish had given them to ask the old salamander, Eli was rehearsing with Rose. Rose, however, was fiddling distractedly with her two-arrowed compass. Of this strange little relic, he understood only that it had a special power—it could somehow show the three girls how to eventually get home.

Seeing his deflated look, Eli tried to involve him in the conversation. "So you really think we can sneak inside without being seen?" Anna dropped back inside to listen.

Romul was feeling sour and uncooperative. "I don't get why we can't just have Cholerish ask a priest in Farwell to let us in."

"But they're different kinds of priests," said Eli sympathetically. "They wear different colored robes to show who they—"

"I know! I been smacked around by enough priests to know that much. But why not find one who wears light-blue ones like Cholerish?"

"I don't think they're light blue exactly," said Rose, looking out the window. "It's more like steel blue or cobalt . . . or maybe cerulean."

Anna gawked at Rose, but Eli ignored her and replied in a very maternal voice. "Whinsom and Cholerish are the only two priests left who wear those colors. They follow Thes, and the rest of the priests follow—"

"No!" Romul stuck out his chin. "I seen one. There was one there, and he was talking to the salamander. I seen him!"

Now all three girls were staring at him. "You mean there's a Thesian priest in Farwell?" said Eli.

"Yes! I guess."

"Well, if that's true . . ." began Anna.

"What d'you mean *if*? You calling me a liar?" Romul tried to stand up, his hands clenched into fists, but the swaying of the coach threw him back into his seat.

"No, no, we believe you. It's just we'll have to find him and talk him into helping us. It was a man, right?"

"'Course it was," he said, sneering. "Not like they'd let a girl in there."

Anna pounced. If Romul had ever believed girls couldn't hit hard enough to hurt, the next thirty seconds cured him of that notion forever.

∽

Romul climbed out of the coach sore all over—partly from the carriage ride itself and partly from Anna. The driver, whose name Romul hadn't bothered to learn, built a fire. The girls offered to help with the rest of his setup, and the surprised coachman accepted. Romul stood stiffly by the coach, as he'd seen Garlandish nobles do, and waited till all was ready.

Soon they had bivouacked, and a savory something bubbled in the crock over the fire, minded by the coachman, who kept casting sidelong glances at him. The girls were off with the horses, watching them graze. Romul still didn't understand what all the fuss had been about. The horses had simply asked what time they were needed back in the morning, and the three girls had gone into conniptions, blathering on about being able to understand them now. *Like there's any four-year-old who can't understand a horse. Equinish ain't that hard.*

The girls followed the horses out to pasture, they'd begun pestering them with questions about what it was like to be a horse. This left Romul in the uncomfortable situation of being alone with the driver. He occupied himself with watching the girls in the field capering around the horses, who seemed indignant at the intrusion on their free time.

Behind him, the metal spoon clanked against the inside of the pot. "Well, little master," said the driver with a feigned sigh of resignation, "I fear we is alone at last."

Romul elevated his nose slightly and sniffed. But he didn't turn around. The driver said no more, but continued to stir. The gentle rhythmic clinks of the spoon against the pot began to wear on Romul. He wandered back to the fire and sat down opposite the coachman.

The old man ignored him. *Clink* went the spoon again.

Romul ignored him in return.

Clink.

He's doing it on purpose. Romul glowered at the coachman, but the coachman's eyes slid slowly back to the pot. He wore a barely suppressed smile on his lips.

Clink.

Romul fidgeted restlessly. *What could they possibly talk to a horse about for this long?* His own brief interactions with horses had revealed them to be rather dull animals, interested only in the qualities of oats or the virtues of being shoed versus going "natural."

He had not long to wait. A commotion of neighing and cries of shock went up from the twilit field. A moment later, Eli returned, guiding a crying Rose by the arm, while Anna marched indignantly behind, shouting back over her shoulder. "And there's no need to be mean about it. It was just a question!" She stomped past Romul and threw herself down by the fire, muttering, "Stupid horse. Rude, stupid, dumb, stupid horse . . ."

Romul was about to ask what happened, but the driver spoke first. "Pay them no mind, little missies. 'Member, they've had a harder day than we. We've had the luxury of sitting while they carried us all behind. They's always a bit out of sorts this time a day. Try them again in the morning, when they's fresh."

Eli and Rose sat down next to Anna.

Rose wiped away a tear. "But I thought they'd be nice like Sazerac was."

The coachman lifted a questioning eyebrow.

"Oh," Eli answered. "Sazerac was a dog we met last time we were here."

"Well, then, there's your answer, see?" The old man prodded the fire with a thoughtful stick. "Doggies can afford to be sociable, 'cause they's so certain of their place. People like dogs. They's like friends to us, see? Companionable, they is. And since we don't expect nothing from them but that, don't cost them nothing to return it. But what's the use of horses? Wouldn't want one sleeping in your bed by night, now would you? Nor would any self-respecting horse want to be there. They's only good to us for riding or working. So we don't think much of them till there's work to be done."

He leaned forward to stir the pot again. "Not so companionable, is it? Nope, 'tis more like a master and a servant. Horses do work we need done, and we pays them. And they knows we'd take advantage of them given half a chance. So they's got no room to be companionable like your Sazerac." He was quiet for a moment, then added, "Normal, I suppose. Tain't unusual for those who are served to forget the burdens borne by those who do the serving."

The old man continued stirring the pot, but Romul was sure his eyes had flickered his direction. He felt his face go hot and pink, and a vague guilt bubbled up in his throat. He thrust the feeling down with a hard swallow.

"When do we eat?" said Anna, whose attention was quickly turning from the horses' mysterious insult to more practical matters.

"'Tis ready even now."

But Romul was no longer hungry.

After a dinner of rich meaty stew and hard biscuit, the driver went off to see how the horses had bedded themselves. The girls had cautiously followed along, leaving Romul alone by the fire with his thoughts. He hadn't enjoyed his first day as a free Garlandian anywhere near like he'd thought he would. The very presence of the Rokan coachman was an intrusion upon his victory.

Now the troop returned, and Romul heard Rose saying, "The horses seem to like you all right."

"Oh sure, me and the horses, we's like brothers, we is." The coachman grunted, resuming his fireside seat. "We understand one another, we do. They know how the Rokan is treated in Garlandium—not half so good as horses. They get paid more than I do making the Halighyll-Umbra run. But they been good to me—given me loans a couple times to tide me over. They's like family."

"Horses are paid more than people?" asked Rose, her mouth twisted into a confused grimace.

"No, no." The coachman waved his hand. "Not more than people, just more than a Rokan. See, horses got privilege 'cause they's needed. If they don't want to pull, nothing moves. But a Rokan—" he clicked his tongue and threw his thumb against his chest—"we's optional. The horses knows the way to Umbra all by themselves. I don't do much—really only along to handle the luggage."

"Still," said Eli, "it doesn't seem quite right. Why do they treat Rokan people so badly?"

The coachman glanced at Romul as if to say *Ask him.* Romul's gaze fell to the dirt. A moment of awkward silence passed. The coachman smiled and raised his index finger in the universal gesture of "just a moment."

The driver rummaged through his pack for a moment and produced a musical instrument. Romul knew it immediately—the

Uilleanus, the traditional instrument of the Rokan. It consisted of a bag made out of goat hide—often with the goat's hair still on it. It had a tube the musician would blow into, inflating the bag. When squeezed with the arm, the bag forced air through a sort of pipe with finger holes. Since the bag could be inflated faster than the pipe could turn it into music, the musician could stop blowing for short periods to sing and the melody would continue unbroken. This the old man now did.

At the first note, Romul's guts knotted. He knew the song—a sort of Rokan anthem. It haunted his earliest memories, and with its melancholy horn solos between each verse, it seemed the very center of all he was fleeing. The girls sat mesmerized by the sound, and the coachman's face was made all the more old and sad by flickering firelight. He sang . . .

> *Come, hear the voice of the wooly pipes*
> *That groan and weep and wail*
> *To tell of how our fathers came*
> *From green lands beyond the vale.*
>
>> *The Queen of Angish sent them forth*
>> *Her kingdom to expand*
>> *To lands beyond the world's own rim*
>> *For to draw them to her hand.*
>
> *So through the door hung upon the air*
> *Did our fathers pass without fear*
> *And came into this hardening land*
> *Filled with toil and pain and tears.*
>
>> *Oh, sore the weight, the Garlandish yoke,*
>> *Descending on their brows—*
>> *The grave demand to renounce their faith*
>> *And abandon all their vows.*
>
> *Yet strong was they in the face of death,*
> *Garlandish gods to disdain,*

But loving still their own good Queen,
Kept faith e'en as they's slain.

So long we waits for 'pointed days
When our Queen's own heir will awake.
In fire he'll rise and we with him
Garlandish bonds to break.

As the music faded, Romul looked toward the sky in a wretched agony of soul. There Lemerrus, his own dear moon, stared down upon him, reddened as with the blood of his forefathers. His imagination saw all the things it had been taught to see at such moments—the green land of Angish, the gracious face of a gentle queen, ancient Garlandish city squares stained with Rokan blood, the promise of revolt and freedom one day.

He hated the images. No, that wasn't true. Even he could not deny it so brazenly. The deepest parts of him, the parts over which he had no control, loved them still. But he hated that he couldn't *help* loving them, and now he saw he would never be wholly free of Rokan. It was beyond his power. And his desire to be free of it made him little better than a traitor to the deepest parts of his soul.

A tear revolted in each eye and wet his cheeks. He lurched awkwardly to his feet and fled the warmth of the circle. He didn't want the girls to see him cry . . . No, it was the coachman who must not see. But there was little threat of that, for the girls immediately began to pester the old man with questions about "the door hung upon the air," and the mysterious kingdom of Angish and its queen, and so on.

It had been a brave thing for the coachman to do. After all, the revolutionary song was forbidden by Garlandish law. But the savvy old driver had realized the girls were not really Garlandish. Nor, Romul realized, had *he* fooled the driver.

He didn't return to the fire that night except once, after the others had all lain down to sleep. He came back to grab his blanket, for though his guilt would not let him sleep in proximity to the driver, he was very practical about dying of exposure. As he crept away from the circle to make his bed between the coach's wheels, he heard the old man whisper hoarsely behind him, "You know the song for sure, little master. You may quit my fire this night, but will you as easily escape the fire that is coming?"

Romul did not respond. He lay down and watched the wisps of smoky cloud drift across Lemerrus's umber face. In the end, it was not the cold that kept him awake that night but his contemplations of fire.

Chapter 7

The city of Umbra was a complete contrast to Halighyll. Resting on the edge of Antumbra Lake, at the meeting of the Waxing and North Wane rivers, it was green and lush compared to parched Halighyll. It was also primarily a center of trade. If Halighyll belonged to the priests, Umbra belonged to the merchants. Thus to travel from Halighyll to Umbra was like exchanging a barren desert tomb for a torrid and sweaty marketplace. At least this was how Romul felt about it. But there was no avoiding it. One could hardly travel north, south, east, or west through Garlandium without stopping there, for all major roads and rivers intersected it.

Romul knew it would have been best to make the journey from the coach station to the wharf on foot. But the girls had pleaded with the driver to help them find their way through the densely packed streets. He'd been understandably hesitant. His papers were sketchy for this kind of travel, and if he'd been stopped, he might have gotten into trouble.

He was, however, more easily persuaded than the horses, who were not in the habit of going the extra mile. But again the easygoing coachman intervened by reminding the horses, in great detail, of the terrible things that could befall unattended children in a city like Umbra. Every inch of every street of the city was open market, where chickens were butchered, wares were both hawked and stolen, and haggling was the universal tongue. The rude, the holy, the counterfeit, and the original—it was all available for a price in Umbra, out under the hot sun or in some dark corner. A wild town that could, in the space of an hour, make you a prince, a pauper, or a corpse.

All in all, the girls may have been better off just braving the streets in ignorance, for after the recitation of possible evils that could overtake them amid those shifty boroughs, they were even less inclined to get out of the coach. Romul thought all this silly. Getting through cities was a simple matter of keeping a low profile, staying out of sight, and traveling as light as possible.

They were now violating these principles in the grandest fashion possible. The coach, built for the wide lanes of the Garlandian countryside, filled most of the street, drawing stares, shouts, and curses from merchants and passersby, who had to squeeze around the hulking carriage. Costermongers had to pull their carts back to allow it to pass. Romul's ears stung with the names hurled at the Rokan driver. Even the filthy street dogs barked insults at the horses, who made more than their share of rude retorts and occasionally kicked at them.

He scrunched down in the seat and tried to block out the angry sounds, but he couldn't escape the odors. Umbra was a smelly city—ripe with closely packed streets teaming with unwashed people and animals but also from the fish and fruit that baked all day in the sun.

Suffice it to say, when they arrived at the northern harbor an hour later, Romul felt thoroughly exhausted with that sort of weariness that comes not from working but from trying hard not to think about something. As they piled out onto the street, he was shocked to find the coachman smiling broadly. He watched with open mouth as the old man pulled their packs down from the coach's roof, whistling a cheerful tune and accepting the girls' gratitude with the carefree ease of one who's done little more than shoo a bee off someone's hat.

Remounting the coach for what was sure to be an equally painful return journey, the driver looked down at Romul and held his eyes for a moment. Romul felt like he should say something, but his mouth had gone dry, nor could he think of anything that didn't sound foolish. The coachman raised his eyebrows, waiting, but when nothing came, he sighed. "Come on, old plugs. Got another long haul before sundown, and we's wasted enough time already." Romul mastered himself in time to raise his hand in farewell, but the driver's back was already to him.

The girls were shouldering their packs and talking about where to go next. The wharf on which the driver had left them was just a long boardwalk extending hundreds of yards in either direction along the shore of the Waxing River. Looking east, Romul could see where the river broadened, dumping into Antumbra Lake. He'd heard the Waxing River was really just a man-made channel dug to connect the northern tip of the Crescent Sea to the lake, allowing barges to avoid the numerous falls on the North Wane River.

So this was the busiest point of the river—called the Great Neck. Barges of ore and wheat filled the river, traveling downstream toward Erintenda or Eddigen. A few steamed upstream, destined for the Crescent Sea and maybe Farwell itself. Smaller fishing boats filled the river's margins in both directions. Romul was overawed by the sight. His last visit to Umbra had consisted of skulking from side street to side street at night. Halighyll had been his destination, and all points in between had been only that. So when Anna looked at him and raised her eyebrows as if to say *now what?* he shrugged and said in his nastiest voice, "How should I know?"

"Some guide." She took off her pack and began rooting through it. "Here it is." She held up the envelope containing Cholerish's letter of introduction and read the words on the envelope. "Pier 27, Umbra."

"Well, that says Pier 11." Rose pointed at a sign.

They began making their way along the wharf. The sun was quite hot by now, and the whole place smelled of sweaty men and rotten fish. Hard-bitten sailors jeered occasionally from the decks of ships as they passed.

When they arrived fifteen minutes later, Romul was hot and sweaty and irritable. They now stood gawking at the only boat that occupied a berth at Pier 27. What had once been a large fishing boat was now such a collection of riggings, cables, and wires that it was barely recognizable as a boat at all. Dozens of shiny mechanical objects hung from booms that projected from it in every direction, like the arms of a squid. The boat itself was bleached, rickety, and sat uneasily low in the water. Its most dominant feature was its mast. It bore no sail, but rather at the top, a large and strangely shaped windmill contraption turned determinedly in the breeze. For all the equipment and tools that lay littered around the deck, conspicuously absent from the whole assemblage were any fishing nets.

As they stood wondering at the thing, two burly sailors sporting acres of tattoos meandered past. They stopped before the great oddity, and one of them yelled, "Hey, Augie, catch anything today?"

The other guffawed loudly. "Didn't get bit by one, I hope." Both broke into coarse laughter. A crash, like the toppling of a stack of cooking pans, echoed from the cabin of the boat, and a moment later a face appeared in one of the round windows. Then it disappeared again, followed by the sound of heavy grunting. The sailors' laughter redoubled. "Looks like he caught something after all!"

Suddenly the cabin door burst open, and a young man with an oil-stained face stumbled out backward. His arm seemed to be snared by something still inside the cabin, and he was yanking and pulling in an effort to free himself. He called out cheerfully in the midst of his struggle, "Oh, hey there, Pike. Hey there, Iggy. Just a minute..." He waved with his free hand while still jerking the trapped one. "The secondary coil's gone and sprung again, and I'm a bit caught up in the whole mess."

While saying this he braced his foot against the doorframe of the cabin and gave a final, desperate heave. With a musically metallic *boing*, whatever had held fast his arm let go. The man stumbled backward, tripped, and fell headlong into the water. The two seamen roared with laughter and clapped each other on the back.

The man floundered in the water a moment before righting himself and making for the dock ladder with a clumsy stroke. A minute later he stood dripping on the dock, his unmanaged hair hanging like seaweed over his eyes. He was tall and stick-like, with an oversized head and an even more oversized nose. A great lump projected from his throat as if an apple had gotten stuck halfway down. This comical voice box danced and jiggled as he talked, causing his voice to occasionally crack as if he were just starting into manhood, although he looked much older. His clothing was ill-sized and hung limp and sodden from his gangly frame like a sail from a cross-mast. He puffed and panted, wearing a sheepish grin.

"Poor ole Augie," hooted Pike, putting his arm around the wet man. "You'll catch your death if you stand round sopping like that. Just let Iggy and me take you down to the inn and get you all cozy by the fire. We'll even let you buy the first round."

"Oh, uh, that's awfully kind of you, Pike." The man grinned, pulling his hair out of his face. "But I've got so much to do here. I'm still hoping to test the new sounder tonight."

The sailors' faces dropped, and Iggy replied in a well-practiced tone, "Oh, well, we sees it now. If you don't want to drink with your old friends Pike and Iggy, we understand. We was just looking out for you, Augie, being your good friends and all. But if you're too busy to return a kindness, well then . . ."

"Oh, now, don't be like that, fellas," said Augie. "I'm still your friend and all. I just can't get away at this precise minute." He looked from one downcast face to the other and then, brightening, reached into his pocket and produced several coins. "Look fellas, I've got two and six right here. How would it be if you went ahead without me, and I'll just catch you next time? That'll be all right, won't it, guys?"

The two sunburnt faces instantly recovered. "Why, Augie!" cooed Pike. "You is a sport after all. Why, we'll drink the first round to your very good health, won't we, Iggy?"

"True as rain, we will," chimed in Iggy. And with the promise of an evening's cheer clutched in Pike's hand, the two men stumped away, down the wharf toward the public house.

The man waved after them cheerfully. "So long, fellas! See you tomorrow!" He looked quite pleased with himself.

Romul, however, was thoroughly disgusted. And he would have walked away right then if, to his annoyance, Eli hadn't already stepped up to the man.

"Um . . . excuse me, sir. Are you Augustus Lambient? We, uh . . . know your father."

Chapter 8

Romul sat on the deck of the boat watching the inventor trot energetically in and out of the cabin and to-and-fro across the deck in his attempt to "realign the secondary coil"—whatever that was. He would disappear into the cabin, scamper out again to grab a tool lying on the deck, only to repeat the same movement a few minutes later and retrieve another tool from the place of its last usage. All the while, he kept up a mumbling conversation with himself, consisting mostly of imprecations about his tools never being where he needed them and how he wished someone would put the *ship* in order. Romul thought "ship" was generous. "Boat" was more honest, but "wreck" was closest to the truth.

What had the priest been thinking to send them here? Did he know about this beat-up hunk of driftwood—or worse, the maze of crazy gadgets built into it by its weirdo captain? Christened *Sea Bellows*, it was a cluttered, unpainted, shabby hulk of a tub whose principal reason for existence was as mysterious as its means of propulsion—neither of which Romul understood.

It was without a doubt the child of its inventor. Augustus Lambient was the smartest and most scatterbrained person Romul had ever met. From the stories he'd heard about his father, the great Professor Ambrosius Lambient, it seemed clear that while his son had inherited his eccentric technical genius, he'd acquired little of his father's discipline and none of his aesthetic style. Romul reviewed the last few hours in his mind, wondering where he'd missed his chance to get out of the voyage.

He'd known they were in trouble from the moment Lambient had read Cholerish's letter. His lips had moved along with the words, a characteristic the illiterate Romul had always found off-putting—like they're saying they were better than everyone else because they could read. But after the first few lines, his jaw simply hung open. At one point, he'd peeked over the top of the letter at the girls with one eyebrow cocked, before continuing. The first words from his mouth when he finished were, "Is this some kind of joke?" And he'd smiled widely as though waiting for someone to jump out and yell, "Surprise!"

Of course, no one did.

When the younger Lambient had finally been made to understand that Cholerish was quite serious about his ferrying the four travelers across the Crescent Sea to the mouth of the South Wane River, so they could then make their way to Farwell in the far southwestern corner of the country, he responded by waving his arms wildly about. "Oh, but I can't. I simply can't, don't you see? I'm . . . uh . . . very busy just at present. Big things! Oh yes, very big things right now." He pointed at his boat with that pride a mother displays when showing off an extremely ugly baby.

Nevertheless the girls had persisted—at least Eli and Anna had. Rose had bypassed the whole debate and climbed aboard ship, where she began picking her way through the clutter on the deck. She picked up this tool or that little instrument with dangling wires, and asked repeated questions, like "What does this do?" or "Is this wire supposed to hang out like that?" And once an "Oops! Sorry." This had the effect of dividing the man's attention, so that one moment he was arguing with the older two and the next attending to Rose with a "Put that down!" or "Hey, careful, that's not a toy."

Inside of ten minutes he was so thoroughly exhausted that he sat down on the deck and put his head in his hands, whimpering, "Okay, okay, I'll do whatever you want. Just don't touch anything." Romul's low opinion of the man was now confirmed. He was a silly, weak person who could be bullied. Now, Romul was all in favor of such persons insofar as he was able to get what he needed from them, but he had little respect for them and was not in the habit of entrusting such people with his life.

The man was apparently made of sturdier stuff than Romul gave him credit for. The moment the coercion ceased, his mood lightened, and he began to act as though the girls' presence on his boat had been a foregone conclusion. He began showing them over the whole boat and explaining with great enthusiasm the exceptional nature of his "research." This rapid change of mood was just as disconcerting to Romul as anything else—cheerful even when used harshly by the sailors, weak when manipulated by the girls, and cheerful again an instant later when speaking of his own interests. This unpredictability made Romul suspicious. Surely one or all of these moods must be a show. When would the real Augustus show himself, he wondered. And what would he be like?

Augustus's conflicted nature was expressed in his work as well. He stood proudly on the deck, surrounded by his disorder, and proclaimed to the children with a theatrical gesture, "I am about to do what no living Garlandian has done! I will be the first to make contact with the merfolk of the Crescent Sea." The bulge in his larynx bounced up and down dramatically as he spoke, as if to underline the seriousness of the claim.

Romul, who knew as well as anyone that no such creatures existed, burst out laughing. The crestfallen look that came over the inventor's face, however, elicited such pity from the girls that Romul fell silent.

"Don't mind him, Mr. Lambient." Eli shot Romul a stern look. "He doesn't know anything about it. I, for one, want to hear every detail."

"Oh, call me Augie, please." He bounced back, mollified. "But I'm afraid I cannot at the moment. I must get the secondary coil back in line before we can sail. Then I shall tell you all about it."

The next several hours were tediously boring for Romul. The

scientist had sent the girls to his flat in the next block "for supplies," which judging from the list of items he gave them, meant to him chiefly foodstuffs. Romul had been volunteered to stay behind in case Augie needed any assistance. But it became immediately clear that the inventor was a one-man show, and he forgot about Romul the minute the girls were out of sight.

So the afternoon wore on till Romul was so out of his mind with boredom that he was just about to abandon his apprenticeship and take a walk along the wharf. But just then, a grease-covered Augie emerged from the cabin and announced the ship fit for launch. "Well, at any rate, it will be once the girls get back with the food." He rubbed his hands together in anticipation. "And they'd best hurry, as I'm all over starved."

At that moment Rose and Anna arrived, carrying large sacks over their shoulders. Eli followed a few minutes later pulling a wagon heaped with tins of meat, a side of bacon, cases of hard rolls and dried fruit, wine flasks, and a five-pound tin of butter.

"Sorry it took so long." Eli heaved a jug of wine onto the deck. "But we couldn't believe you wanted us to bring all this."

Augie surveyed the contents of the wagon with a look of disappointment. "I thought there'd be more."

"More?" Anna was hot and sweaty from carrying the heaviest sack. "There's enough food here to feed my whole school for a week! Plus the cabin's already packed so full of beans and fruit and boxes of I-don't-know-what-all that you can hardly move. I don't even see where we're supposed to sleep!"

Augie sighed. "Well, it'll have to do. You four go store it all in the cabin wherever you can find room, and I'll cast off. And once we're under way . . . supper!"

Romul was thus conscripted to help stow the provisions, and he was shocked by what he found in the cabin. A single hammock swung in the space overhead, and the floor was so littered with empty tins, tools, and paper wrappings that one could not tell whether the floor was wood or carpeted. No sink could be found—just two metal buckets against the wall—one marked with a plus sign, the other with a minus sign. Presumably you took water from the plus bucket for whatever use, and drained it into the minus bucket as waste water.

Romul's hard life had given him admittedly low expectations, but even he was appalled. What the boat lacked in amenities, however, the larder more than made up for. It seemed Augie had disposed of even the toilet for the sake of increasing his food stores, and within the hour Romul understood why.

During the supper that followed their departure, he watched with wonder as the scientist put down more food than Romul believed any person could hold and with room to spare. In fact, over the coming day, he not only ate twice the fare of a man twice his size, but finished off everyone else's leftovers as well. He even kept a flock of eager spatulas at the ready to scrape clean any container that neared empty. There seemed little use in washing his dishes, as they looked as clean after the meal as before. If it was even technically edible, it had a place on his menu—the brine from the pickle jar, the oil from a sardine can, apple cores, and even the rinds of oranges. And this gorge was apparently repeated several times a day. It was inexplicable—very nearly magical—that so much food could be poured into the lank and boney man without creating a single bulge anywhere on his frame. Having little respect for the scientist in other regards, Romul, who knew something of hunger, had to marvel at their host's infinite capacity for food.

The sun was setting behind them as they cleared the mouth of the Waxing River, against whose flow they had been slowly beating for several hours. The first waves of the Crescent Sea were beginning to pitch the ship unpredictably. Romul, who had never been on a boat before, was finding the new sensations most unpleasant. One moment his stomach was situated normally in his middle, and the next it was in his throat. His forehead bore a ring of perspiration that had nothing to do with the heat, and he desperately wished he'd eaten less than he had, thinking that in a minute or two he'd be seeing it all again. He clutched the rusty railing at the bow of the boat, looked out to sea, and cursed whatever devilish powers had tricked him into this horrible adventure.

Suddenly the movement of the boat changed. Where a headwind had been a moment ago, now there was none. The ship seemed to have lost its forward momentum. He looked behind him. The mouth of the river was already lost from view in the indistinct detail of the seashore. Yes, they had stopped moving. The ship was drifting, turning toward the shore as the waves struck it. Broadside to the waves, the ship not only pitched up and down but now rocked from side to side as well. His knuckles whitened as he tightened his death grip on the railing.

The door of the cabin flew open, and out shot Augie with crumbs on his lapel and a meat roll in his hand. Cramming it into his mouth, he stumbled to the bow and fell on the deck next to Romul. He heaved on a lever, and Romul heard a splash. He looked over the side just in time to see a big anchor disappearing into the sea, dragging a heavy line behind it.

The inventor turned to him and grinned. "Well, time to refill the bladder." And without another word he scurried toward the cabin. Romul, assuming he was off to get a drink, rolled his eyes. A moment later he was joined by the three girls, who'd been sitting in the stern talking quietly.

"So is it time to refill the bladder?" Eli said it so casually that Romul was impressed by her ability to not snicker.

"Must be," said Anna. "It feels like we've stopped moving."

"What's that got to do with his bladder?" Romul was immediately sorry he'd asked, for the girls burst into laughter.

"No, silly," said Rose. "The ship is out of water."

Trying desperately not to display further ignorance, Romul cast a cautious glance overboard to see if the ship really was out of the water, and how it was possible. The laughter broke out again.

"Weren't you listening when he explained how the ship works?" said Anna.

"Oh, poor Rommie," jumped in Rose. "He couldn't know. Remember, he was up here being sick when Augie told us."

"I ain't sick," began Romul, when a wave heaved the boat up several feet into the air. Romul tried to finish his sentence but knew it was no good. He no longer doubted that he was going to be sick; it was just a matter of when. To cover for his greenish feeling, he motioned for Eli to continue.

"See the big prop up there on the mast?" She pointed to the propeller high above the deck turning slowly but evenly in the sea breeze. "That turns a pump in the hold that sucks in sea water and pushes it into a huge 'bladder' that takes up most of the hold. He puts that huge sack of water under pressure . . . somehow—I didn't quite get that part—and then shoots it out small nozzles in the back like a jet. It's quite ingenious, really. He's more like his father than I thought."

"More or less." Anna scanned the cluttered deck.

"He said we can run for several hours on a single charge in calm water," continued Eli, "but when the pressure gets down so far, it won't move the boat anymore, and we have to let the turbine catch up. More wind means a faster recharge."

"I don't think Rommie wants any more wind." Rose patted him on the head. This infuriated Romul, but he dared not open his mouth to respond.

"Okay," came Augie's cheerful voice from the cabin. "We're recharging at a good rate. We'll be ready for another run in about twenty minutes. I'm thinking of a sandwich."

"Geez!" cried Anna. "He eats like a hobbit!"

Augie regarded her for a moment. "Uh . . . okay. Anyone want to join me? I've got a big juicy piece of salt pork that's just—"

The suggestion was too much for Romul's roiling belly. He threw his head over the side and gave himself up to the inevitable . . . several times.

Chapter 9

Romul lay faceup on the deck, looking at the moon. Augie had finished his bedtime snack, which he called his "final fête"—whatever that meant—but really constituted a second supper. Now he was preparing for bed. He emerged from his cabin carrying his two buckets. He drew up a bucketful of water in the "plus" bucket, emptied the "minus" bucket over the side, and disappeared back into the cabin, whistling the whole time.

He'd acted like he was actually enjoying himself. Now that Romul and his guts had reached a relative truce, he could very well begin to appreciate the inventor's life—bereft of luxuries as it was. The night was fine and clear and warm. Other than the rhythmic sloshing of water against the sides of the anchored boat, it was peaceful. Indeed, it was the quietest moment Romul had enjoyed since his conscription and the first in which his mind wasn't filled with troubling thoughts.

No one had wanted to sleep in the squalid cabin with Augie, nor was he apparently interested in company, for he'd produced a stack of blankets for their use without being asked. Now the girls were bunked down on the stern deck and already asleep—or so he supposed. A few minutes later the light in the cabin went out, and Romul was alone with his thoughts.

He stared at Lemerrus high overhead. It looked larger and closer now than at any time Romul could remember. He passed the firebrand from hand to hand, looking first at it then back to the great red moon. He pondered what the priest had said of a connection between the two. Lemerrus—god of the poor and resourceful and of fire, was that it? No, not "god." Cholerish hadn't said that, but Romul couldn't remember what the priest had called Lemerrus. But certainly everything else fit—poor, resourceful, fire-loving. Romul wondered if that was why he'd always felt so connected with the moon. Was it some sweet influence pouring down upon him from that red disk his whole life, without his even knowing? Was this why he'd always preferred night to day? Or was that only a result of his skulking existence? But that, too, was part of poverty and resourcefulness, wasn't it?

He looked again at the firebrand. Was this Lemerrus himself? The great fire-moon come down from his place in the heavens to earth to do . . . what? It made little sense to Romul. A great threat arising, heavenly powers descending, and all this to be clarified by a conversation with a salamander. It was madness. How could any of it even be true?

No, it was Garlandish legend. It had nothing to do with him. He was Rokan . . . unavoidably, it seemed. If he belonged somehow to the Queen of Angish, then all this talk of heavenly emissaries —*that's* what the priest had called them!—was mere Garlandish rubbish. And yet as he stared at the crimson circle floating high overhead now, he felt he couldn't be certain of anything.

Even with the unfamiliar rocking of the boat or perhaps because of it, it took less time than one might expect for all this to pass through his mind and be washed away into a sleep where even his dreams were colored by a comforting red hue.

∽

Apparently Augie needed only about four hours of sleep. Romul awoke several times to knocking and clattering from the cabin. Now the inventor was up before the sun, bustling around on deck. He'd heaved up the anchor for the "severalth" time and set the ship in motion before Romul had managed to pick his head up off the deck boards. Even more to Romul's annoyance, Eli and Rose bounced forward a few minutes later, arms loaded with breakfast goods and chattering like birds.

"Rise and shine! Today's the big day," cried Augie.

Romul's reply consisted of a grunt and a burying of his head into his folded arms. When he felt someone tousle his hair and say, "Good morning, Rommie," he flew into a fit of pique. He sat up ready to behead the offender, but Merris chose that exact moment to cast her first rays over the liquid horizon. That beam poured the full glory of the morning into Rose's blue eyes, making them sparkle with the innocence and laughter that lived there. In that moment she was a vision of the morning sky, limitless and free, winged and soaring in empty halls of air.

Romul was shaken to his soul by a sense of beauty that went way beyond Rose, but for which she, in that moment, was the lens. Ignorant of her own transformation at the hands of Merris, Rose laughed and retreated, taking the aura of the dawn with her. Romul felt dizzy and faint, like a man forcibly awakened from a vision.

When his head cleared, he found Augie, Eli, and Rose sitting on the deck, already eating. The scientist was talking rapidly between mouthfuls, all the while pointing wildly at various contraptions surrounding him. Romul suddenly found himself hungry and joined them.

Perhaps it was the sea air or perhaps something else, but the tinned biscuit and dried fruit he was munching tasted better than usual—sweeter and more nourishing. His imagination could almost sense the fields of golden grain from which the biscuit flour had come and the orchards that had labored to produce the figs.

A gratitude for humble pleasures like eating, breathing, and simple sight welled up within him with such force that his eyes grew uncontrollably moist. What was happening to him? He'd never been the reflective type, but in this moment, the whole world seemed to be speaking to him of his own smallness and insignificance—and for that reason, of the greater glory of undeserved blessings. Was this what the old men of Farwell had spoken of when they gave thanks to the Queen of Angish for "gifts great and small"?

The next moment all the glory of the morning was shattered and made commonplace by Anna. Like a cow stumbling through a picnic, Anna staggered up from the stern, bleary-eyed and sour-faced, and threw herself down in a huffy pile next to him. Apparently she enjoyed the morning about as much as he did.

"Geez! Are the fish even up yet? If you guys want to get up at the butt-crack of dawn, fine, but I don't see why I—"

"Oh, pipe down," said Eli. "Augie was just telling us about his new invention. We get to be the first ones to see it in action." She looked expectantly toward the scientist. "Go on, Augie."

As she reached for the coffee, Anna only muttered, "Yeah, that's what he needs—a little encouragement."

He proved her right in this by continuing his explanation more or less unabated throughout Anna's arrival. He was now pointing at a long metal tube about the width and height of a man strapped to the starboard side of the deck. "So first the sender unit gets lowered into the water. Then when I throw the switch—" he pointed to the cabin—"it emits a particular kind of sound into the water. It's so high-pitched that we wouldn't be able to hear it, but I believe the undini can."

Romul burst into laughter. "Sound we can't hear? That's nonsense. It wouldn't be sound if we couldn't hear it!" Thinking himself very clever, he was shocked to find that the girls seemed to understand what the inventor meant very well.

Augie didn't even notice the interruption but rattled on. "So this is the first device I believe capable of enabling communication with the merfolk and other undini. We don't believe undini speak, but they probably have very keen hearing. And they may come when 'called' in such a way."

"They don't speak?" asked Rose. "How do they talk to each other?"

Augie raised a knowing finger and said "Ah . . ." He bounded off to his cabin and returned a moment later carrying a weathered book. "My secret weapon." He patted the cracked and moth-eaten leather. He set it down on the deck and gingerly opened its yellowed pages. "I have Cholerish to thank for this. Although he, too, considers my quest madness, he told me that if any merfolk still inhabit the Crescent Sea, this book would be of inestimable value. I have practically memorized it."

Romul had the worst angle on the book, but it seemed to contain page after faded page of tiny sketches. Without closing the book, Eli lifted its cover and peered underneath. She read slowly, *"On the Speech of the Therran Undini or more particularly on the modes of gesticulation and courtesy among certain Oceanic Therran Merfolk complete with integrated visual indications," by Dr. Algeaus Salmankindia."*

"That's a mouthful," mumbled Anna.

"Gesticulation?" said Eli. "That's like a *gesture*, isn't it?" A light dawned on her face, and she grew excited. "Oh, does this mean they use sign language?" She and Augie shared a look of mutual appreciation, which Romul felt was a bit smugger than necessary—an opinion clearly shared by Anna, who rolled her eyes.

"You've hit it on the head, shipmate! Yes, this most ancient book is of Azhionian origin. It would have to be, for no one in Garlandium has thought of such things in hundreds of years. It catalogues the communication methods of the merfolk who live in the oceans. It theorizes that merfolk use high-pitched sounds— much like my sounder—for general long-range communication and a system of gestures for close and detailed communication. I've spent the last year studying it. I'm now pretty sure that, with the signs, I can communicate with them . . . if I can just get their attention."

"But would the merfolk in the Crescent Sea use the same signs as the ones in the ocean?" said Anna skeptically.

Augie's grin wavered a bit. "Perhaps. I mean, I have to admit, it's not exactly a perfect plan. But it's the only one I've been able to think of."

"I think it's just super!" said Eli. "Imagine, a real mermaid!"

The rest of breakfast consisted of Augie describing—in agonizing detail—how the sounder made its sounds that could not be heard. Romul understood little of it and quickly lost interest.

An hour later they were almost ready. The girls were all in the stern, waiting for the sounder's deployment. Romul had been conscripted to help Augie drop it over the side without damaging it. It was heavier than he'd expected, and lowering it involved a sweaty and prolonged effort by them both. Finally it hung suspended over the water by a boom, but Romul couldn't leave because he had to hold it steady as the scientist made final adjustments to the dials and knobs that covered a whole side of it. Romul felt awkward in such proximity to the inventor. He could feel Augie's breath on his hand as he labored over his precious device.

The inventor must have found the close silence awkward as well, for after a few minutes of silent tinkering, he mumbled in a casual tone, "So you're . . . uh, headed home, are you?"

Romul's heart double-beat. "What?"

"Back to the Ward in Farwell. That's where you're from, isn't it, being Rokan and all?" he said with the awkward air of one who's distracted.

"How did you . . ." Romul collected himself and tried to sound offended. "I'm not Rokan. I'm . . . um, pure-blooded Garlandish." And he thought he sounded rather grand saying it.

The scientist smirked but continued his tinkering. "Suit yourself. I spent most of my childhood denying I was the son of a mad scientist. Didn't get me anyplace particularly worth going in the end. But I guess we each have to walk our own road."

This irritated Romul. "You don't know what you're talking about. I said I ain't Rokan."

"Look." The scientist shrugged. "I'm not trying to fight. It's just obvious that you're not quite . . . uh, native to these parts, and I—"

This made Romul mad, and he spat out venomously, "What do you know about it? What do you know about anything, you . . . you crazy milksop! I'm telling you, I am not one of those dirty little . . . Opsies." He stumbled a bit over the final word. He'd never actually said it out loud, and it came hard.

Now Augie was looking him right in the eye, for the moment very unlike the namby-pamby person Romul had seen so far. "All right. Back up! I know you don't like me . . . or at least, you don't respect me, which is probably worse. But I know what it's like to hide from yourself. You think I like pretending to be stupid and clumsy with Pike and Iggy? You think it's easy to act dumber than you are? Do you know what the sailors or city officials would do to me if they thought for a moment I was smart enough to actually succeed? They'd run me out of Umbra on the next coach, like they did my crazy father. They don't want to know what swims beneath us. There's no money in it, but if a tenth of the legends are true, there's plenty of risk. So long as I'm a sideshow who pays for everyone's ale, they leave me alone."

It seemed like Augie had poured all that out in a single breath. Now he inhaled a great gust of air for another run, as if in sympathy with his ship, and continued. "But then you show up out of the blue, beg passage on my ship, eat my food, and then have the nerve to put on airs and lie to my face?" Now it was Augie's turn to be angry. "Hell, kid, do you think I care where you come from? Or what you think of me? You think I don't know what it means to run from your past? Well, I've been doing it longer than you've been alive, and apparently I'm better at it than you'll ever be. So if you want to go on pretending you're not Rokan, you go right ahead. But don't try to play me for a fool. Nobody plays a fool better than me."

He threw his wrench down on the deck and stormed away. A few seconds later the cabin door slammed.

Romul stood frozen, unable to move.

"What was all that about?" asked Eli. The shouting had brought them forward.

"I . . . I . . ." He didn't know what to say. "He knows I'm . . ."

"Of course he knows." Anna crossed her arms with an exasperated air. "He asked us about it last night."

Romul whirled on her, but Rose spoke first. "But we didn't tell him anything, Rommie."

"Yeah," added Anna. "We told him to ask you. It's not our business."

"But you shouldn't have yelled at him like that," said Eli. "Don't you know the pressure he's under? He's out of money. If this doesn't work, he'll have to quit and go back home. You shouldn't antagonize him."

Rose jumped to Romul's defense. "Get off his back, Eli. He didn't know, and he'll apologize, won't you, Rommie?"

The suggestion sounded so sensible, so innocently offered, like a rescue. He nodded numbly and even took several steps across the deck before he came to himself. He turned to insist he hadn't done anything wrong, but Rose had this look on her face that said, *Go ahead. I know you can do it.*

He wandered around to the cabin door. Not knowing how to proceed, he knocked.

"Yeah?"

He pushed the door open. The inventor was standing in front of a bank of controls amid a cascade of wires and switches. "Oh, it's you."

"Yeah, I'm, um . . ." He'd never apologized in his life, and didn't know how to do it.

The inventor looked up at Romul's face, smiled sheepishly, and said, "Yeah, me too."

Romul knew he need say no more. Everything between him and Augie was okay. Even more, in that thin goggling face and oversized nose, he saw someone, maybe the first someone, who really understood him.

"How did you know?"

Augie laughed. "There's more to being Rokan than white hair, kid. For one thing, Garlandians don't refer to themselves as Garlandish. That's usually an insult used by Opsiercoms and the Azhwana."

Romul didn't even flinch at the O word now, but he was still a little unsure. "Is it okay that I'm . . ." He let the question drop. It would only sound silly.

Augie looked him in the eye. "People who have time to concern themselves with such nonsense have too little to do. People busy with great affairs have no time to worry about who's better than who. The proof of your worth is in the size of your dreams . . . or today, in the dream's doing!" He grinned and went up on deck.

The next sound Romul heard was a tremendous splash, followed by the scientist's joyful cry, "Sounder away!"

Chapter 10

Augie had only a vague idea of how far the sounder's transmission could travel under water, and even less of an idea of where merfolk were likely to be found. So the best strategy was to drag the sounder over as much of the Crescent Sea as possible—which wasn't much. It was like towing a huge anchor. So they actually made very little forward progress.

Hours passed, and the initial excitement wore off. Eli had apparently expected mermaids to begin jumping into the boat like fish the moment Augie toggled the switch. She grew snippy with disappointment as the afternoon wore on, even telling Augie his sounder wasn't "turned up loud enough." While part of Romul wanted the experiment to succeed for the sake of his newfound sympathy for Augie, he still didn't believe merfolk existed. It was the sort of conflict that muddled his mind. How does one hope the impossible is true after all?

Eventually Augie had to concede that Eli's point might have merit. He decided to risk burning out the sounder by broadening the frequencies and boosting the signal with more power than he was confident it could handle. He returned from the cabin with a worried look on his face. "Well, that's all she's got. If that don't do it, then nothing—"

Anna's cry cut him off. The rest of them looked up to where she stood at the bow, on lookout, pointing toward the horizon. A tiny atoll of land was just visible above the surface.

"Oh, that's just one of the Insula Plura," said Augie, unconcerned.

"There are several collections of them in the Crescent Sea. I could show you on the map where we—"

"No!" Anna pointed again. "Closer than that!" Romul looked hard and saw troubled water a few hundred yards from the ship. The surface broke, and white foam burst into the air. Then the geyser was gone, but the troubled water was now closer—a hundred yards, maybe. The water roiled. Something was moving rapidly right below the surface in their direction.

"Um . . . um . . ." stammered Augie. "Everybody get to the center of the boat . . . and, uh, grab on to something." The goal of the experiment had been to summon merfolk. Romul now realized that other, less-pleasant things in the Crescent Sea might be summoned the same way.

The white wave burst again a mere fifty feet from the boat. There was no question now. They were about to be rammed. Romul threw himself to the deck and searched for something to hold on to. His hands closed on one of the heavy wires that crisscrossed the deck.

Romul never remembered the exact moment of impact; he simply found himself airborne. The boat, too, seemed to be out of the water. It was lurching upward as he was coming down, and he was driven into the deck with a sickening crunch. One of the girls was screaming, maybe all of them. Romul maybe was, too—he didn't know. The boat creaked horribly under him, cables snapped and twanged around him, and he realized something was wrong with the sky. It seemed to be tilting sideways—no, the whole world was tilting with it.

Then his head cleared, and he saw what was happening. The horizon seemed to keel over sideways, but he knew that wasn't the case. It was worse. The boat was listing.

He picked himself up groggily. Anna lay to one side of the deck groaning from unknown injuries. Eli lay on the other, weeping and pointing. Augie was leaning over the side shouting, but Rose was nowhere to be seen. He scrambled to his feet and struggled to

Augie's side, which felt increasingly like an uphill climb. Rose was bobbing up and down in the water. Augie threw her a little float-bob pillow, telling her to grab on to the handles.

Romul turned now to survey the damage. He was stunned. The *Sea Bellows* had been nearly torn in half by the impact. She was buckled right in the middle, and the bow and the stern seemed to be sinking toward each other. Only then did he understand their peril. They were all going into the water. It was only a matter of minutes.

He turned and yelled, "Augie, we've—" But he was cut off by a float-bob hitting him in the face.

"I know, I know!" yelled the scientist as he threw another of the pillows to the wailing Eli. He picked Anna up off the deck. She seemed lethargic, and her forehead was bloody. Her legs would not hold her up. "But, Mom, the mermaids will be nice to *me...*" Anna mumbled incoherently. But even as Romul attempted to parse the gibberish, he saw white foam burst again off the port side.

"Augie! It's coming back."

"I know, I know!" Augie yelled again, hoisting one of Anna's drooping arms over his shoulder. "We can't be here when it hits."

Romul was aghast, but it was Eli who spoke—or rather, shrieked. "You mean get in the water with it?"

Augie rounded on her and spoke in a calm but authoritative voice Pike and Iggy would not have recognized. "No debate, now. We jump or become flotsam ourselves." Eli fell silent, but didn't seem able to move. Augie looked at Romul, who understood and went to her.

"Come on." He took Eli's arm, intending to lead her to the edge, but at that moment the boat lurched and tilted further over. Romul nearly fell on her as they slid to the edge. The gunnel on the starboard side was already under, so there was little persuading to be done. He simply pushed her away from the boat as she slid into the water.

Then Rose came paddling into view around the bow of the sinking boat. "Don't worry, Eli. The water's fine."—as if the temperature had been Eli's sole hesitation. Romul had no time to ponder the enigma that was Rose. Augie needed help with Anna. She'd recovered somewhat, but was still woozy and weak-kneed. One on either side, they guided her into the water and pushed away from the submerged deck, each with a float-bob under them.

Suddenly a great shadow fell across them. Between them and the sun, a huge head on a long neck—a neck so long that it looked like a snake—rose out of the water. Upward it went to an impossible height, where it opened its maw and let out a terrible scream of rage that shook the sky. Instinctively Romul put his hands to his ears, but in doing so he let go of his float-bob. He sank momentarily, resurfacing just in time to see that neck, thicker than an oak, rear as snakes do when preparing to strike. Romul was sure it was the end.

But to his amazement, the monster plunged headfirst into the sea behind the wreckage. With a splintering and cracking of timber, the stern of the boat was torn loose and began to move bizarrely away as if under its own power. Then the beast's head emerged again a hundred yards away, and he saw the glint of silver metal in its teeth. It had grabbed the sounder like bait and was now swimming away, dragging the stern of the boat with it like a bobber. Then it dove, and the stern dipped under the waves and was gone. A final *glub* behind Romul told him the bow had come to a similar end.

Eli and Rose paddled up to them, their pale faces revealing worry and wonder respectively. Five people now treaded water in the middle of the Crescent Sea without ship or rations.

True to his form, the panic was already draining from Augie's face, leaving a cheery smile in its place. "Well, here we all are. No two ways about it, we were just plain lucky." Romul looked from the swooning Anna to the grinning scientist. Apparently Anna wasn't the only one with a head injury.

Chapter 11

"Oh, my head," groaned Anna. She was treading water on her own now, but Augie held her fast to him since she had no float-bob. Romul was not a great swimmer, and staying afloat consumed all his attention. He regained his own float-bob, which gave him the luxury of wondering what would happen to them now.

Eli was weeping softly. Even Rose's cheery demeanor had slumped, and she was looking forlornly about them. Augie alone refused to allow the Crescent Sea to dampen his spirits. He was mumbling encouraging words like "It's okay" and "We're going to be just fine" to no one in particular.

Romul found such buoyant optimism incredibly unrealistic and was about to say so when suddenly Rose cried out and disappeared. Her float-bob bobbed away. Before Romul could register what had happened, Eli screamed and sank as well. Then Rose popped back up, a wild terror in her eyes. She managed to say "Something's got—" Then was gone again. Next Augie yelped and went under, but now Eli had resurfaced, screaming, "Let go, oh please, let—" She disappeared once more.

Romul felt something grab his ankle, and a powerful pull drew him into the deep. Only instinct kept his mouth closed. His mind screamed in terror as a cascade of bubbles whirled around his head. His arms flailed frantically before his face as though they belonged to someone else. A form bobbed upward next to him— Eli again? Then the hold on his ankle released, and he, too, rushed to the surface.

He was only in the world of air long enough to take two gasping breaths before the grip returned and drew him down. Again he was released, and again he surfaced. This time he heard Augie cry, "It's them, they're—" His voice was cut off mid-burble. A moment later, and despite frantic kicking, Romul was again dragged under.

This time he was pulled down deep. He heard a thudding in his ears, and his body heaved, demanding breath. His mind overruled it, and his mouth remained closed. Yet through his panic, a wholly different part of his mind now awoke. Most of him was consumed with survival, but unexpectedly, a part of him experienced curiosity about their assailants. This other part of him swiveled his head back-and-forth and was struck by the clarity of the water. He actually took stock of things. Eli and Rose were momentarily free, swimming wildly for the surface. Next to him, Augie was being dragged down by . . .

Romul's eyes nearly stared out of his head. From out of the stories of his infancy, he recognized it—the long fish-like body, lithe and iridescent, the length of a man plus a half, yet with long arms and a head. A merman. The creature had pulled Augie down to its level, stared into his face for a moment before releasing him. Romul's own captor now did the same. He found himself staring into two great lidless eyes—colorless but reflective, with large, black pupils. He also had the impression of a sadistic grin. Then he, too, was released, and the face faded as he fought to gain the surface.

In his upward rush, he blundered into Anna who was being pulled down. She was giving only feeble resistance. He grabbed vaguely at her as he passed with no clear idea of what he could actually do for her, but his fingers caught hold of the chain around her neck. It checked his momentum slightly before being jerked out of his hand. Anna sank, and he continued to rise.

He broke the surface and gasped for air. Again he kicked his feet frantically in a hopeless bid to prevent being seized again, but the groping hands did not return. Augie, Eli, and Rose were also on the surface. They exchanged wild-eyed glances, having no strength for words.

After a whole minute of exhausted treading, however, no attacks came. Eli and Augie both recovered their bobs, and between them all four were able to have a moment's rest.

"Don't understand," panted Augie. "They're just playing with us."

"Where's Anna?" Romul turned round in a circle looking, but she was nowhere to be seen. Eli's face twisted in grief, and Rose finally decided it was time to cry.

No one spoke. What was there to say? Romul knew nothing could be done. Anna was gone, and now they all awaited death on the timetable of the very creatures they'd been foolish enough to seek.

Then he had an idea. "Augie, hold me down. I'm going to look." Before Augie could ask what he meant, he'd taken several quick breaths and ducked into the water. Romul could feel Augie's hand on his back, holding him down. He looked around, amazed again at the clarity of the water. He could see at least thirty feet in every direction.

Then he saw her. Anna was down at the center of a swirling cloud of the fishy shapes. Between their flitting forms, he could see she was being held by all four limbs. Romul was confused. She wasn't fighting her captors, nor did she look very drowned. This alone seemed a minor miracle, for she'd been under nearly five minutes.

She was being examined by the creatures. The largest of them, a mermaid with long, reedy hair that swirled around her head, was darting back-and-forth in front of Anna. She would pause every pass or two and grab at something around Anna's neck—her amulet. She would seize it, pull it tight on the chain, and peer at it closely. Then she'd drop it and begin gesturing wildly to the others before starting the sequence over again.

Romul was feeling the need to surface, but just as he'd decided to do so, Anna cast her eyes upward. Something was wrong with her face. Something dark and mushy-looking clung to it, making her look as if she were eating a giant mushroom. Her eyes met his, and even from this distance, he could see the fear in them. But her movement caught the attention of the mermaid. She, too, lifted her head and spied Romul. She threw out a finger toward him, and the whole group of merfolk turned and looked at him.

Then they came.

He panicked and struggled to rise. He got his head above water just in time to get a breath and cry, "They're coming!" when hands closed on his ankles and down he went.

Fighting was futile. His arms were grabbed and his head pulled back. He was vaguely aware of a similar struggle going on near him with the other three. Whatever he expected to happen next, what actually happened was such a surprise that he forgot to hold his breath.

Something was shoved into his face. Green, gritty, and spongy, it latched onto his mouth and nose with a remarkable suction. He screamed, and the sound of his own voice sounded dull and hollow. But then he realized he'd inhaled.

He had inhaled!

The creatures began to drag him down to Anna's level. He was determined not to let go of the lungful of air he'd somehow gained, but he grew light-headed with the effort of holding his breath. Panic rose again, but now Anna's face came into view. She looked at him, blinked, and nodded as if to say *It's okay*. She was very much alive, and the deformation on her face, he imagined, was of the same sort he now wore. A line of bubbles burst out of it as if she'd just exhaled through it. He was slow in comprehending.

He looked from side to side and saw that the other three, also held by strong hands, were all wearing the same spongy growth. Augie was showing signs of fainting, but Rose seemed to have regained her ease. Romul could hold his breath no longer. His vision began to fade, and he felt the air leave his body against his will. His body again refused his mind and drew in a breath, but Romul was immediately refreshed. Again it was air and not water that flooded his lungs. Now his body revolted entirely and began breathing without his consent. Whatever the stuff was on his face, it was allowing air to pass into him.

Augie's head shot up with surprise. He was having a similar revelation. He began to struggle, which initially Romul thought foolish. After all, if the merfolk wished them dead, they would be already. Then he realized Augie wasn't trying to escape but to get his arms free. In this he actually succeeded. For several seconds his right arm was free, and he was making gestures.

The great mermaid who had been examining Anna swam slowly up to him, her head cocked to one side like a dog listening hard to a far-off sound. Romul now saw the creature's face distinctly. The eyes did in fact have lids, but they seldom closed. While a slight bulge gave the impression of a nose, she had no nostrils, nor did he see any ears amid the wild and tangled hair that flowed down over the top third of her body. Her skin was green and glossy, not like a fish but more like a shark's. She was larger than the mermen, yet Romul realized that, except for the long hair, she was nearly indistinguishable from the males. Yet something in the face, in the look and manner, seemed to him very feminine.

She was making tentative gestures now before Augie's face. Both his hands had been released, but his legs were still being held fast together. She paused, and Augie's face contorted as if trying to remember something. He made a quick gesture in reply, and she drew back in dismay. Augie shook his head violently and made another. Then she relaxed.

And so it went for several minutes, with her making confident and fluid circles and signs with her fingers and Augie struggling with much effort to make appropriate countersigns. The exchange climaxed with Augie throwing his hands over his face and his whole body beginning to shake as if he were crying.

Anna's amulet was again held out in front of him as if demanding some explanation. But Augie's eyes were unseeing. His arms floated limply in front of him. He looked like a soldier in war who sees one tragedy too many and is thrust into shock. He stared without comprehension and made no reply. This at last frustrated the mermaid beyond her tolerance. She began making more complicated gestures to her companions than Romul had yet seen. They seemed to all be males. But again, Romul was not exactly sure why he thought so, other than that they lacked the long flowing train of hair—and they were all smaller than the mermaid.

A moment later he felt the hold on his legs release. The mermaid had turned and was flitting off, and her mermen were following. The two holding Romul's arms made powerful forward lunges that made his head snap back. At great speed, they were all being borne along by mermen in procession behind the mermaid. It was really unpleasant. He felt like an anchor being dragged through the water, and the rush of the current forced him to close his eyes. This made him lose his bearings. If he'd been blindfolded and spun in circles, his disorientation could not have been more complete.

Nausea welled up in his belly, and he wondered what happened if you barfed under water.

Chapter 12

After what seemed like hours of being dragged along like a toy on a string, Romul, his eyes still tightly shut, felt a change. They were descending. It grew more uncomfortable—weight on the chest, ringing in the ears, pressure in the temples. The discomfort turned quickly to pain. He was on the verge of crying out when they suddenly changed directions and began to ascend. Romul was so discombobulated by now that he wouldn't have known even this but for the immediate easing of the pressure on his ears.

Almost before it could register, all forward motion stopped. He was given a shove and released. He opened his eyes, and a strange sight presented itself. It took him a moment to realize that he was having a fish's perspective of a shoreline. A broad but strangely illuminated stretch of rocky coastline ascended steeply before him toward the surface.

Oh sweet Angish, he thought as he scrambled forward. He scraped his hands on the rocks as he clawed his way through the water and up the steep slope of gravel.

He broke the surface of the water and dragged himself forward to the shore, where he lay like a half-drowned animal. He experienced a brief fright in finding he couldn't breathe, but then he remembered the spongy apparatus on his face. He tore at it, but it was already drying out and losing its grip. It came free with ease and melted into a green jelly in his hand. Disgusted, he threw it away.

Now he perceived others panting and coughing around him. He lifted his head and counted the bodies. Four plus himself, all sprawled on the sand. His relief was so great that he laughed aloud. The sound of his own voice surprised him—strangely hollow, producing echoes. It took him a full minute to realize they were in a cave with a high ceiling. A sliver of daylight came down through a fissure in the ceiling, but otherwise the cave was dark. The only noise was the repeated crash of breakers outside, sounding rather like thunder yet coming every few seconds without pause.

Suddenly the relative quiet was rent by a cry. Augie had drawn himself onto his knees and was crying out as if he were dying. Romul jumped to his feet, but he couldn't see anything wrong with the scientist. Augie threw his forehead down into the sand and collapsed in melancholy sobs. He moaned wretchedly and rolled onto his back, crying out again.

"Augie, Augie!" Eli crawled over to him. "What's wrong? Are you hurt?"

He shook his head fiercely and gnashed his teeth. He grabbed handfuls of sand in writhing hands and pitched them into the air.

"Augie!" bawled Eli into his ear. "Tell us what's wrong!"

"Oooooh," he moaned. "All my life . . . all my life . . . I looked, I studied, I prayed. And now . . ."

Romul looked around the cave. The threat of immediate death seemed to have passed, but their situation had only marginally improved. This was no time for compassion. They couldn't afford to have the only sea-wise member of the team—and the only adult—lose his mind.

He ran to Augie's convulsing form, straddled his chest, and shook his shoulders. "Hey! Hey! Get hold of yourself. We don't got time for faking right now. If you ain't hurt—"

But Augie rallied with unexpected strength, grabbed Romul by both wrists, and threw him off with the ease of a man in a great fury. Romul lay stunned on the sand next to him. The girls, who'd been gathering their courage to try to help somehow, now shrank back and sat in a little half circle around him. Nothing to do but let the fit pass.

This it did, but only after several more minutes of convulsive outbursts. Eventually Augie's weeping ebbed, and his reason returned in a torrent of clarity. He jerked upright and blinked at them.

"I . . . um . . ." he began, but got no further.

All three of the girls began saying encouraging things like "It's okay" and "We understand." Romul did not understand, did not think it was okay, and said so.

"I'm sorry." Augie shook his head. "But you *don't* understand. I have worked to make contact with the undini since I was a child. It was my dream. I chose the Therran academy so I could specialize in merlore. It's all I've ever wanted to do, to understand how they think and why. And now . . ." His lip quivered.

"And now they don't seem nice after all—" began Anna.

Augie cut her off. "No, no, you really don't understand. I mean, yes, they don't like us, that much is true. But it's my fault we're here. That they . . ." He swallowed hard, but continued. "It was the sounder. I never imagined . . . They said it hurt them. The sound was painful to them. They thought . . . they thought I was trying to kill them. But all I ever wanted was to make contact. And now I've ruined everything." He put his face in his hands again.

"That's probably why the other thing attacked too," added Eli.

"Yes," came his muffled voice from between his palms. "The eachey has very sensitive hearing, just like the merfolk."

"Well, that's just great!" huffed Romul. He was not at all moved by the shattering of Augie's dream, but he did recognize a prison when he saw it. It was obvious this place was meant to contain them, but why and for how long? He explored the cave just to be sure. It was actually a hollow space inside an island mountain completely enclosed by rock. The watery tunnel they entered by looked from here like an innocent pond. But no threat or bride in the world would get any of them to enter it again. They were trapped.

The light filtering in from the hole in the ceiling grew slowly golden, dimmed, and disappeared. Night came with all its predict-able gloom. Romul produced his firebrand from his pocket and conjured a wick of flame. They huddled together around the tiny light as the only source of comfort in the dark. No one wanted to sleep, but eventually they all grew weary.

They decided to take turns at watch. Eli would go first and stay up as long as she could. When she couldn't last any longer without risking sleep, she would wake Augie, who would in turn wake Anna. Then she would rouse Romul, and he would wake Rose. And so began as fitful and uncomfortable a night's sleep as Romul had ever had. He was used to sleeping on the ground, but the waves thundering outside constantly disturbed him.

He must have slept eventually, for there came a moment when he felt a finger digging into his ribs. He groaned.

"It's your turn," hissed a voice in his ear. It sounded like it was coming from a long way off. Then a not-so-gentle thud on his rib cage brought him to full consciousness. "Get up! It's your turn!" He registered the frustration in the voice, as if it had been saying the same thing for some time. It was, of course, Anna, waking him for his turn at watch.

He sat up and looked about, but it was so dark he couldn't be sure whether his eyes were open or closed. He heard Anna flop down in the sand next to him, and in a few minutes she was breathing softly. The pounding surf outside had become merely background noise, so despite it, the cave felt very silent.

At some point, Romul's head shot up, and he knew he'd nod-ded off. He looked around to see if anyone had seen. But even the possibility of being seen meant something had changed. Everyone was still asleep, but he could see them as dim forms lying on the sand. It was not so dark now. The cave was filled with a dull gray light, not quite morning light, and certainly not sunshine. If it was morning outside, it was a dark and cloudy one. He thought about rousing Rose for her watch when something happened that put all weariness to flight.

A green iridescent glow shimmered from under the water. It grew stronger. Romul began slapping at the various arms and legs that lay about him. The sleeping forms stirred and grunted with annoyance, but as each cracked open an eye, they popped up and stared at the glowing water with him. The five travelers watched with a mixture of wonder and terror as the light grew stronger and brighter. Then it separated into two distinct patches, and a moment later, two glowing green globes emerged from the water a dozen feet from shore.

They all blinked at the change of light. The globes illuminated the whole cave and bathed them in soft but steady green light. At first Romul thought they were hovering some six feet above the surface of their own will. But then he realized they were on thick, reedy poles carried by mermen. The two mermen struggled to rise from the water, which was too shallow for them. Their faces were aglow in the light, and it made their already greenish flesh look pallid and sickly. They glanced about nervously, apprehensively. They hastily thrust the poles into the gravelly ground and dove away as if fearful.

"It's the cave," whispered Anna. "They don't like it."

Eli inhaled sharply in understanding, "That's right! They can't come up here. Everything underground belongs to—"

"Shh!" hissed Augie. "Look!" Two more mermen had appeared above the surface. They were struggling with a large cumbersome object. They heaved the thing upright between the two lamps, then they, too, dove away as if they had not a moment to lose. The thing was a sort of bench, raised on one end.

Then all was quiet again. They waited, but when nothing happened, they looked at one another and shrugged. Suddenly Romul heard a growling sound, like an angry animal, but it wasn't coming from the water. He looked over to find everyone staring at Augie, who was rubbing his belly and smiling self-consciously. "Sorry. It's been too long!" His stomach gave a final reminder of its need and was silent.

They went back to watching the water.

After an unreasonably long time, the surface moved again—seemingly of its own accord. It seemed to recede from the shore, drawing itself back almost reverently, as if in preparation for some great or catastrophic event. Then the water obediently parted as the form of a mermaid ascended slowly, majestically, out of the sea and planted itself upon the bench.

She was nearly twice the size of the mermaid Romul had seen earlier. Her head stood at the height of the lamps, while her long, lithe body spread itself out upon the bench as if on a couch, and her arms rested casually on the raised end. Her tail was still under the water, making it impossible to guess its total length. So immense was the bulk that if someone had told Romul he was seeing not a mermaid but a young whale, he would not have argued. And yet there was the hair. It flowed down in massive tumbles around her shoulders and into the water behind the bench.

She looked upon them with great eyes that glowed with the pale-green light. Romul couldn't decide if they reflected the light from the lamps or gave off their own, but they silently scrutinized the five land creatures as if looking for evidence of something.

"Sweet merciful Therra," whispered Augie in an awestruck voice. He rose awkwardly to his feet and wiped his sandy hands on his sandy pants in an unconscious expression of uncleanness. He turned and whispered viciously at the others. "Get up! Get up! That's no mere mermaid."

"It's not?" Romul got up slowly. The girls staggered upright as well.

"Don't be a perfect fool," said Augie out of the side of his mouth. "That's the queen, and we're probably the first people in a thousand years to see her and live . . . *if* we live."

Romul, who couldn't have torn his gaze from the creature if indeed his life had depended upon it, felt his head nodding in involuntary agreement. Of course! Who else could she be?

Chapter 13

"What's she waiting for?" asked Anna anxiously.

The question dissolved Augie's enchantment. "Oh, she's waiting for me. In formal settings the weaker party has to speak first among the undini—make its case, so to speak. Then she decides whether it's worth answering . . ." His voice faded to a mumble, but he made no gesture.

After an awkward moment, Romul whispered, "Um, ain't we the weaker party here?" Augie grunted an affirmation. "Then we ought to say *something*, don't you think?"

Augie remained silent.

"Um . . . Augie?" said Romul without turning his head.

"Just a minute," he hissed. "I've got to do this exactly right. I don't want to offend her."

"And ain't just standing here like a stick going to do that?" Though he could identify no actual change in her behavior, Romul felt the creature was growing impatient. She continued to stare—to evaluate—as if her whole existence was to extract the last particle of significance from the five frozen land creatures.

Finally Augie took a step forward and lifted his hands slowly above his head till his arms pointed straight up. He then bowed in that position like a man getting ready to dive. Then he knelt and began to make slow and deliberate gestures. Several times he paused, thinking. His gestures climaxed with a dramatic spreading of his arms wide, as if in supplication. Then still on his knees, with his head bowed, he motioned for the others to kneel beside him.

Silence again. As they waited for the merqueen's response, Romul noticed she was not absolutely silent. She made periodic gasping sounds, like hiccups, at a consistent frequency. She was breathing air—something she could clearly do but not without conscious effort.

Still they waited.

After what seemed an eternity, she stirred. Her hands burst into meaningful motion. Augie's head bobbed around in unconscious nods as his mind tried to keep up with the rapid motions his eyes were following. Finally he put his hands to his temples and shook his head.

"I can't . . . I can't. It's too much. It's too fast!" The queen's hands paused in mid-sign, and her head tilted sidewise in a gesture common to all confused creatures. She waited.

Augie attempted to explain. He also began to translate as he moved. Romul couldn't tell if he did this for their sake or to aid his own understanding. He didn't care so long as he understood what was going on.

"I'm sorry," signed Augie, rising slowly to his feet. "I cannot understand all you say. My knowledge of your words are small. But we did come in search of you."

"Then you have come at your peril," she replied, and Augie translated. "There is no love between my people and the fish-killers."

"We did not come to kill the fish, but to find you," said Augie.

"And to give great pain, I am told."

"No! I was foolish, but meant no harm. I intended only for my . . . sound-thing to call you. I did not know it would hurt you."

"You know much about our hands. Did you know nothing of our ears?" Her hands moved in soft liquid motions, and Romul could not distinguish any particular sign in it. Yet the comment seemed to increase Augie's confidence.

"Little is known of you among my people. Only very old books remain that speak of you. Many do not believe in you at all."

"This shall soon change." Augie made no reply to this but stood frozen in surprise, hands still outstretched. She waited, but Augie still made no answer. He didn't know what to say. After a moment she continued. "Do you not know the times in which you live?"

"I . . ." Augie began, and Romul saw that it was possible to stutter even with one's hands. "I don't suppose we do. We may not count time as you do."

"There is only one time. It is now. In this time the Great Change flows backward."

"I do not understand." Augie turned to the others. "I may not have gotten that last part right. I don't exactly understand the words."

But here the merqueen betrayed her first sign of impatience. "Have the children of men so forgotten their place in the affairs of the heavens that they do not even remember the evil they visited upon us?"

"As I said, we did not come to kill the fish or harm—" began Augie, but the merqueen silenced him by hurling her hands together in a mighty clap that echoed through the cave and hurt their ears.

"You have forgotten the Diminution!" This was not a question, Augie explained. "My people became few, were lost and scattered. The seas were silenced, no storms, no births—a great dwindling toward extinction. Yet you, the children of men, do not remember your part!"

"No!" Augie signed with a vigor even Romul could see. "No, we do not know of what you speak. It was others, not we who did these things."

"No matter." The merqueen ignored his interruption. "That time is passing. We are renewing. There have been many storms in recent seasons, and many births. We wondered if the time was drawing near. We searched amid the deepest lore of our people for the meaning. And now we understand." She concluded with a dramatic gesture—her long arm outstretched, her index finger extended in the universal sign of pointing. It was aimed at Anna's heart.

Anna's flush was visible even under the green glow. She understood, and her hand clutched at the amulet.

Augie didn't. "Her trinket?"

"Therra has returned, and her people shall be renewed."

Augie was at a loss. He knew nothing of the amulet, other than that it belonged to Anna. Anna seemed strangely emboldened and stepped up beside him. "Augie, can you translate for me?"

"Um, I guess, but this is very sensitive—"

She cut him off. She looked determined, confident, even older, and when she spoke, it was not as Augie did—as one making a supplication. It was as to an equal, with even a bit of condescension at moments. Her audacity was both frightening and awe-inspiring. "Your majesty, I have never before heard the story you have told us—of your suffering and loss—but I am sorry for it. We have come on a journey seeking answers to the riddles written on the walls of the temple in Halighyll. We were sent to the cities of the western mountains, but it is good that we have come instead into your kingdom. Will you aid us in our quest?"

Augie, who was struggling to keep up, paused and looked at her. "Say it, Augie." Anna did not take her eyes off the queen.

The mermaid was taken aback by this new approach and said nothing for a long time. Her head rocked to the left, then to the right, considering Anna. Then after a long while—"What help?"

"Will you tell us more of this Great Change? What do you know of the dragon bones at Therra's well? Or the prophecies in Halighyll?" She may have continued to rattle off questions had the queen not cut her off.

"Dragon!" The queen was instantly agitated. "Bones? So he has finally . . . No. I will not tell you of such things. You speak strangeness to me. My people's ancient lore is not for your eyes. Therra, I know; you, I do not. The debt your people have with us is deep.

We have not forgotten your betrayal in the ancient days. You shall learn nothing of these things from me. You do not deserve it."

Now it was Anna's turn to pause and think. "You will at least help us to pass beyond your realm safely so we can continue our journey." She whispered to Augie, "That is not a question." He looked at her nervously, sighed with resignation, and began. As he did so, Anna produced the amulet and held it out in front of her.

The queen stared at it while Augie translated. She sat motionless for a long time afterward before making a single, slow gesture. She then slid from her throne into the water and disappeared.

Augie's frame went watery, and he melted onto the sand, exhaling in relief. "She will."

Chapter 14

The daylight refused to grow any stronger—or else the green lamps overruled it. Romul was starting to question the merqueen's intentions. An hour or more had passed since her departure. They were all feeling hungry as they'd not eaten since before the ship went down. Augie's disproportionately large appetite was causing him disproportionately large hunger pangs. He laid on the beach looking up at the cave's ceiling, moaning softly to himself.

Without warning, a great flash of light transformed the cave into daytime—then it was gone. It was followed a second later by a muffled boom. It took Romul a moment to recognize it as lightning and thunder. A storm was brewing outside the cave. He wondered what new trouble this would mean for them.

A splashing sound diverted his attention from the weather. A mermaid and several mermen had risen from the water and seemed to be waiting for them. The mermaid began making signs. Romul kicked Augie, not quite as gently as he could have.

"She's telling us to go with her," Augie said after staring blankly at the entourage for a moment, "and—oh, thank all that's high and holy, they have food." Without waiting for the others, he splashed out to meet the merfolk. Romul hesitated, then realizing there was nothing to be gained by waiting, stepped into the water as well. The girls followed.

It was a strange and disconcerting meeting. He recognized them as the same crew that had originally attacked them. It was clear from the sour looks on their faces that they didn't relish the current hospitalities they were extending. One held up a bowl filled with a dozen or so strange, green, pod-like fruits . . . or vegetables. Romul couldn't be sure which. Showing no hesitation, Augie grabbed one and put it to his lips.

"Oh!" He chewed once or twice slowly. "Oh, I don't know about this . . ." He took another bite. His eyes took on a funny, glazed look. "It's . . . it's . . ." He chewed silently, holding the pod up before the mermaid and smiling a distracted and flabby sort of smile. "Wow, now, that's something . . ." Then noticing he was the only one eating, he said, "Oh come on now, tuck in. It won't hurt you . . . I think. It just takes a little getting used to . . ." He took another bite.

Romul hesitantly took one, and so did the girls. He held his up and smelled it. The odor was strong, but he couldn't place it. It smelled fishy yet sweet. He took a small nibble, then he, too, said, "Oh!" His head began to swim. Next to him Eli put her hand to her forehead and echoed his sentiment. The effect of the fruit, for surely that was what it was, was strong. It muddled his head and sent warm sensations coursing down his limbs.

His perspective changed on the objects he saw around him. The merfolk no longer looked strange or threatening. Their greenish skin now seemed entirely natural; their eyes, which he'd thought looked too large for their faces, now seemed bright and wonderful—like deep pools of water themselves. Even the water moving about his waist beckoned him to come under, to swim and frolic in the eddies and currents, to let the luxurious liquid life have its way with him. His eyes roamed distractedly. He saw Augie and the girls and shuddered. They were pale and otherworldly, with tiny piggish eyes and strange bulbous projections for noses. How ugly, how unnatural, how—

By then he'd devoured the fruit. As the juices drained down his throat, his head cleared a bit, and his terrestrial instincts reasserted themselves. He looked at the fruit in the bowl. It might have been alcoholic, for all he knew. Augie was already eating another, but strangely, Romul no longer felt hungry. The girls likewise ate no more, but Augie continued to eat piece after piece till even the merfolk stared in disbelief. When Augie had gloried in the last of the fruit, he stood, a little wobbly on his feet, looking at the merfolk as if waiting for the next course. But no more came.

The mermaid began a long series of gestures, then turned and dove away. The mermen who remained held out their hands in invitation. Augie translated. "She said to come down with them. They have *something* for us. I don't know the word, but it's related to the word 'breath.'"

"You mean the jelly stuff they put on our faces before?" said Eli with a shudder.

"It was kinda gross," added Rose.

At the urging of the mermen, they walked out. The gravelly bottom continued to drop away till the water was up to their chins. The mermen gestured and disappeared.

"Um . . . they said to go under and get the . . . whatever-it-is." Augie looked at them, shrugged, took a breath, and went under. They all did the same. As soon as he was under, Romul saw a merman putting his hand out toward his face. He drew back instinctively. The merman paused and tilted his head to one side in confusion. Sure enough, he held one of the green sponges in his hand. Romul willed himself to lean forward and receive the disgusting mass. He felt it latch onto his face with a sickening suction. He exhaled, and a small bubble emerged from the sponge. He tried a tentative inhale. As before, he could breathe.

Before he'd actually resigned himself to it, however, he found himself pinioned by the arms once more by two mermen. They dove and whisked him off his feet. Again they descended to the point of discomfort, then he felt the water change all around him. It was colder and surged unpredictably as if angered by their return. He tried looking around. A dim light shone many feet above him, but things were mostly dark.

Then a great white light tore across the watery roof of the

world, and even that far below the surface he heard the muffled boom of thunder. The mermen were struggling to make headway against the surge of currents sucking them back toward the rocky coastline.

Total confusion overtook them. All forward movement stopped. The mermen released him so they could gesture wildly to one another. Romul shot upward, but was caught by the foot and pulled back down. The mermen made Romul and the three girls hold hands. From then on two mermen kept the little human chain from rising to the surface, while the others began swimming in violent circles around Augie a ways behind them.

Romul looked and then stared. Something was happening. The currents had drawn themselves into a kind of vortex, like a tornado underwater. The funnel seemed to dance and move of its own accord. Sometimes it would intersect one of the mermen, and he would go spinning off into the watery darkness like a rock hurled from a giant's hand. Lightning flashed again, and by its momentary light he saw that at the center of the twister a small shape was taking form.

Romul's heart leapt within him. He knew what he was witnessing, and yet knew it couldn't be so. A verse he'd learned by rote in school flooded his mind and staggered him. *"Where e'er there is disturbance in the earth, the elementals give longaevi birth."* Even the Rokan knew the first principle of science. He had met people—liars, to be sure—who'd claimed to have seen these elemental principles at work. He had never believed them. It happened, he'd supposed, but so rarely and privately and . . . well, not to him. Yet even as he watched, the form at the center of the vortex assumed a familiar shape.

The cocoon at the center of the swirling water now gave off a faint light of its own. The embryonic form at the center seemed to grow every time the vortex jumped. It was already as big as the mermen. Lightning flashed again, and Romul thought he saw a face—the eyes closed but already bearing a long mane of hair. A mermaid. The merfolk darted in and out of the typhoon's path, risking its fury.

He didn't know how he knew it, but he could tell the event was reaching a climax. The vortex was swirling at an almost audible frequency. The light grew rapidly. Arms began to extend from the center of the watery womb. Then the vortex made a final leap. The whole thing jumped almost directly into the space where Augie hovered. In fact, it *did* spiral into the mermen that held him, and Augie was ripped free from their grasp as the mermen were tossed away. Augie began to rise, but at that moment, with violent force, the elemental womb expelled its infant charge right into Augie's line of assent.

The newly born creature collided with Augie, and they went rolling and spinning through the water in each other's arms. The typhoon dissipated almost instantly, but Romul couldn't see anything of Augie's condition because the writhing pair were instantly surrounded by a score of merfolk, gamboling and frolicking with an obvious mixture of joy and agitation. At first he thought the joyous merfolk were drawing nearer, but then realized they were instead being dragged toward the chaotic dance. Their two stewards were, perhaps unconsciously, swimming slowly forward, dragging them all toward the heart of the action.

What Romul saw as they drew closer made him first groan, then laugh, though awkwardly under his spongy respirator. Augie still embraced the newly "hatched" mermaid. Her head lay contently on his chest as if in peaceful repose. He was unable to dislodge her, and she clung to him as a child to its mother.

When their eyes met, Romul needed no words or gestures to understand the meaning in Augie's frantic look. His eyes screamed *What have I done now?*

Chapter 15

The undini of the Crescent Sea were far cleverer than Romul would have guessed. They had worked out that heavy items could be more easily transported if they were floating on the surface. They also knew the thick stalks of a certain tall undersea plant would shoot to the surface when cut. They bound this spongy "lumber" together in rafts or barges, which they tethered below the surface till needed. This technology became the means of escaping the underwater world for the five travelers.

A glorious sunset was developing. They watched it as they all lay on one of these springy rafts. Romul's skin was still puckered from nearly half a day underwater, and he was glad to be out of it. The last half day had taught him more about the ways and intelligence of the longaevi than he'd learned in his eight years.

Or was it nine?

Yes, he was feeling nine today. Today he would be nine.

Ropes of thickly braided seaweed—or something like it—led from the bow of the raft down into the water, where fierce-looking seabeasts drew it southward. When looking over the bow, Romul could only just make out the shapes of the creatures in the evening sun—heads like great seahorses, oversized eyes like the merfolk, fish-like hindquarters, and most interesting of all, powerful front legs like farm horses but ending in great fan-like fins with which they beat forward in the water. They were called the each-uisge, and their strength was awesome. They dragged the raft forward without pause at a far greater speed than the *Sea Bellows* had produced under full pressure.

Augie was in a mixture of delight and horror. Unable to contain his wonder at the horses, he would look eagerly over the side, only to draw back with a groan.

"She still there?" asked Anna.

Augie just sighed.

The mermaid birthed into Augie's arms shadowed the raft a few feet below the surface, hoping for a glimpse of his face. Her name was Murgen. Apparently merfolk came into the world knowing a bunch of things already—"ancestral memory" Augie had called it—among them, the merfolk's sign language and their own name. Whatever knowledge came with birth, however, newborn undini were still newborns. They formed an instinctual, almost parental bond with the first merfolk with whom they had meaningful contact. Thus the merfolk tried to have a mermaid be the first contact, for the females of that species seemed to have the same nurturing instincts most human females had.

Most.

A pang of longing sounded in Romul's heart as he was reminded of his abortive search for his own lost mother. He shook his head to clear the thoughts away. They were no good to him at the moment.

He'd learned all of this trivia about newborn merfolk, because in Murgen's sad case, her maternal bonding had been with a crazy human scientist who possessed the parenting instincts of a sea anemone. Romul looked over the side. Murgen's face lit up with a hungry longing he associated not with parental love but with romantic desire. But it faded to disappointment the moment she realized he was not Augie. It was funny . . . No, it was disturbing!

"What's the matter, Augie?" Romul goaded. "I thought you wanted to get to know the mermaids. Looks like this one's up for the job."

Augie groaned and put his head in his hands.

"Rommie," cried Rose, "that's mean!"

"Stop calling me that!"

The sun now sat on the rim of the sea and bathed them all in such glory that all talk ceased. They all rolled over to watch Merris cast her final rays on their foamy wake.

After a while Augie sighed. "Land tomorrow."

"Really?" Eli sat up and looked at him.

"Yup."

"That's what they said?"

"Yup."

"What'll happen then?"

"Don't know."

"Don't you think we should talk about it?"

The only answer she got was a snore. Augie was asleep.

∾

What awoke Romul the next morning was not the sunrise. Rather, into all the rocking and heaving of his dreams had crept a strange silence—a lack of movement—like when the carriage you've been riding in comes to a halt. Their seaborne carriage had ceased its forward surging with the same result. It was now bobbing up and down in relative calm.

Romul sat up and groaned. He'd slept on just about every surface imaginable and yet nothing compared to the exquisite soreness produced by sleeping—off and on—on a pile of sea-logs being dragged across the water. He was both cramped from lack of movement and bruised from too much of it.

Augie and Rose had slept like slabs of wood themselves and bounced up cheerily. "That's what I call a water bed," said Rose, beaming.

The others, whose memories were also of long hours awake as the waves bounced them without mercy, felt differently. "Now I know what the shore feels like," grunted Anna, massaging her temples.

"Speaking of . . ." said Eli. Sure enough, the raft was holding about twenty feet from a sandy beach. The seahorses were gone, and their raft was being held stationary by several pairs of greenish hands.

"Hey, she's gone," said Augie, very much relieved. He scampered around like a monkey, looking over every side of the raft.

"Lost your girlfriend, eh?" said Romul.

"Yeah, I guess so. That solves one problem, at least."

Romul was about to needle him further when a greenish face rose in the water beside the raft. It was a mermaid—not the queen nor one they'd seen before. Romul was surprised to discover that merfolk faces came in the same diversity as human ones. This one was thicker than the others. Not obese, just bigger in the bones. Her "nose," however, was a barely discernible bump between her eyes, which themselves were a shocking, nearly fluorescent shade of blue.

She began to sign immediately. This sobered Augie, and he watched with rapt attention, nodding periodically. She paused for a moment as if to give him time to translate to the others. Rather than doing so, he immediately began signing back at her. She seemed surprised, then sarcastic. She fluttered a few signs in return, and Romul saw Augie's face brighten ever so slightly. Now he translated.

"They're restraining her," he said.

"Who?" said Eli.

"Murgen. They say since she can't come along, they had to keep her away. Apparently she's . . . uh . . . somewhat smitten." He ended with an embarrassed grin, as if a female of any species being attracted to him was a strange new experience.

"Aww, Augie's first girlfriend," said Anna. "Now ain't that . . . awkward."

Eli groaned. "Who cares! I've had enough of the water. What happens now?"

"We get off," said Augie. "They've brought us as far as they can or plan to. That's all the help they're going to give." He exchanged more signs with the mermaid, who abruptly turned and disappeared beneath the water while Augie was still in mid-sentence.

"That was rude." Anna clambered down into the water and found it waist deep.

"Yeah, well . . ." Augie's hands were still raised in the final sign. "Her last words were a sort of *and don't come back*, so I guess they've had enough of us."

"Mutual, I'm sure! Crummy ocean," grumbled Eli as she waded ashore.

"Sea." said Rose.

"Whatever."

It was an awkward homecoming for them all. Never having gotten off a boat before, Romul didn't understand why the ground felt like it was heaving under his feet. Rose took two steps, hopped sideways on one leg, and fell over.

"Come on, noodle legs." Anna tried to pull her up, lost her balance instead, and collapsed on top of her with an *Oomph*. Augie hoisted Anna off her sister, and they all ambled unsteadily toward the small dune before them. They climbed it without too much difficulty and stood looking out to sea. No sign of the merfolk remained, and the raft was gone as if it had never been. Long sparse grasses grew around them, and a strong wind blew in off the water.

"Well, what now?" asked Eli again, still in a wet and sour mood.

"On to Farwell, of course!" cried Augie.

"But I thought you were only supposed to get us across the sea?" said Anna.

Augie pointed at the dune on which they stood. "And I did."

"Yes, I see that. But you weren't planning to come with us after that, were you?"

"Plans, plans." The inventor shrugged. "Honestly, what do you think I'm supposed to do now? Swim back to Umbra?"

Anna shrugged.

There really was no reason for Augie not to come, Romul supposed. He had nowhere else to go now that the *Sea Bellows* had bellowed its last. He'd been more successful in contacting the *Undini Crescentia* than he could have desired in his wildest dreams. The knowledge that the encounter had almost killed him seemed not to affect him. He was acting now as if he had fulfilled the big dream of his life and had a completely free schedule.

"Well, madam." Augie bowed to Eli, who blushed. "Shall we be going? I'm feeling a bit peckish. We should find something to—"

"Look," Anna whispered hoarsely, pointing back toward the shore.

They looked. A great fish-like form was struggling out of the water. It was Murgen. Augie's suitor was dragging herself out of the water, crawling like a half-drowned animal, arm over arm across the sand. Her eyes, miserable with pleading, were fixed on him.

"Oh, gods!" the scientist moaned. "She's trying to come with us."

Chapter 16

"She can't come with us," said Romul matter-of-factly. The idea was preposterous. She was a mermaid. Of course she couldn't come.

"The surface belongs to all," whispered Eli.

"What?" Romul rounded on her.

"It's something we were told last time we were here. I never thought about it with mermaids, but I guess if it's true, then . . ." She turned to look at Augie.

"Yes, yes," said Augie with wide eyes. "She *can* come. It's horrible! What have I done?"

"What do you mean?" said Romul. "She can't come. She—" His protest was cut short by a cry from the mermaid. She screamed as if stricken. It was the first sound he'd heard a merfolk make, and the treble of the scream froze his blood. It sounded as if she were being murdered.

She screamed again and floundered on the beach like . . . well, yes, like a fish out of water. Her tail thrashed back-and-forth as if searching frantically for moisture. Her eyes scanned the heavens in terror even as she clawed forward across the sand with her arms. The strength in those arms was astounding. She was already at the verge of the long grass.

She cried out again and turned to survey her own body. The fishy tail seemed to move against her will, but something was happening. The fins had grown thick and stumpy; the lovely iridescent scales of her body were falling from her like leaves from a tree. A sort of indentation ran down the tail, and it was growing deeper every minute. To Romul it looked like when you push your thumb into your thigh, then keep pressing harder and harder as if to put your thumb right through your leg. He imagined how it would hurt. That's what it looked like, and that was the nature of her cries.

She gasped in agony, and threw a hand out toward Augie. She looked at him with begging eyes. It was more than he—more than any person—could stand. They rushed down the dune to her. Augie knelt beside her. She rolled into his arms, her face toward his, and he held her.

"Should we get some water or something?" said Eli.

"No!" said Augie between her groans. "It would only prolong it. She has to endure the stegnoma—" he swallowed hard—"the drying out."

She moaned and cried piteously. Through the agony of his own helplessness, Augie whispered, "It's okay, it's okay. It'll be over soon." He stroked her forehead—the only part of her still damp.

Romul could not fathom what was going on. But that line down the middle of her tail continued to deepen as if it intended to cut her in half. And in the throes of a final, desperate scream, that is exactly what it did. The tail flopped hideously, but bloodlessly, into two long lengths. These continued their wild thrashing movement, but now independent of each other. To Romul's horror and wonder, they each grew round and stiff, except at certain points. At these points they flexed in oddly familiar ways.

Then he understood. Legs. Of course! Now she kicked at the sand with very human-shaped legs. Her cries subsided into mere weeping. Augie, not knowing what else to do, held her close and tight. For all his desire to make contact with merfolk, this was clearly a level of contact he'd never anticipated or wanted.

Then the surface of the sea broke in a torrent of foam. Faces— angry faces, murderous faces—emerged from the water. Spears and clenched fists were held aloft. It took Romul a moment to realize that the whole contingent of merfolk had returned. They boiled in the waters off the coast, but not one would venture a fin upon the sand.

Eli and Rose had knelt next to Murgen, but now drew back. Augie stood and waved frantically, shouting idiotically at the merfolk, "No, no. We didn't want this. We were—"

Then, as suddenly as they'd appeared, they were gone, and the waves resumed their normal assault on the beach. Augie, his hands still held out over the water like a priest giving a blessing, turned his head and stared back at Romul and the girls, terror and confusion overrunning each other on his face.

Then the surface broke again. The mammoth form of the queen rose from the water. She didn't seem any smaller for appearing now outside the cave. She drew herself up into the shallows like a slug—no, like a snake—and raised her head to look at them. She didn't appear angry as had her people. Rather, her face was set in a determined resolve.

The queen made a gesture toward Augie, and he staggered forward—as if he had lost control of his limbs—till the toes of his shoes rested in the dark, wet sand of the shore. She began a series of firm gestures, but before she could have said much of anything, Murgen herself had struggled—crawled, actually—into the fray. She cast herself down atop Augie's feet and began throwing counter gestures toward the queen. The queen was taken aback by the cheek of it, but recovered herself, and a battle of gestures commenced.

Augie contributed nothing but wild stares, first at one then the other. To Romul the debate had the appearance of hand-to-hand combat, except the combatants were separated by a dozen feet. He could almost imagine one gesture by the queen being blocked by Murgen's counter-gesture. Though Romul had no idea what was being said, it was as if she was defending Augie against the queen's assault—a battle of words rather than blows.

Eventually a moment arrived when the queen did not respond.

Murgen continued her frantic defense for several minutes. When she'd finally worn out her fingers with words, the queen thought for a moment, then looked at Augie and waited.

He, too, stood frozen in place for a moment, and then slowly made a single gesture. The queen smiled in a not-so-pleasant way, slowly rolled her great bulk over, and disappeared into the waves.

Augie remained a statue, looking out to sea after she'd gone. Murgen clutched at him, drawing herself onto her unstable feet and turning her gaze to follow his. His arms instinctively encircled her waist to help her stay upright. But for the hint of green tint of her skin, they might have passed for two lovers enjoying a sunrise at the beach.

The vision evaporated when Anna broke out in a huff, "What the flying fish is going on?"

Augie's voice came back to them, but he did not turn or stir. "They're sending me a challenge."

"A what?" said Eli.

"A seabeast," he said without emotion or inflection. "I have to tame it, or they won't let her come with us."

"Great!" cried Romul. "We don't want her to. You said no, of course."

Augie was silent.

"You did say no, right?" said Anna.

"I have to do it."

"Why?" they all cried at once.

"Murgen said if she cannot come with me, she will suicide."

No one said anything in reply.

A few moments later a great foaming whitecap appeared on the surface a hundred yards offshore and came toward them at a terrifying rate. As it neared the beach, a form arose from the water. The great equine head of an each-uisge thrashed about as if trying to free itself from the confines of the water. By the time it hit the beach, great blowing nostrils had formed in its long face, and its long front legs sported heavy hooves instead of fins. As it came full out of the water, to stamp and snort on the beach, it was, but for a slight oddity of color, indistinguishable from a huge farming draft horse—except that Romul had never seen a horse as proud and terrible as this.

The seabeast's transformation left the mermaid's looking like an awkward and clumsy affair. It transformed easily, willfully, even eagerly. If it experienced any pain comparable to the mermaid's, it had channeled it into rage. And it *was* enraged! Its eyes showed murderously red. It reared on its hind legs and screamed so that everyone covered their ears. It was a scream without an ounce of speech in it. Romul understood Equinish as well as anyone, but this was a foreign sound. Either the creature could not speak, refused to, or its elemental nature left the human ear unable to decipher its language.

It was frightening, to be sure, but Romul also experienced a sense of relief. After all, this was not the great sea serpent or an even more unfathomable terror. Breaking a horse was something any farmhand could do. So he loaded as much confidence into his voice as he could muster. "It's okay, Augie! I seen bigger horses than that busted! You can do it."

The inventor simply stared at him with wide eyes, his great gulping Adam's apple rising and falling like a bobber on a fishing line. "That's no horse, you idiot!" The creature reared on hind legs and pawed the air. "I can't ride him."

"Sure you can. You just gotta—"

"No!" yelled Augie. "That's an each-uisge! Once I'm on its back, I'll just stick to him, and he'll drag me out to sea. I've heard legends of sailors lost that way."

"How are you supposed to break him, then?" asked Romul. That, of course, was exactly the problem. How do you ride a horse that can't be ridden?

Thinking its prey had been given sufficient time for talk, the horse charged. Murgen fled before it, staggering clumsily up the dune with the girls.

The horse thundered straight at Augie as if it knew the terms of the contract. Augie seemed unable to move, till at the last second he dove to one side as the horse galloped through the space where Augie had just been standing. It rounded, reared, and screamed again.

Forms rose out of the sea. The colony of merfolk had returned to watch the sport. Though they didn't cry out like people at a match, they wore eager faces and motioned constantly to one another in flamboyant conversations.

The horse charged once more. The girls screamed as Augie dove again. The beast missed him by a hair in its forward rush.

Augie did not rise from the sand. He shook his head as if trying to ward off a cloud of gnats or clear his head. The each-uisge did not charge again. It stood stamping impatiently, almost chivalrously, waiting for him to rise. Augie slowly rose to his knees and looked helplessly up the dune to them. Romul could tell the horse's patience was being taxed and that it would soon charge again whether or not Augie stood.

Next to him Anna had been doing something with her hands. Romul was not, of course, paying any attention to her, but she was mumbling, "Let go, darn you" as her hands fidgeted. "Ah!" She ran down the dune, yelling, "Augie, Augie!"

He looked up at her with despairing eyes. Anna reached him and knelt next to him for a moment. Resenting the intrusion, the horse screamed and charged, but Anna was away again and back up the dune in a heartbeat.

"What good was that—" began Romul, to which Anna only pointed. Augie was back on his feet, facing the charging beast. It bore down on him with powerful strides, ready to grind him to powder. Murgen cried out senselessly. Moments before the rending hooves reached him, Augie set his jaw and held out his hand toward the beast like a soldier ordering a coach to stop. To Romul's wonder, the horse locked its front legs, plowing great furrows in the sand as it drew up a foot from Augie, its nose almost pressing on the inventor's outstretched palm. Even the watching merfolk let out audible gasps.

Augie extended his other hand toward the horse to touch its nose. The horse shied, but Augie thrust his first hand forward into its face. Romul now saw that he held something in it. He turned to Anna and saw her amulet chain swinging empty around her neck. Augie had it, and he was using it to back the horse. It yielded to the amulet, giving ground, one awkward step after another.

Now Augie spoke to it in low tones no one could hear. Even though he used landsmen's words, the horse seemed to understand. It bowed its great head and allowed Augie to stroke its nose. One hind leg stamped the ground in great displeasure. Slowly Augie moved the hand up the head and onto its neck, all the while keeping the amulet within its field of vision. No sound or movement was discernible from either the human or merfolk spectators. All were waiting, holding their breath, as Augie held the horse's gaze with the amulet.

When he had moved his hand down from the neck to the body toward the place he would have to mount, it became clear that he could not keep the amulet within the horse's field of vision. He paused before slowly withdrawing it. The horse shied again, but Augie thrust the amulet back into view as if to remind the horse it was still present even when it couldn't be seen. Then he vaulted to its back in a single move.

It was almost gracefully done, but that didn't matter. The horse shivered as if trying to free itself from its enchantment. But slowly its head came up, and it uttered a frustrated but calm whinny. The next moment the crowd of merfolk were wildly gesturing at Augie with a vigor that made Romul think very derogatory things were being said. Augie paid them no heed. He stroked the beast's neck and continued speaking to it.

Now Murgen was stumbling down the dune toward him on unsteady legs, her face beaming with pride and possessiveness. She drew near to the horse, who ignored her as a familiar thing, and caressed Augie's leg. Augie's face was different. Something in it had changed. That awkward humiliation so evident on the docks of Umbra had fallen away. He was now the master—not just of the great steed but of himself as well.

He stretched his hand down with an almost regal gesture and caressed Murgen's cheek. Her response to him had seemed at first that of child to nurse, then lover to beloved, then mother defending her young. But it was now almost the devotion of a subject to a sovereign.

Romul had never been in love, and he couldn't understand how all these roles could exist in the same space much less dwell together happily. The depth of it left him feeling on the outside of some great mystery. If this was love, he thought it the strangest thing he'd yet seen on his adventure.

BOOK 3

The Old One of Farwell

How shall I explain the historic mistreatment of the Rokan by Garlandian society? I confess, I cannot. No race *deserves* a place above another, and if the gods know better, we should not speak on their behalf. Yet if each will consider his own heart, it is clear that we each *desire* such a place. Any man with power over his peers will misuse it. It is a kink in human nature. But why? Why, if we know it is wrong, do we do it anyway, even relishing in the particular flavor of the wrong? Ultimately these are questions for idle poets, like my brother. The historian's interests are more concrete. Given that the longaevi suffer from the same tendency to misuse power, did we learn the craft from them, or were we the teachers?

DR. SONJI RAZHAMANÌAH, *An Attempted History of the Halighyllian Prophecies and Their Fulfillment*, Vol 2: *Legends from the Dawn of Rokan*, 54v.

Chapter 17

When the merqueen finally slithered away into the surf and disappeared, she left five humans, a weeping mermaid, and a humbled each-uisge standing on the beach. While the terms of the challenge had been grudgingly honored, the queen was in no way pleased with the results. She had warned of great abuses Murgen would suffer at the hands of the "fish-eaters" and that she should not presume to receive welcome among any longaevi she might encounter or even from her own people should she ever return.

"And your first indignity will be the need to cover yourself before them." At a wave of her hand, one of the mermen in the shallows threw upon the beach a sodden set of fatigues from some poor lost sailor. They were in pitiable condition, but would serve till they could find her sturdier clothing.

Murgen had endured all the dismal predictions patiently and without response. She had clung to Augie's arm, staring adoringly at him throughout the homily. The whole affair had reminded Romul of a wedding he'd once seen, where the priest had droned on and on about the challenges of marriage even while the couple ignored him.

The end result for them, however, was a fortunate one. So concerned was the queen for Murgen's safety that she had given the each-uisge to her as a sort of bodyguard. The horse had received its new commission with silent resignation and a fuming eye turned occasionally toward Augie. It was a lavish but extreme gift, fraught with its own kind of peril, for the queen had warned them to beware the nixie—at all costs.

This required some further explanation from Augie. The nixie were a genus of undini who dwelt in rivers—like nymphs but more malicious. Their closer proximity to human dwellings meant they often suffered the befouling of their habitat. Thus they were, if possible, even more inhospitable to humans than the merfolk. They would also highly prize an each-uisge if they could obtain one. If possible, they'd cry out to it and beckon it to return to the water. "And woe be to the rider who sits upon its back in that hour," warned the queen. "Murgen is your only sure hold over the creature. But for her, it will heed the longing of its heart and return to the waters."

Augie had replied, "We still have the amulet if it should come to that."

The comment had filled the queen with a sort of trembling rage that turned her skin rather pale, and she uttered her most passionate warning. "It was an act of cowardice to use Therra's power to overturn the each-uisge's will. If a mother so abuses her power, there may yet come an hour when even her children will no longer honor her." And her eyes flitted maliciously between Anna's amulet and Anna's defiant eyes.

Anna was naturally unrepentant, having concluded that the queen arranged the duel only to kill Augie and force Murgen's return. Anna in particular had a growing respect for this sea maiden, who was ready to defy all authority and convention for the sake of her passions.

Now the sea had returned to its eternal rhythm upon the shore, and the travelers were trying to decide how to proceed.

"We have no food," said Anna glumly.

"No, we don't," said Augie even more glumly. "And we shan't so long as we stand here."

"What about her?" Eli pointed to Murgen. Her legs were unreliable. Though she could stand easily now and even execute a wobbly stride, her new limbs were weak and tired easily, plus she had no shoes.

"That shouldn't be a problem." Augie put his hand on the horse's back. The horse, having resigned itself to its fate, merely snorted with distaste. "The each-uisge can easily carry the two of us and probably one more." And so the journey began with Augie, Murgen, and Rose riding and the other three walking alongside.

Beginning a journey, however, implies that you know where you're going. On this delicate point, a choice presented itself. They knew they were headed to Farwell, the largest city in western Garlandium, nestled in the foothills of the Aracadian Mountains and straddling the South Wane River. But they didn't know where they were, other than somewhere on the western shore of the Crescent Sea. Augie had map knowledge, and Romul had traveled through here before, so between them they logically worked out the following:

Farwell was the great industrial city of the country. It smelted all the ore and processed most of the mineral wealth from deposits in the Aracadians. The raw goods were then sent down the South Wane River to the Crescent Sea and on to seaports like Umbra on the eastern side. The South Wane entered the sea in the far southwest. Therefore they were probably still north of the river mouth. Once they'd found the river, they could simply follow it westward right to the city gates. But therein lay the problem. They were still acutely aware of the queen's warning about the nixie. To intentionally follow the river invited trouble.

In the end, no alternative presented itself, so they decided to make for the river mouth and do the best they could from there.

Their immediate difficulties were a lack of food and supplies, plus their clothing was in dismal condition, especially Murgen's. But Romul knew the countryside from Farwell to the sea was dotted with farms down both sides of the river which could serve their needs. He'd made use of them on his last journey. Their immediate locale, however, consisted only of pine forest on their right and dunes, beach, or sea on their left. He knew from experience that pine cones were not a subsistence food. But for the fact that the sea was freshwater, their situation would have been dire.

As it turned out, all their concern was unnecessary. By early evening they'd arrived at the edge of a forest that looked out upon a neatly tilled field. Here, Romul had to give them the lay of the land. This part of the country wasn't noted for its agricultural production. Its proximity to the mountains put arable land at a premium. The flatlands out east were the country's true breadbasket. Farwell didn't produce food so much as wealth. It was home to some of the most well-heeled merchants and industrialists in the country. Nearly every farm they would pass was a supplemental holding of some member of the upper crust, whose larger estate was somewhere closer to the city. They could expect luxury crops here—fruit, tobacco, wine, that sort of thing.

From their place of minimal concealment, the troop looked out over a tired field of short and meaningless green crops. Part of the half-mile-wide strip of land was still being worked even this late in the day. Romul explained this was because the sun didn't clear the western mountains till late morning, so the workday in the shadow of the Aracadians was always started and ended later in the day than out east. Dusk also came later as Merris prolonged her rest-taking by sinking low on the Crescent Sea.

Workers now moved hurriedly through the rows, harvesting by hand, trying to get the most out of the remaining daylight. A great manor house stood at the far end of the field, and other fields were visible beyond that.

A hard lump formed in Romul's chest as he watched them work. The heads of the men and women, and even a few children, glistened white in the eastering sun. They were Rokan field-workers—not actual slaves but tied to the land in ways they could not control or change. They worked the land of the Garlandish wealthy for subsistence wages. Romul had spent time in fields like this, though not often, partly because his maternal stand-in had been a midwife, but more so because he'd been reared west of Farwell, farther up in the mountains where sheep and goats were the dominant "crop."

They'd stood in the shadow of the trees watching for several minutes when Augie broke the silence. "We can probably forage at that plantation, but we should wait until it gets darker."

"I'm hungry," whined Rose. No one replied, but someone's stomach growled in agreement.

It was a long, dull wait till it was dark enough for the raid, but when all was said and done, Romul had appropriated some farm clothing and shoes for Murgen, and Augie had stripped several pear trees near the house bare of their produce. Thus minimally provisioned, they continued their journey down the coast.

They foraged similarly for the next two nights, and thanks to Romul's firebrand, had a reliable source of fire.

Murgen proved adept at human language. She still would not speak, but she understood everything said to her. Augie recalled sea stories from Umbra public houses about men who claimed to have heard mermaids sing. The sound would throw men into such swooning fits of love that they would cast themselves from the sides of ships to reach them. Eli recalled similar tales from her own world.

The sea maiden fell into a special rapport with Anna, perhaps because of the Therran amulet she wore. When allowed to examine it, she caressed it lovingly and even whispered tiny tender words to it as if to a sleeping infant.

No one was much inclined to conversation during those days of wandering. The girls would gather nightly and put their heads together over the little glass ball Rose had carried in her pocket all through their adventures. They would chatter softly over it, pointing and gesturing in various directions. Even hearing them discuss the compass with Cholerish hadn't provided him any clarity about its purpose other than having something to do with getting them home. He ignored them.

He was consumed with his own conflicted feelings about being Rokan. Returning to his hometown was reopening a lifetime of uncertainties. While foraging at the farm that first night, he'd been forced to sneak around the collection of Rokan hovels on the outskirts of the property to reach the manor. He'd found himself frozen in the bushes, listening as a hauntingly familiar melody went up around their cooking fires. *Come, hear the voice of the wooly pipes that groan and weep and wail . . .*

He didn't want to return to that life, to be sure, but he wasn't as enamored with Garlandish life as he'd once been. He saw it now not as an escape into glorious opportunities but as an act of treachery against his Rokan heritage. No going back. No going forward. He felt cut off from all worlds. He didn't belong anywhere.

The change that came over Augie was equally tidal. He still ate the largest share of the foraged food and anything left over—as well as a number of things Romul thought inedible—and he still lapsed into goofy melancholia on occasion. On the whole, however, his temperament had evened out, and he became a more serious and thoughtful creature. He began, whether intentionally or no, to mimic that same alternating sense of protection and humble deference Murgen in turn showed him. He wasn't yet accepting her affections, but he was no longer resisting them.

On the morning of the third day, they came upon the mouth of the South Wane River. Thus they also discovered the main road through those parts. It roughly followed the river westward, though at times it wound far away from it to accommodate pleasure houses and docks that bordered the water. Their journey now became riskier, for the road was well traveled by Rokan workers, wealthy Garlandish businessmen, and even soldiers. It could not be avoided, however, unless they wanted to wander directly across fields and private property, which would be just as perilous.

They bundled Murgen with extra layers of stolen clothing to hide her greenish tint, though anyone who examined her face closely would know she wasn't quite human. The each-uisge, whom the girls had taken to calling Eachy, could not be hidden at all. Fortunately, full daylight muted his slightly-off pigmentation, so he could generally pass loose visual inspection as a normal horse—well, not quite normal. He would still be the finest stallion those parts had seen in many generations.

For the better part of the day, the ruse worked fine. Nearly everyone they passed stared at the horse with wide eyes, but no one said anything. Nor did Eachy's proximity to the river seem to tempt him in the slightest, although Murgen said the nixie were usually more active at night.

Late that afternoon, the road began ascending and gently winding away from the river. They were now in the foothills of the Aracadian Mountains, and Romul was on turf he knew well. When they rounded the next bend, he knew the trees would give way to reveal the sooty city of Farwell before them. But they never made it to the bend.

As they approached the forest edge, six soldiers emerged from the trees onto the road. All were well-armed and wore cocky looks. They were led by a thin, sallow-faced lieutenant who was a hand-and-a-half shorter and several years younger than any of his subordinates. He had a mean little face like a mouse that lit up when he spied the travelers. When he began to saunter toward them with his hand uplifted in the universal "halt" sign, Romul knew they were in for trouble.

Chapter 18

Instinctively, Romul looked around for Murgen, but she wasn't there. A small movement in the bushes told him she must have slipped off the road unnoticed. This made for one less problem. He willed himself not to look after her and hoped the others would have the good sense to do likewise. The lieutenant was too busy to notice. He was slowly removing one of his black leather gloves, tugging one finger at a time, eying Eachy carefully, and, Romul thought, greedily.

He cleared his throat in an unnecessarily loud way, as if to get a crowd's attention and sang out, "Papers." His voice was lazy and annoyingly high-pitched, and he overemphasized the p's as if trying to put on an accent far above his social class. From that one word, Romul knew he was from out east, probably the coast or even Garlandvale itself. The soldier thrust out his naked hand and waggled his fingers impatiently.

Like most educated persons, Augie had papers enough to clear the lot of them all the way to the city. But most educated persons have not spent the better part of a week being shipwrecked, dragged through water, assaulted by merfolk and seabeasts, wandering like nomads, and finding true love—or something like it. Of course, he had no papers, and worse, he looked like he'd never owned any.

He did his best, though. "I'm sorry, officer, but I have none with me. They were lost when my ship—"

The soldier had already dismissed him with a wave of the hand

and a "nuh." He glanced at each of the others, his eyes coming to rest for a moment on Romul, then his hair. He said nothing, but must have decided the rest of them could not possibly have any papers either, so he continued in a practiced and almost artificial way while removing his other glove. "Rokan indigents are to have papers with them at all times. Those without shall submit to the severest of—"

"No, no," argued Augie. "I have them, but they were lost when—"

The lieutenant sneered at the interruption, but before he could say anything, Augie yammered on. "I'm not Rokan. I am a scientist, a member in good standing of the Therran order in Umbra, and I—" But once again he was cut off. The soldiers were all laughing at him.

The lieutenant wiped a fake tear from his cheek, and sighed. "Ah, if I had a dynar for every ... Well, Droge—" he gestured to the tall soldier at his left—"you warned me how inventive the Opsies are, but I never suspected they would be so bold as to—"

"Now look here," pressed Augie, losing patience. "I'm not Rokan. Look at my hair. Does it look white to you?"

The lieutenant ignored the question. He thrust his finger into Augie's chest, even though he had to reach up slightly to do it. "Without papers, you're only who I say you are. And the lot of you look to me like a group of rogue Opsies trying to make off with your master's prize horse."

Augie was so taken aback by the accusation that he stood with his mouth hanging open. His great epiglottis succeeded in bouncing up and down dramatically but produced no sound except a faint gurgle. Having grown up near Farwell, Romul knew arguing with soldiers was a waste of time at best—and usually dangerous. It was probably for the better that Augie was rendered speechless. Did he think he had any power in this situation? Without papers and accused of being Rokan out of dress, they had no one to turn to. It was not as if the Rokan had lawyers. They would suffer whatever indignities the soldiers felt like handing out. It was wisest just to let it happen, get it over with, and hope for the best.

But even Romul did not expect what happened next.

The lieutenant shrugged as if Augie's response was irrelevant. "No matter. I'll just ask the horse." He turned his attention to Eachy. "Eh, horse!" he shouted. "Come on, answer me. You don't want any trouble from these Opsies now, do you? Who's your master?"

Eachy just eyed him and made no sound. One of the soldiers guffawed when the horse did not respond. The diminutive lieutenant wheeled on his men. "Who was that? Who laughed? If I find out, he'll be on B & W for two days!" Turning back to the horse, he yelled, "Don't play dumb with me. I've never yet met a horse that could hold a civil tongue in its teeth, so out with it, and don't spare me the niceties."

Either Eachy truly did not understand human speech or he liked the soldier even less than he liked Augie, for he merely snorted and turned his head away as if shooing a fly. It was probably the worst thing he could have done, for the whole troop snickered for one brief second. The lieutenant rounded on them again and shrieked for them to be silent.

"That's it, now!" he cried, marching up to Romul and the rest. "I'm detaining this here horse for further questioning."

"But you can't—" Augie began. This, too, was the worst thing he could have said. For while he'd probably intended to give a warning, the uptight lieutenant took it as another challenge to his tiny authority.

"Can't I?" His face purpled with rage. "Can't I? And who's to stop me? You, you stinking Opsy and your herd of stinking baby Opsies? You're just lucky I don't throw the lot of you in the workhouse to teach you respect for your betters." He reached out for the horse's reins, then stopped because there were none. This by itself was not unusual because horses who were well-paid or at least willing didn't need them. Eachy was neither.

The lieutenant was only slightly put out by this and yelled over his shoulder, "Droge, rope!" He was absolutely raving now, and his voice broke into an adolescent screech as he said it. Romul saw several of the burliest soldiers exchange amused glances, but no one laughed out loud. In two shakes a rope was produced, complete with a loop to serve as a bridle. The lieutenant stepped up to Eachy preparing to toss the lasso over the horse's head. Eachy snorted and pulled back.

At that moment, Rose ran up to the lieutenant and grabbed at his leggings, crying, "No, no, you can't take him! He's not a real—"

The intrusion further enraged the soldier, and his hand flew out. Rose was knocked to the ground. At this, both Augie and Romul flew into fits of anger and charged the lieutenant, Romul crying, "Why you—" and Augie shouting, "Now, that's totally uncalled for!" But it came to nothing. After the briefest tussle, both Augie and Romul were lying on the ground. Romul was doubled over with rat gut from the butt end of a spear, and Augie was swooning from a blow to the mouth.

As the soldiers were dealing with these two, the lieutenant had succeeded in getting the lasso around Eachy's neck. The horse had reared and would certainly have removed the lieutenant's head with a kick but for Murgen. She'd risen from her hiding place just enough to catch the wild horse's eye, and by some means Romul never understood, had ordered him into a resentful submission. She then sank out of sight again. The soldiers had all been so busy that they hadn't noticed her.

Even with Murgen's command upon him, Eachy pranced back-and-forth on the road in agitation. It took three of the soldiers tugging on the rope to lead him anywhere. But it was done. Even before Romul and the rest had reached Farwell, Eachy had been taken from their company. The soldiers moved up the road toward the city with the lieutenant crying out, "Magnificent! Simply magnificent! Wait until the colonel sees him!"

Eli and Anna helped Rose and Romul up off the ground, and as soon as the soldiers were out of sight, Murgen emerged to nurse Augie's split lip. Augie was dazed and could hardly stand, so they decided to set up a rest camp off the road in the trees till he came round. They were a very gloomy lot as twilight fell on them.

Chapter 19

"What do you mean we can't get him back?" said Augie, slamming his fist into his palm. "You said you knew where the soldiers' paddock was."

"Yeah." Romul sighed for at least the fifth time. "But knowing ain't the hard part. Garrison's got a hundred men at least, and unless you're better at fighting than you showed today, it'd be crazy. Besides, we're better off without him. Remember, this whole stupid trip is about sneaking in to see the Old One. And horses don't sneak good."

Romul was surprised that he had an ally in Murgen. She waved her hands for a few seconds, and Augie deflated. Apparently merfolk had a strong enough sense of fate for her to believe Eachy's parting was what was supposed to happen, or that he had his own destiny, or something like that. Romul was not exactly confident in Augie's mumbled translation.

After Romul offered a depressing litany of all the things soldiers had been known to do to undocumented Rokan migrants, they all concluded they'd been rather fortunate. No one had been seriously injured or killed, nor had the soldiers taken their sack of meager foodstuffs, which had toppled off Eachy's back while he was bucking the lasso. Nor had they been arrested or even searched.

Now that the question of rescuing Eachy was off the table, however, everyone fell into a grim silence. Though they couldn't see it in the early dark, they could hear the South Wane through the sparse trees as it chattered its way down toward the sea. As they sat at the outskirts of Farwell, their mission was coming to a very practical point. Cholerish had charged them with finding a way to interview the ancient fire lizard that inhabited the furnaces of the great foundry at Farwell. But how was this best achieved?

As the girls again rehearsed the details of the task, Romul once more felt the injustice of what was coming. He was the only one who knew the city of Farwell at all. He was the only one who'd been inside the foundry before. And because of his firebrand, he was the only one who might be able to get the cooperation of the Old One. The weight of the work that would soon come down on his shoulders made him feel queasy. None of this had anything to do with *his* main concern—finding his mom. It was all one big distraction.

"Here's the problem as I see it," said Augie. "First we have to find this priest Romul saw, to see if he'll help us. That's got to be done during the daytime. Then we have to sneak into the foundry—"

Eli finished his thought. "And that has to be done at night."

But Romul's recent reunion with the Farwell establishment had settled that option for him. "You think a priest'll be more helpful than the soldiers? We got no papers, no money, and no luck. He'd throw us out in a minute. I say we go straight for the foundry—and do it tonight."

He'd been planning to say more, specifically about the problem of getting into the city at all, since the gates were sure to be double-guarded after nightfall. But at that moment the wind changed. It now blew from the river and carried with it a strange sound. He heard it, but not with his ears—a high-pitched and haunting melody went straight to his brain, his heart, his gut.

Clearly, everyone else heard it too. The girls were looking around wildly, trying to find its source. Augie's mouth hung as wide open as possible, as if he were trying to eat it. Murgen sat upright with a grimace on her face. She turned to Augie and made a sign. When he gave her no response, she shook him.

"Wha . . . what?" he said, like a man under a spell. Romul, too, was having trouble thinking. It was as though his mind had been opened up and filled with things without any of it actually passing through his senses. He felt cool water around him, slick pebbles under his feet, a glorious gurgling and chattering of happy water over stones that formed a harmony with the music.

Murgen began waving her arms frantically in front of Augie's face. His eyes followed the hands like a hypnotized man watching a pendulum, but he made no other response. Casting caution to the wind, she bent close. Her lips parted, and she began whispering in his ear—actual words of which Romul could hear nothing.

The result was immediate. Augie jerked free of the spell and looked her in the eye. "Nixie? Really?" he replied in the clear, concerned voice of one who finally understands. He turned and said something to the girls, who responded with equal clarity, as if the music's effect on them was much less. But Romul's mind was growing muddier by the moment. He was a sponge, basking in the fundamental nature of the sweet river.

He'd never realized how beautiful rivers were—how beautiful it was to *be* a river. Moonlight plashing off his rippling surface, never still, always moving, moving . . . no questions, no uncertainty, only purpose . . . absolute and sure purpose . . . to flow, to pour himself out with abandon upon the rocks, to cleave the mountains and earth like a gentle and loving sculptor. Great leaping fish broke his surface in momentary flight, desperately fighting his current, but he pulled them back down into his liquid belly, where they squirmed and made him laugh.

When a part of him began to feel weary from his incessant running, he cast it aside to eddy and pool in some side corner of his reedy self. But his central spirit continued on, always on, downward drawn, seeking the absolute bottom of all worlds—down, down to lose himself in the eternity of the sea.

Part of him was aware that he was being hauled to his feet and pulled—oh, horror—away from the music, away from the call. He struggled, but only weakly, like water resigned to being hauled up in a bucket. Anything stronger than gravity could have its way with him. Oh, for a hole! His legs went loose. His arms flailed at the parched, empty air looking for a hole through which to pour himself out. He wept at the cruelty, hoping at least his liquid tears might escape—to flow once again.

To no avail. Strong arms dragged him forward till something hard and horrid was under his feet. He struggled for the word—*road*—like a word from a foreign language—a dry and terrible word, thick and impenetrable under him.

Then a pair of hands caught his head, covering his ears. The music faded, but not entirely. It still soaked in through his eyes, his nose; his very pores drank the draught. But as his mind cleared a little bit, Augie hoisted him feet first over his shoulders and began running. Murgen, stumbling to keep pace, was crushing his ears in a vice-like grip.

He became more and more aware of his surroundings. Augie and Murgen and the girls were running up the road toward Farwell, carrying him like a sack of coal. The tree line was behind them now, swimming in the ambient lights of the city. He could make out Augie and Murgen's long shadows bobbing on the road behind them. They passed occasional people on the road, all standing motionless, facing the river, caught up in the nixie music as well.

They must have been within a few paces of the city wall, for the road was now cobblestone under Augie's feet. He was puffing hard. This final leg of the journey had all been uphill to the gates. Romul heard the pounding of horse hooves but couldn't tell from what direction. Suddenly Augie heaved himself off the road, and they tumbled into the gutter. Murgen's hands came loose, and Romul had one fleeting look at a great horse—was it Eachy himself?—gallop wildly by, accompanied by the frantic cries of a human rider. Then the music took him again. Murgen threw herself upon him, pinning him to the ground, again covering his ears.

As his head cleared once more, he could see that a whole company of soldiers stood swooning in the city gates. Spears and swords lay scattered on the ground. Looking back down the road, Romul saw the horse—it was certainly Eachy—leave the road and head toward the river, galloping at a terrifying rate. The rider on his back was having trouble. His legs didn't bounce against the horse's side as they should have at full gallop. They moved rather as part of the horse in a most unnatural way. Then he understood. Eachy was responding to the nixie call, just as he himself had longed to do. He was heading for the river, and the rider—

Romul didn't have time to think about his fate, for Augie was pulling him back to his feet. They were back on the road, Murgen struggling to keep her life-hold on his ears. The girls were there, too, looking scared and dazed but running under their own power. With Augie tugging at all of them, he dragged them through the cluster of soldiers, who stared blankly out toward the river as if drugged, through the city gates and down a shadowy side street, then another. He had just thrust them all into a close dark alley between buildings and made them all sit when Murgen released Romul. The music was gone, and his mind snapped fully back into its proper shape—although he had a terrific headache.

He grabbed his temples and yelped, "What the—"

Augie silenced him, knelt, and motioned for them all to come in close. When they'd formed a little knot together, he whispered, "We have just had a most remarkable experience."

Romul wanted to laugh. After all they'd been through, very little felt remarkable. But he held his tongue because his head was still swimming.

"We have just heard what few living men have heard—the song of the undini."

Here, Murgen produced a flourish of signs that Augie translated. "As soon as I heard it, I knew you would be overcome. The voice of the undini has strange power over humans—especially men. They are easily subdued by the song."

"Wait." Finding he was more or less master of his mouth again, Romul continued, "Augie's a man. Why didn't it bother him?"

"Oh, it did." Augie shuddered. He looked at Murgen and smiled in an abashed sort of way. "But if you think the nixie voice is powerful, you ought to hear a mermaid's." A silent something passed between Murgen and Augie.

Now Anna jumped in. "I felt a little disoriented, but I didn't become a cripple like Romul."

Before Romul could protest, Murgen responded. "That is because human females are less susceptible to the overthrow of reason."

Here he did manage to mumble, "That's 'cause they got so little to overthrow." This would have marked the beginning of another "debate" between Anna and himself, had Augie not put hands between them and finished translating Murgen's signs. "In this case, however, the nixie were singing to attract a male each-uisge. Therefore it was the female's song. Had a male nixie chosen to sing, you would have fared differently."

"As it is," continued Augie on his own, "this has worked out to our great advantage. We have managed to steal past the city gates, and it's unlikely the soldiers will even remember our passing." As if to underscore his point, a chaotic murmur could now be heard coming from the direction of the city gates. The soldiers and way-farers alike must have been waking from their stupor.

Augie looked hard at Romul. "How do you feel?"

"Like I been kicked by a horse."

"All right," said Augie as if Romul's answer didn't really matter. "Then, worthy guide, I need you to find us a quiet place to rest and plan . . . and eat!"

Romul shook his aching head. That was no small order given the size of Augie's appetite.

Chapter 20

Farwell was an inefficient and wasteful city. Half of it was clean and robustly built, with smart shops, taverns, and apartments. This eastern part of the city was wealthy and expansive, with wide streets and brick buildings. Thanks to the steam and gas works of the foundry, it was also well lit by garish streetlights that blasted the nightly stars out of existence just to prove they could.

As one moved into the looming mountains, however, the metropolis gave way to squalid shantytowns made mostly of canvas, rubble, and wood dotting every habitable plateau—and even, at its highest edges, caves. While Romul had grown up in one of these small nameless communes on the distant slopes, he'd also been down in the city frequently throughout his youth, so he understood how things worked.

He explained that the affluent portion of the city they were now in—the Ternion—was almost exclusively Garlandish. The Ternion was a bare one third the size of the other part—called simply the Ward—which was entirely Rokan. It was said by the Rokan that the Ternion threw away more goods each day than the Ward received.

"Why is it so much bigger?" asked Eli, looking cautiously out into the street through the front window of the bakery Romul had broken them into.

Romul sighed. "Well, what d'you expect? It takes a lot of servants and hired hands to run one of them big mansions you saw down there. And more to run all the icky parts of the city."

"Disgraceful." Augie's mouth was full of pastry. He said more, but since he'd just shoved the remainder of the bread roll into his mouth, it came out as a series of garbled grunts. Rose leapt away from him as a fountain of crumbs flew in her direction. He covered his mouth with one hand to stop the heel from flying out, while his other hand reached for another.

Romul had initially wanted to break into a whiter's shop. It was the safest choice, as these little stores where Rokan received the albsignum were nearly the only shops in the Ternion that would be owned by a Rokan. At Augie's grumbling insistence, however, he'd steered them into the bakery of a particularly wealthy and disagreeable Garlandish gentleman. Now, in a place where Augie's true nature could function without restraint, Romul watched in awe as several months' worth of the baker's profits were consumed with the ease of fire consuming wood. Even Murgen watched in wordless fascination the feeding frenzy that continued long after everyone else was full.

"Nice geography lesson, but how does it help us?" asked Anna.

Miffed, Romul replied, "Well, like I was saying, the main entrance to the foundry is in the Ternion, and there ain't no getting in that way. It's guarded every minute, like more than the city gate, even. So the only way in is through the sewer pipes I mentioned. And they dump out in the Ward. Once we're in the Ward we won't have to sneak around anymore."

"But . . ." said Eli tentatively, "won't we be noticed because we're . . . uh . . . different?" She tugged at a strand of her dark hair.

Augie, who was in the process of consuming a large berry pie, pointed at her and nodded his head as if to say *Good point.*

Romul stared at the man in amazement. He was always amazed at how ignorant Garlandish people were about the Rokan who moved in their midst, ignored and unseen.

"You don't think we dye our hair because we want to, do you? Only Rokan who have to go into the Ternion or down-country wear the albsignum. There'll be lots of people who look just like you in the Ward."

"But the law says all Rokan have to—"

"Geez, Augie!" cried Romul in frustration. "Do you think Garlandish go into the Ward to check? Did you forget that we're not actually part of your nice little country? We have our own places, too, you know! Places you wouldn't be welcome. Most of us are only here because we got no money to go anywhere else!" Hot anger on behalf of his people arose in him, as well as confusion as to why he suddenly cared. "You can go anywhere you like, be around anyone you like. You can go your whole day and never see a Rokan, can't you? Whole weeks!"

He was impassioned now and blind to the fact that everyone was waving hands to get him to lower his voice. "But where can we go to get away from you? If I want to go anywhere nice, there you are, looking down at me, wondering if I'm allowed to be there. You're everywhere. The only place I can go to get away from you people is the Ward. But it stinks! All I can do is be your slave or go be poor in a slum. It ain't right, I say! It just ain't right!"

Romul was so inspired by his unexpected rage, but so ignorant of its source, that he nearly suffocated under all the horrible things he wanted to say. It was as if the real difference between the Rokan and the Garlandish—a difference he had known his whole life but accepted as normal—had suddenly stood out in true relief for the first time. The absurdity of it burned his insides, and troubling images clawed unbidden from his memory—weary, white-haired girls laundering clothes that didn't belong to them, weary, white-haired men gleaning grapes for wine they'd never drink, weary white-haired carriage drivers paid less than the horses they led . . .

An involuntary sob choked him, and he stood openmouthed, his jaw working noiselessly. But oh, horror! On the heels of all the anger and frustration came shame. Horrible shame. The kind that empties the gut and robs even righteous anger of its dignity. He felt ashamed—ashamed of the moisture in his eyes, ashamed of saying such things, and ashamed of not saying more of them.

The whole group sat on the floor looking at him in astonishment. Only Murgen reacted by rushing to embrace him. She pulled him off his quaking legs, drew his head to her breast, and uttered a soft "Shh" into his ear. The common sound and motherly touch loosened the cords of his strained conscience, and he wept into her shoulder.

After several long minutes, Romul looked up to find Augie standing next to him. "Oh, Romul." He sighed and put his hand on Romul's back. "I'm sorry. I . . . I just don't know all the . . . um, what it's like. Everybody knows the Rokan aren't treated very well, but no one really . . . really knows, I guess. How could we?"

He meant well, and Romul knew it. But he couldn't help making a final jab. "You *could* know. Anyone could. You just have to look." Pulling away from Murgen, he stalked off to the other end of the shop, where he peered cautiously out the window into the street. He knew he mustn't dwell on what just happened. It would only make him hesitant, and he hated feeling like he wasn't in control of himself.

He turned to face the silent group. "We can't stay here. We have to go. Now."

Anna had the dignity not to comment on the recent spectacle, but said only, "Well, where to?"

"The Ward. The best time to get into the foundry is just before dawn. Things are coolest then, before they crank it up. So we needs to get somewhere tonight so we can sleep first."

Ten minutes later they were again skulking their way through deserted alleys, gradually making for that place ahead where the city lights, like a curtain, drew the line between the Ternion and the Ward. Electric lights were not permitted in the Ward, under the belief that they allowed people to stay up later, making them less able to rise for work in the morning.

Thirty minutes more and they were done sneaking from

shadow to shadow, because the Ward after dark was all shadow. The two parts of the city were divided by a wall, punctured periodically by gates. He knew the few that remained open after dark were guarded by some of the surliest guards. In two places, however, streams cut through the city on their way down to the South Wane River. One of these flowed through the wall, serving as the waste stream of the Ward, and fell into an underground system as soon as it entered the Ternion. It then traveled the rest of its fetid journey to the river, out of sight and mind of the Garlandish citizens.

They sloshed up the smelly stream. Romul was used to such odors. This was the smell of his childhood. But the others gagged and wretched behind him in the dark, and someone, Romul didn't know who, tossed all their bakery treats.

The grate that was supposed to bar the way had rusted away entirely, and passing through the duct, they found themselves in instant twilight. Romul stood reflecting on what he knew lay before him, but could see only by the light that bled over the wall from the Ternion.

He had returned. He was home. And he hated it.

Chapter 21

"What!" Romul sat up with a jerk.

"Sorry," whispered Eli. "Augie says it's time to go, and you wouldn't wake up, so I had to . . ."

Romul rubbed his arm where she'd pinched him, but he rolled off the mat and got up. He looked around the long low room. It was a flop—one of a number of very humble facilities in the Ward for Rokan who had no other place to sleep. The fortunes of a Rokan changed so unpredictably that it wasn't unusual to find oneself without lodgings. So the residents of the Ward had appointed several locations as flops—large common sleeping rooms where anyone could come and "flop" on the floor for the night, no questions asked.

They were stigmatized in the Ternion as places that housed criminals—not without some justification—and were frequently raided and shut down by soldiers only to reopen elsewhere in the Ward. It wasn't as though anyone liked sleeping in a flop. They were smelly, uncomfortable, and had no amenities. The only thing worse than a flop was having nowhere to sleep at all.

They assembled outside in the early morning dark. The stars were just starting to wink out, and a rustle of predawn sounds was beginning around them as Rokan servants struggled to get themselves up and into the Ternion to wait on their employers when they arose. Candles were appearing in windows, and shadowy figures clopped along the narrow streets toward the Ternion gates.

The short three hours of sleep had left Anna grumpier than

when they'd bedded down. "I wonder which one Katniss lives in?" she grumbled as she looked around at the dilapidation. Even Rose wore an unusually surly look.

Despite his late-night gorge, Augie's stomach was already grumbling loudly. He cast about, looking for something to silence it with. But breakfast was another amenity the flop didn't offer. So he dipped into his rucksack and passed around a few morsels of pastry he'd liberated from the shop before leaving. Then they trooped off between the buildings in a general northeast direction, with Romul in the lead.

They left the shabby shops and decrepit hovels of the Ward behind them and began to hoof it along the foothills. As they crested the last hill of their journey, Romul stopped and looked about. To their right Farwell lay spread out before them. Everyone's attention but his was pulled toward the brightness of the streets that cascaded down the foothills toward the main gates they'd snuck through the night before. Romul, however, looked across the little valley ahead and up into the ascending foothills toward the mountain heights. The cave where the bodacha lived was beyond the next rise and further up still his old home.

He was filled with two sudden longings. First to see again the place that had been his home, however atrocious it had been. And second to give the bodacha a piece of his mind for sending him all the way to Halighyll to find a mother who hadn't even been there. He resolved to do both once the business at the foundry was over.

"Come on," he muttered.

They left the knoll and walked down into the pine forest that filled the little valley. The forest was clearly man-made, for not only did the trees end in a perfect line just shy of the crest of the hill but throughout they grew in straight geometric rows every ten feet or so. They had shed all their lower branches, so Romul could see all the way down to the stream, whose centuries of steady progress had cut a gouge through the hill.

When they reached it, he could smell the acrid odor of the

foundry waste and knew they were close. The river poured down the steep sides of the foothills into this valley, where it bent toward the Ward. At this bend, sheltered by a spur of rock, a great metal culvert emerged. Nothing grew around or in the pool, and from the bare ground it was clear that the water was frequently much deeper than at present. The small stream of rust-colored water dribbled out the end of it, forming a small rivulet that wound down to the pool.

The sulfurous odor was stronger here. Rose crinkled her nose. "Phew!"

"Well?" Romul pointed across the pool to the culvert. "This is it. You still want to do this?" He looked around at the little group, all of whom now wore discouraged and nervous looks—all except Murgen, who stared with wide horror-filled eyes at the maw of the culvert, as though it were a serpent about to swallow her. She turned and buried her head in Augie's shoulder.

Eli and Anna had begun a heated conference, while Rose held her nose and looked back-and-forth between them. It appeared Eli was having second thoughts about the plan. The argument ended with Anna delivering a long, whispered rant and pointing dramatically at the tunnel, Eli giving a great heave of her shoulders, and Rose wandering over to the mouth of the culvert to stand next to Romul.

"She'll come," said Rose softly. "She knows we have to." The two girls crossed the stream and came toward Romul. He turned to go, but a new clamor arose behind him. Augie was standing midstream, tugging on the mermaid's arm. She, however, was not to be moved. Her feet were planted in the mud at the edge of the stream, her eyes fixed on the tunnel entrance.

Eli's hand went to her forehead. "Oh, that's right. She can't come."

Augie looked from Eli to Murgen for a moment before his eyes went wide. "Of course. How stupid I am. Of course she can't come in."

"I don't get it," said Romul impatiently. "We need to get—"

"She's undini," Augie replied as if this answered everything. Seeing it didn't, he continued. "She can't go underground—into the realm of the gnomi. It would kill her."

"Well, leave her behind, then. We don't got much time." Romul stepped up into the culvert, took two steps and looked back.

Augie was looking torn and forlorn. He'd taken a single step toward the tunnel, then stopped. Murgen made frantic signs to him. He looked at Romul with agonized eyes, which then fell downward, along with his shoulders. "I can't leave her. She's not even a week old."

"She ain't no baby. She's stronger than you."

Augie didn't move. His eyes grew hard. "We'll stay here. Meet you when you're done." He stepped back across the stream to receive the trembling mermaid into his arms. "Get on with you. You don't have much time."

With tears in her eyes, Rose whispered, "It's so beautiful. The way he—"

"Oh, come on," barked Romul. "Get a move on or they'll all be up before we're done."

Romul wasn't bothered by the tunnel, which grew inky dark within a dozen feet of the opening. He'd done this before. But the girls held hands and—particularly Eli—twittered annoyingly behind him, bemoaning the smell, the black, the wretched state of their lives till he couldn't stand it any longer.

"Look, shut up, will you! Almost there, and if you don't pipe down, we'll be caught before you get to see your little red friend."

The foundry in Farwell was strategically placed. Here at the foot of the Aracadian Mountains, the world's deep furnaces burst forth. Centuries before, the Rokan had first harnessed the heat of this natural inferno, only to gradually lose control of it to the annexing power of Garlandium till they were little more than servants in the city they'd founded. But in those subsequent centuries, the Garlandians had expanded the operation to many times its original size, including a garrison, dormitories, and even a small Lemerrian chapel—for the whole complex was dedicated to Lemerrus, god of heat, fire, labor, and cunning. The foundry was like a small iron city, half of it dug into the mountain and half jutting out into the larger city. It was generally understood that the production of the foundry would pour into the Ternion and Garlandium, while its waste would be poured out into the Ward.

Romul was only grateful that the place still slept, for soon hot and toxic waste would pour down this stinking shaft in which they now walked nearly doubled over. Reddish light grew some deceptive distance ahead of him. A few minutes more found them struggling out of the open culvert onto a kind of loading dock. Vats of brown sludge surrounded them—the previous day's waste allowed to cool to a manageable temperature before being emptied from a dozen ports into the culvert.

The room was empty. Although not ungrateful, Romul was surprised. He'd expected the room to be guarded like the last time. It had required a great deal of stealth from him. He'd woven and bobbed around barrels, vats, and pressure valves till he'd won his way onto the catwalk system that ran throughout the complex.

He carefully popped his head up out of the open culvert and immediately knew things were different. Steam still hissed from valves in the dark overhead, sooty red lights still cast their Lemerrian glow, and rusty metal girders groaned periodically overhead, but no human sound could be heard.

He'd just finished explaining the oddity and his concern about it when Anna cut him off. "Just be grateful and get on. We can't expect the luck to last."

So rather than creeping in with feline stealth on a catwalk, Romul led them right through metal-shod hallways. He still moved cautiously, peering around corners before continuing, but they saw no one. In ten minutes they stood before a set of high metal doors, which bore engravings of serpents, lizards, and other reptiles gamboling and twisting in what may have been intended as playful abandon. In this dark and industrial setting, however, the effect was ominous.

Romul had pulled the bar and was pushing one of the doors open when Rose pointed at the bottom of the doors. "Oh look, a dragon!"

They all stooped and squinted in the ruddy light. The engraving at the bottom featured a long, twisting, snaky figure possessing both four legs and two wings. Its head was turned upward toward all the other creatures. Romul thought it looked hungry—or maybe even jealous.

"Look here." Eli ran her finger over the engravings above the creature. The dragon, if it was a dragon, was separated from all the frolicking lizards by several wavy lines that looked like smoke or water or sand. She continued feeling her way over the shapes. "The light is just so bad, I can't make out whether—"

"Whatever!" Romul pushed the door away from her. "We just need to get inside. Then we'll be safe . . . at least from guards. They won't come in unless they're called for. They're scared of the place."

They piled through the door and stood gazing in wonder at the cavernous hall. Romul's eyes went upward to the catwalk he'd occupied on his last visit. It was obscured by countless metal lines and girders. The room felt much larger and more open from down here . . . and less safe. All the walls were metal except the one on the far side, which was rock, as though the room had been built directly against the mountainside. From the rock protruded a great iron proscenium inset with large iron doors that leaked a dull red glow around their edges.

They stood in a sort of gallery that sloped down to a rail. Beyond the rail a small dirt arena sank into the floor about six feet. The gallery circled around to the rock walls, creating the effect of a dark amphitheater or stage.

"It's like the lion exhibit at the zoo," whispered Anna.

Most dramatic of all, a large iron pedestal with branching arms, like a misshapen tree in winter, stood in the middle of the arena. Black rock and bits of burned-out charcoal littered the area. And the whole room smelled of sulfur and baked earth.

"I don't like this place," whispered Rose.

"I don't think you're supposed to," said Anna. But she squared her shoulders, pointed at the iron doors, and added, "Okay, what do we do? How do we get inside?"

"Oh, you don't go inside. That's the living fire in there. You get any closer than that railing when the doors open and you're toast."

"Literally," added Eli.

"Fine, then," said Anna. "What do we do? Knock politely?"

"I kinda missed that part," said Romul, "but I think we have to pull that." He pointed to a thick metal chain that descended out of the gloom and made a serpentine pile on the floor. He walked over and took it in his hand. It felt dense and heavy, like iron. "I suppose it rings a bell or something . . . in there." He nodded toward the iron doors.

"Someone will hear?" asked Anna, still skeptical.

"Nah, I don't think so. Those doors are awful thick."

"I don't know . . ." Eli was looking around for another solution.

"Look, if you weren't going to believe me, then what'd you bring me for?" Romul snapped.

"All right, all right." She sighed. "Let's do it."

He was already putting his weight into the chain. At first it didn't move. Then he felt a link somewhere high overhead slip round a pulley, then another. A single deep, hollow gong sounded somewhere far off in the depths of the mountain. Suddenly unnerved, he let go of the chain and spun to watch the door they'd entered by, expecting soldiers to come piling in.

None did. In fact, nothing happened for several minutes.

"I hope he's not as hard to reach as a dwarf," muttered Anna. "We haven't got the time."

Feeling less confident, he grabbed the chain once more and looked at the three girls. He waited for each of them to nod their assent then bore down with all his strength. Again the gong reverberated through the mountain. He released the chain and pulled again, and again, till the heavy peal had sounded three times. Winded by the effort, he let go.

Again there was no response.

"Well, ain't that just ditty," muttered Anna. She began pacing with frustration and kicked a small lump of charred rock out into the arena.

Rose sidled up to him. "What's he look like?" she whispered, sounding more awed than scared.

"I never saw him. He just talked from out the fire on the other side of the door—"

They all jumped in unison as a great rasping noise came from behind the doors. Hot air blasted from the widening crack as they parted. Jets of orange flame shot out and enveloped the iron tree for a moment. When the flames withdrew, and Romul could see a bit again, the tree glowed like the tip of a sword on a forge. But there was no seeing through the doorway, which blazed in gold and white flames. Yet Romul knew something moved in the midst of the inferno.

Having heard the vulcani speak before, he knew what to expect. But it still raised the hair on his neck when it came.

A voice, deep and raspy, hissed from the glowing cavern beyond the archway. "It is not the appointed time. Why am I summoned? It is not the agreement." It was like a withering hot wind in the face, taking one's breath away, but utterly dry, as if issuing from a throat that had never known moisture. Yet for its scorching and arid quality, it was still rich with inflection, sentiment, and even guile.

You wanted to believe whatever it said. And at the moment, it was making Romul believe they'd made a terrible, terrible mistake.

Chapter 22

If the salamander was surprised to find itself looking at four mere children and not a sage or a soldier, Romul couldn't tell. While his eyes were becoming accustomed to the brightness of the gallery, no distinct form could be made out within the fire itself—only a vague undulating motion half seen and half felt in the waves of the heat that washed over him in varying degrees of hot, hotter, and scorching. But the creature was silent for a moment as if considering them.

Of course, none of the children spoke. They all stood frozen by the heat and light that emanated from the archway.

Eventually the voice sizzled again from the fire, but this time it was preceded by an even more disquieting sound—like that of lips smacking hungrily together. "So seldom have I visitors, especially ones so delicate and dainty. It would seem wasteful to deprive myself by summoning the guards." A long hiss followed, and to Romul's increasing discomfort, a head the size of a horse's emerged from the blaze.

Then came a supple red body—thirty feet long, at least—covered by thin silver lines so intricate that Romul couldn't tell if they were actually part of its hide or if they'd been inked on by an artist. They glowed with heat as the Old One emerged, but the glow faded as its skin cooled. Long, vicious claws furrowed the ground as it glided forward and lithely encircled the iron tree, climbing with the grace of a snake, till it reached a place where its great head was level with theirs.

The jaws smacked again, showing row upon row of sharp, snow-white teeth. The head swiveled back-and-forth slowly as if trying to see them out of each eye separately from a distance of a dozen feet.

Romul felt something next to him and jumped. It was Eli, eyes locked on the salamander but leaning in to say something.

"The firebrand," she whispered. As she said it, the creature's hindquarters began inching up the iron tree, its body contracting like a coil preparing to spring.

Romul's mind was muddy with fear, but Eli's words unlocked something inside him. His hand went to his pocket. Part of his brain realized the pocket was hot, and when his fingers touched the firebrand, they instinctively drew back. He was sure it had burned his fingertips.

"Hurry up," hissed Eli frantically. The salamander was now hunched over its front claws like a cat, its hind legs gathered, ready for the lunge.

Panic forced Romul's hand. He jammed it down into the pocket and grabbed the firebrand tightly in his fingers. His mouth opened in a silent howl of pain, but his hand grasped even harder as he dragged it up and out. He threw his arm out in front of him as if to get rid of the thing, but he couldn't have dropped it if he'd tried. His fingers curled around it of their own will.

Suddenly and without warning, the firebrand burst into flame in his hand—not the comforting little flame he'd shown Cholerish. Not even the more torch-like flame by which he'd scared away the panther, so black it looked purple. This was a jet of orange and red shooting upward, a pillar of fire three feet high.

Romul stared in horror at the ball of fire that was his hand. He wasn't even worried about the salamander anymore. The more immediate peril of the fire had driven everything else from his mind.

The great head of the creature drew slowly into his field of vision, stopping less than a foot from the burning hand. Its mouth opened, and with all the ease of a man blowing out a candle, it extinguished the towering inferno with a single puff of air.

Romul remained petrified, frozen, his hand still outstretched before him. It took him a moment to realize that his hand was not burnt. The firebrand had become inert again. What did that mean?

The creature spoke slowly, almost casually. "The game is afoot, I see. I knew it would not be long before Lemerrus descended, considering that Therra has been here for some time." Its yellow eyes scanned each of the girls before affixing themselves to Anna as if she had a tattoo on her forehead. She stared back with wide eyes for a moment before pulling the amulet from under her shirt. She held it up alongside Romul's firebrand.

The creature sniffed at the two objects, gave a long reluctant sigh, and swung away. It muttered as it slithered lazily back up the tree, "Very well, I shan't eat you . . . yet." It came to rest as if out of habit among a particular arrangement of limbs.

It sat for several minutes, blinking at them, waiting for someone to speak. When no one did, it smiled broadly, showing its fangs, and said in a syrupy and condescending voice half to Anna and half to her amulet, "Such a quaint and happy little family you make, little one. Where is your other brother and your sisters?"

Anna pointed to her sisters. "These *are* my sisters. And he's not my brother. He has no family."

Romul resented the statement and would have corrected it immediately if the salamander hadn't uttered a long staccato series of hisses Romul took to be laughter. It made an elegant if dismissive gesture with one claw and hissed, more to itself than to them, "Oh, how rich—the youth, the presumption, the utter ignorance . . ."

Eli seemed to have collected herself, for she stepped forward. "No, you don't understand. We were—"

The lizard cut her off and fixed Anna and Romul each with an eye that blinked independently of the other. "The longer I must stare at you, the hungrier I become. Best get on with whatever you seek. Did the priest send you?"

"Yes," said Eli with a little heat of her own.

But still the salamander took no notice of her and continued blinking at Anna and Romul till Anna repeated the word. Then it gave a sniggering hiss. "He did not like my previous answers?"

Now all four exchanged puzzled looks.

Anna said it for all of them. "Cholerish was here?"

This time the salamander responded by spitting a glowing gobbet to the floor that exploded in small liquid sparks. "Not the dark-minded invalid. It was the other, the more practical one."

Eli was thinking hard. "Do . . . do you mean . . . Whinsom?"

The fire lizard said nothing but grinned again, showing its brilliant dagger-like teeth.

Fear was beginning to ebb from Romul. His mind was catching up, and he suddenly understood. He looked at the others triumphantly. "See, I told you! I said I saw a priest when I was here before. And I did!"

"Yessss." The lizard lifted its nose from the limb and sniffed right and left. "That's it. I remember your smell. You were here before. Were you not apprehended then? How interesting. You are craftier than I expected."

Eli chose this moment to try taking control of the conversation, "Look, um . . . we need to ask you some questions . . . if that's okay, um . . . with you."

The salamander finally condescended to acknowledge her presence—but only by means of a prolonged hiss that concluded with, "Why don't you ask the dried fish who travels with you?"

"Murgen? How do you know about her?"

It gave a disinterested sniff. "You bear the stench of the undine all about you. You have the look of ones who have eaten their cursed food."

Anna was thoroughly over her fear now, ready to lock horns with the lizard. "Look, she was just . . . uh, born recently and doesn't know very much. And anyway, we were sent to talk to you. So we'd like to ask you some—"

"Born recently?" The lizard took in this piece of information with great interest. "Well, it seems the vulcani are not the only ones who have begun to multiply again. I suppose one must take the bad with the good."

"The salamanders are multiplying?" asked Eli.

"Your powers of deduction are staggering. How do you think I knew Father Lemerrus had descended?"

"Didn't Whinsom tell you—?" began Anna, but Eli cut her off.

"No, he couldn't." She began to pace, thinking hard. "He doesn't know about Romul. He only knows about you, and so he couldn't . . ." She started and looked back at the salamander. "What *did* he want? Whinsom, I mean. What did he want to talk about?"

"That is not your concern." It snapped its jaws together with such a crack that Romul could tell that line of questioning ought not be pursued.

Thankfully, Eli recognized it too. "Okay, okay, fine. Um . . . what do you know about the Legate of Hamayune?"

The lizard resumed its nonchalance. "Which one?" It licked a claw lazily, and a careless flick of the tail made it clear it had no intention of cooperating.

"There's more than one? But . . ." Eli was stunned to stillness.

The salamander blinked both eyes at her in succession and gave a dismissive hiss.

Anna nudged Romul. "Look, doofus, you're holding the dang key to this thing. How about you say something now."

Only then did it become clear to him. She was right. He lifted the firebrand out in front of him again, and spoke, trying to sound confident. "Look here, uh, lizard. This is Lemerrus here, and, uh, he wants you to answer our questions. So quit your stalling and—"

The creature thrust its tongue out at Romul and made a sound he would have associated more with a three-year-old blowing raspberries.

"I find you human creatures very diverting. You are quite good at acting knowledgeable while in the midst of profound ignorance. Yes, I will answer your questions because of the presence of Father Lemerrus in this hall, but I will not be trodden under by one whose mother has forgotten her own children."

Romul blinked. "My mother? What do you know about my mother?"

But Eli was now in full career through the questions Cholerish had given her and was not to be denied. "What about the legate? What do you mean by *which one*? How is there more than one?"

The lizard gave a resigned hiss. "There is the one who came and was defeated and the one who is coming but shall not be."

"Okay, you mean the dragon. Did Whinsom tell you about the dragon?"

"Of the dragon, I told him!"

Eli was visibly shaken by this revelation. "But how did you . . ." She tried again. "But that means . . ." The lizard smiled as if daring her to solve the puzzle. Her final attempt succeeded. "You're that old?" she whispered.

A soft hiss confirmed that its knowledge of the mysterious dragon was not secondhand.

"The dragon was the *first* legate?'" Eli asked in a tone as soft as the hiss.

For a moment the salamander seemed to lose its guile, as if now that it came to it, it really wanted to talk about this after all. "Yes, I know of the things of which you speak, but my brother would know more, as they took place within his lands far in the north. No tiding comes to me as to whether he yet lives, but these things happened generations before the plains became desert."

Eli pressed for clarity, even risking so far as to interrupt. "So the dragon *was* the one who '*took the water from the earth*,' like in the prophecy?"

"Yessss, and more!" The Old One's voice rose in feverish recitation. It rose on its forelegs, lifting its head toward the ceiling in keening lamentation. "*In guile, he tears the elements asunder . . . Everlasting war shall be his offspring. It is the dawn of Hamayune.'* Yes, I know of how he arose from the pit, desiring to wrest us from the control of men—our liberator, our..." It waved its head back-and-forth in a kind of anguish but said no more.

"Liberator?" pressed Eli.

But the spell was broken. The lizard mastered itself, shrunk back into its previous position, and stared at her in enigmatic silence.

She tried again. "Liberator?"

The salamander looked at each of them in turn before pausing on the silent Rose. Romul followed its gaze and was shocked to see her looking not at all frightened but wearing the look of a mourner at the funeral of a beloved pet.

They held each other's eyes for a long time before she whispered, "You're so sad. Why don't you leave this awful place?"

Of everything that had so far been said to the Old One, this produced the most dramatic effect. The creature reeled as if struck and cast itself down from the tree. It raged about the sunken arena. It grasped a section of wood rail in its teeth, tore it loose in a single heave, and cast it aside. It clawed at the rock wall of the archway, cleaving ugly furrows into the solid stone.

"Why?" it shrieked. "Why, you ask? Why have I not quit these fetid fires for a millennia? Do you think I desire it not? Do you think the vulcani—or any of the longaevi—delight in their submission to you? You who pollute our fires, hew our rock in pieces, slay Father Lemerrus's children, and bind us with the elemental promises! Do you think we delight to be your slaves?"

Here the rampaging creature threw itself into the trunk of the iron tree with such force that several branches bent, and one broke entirely. The collision both dazed the creature and drained it of its fever. It lay in a heap at the foot of the tree, panting and hissing.

Now they all had their backs against the exit door, having fled as far away as they could from the terrible frenzy. But when the creature did not rise after several minutes, they began to find their courage and come slowly back to the rail.

Eli spoke first, and from the moment the words left her mouth, Romul knew they had overstayed their welcome. "Um . . . we have a few more questions."

"I have no more answers." The lizard rose with a ponderous and world-weary tiredness.

"But what about this other legate? Who is it?" Eli's voice rose in panicked shrillness. "When is its—"

"I go to summon the guards," interrupted the creature, deaf to her now. "But for Father Lemerrus's sake, I will count before I do so." The blast doors split open, and they were plunged again into dazzling blindness.

"To what?" cried Anna, stepping in front of Eli. "Count to what?"

It smiled and turned toward the fire. At least Romul thought it smiled, for white teeth were now the only thing he could make out in the brilliance.

"But . . . but . . ." Anna grabbed the rooted Eli and dragged her toward the exit. With her other hand she did the same to Rose, who was also fixed in mesmerized pity.

Romul likewise turned to go, but as he did, a question stormed back into his mind. He shouted at the retreating lizard as loud as he could over the blast. "What do you know about my mom?"

The creature paused. Its head emerged one last time from the blinding glow. It hissed, "What *would* I know of such things? Look for her in the east among your own kind."

Deciding this was no time for timidity, Romul shouted back, "You mean west, right? 'Cause I'm not Garlandish. My mom was Rokan."

"You are not Rokan any more than they." The lizard gestured toward the three sisters, who had stopped in the open doorway to watch the exchange. With that the creature's head withdrew into the fire, and the iron doors slammed shut.

Romul stood dazed and blinded amid the renewed blackness of the room. He was also mortally confused. He had been pretending to be Garlandish since the beginning of the journey. He had not so far fooled anyone. That a creature so supposedly old and wise would fail to see what no one else had missed gave Romul a queasy feeling.

He was given no time to muse on it, however, for a piercing whistle suddenly went up all around them. It blasted for a second, then fell dead, only to resume a moment later. Romul cursed and broke into a run—out the door, past the stunned girls, and down the hall. He glanced over his shoulder to make sure they were following. All three were running hard behind him. Above all the questions now swirling around in his disordered mind, the whistle continued to wail like death itself.

Chapter 23

Romul could never remember the flight back to the drainage duct or the dark splashing journey through it. His mind didn't catch up to his senses till they emerged back into the forest and had run through the trees back up the hill, yelling for Augie.

They found him and Murgen standing at the crest, looking down into the shantytown.

"What's going on?" demanded Augie with far more concern than Romul would have expected.

"I don't know, but we need to—"

"But what's happening?"

"I said I don't know! But we gotta get back into the Ward and hide."

"I'm guessing not." Augie pointed down into the mass of hovels.

Romul's labored breath caught in his throat. Smoke was rising all around the Ward. Although the sun couldn't yet be seen over the mountains, it was full morning. He could just make out individual forms on horseback, riding through the narrow streets with torches. Everywhere they went, flames leapt up. By straining his ears he could just detect the sound of screams and shouts.

Now it was his turn to ask "what's going on?" But it came out in a hoarse and grief-stricken croak.

Augie shook his head. "It started a few minutes after you went in. I almost left Murgen to come tell you, but . . ." He looked at the mermaid still clinging to his arm and fell silent.

"A few minutes?" Eli was the last to gain the hilltop. "But that's long before we even got into... It doesn't make sense. They can't be looking for us. It must be something else."

"Well, whatever it is, I'm not going down into it." Anna crossed her arms.

"Then what do we do?" Rose asked.

Romul still couldn't speak. The smoke rising over the burning buildings flowed past his eyes and into his muddled mind. He didn't understand. Everything was going wrong. What could possibly possess the garrison to burn the Ward? Didn't they know children and old women lived there, that they had no other place to go? The world was turning to madness.

He felt a hand on his shoulder. It was Rose. "Rommie, are you okay?"

His head cleared, and he knew what to do.

"This way." He turned away from the burning Ward and marched down the hill back toward the culvert, and as an afterthought yelled back over his shoulder, "And don't call me that!"

No one moved. "Where are you going?" called Anna.

"To get some answers," he yelled back as he marched into the trees. He heard the sound of stamping feet behind him as the rest scrambled down the hill to catch up.

"But we can't go back in there," said Eli as the culvert entrance came into view. Romul made no reply. He splashed through the stream at its narrowest part, but instead of going into the tunnel, he began following the stream up the far side of the valley.

"Romul!" Augie called from behind him. He continued his march uphill. Again, "Romul!"

Romul heard a heavy huffing and puffing from behind, and a hand grabbed his shoulder. Romul shrugged it off and marched on.

Then from further back came Anna's irritated voice. "That's it! I'm going to tackle him again."

He spun around. Augie stood right behind him, a bewildered look on his face. Murgen stood behind Augie, holding on to the sleeve of his shirt, unwilling to endure any separation. Right behind them stood Anna, looking ready to carry out her threat. Further down, Rose struggled up the hill, looking tired, with a nervous Eli trying to help her. They both looked up and caught his eye.

He suddenly felt lost in the world. He had no sister to cling to, no adoring mermaid to cling to him. Thick curling smoke was now visible above the trees. The only town he'd ever known was burning. He was alone.

"Look." He had to choke back something in his throat that wanted to get out. "I don't know what's going on back there. It's all so . . ." But he couldn't think of the right word. Big? Crazy? Out of control? He gave up trying. "The only thing I can think is to go to the bodacha. She lives up this way. She may know . . . something."

He turned and trudged on. He knew there was a road at the top of this hill—a path, really—leading up into the foothills to the tiny Rokan settlements on the small plateaus dotting the eastern side of the Aracadians.

They traveled on without words till they stood on a small heath of level land, covered in short scrubby grass and a collection of wattle-and-daub shanties. A dozen or so people, many with hair dyed snowy white, were trying to corral a bunch of sheep and goats that had escaped from somewhere. They wandered bleating throughout the village, breaking into short-lived spurts of motion every time someone tried to grab them. Somewhere a dog barked an angry *It's not my fault.*

Romul knew this village well and knew where he had to go. He plowed into the commotion without hesitation. The others followed. He made his way through the collection of buildings toward the sheer wall of mountain that formed the back of the plateau. Upon reaching it, he stood before the mouth of a cave, covered by a red cloth bordered with tassels. Most of these had worn away, however, and the cloth was now shabby and faded.

He stood unmoving, as if the curtain were a door of iron. He was trying to keep his breathing normal. His last visit to the strange old woman had resulted in his miserable trek to Halighyll and back again, without the benefit of a single answered question. He felt a surge of anger, and embracing it as motivation, grabbed the two wooden sticks lying next to the doorway. He rapped them together several times, as was the custom for homes without wooden doors.

The loud clack of the wood had barely sounded when an aged voice, strong and clear for its years, rang out. "Come in, oh Son o' the Moon. Come in, young seeker and all the host of heaven with ye."

He had no idea what that meant, but he'd gotten the first two words, so he pulled the curtain aside and stepped into total darkness. He paused but was immediately thrust forward by the others piling in behind him. A great deal of grunting and shoving followed as everyone stumbled over everyone else in the darkness of the cave. *Geez, why don't the old hag put on a light?*

As if in answer to his unspoken question, the voice sang out again. "I could not see wasting strength on the flint this morning when I knew I were to be visited by the Red Father himself." Romul heard the others begin whispering around him.

Oh for the love of Angish! He reached into his pocket. Producing the firebrand, he held it out before him and thought about fire. The firebrand warmed in his hand, and a moment later, with a little popping sound, a tiny flame, the size of a match, shot up from the piece of metal. Unlike the eruption in the hall of the Old One, this was a patient, friendly, even playful sort of flame. It danced upon the surface of the firebrand as if looking around the cave for something of interest. And it must have found such a something, for it leapt from the firebrand out into space, like a man diving from a cliff, and landed on the very tip of a candle sitting on a table before them. There, it blazed up, and everyone gasped and drew back.

In the immediate glow, nothing could be seen but a single great eye, staring at them from inches behind the flame. Romul stood mesmerized as the eye passed slowly over them, unblinking. Even Romul, who knew somewhat better what was going on, was still overcome by its appearance.

Eli whispered in a petrified voice, "It is the beating of his hideous heart." Whatever that meant, it broke the spell, and he turned a raised eyebrow toward her.

The candle moved, and the eye disappeared. Its glow passed off to one side and was thrust down out of sight for a moment. Then a blaze sprang up in the fireplace, and the blackness suddenly had shape, color, and depth. Romul saw that almost nothing had changed. The room was still mostly empty save for the single chair and its table and a small trunk against the wall from which he knew she drew out various things for her twisted trade. A second curtain of indistinct color hung further back in the cave, setting apart her sleeping place, which Romul had never seen.

The old woman now seated herself at the table, twisted the candle into a candlestick, and looked at them again. A stout and heavy silence descended, in which she was the only comfortable participant.

Her eyes were still her most disturbing feature—overlarge like an owl's with great glassy blue irises, staring, staring, not at you but through you, as if you were a mere ghost, casting a faint shadow over things she really saw—things more profound and real. The eyes overwhelmed all her other features, making her nose and mouth and even her head seem small and underdeveloped—like an infant's. But he knew her to be of a great age. As evidence of this, her hair was snowy white and had been for as long as Romul had known of her—not, he was sure, from the albsignum.

He now wondered if she were Rokan at all. He looked to the hearth for confirmation and was not surprised to find it bare. The eregina was missing. Every faithful Rokan hung the eregina—the Creed of the Queen—above their hearth if they had one. Or at least on the wall if they did not. It looked different in every home—sometimes illegibly scrawled on a piece of wood, sometimes an ornate family heirloom, and in the poorest houses scrawled in mud or blood upon the wall. But the words were always the same—*Semper Eadem*.

He couldn't read what the letters said, but he didn't need to. Every Rokan child was taught to recognize these words. They were not Garlandish, Azhionan, or even Mulekese. They were an even more ancient tongue—the language of the world from which the Rokan had first come into Errus. They were the very words of the Queen of Angish to her people as they left for distant shores. They meant—"Always the Same."

It was the single greatest identifying mark of the Rokan. Not the albsignum; that was a mark of slavery and ridicule imposed by the Garlandish. But this . . . this was their own testimony of their enduring faithfulness to the Queen of Angish. It proclaimed their defiance of the Garlandish gods and their unwillingness to bend or be changed. It was the first thing hung in a Rokan home and the last thing removed. Romul had even heard stories of people running into burning buildings to rescue the eregina. This caused a hard knot to form in his stomach as he thought about the flames now ravaging the Ward. He wondered how many might die simply because they refused to leave the eregina behind in their burning hovel.

That this testimony was missing from the bodacha's wall almost certainly meant she was not Rokan—or at least not one of the faithful, which was worse. Knowing what she wasn't left the question of what she was. Cholerish had called her a "superstitious fool of a sorceress."

Romul's thoughts were interrupted by a scuffling behind him. He turned and realized that only the three girls were with him. Augie stood at the entrance of the cave tugging at the arm of a stubborn Murgen. Although he was speaking soothing words of comfort, she shook her head vigorously and resisted with all her strength, which of course was far greater than his. He might as well have tried to pull the mountain into the sea. Her eyes were nearly as large as the bodacha's.

Augie finally gave up. "She won't come in. Won't even come behind the curtain. I guess I'll have to stay out there with her." He swallowed hard, and the unnaturally sized lump in his throat jumped involuntarily with emotion.

"Of course she can't come in," said Eli. "It's a cave."

"I know that," snapped Augie, "but it means I'm going to miss what happens . . . again!"

"Well, if she can't come in . . ." began Anna.

The raspy voice of the bodacha interrupted softly. "Oh, but she can."

Chapter 24

All eyes returned to the old woman sitting calmly at her table. She smiled and pulled a small leather bag up from somewhere beneath the table. She reached into it and produced a handful of beads. She nonchalantly threw them onto the table and bent the candle to examine them as if she'd forgotten her guests were even there.

Augie was first to recover. "What do you mean she can come into the cave? She's undini. If she comes in, she'll die. Longaevi can't cross into each other's—"

"She'll not die." A bony finger jabbed at one of the tiny beads. They seemed to be of every shape. It looked to Romul as if each side was marked with a symbol. He took this in without thinking about it, for Augie was speaking again. He sounded excited.

"Do you mean there's a way for longaevi to move between elemental realms?" He paused, his mouth hanging open. He shifted from foot to foot excitedly, his mind visibly racing ahead to implications. "Do you . . . do you mean you've discovered the Unitas? We've been looking for that for—"

"No." The reply was flat, almost sarcastic. The old woman sighed and looked up at him. "Ye do not understand. Yer kind never does. There is no reason to *seek* the Unitas. Science cannot unite the elementals. The unity don't exist the way ye think. The children be united in their parents or not at all." She returned to her beads.

Romul understood nothing she'd just said, but apparently neither did Augie. He opened his mouth to press whatever his point was, but Eli got in first.

"Please, ma'am. What do you mean she can come in? How?"

With a single gesture the woman swept the beads back into the bag. She looked, not at Eli, but at Anna. "Her love of Therra is stronger than her fear of Berducca." She paused, staring hard at Anna, who fidgeted uncomfortably but held her gaze. "Hm? Do ye not see? She may safely go where'er Therra goes."

Anna's hand went slowly to her throat, and she produced her amulet on its chain.

"Ah!" The bodacha clapped her hands together. "Ye understand, then." She waved her hand at Anna, shooing her back toward the cave entrance. "Go to her, daughter of heaven and earth. Comfort her, and she'll follow ye."

Anna looked back, one eyebrow raised, then slowly turned and pushed past Augie, pulling the curtain back wide. "Murgen, come with me."

Fear remained etched into every line of Murgen's face, but remarkably, like a child afraid of being parted from its mother, she thrust out a hand and clutched at Anna's sleeve. She pulled herself slowly toward Anna till she stood next to her at the mouth of the cave, now holding Anna's arm in a death grip with both hands. Anna turned and took a tentative step into the cave. Murgen hesitated for a moment longer, biting her lip in terror, then put her foot over the threshold into the darkness. The mermaid was underground.

Romul realized he'd been holding his breath. He sighed and found the others, too, were exhaling. It took a full minute for Anna to get Murgen over against the wall and seated on the floor opposite the fire. When Anna tried to step away to rejoin the others, however, she was pulled off her feet by the mermaid, who had not yet released her arm.

"Ye must not leave her. Nor do I suspect she'll let ye." Now the old woman waved her hand above her head as if shooing a bug. "But come, ye have very little time in which to ask yer questions."

"What do you mean?" asked Romul.

"The soldiers. Even now they come."

All the voices chorused out their questions at once. "What?" "Here?" "Why?"

Again the old woman waved dismissively and struggled to her feet. She hobbled round the table toward Anna and the mermaid. She thrust the bag of beads toward Anna and held it there. "Come, come, take some, or I shan't be able to tell ye anything." Anna put her hand hesitantly into the bag and withdrew a few beads.

"But why are the soldiers . . ." began Romul, but the bodacha turned next to him and thrust the beads under his nose, her great eye fixing him in its glassy gaze. "Um . . . okay." He took a few beads.

Only when everyone had taken some beads did she speak. "I have heard," she began in a conspiratorial whisper, "that last night in Farwell, the commander of the Western Province himself was assassinated. Now they be burning the Ward looking for his killers, for they believe the perpetrators to be Rokan."

"'Course they do," muttered Romul.

"How was he killed?" Augie asked, his voice full of trepidation.

"It would seem—" the old woman nodded knowingly—"that someone tricked the garrison's lieutenant. He was given a magnificent horse, which turned out to be not a horse but a rather troublesome undini—a kelpie or worse."

"*Given!*" Romul now knew what Augie must have suspected. "Stole's more like."

Augie waved him silent. "It was an each-uisge, and the commander was carried into the river and drowned, wasn't he?"

The old woman nodded brightly at him. "And all they finds of him this morning was his liver lying on the bank of the river." She began to cackle with mirth, while Romul shivered at the thought.

Augie collapsed with a sigh next to Murgen, who for the first time seemed conflicted as to whether to maintain her death hold on Anna's arm or transfer it to Augie. "It's our fault," he muttered.

"No, no, it isn't!" said Anna defiantly. "Romul's right. We tried to warn him, that stupid little idiot. He stole Eachy, and it serves them all right."

"Either way, the Ward burns." Augie's words silenced everyone again.

Only the bodacha was unruffled. She dropped back into her chair at the table and watched them as if entertained by it all. "Come, come," she called cheerfully. "Thes guides every hand and every bead. So come forward, and let's just see what the *fortuna aleam* have to say. "

Everyone seemed too troubled to pay her much mind except Rose, who stepped up and dropped her four beads onto the table with a clatter. The noise jolted everyone out of their stupor, and as the bodacha bent to examine them with her candle, curiosity drew Romul to the table.

"Hmm, soooo . . ." the old woman began, "it has returned. Most precious, most mysterious of the Berducca relics." Without raising her head, she thrust out her hand toward Rose, who, without hesitation, took the small globe-shaped compass out of her pocket and dropped it into the waiting hand. Eli let out a small gasp but said nothing. The old crone brought the orb under her nose and into the candlelight.

"The *shemaroon-demageen* as it were called in the dwarf tongue of old. I thought it perished in the Great Change. Yet here it be." She rolled it around in her hand like a great marble before giving it back to Rose and fixing her with her rookish gaze. "What is it that ye seek, oh youngest?"

"I guess . . ." Rose thought a minute. "I mean, sooner or later, we have to go home. And I want to know where the window will be."

The bodacha did not look at the beads nor even at the arrows of Rose's compass. "It awaits ye at journey's end. Ye needn't me to answer this. Just follow the iron arrows. "

"But why . . ." Rose looked imploringly at Eli, who stepped up next to her.

"I think what my sister is trying to say is that last time the window was right where we needed it. I mean, it was right in the cave with us. And now the compass hands point west, but we were supposed to go west anyway. Why does the door always seem to show up in the place we need to go anyway?

"The door will always lie at the end of the journey. It cannot help but do so. That is what a door is—an entrance or an exit. Where else should it be but where 'tis needed?"

Now Anna's agitated voice rose from the wall. "But how does it know where it's—"

"Silly child! Do ye think the world is without direction?" She ignored the combined protests of Eli and Anna and bent over the beads. "Very well." She sighed. "What ye seek now rests in the birthplace of the Rokan. The place of their entrance is now the place of yer exit. Look ye between the White Rocks of Rokehaven."

"Rokehaven!" Now it was Romul's turn to be unconvinced. "That's way over the mountains. *I've* never even been to Roke-haven! No one has!"

"Then it is time for ye to go! There is more here, but I wish to see the sister's first." She looked at Anna, who tried to stand.

"Ugh." She was yanked back down by the deceptively strong hand of the mermaid. "Well, I guess I'm not allowed to show them to you." But Eli had already crossed to her. She took Anna's beads and deposited them on the table.

The old woman looked at her with interest. "Yours, too, oh eldest. I suppose I shall have to read them together now."

"Why?"

"Ye have touched her beads. They has become yours as well. Let me see them all." When Eli had produced them, she bent to examine the two piles of beads. She poked at them for a full min-ute—mixing them together, teasing them apart—before clapping her hands together and crowing with delight.

"What?" said several voices at once.

"Oh-ho!" She clucked again, making a sidelong glance at Ro-mul. "Some mysteries are too wonderful to be spoken of. No, no, they's being made plain of their own accord. Of this alone shall I speak: A day will come—years from now—when ye sisters will be parted from one another by an expanse of sand, and the fate of two nations will rest upon yer doing justice upon earth and sea."

"'Expanse of sand!'" moaned Anna. "Not that stupid desert again."

"Come, come! We's almost out of time. The boy is next."

Romul stepped up and dropped his beads on the table.

She scrutinized them all for a moment, then sat back in her chair and scrutinized *him* for another minute before producing a flat, "Yer mother lives again."

"What? That's it? That's what you said last time. I went all the way to stinking Halighyll, and all I got was these three." He threw his thumb out indignantly at the sisters.

The old woman quelled their protests with a look. "Ye do not yet know why ye was brought to them?"

"No!" He knew he'd been their guide to Farwell. He knew Cholerish had given them a mission. But so far as he could see, he hadn't gotten anything out of the deal except sore feet.

The bodacha raised her eyebrows but said nothing. She leaned again over the beads. "Ye must cross the mountains three times to find her."

Romul felt only frustration at this new quest. His temper rose in answer. "Look, if you don't want to tell me how to find my mom, just say so. But I'm not climbing the mountains of the whole world just because you says I got to."

The woman was patient and thoughtful. "But, dear Lemerrus, how shall your fair sister Therra—" here she nodded toward Anna —"find her way to Rokehaven?"

He heard himself yell. "That's *her* problem! I'm done. I'm sick of being led on by everyone else. I just want to find my mom, I just want to know about who I am, and—" Suddenly two distinct and new questions appeared in his mind and sobered him with their possibilities. "What about my . . . my stepmom? She'll know something. She can tell me."

The old woman sat back in the chair and crossed her arms. "Ah, so thought of Leaserae at last, have ye? Well, your fortuna aleam say nothing of her. But—" she raised a bony finger like a poker and fixed him with her eagle's eye—"some weeks after your last visit, she came to see me. She was searching for ye. She told me many things . . . strange things. She sought forgiveness."

"Forgiveness? For what?"

"Child, it is not my place to tell ye the sins of another."

Romul felt like banging his head against the stone walls with frustration. "Not *yer* place! Even if I'm the one she did her sins against?"

The bodacha continued to stare mildly at him. Her fingers danced together in front of her withered face as though she were thinking hard about something.

"Why, child, do ye think *ye* are the one she most wronged? What of your mother and the one ye know not of . . ." The last few words trailed off into a whisper.

Romul couldn't have heard her right. "Of what?"

"Why should ye believe ye was her only child?"

A roaring filled Romul's head, and his legs went watery. He slid to his knees before the table. The roaring was loud now. He heard screams.

"What's that noise?" squealed Eli.

Romul was confused. The part of him still able to think knew the awful chaos could only be in his own head, but all the others were on their feet now, rushing toward the cave entrance.

"They has come," said the old woman quietly. "Our time be gone."

As another scream tore the air, Romul realized the pandemonium was outside his mind as well. He faintly heard the galloping of hooves mingled with cries of terror.

Augie was back at the table in an instant. "Quick, old woman, what do we do now?" He slammed his two beads down.

She looked at them impassively and said only, "Ye must be a fool."

"Yes, I probably am," said Augie through clenched teeth. "But what . . . do we do . . . *now*?"

Dogs barked wild warnings outside, and Romul caught a whiff of smoke. The bodacha turned casually and pointed to the curtain hanging over the back of the cave. "The tunnel goes up and up. Stick to the main passage, and ye shall come to where ye needs be. Yer way has been long prepared."

"Fine." Augie pushed Rose and Eli toward the back of the cave and went to help Anna with Murgen.

Romul knew he had just seconds, so he blurted his second question. "The Old One said I weren't Rokan. What'd he mean?"

The great eyes rotated back to him. "He sees much even I cannot tell. He can be wrong, but he would never jest."

That was all. Augie caught him by the arm and began dragging him deeper into the cave.

"Take the two sacks in the hall," she cried after them. "I have prepared them against yer journey."

The girls had already passed into the darkness beyond. As Augie pushed him through, Romul looked back, wondering at the old woman's foreknowledge of this dark necessity.

They locked eyes a final time, and she read the question on his face. She held up a single bead between her bony fingers. "I can read me own fortune as well. Goodbye, dear Lemerrus."

BOOK 4

Gnomi Aracadia

How came your fate, oh Rokan,
To be so bound up with Garland?
Your prophecies of no common ancestor,
Yet thine and theirs lie tooth and bone together.
Is this the proof that the world's movements are not
    random?
How persistent Time is in her suggestion that,
Whate'er God's proper name may be,
It is not "Chance."

> FRANKO RAZHAMANÌAH, from "Of Queens
> and Gods" in *Songs from the Rokan Highlands.*

Chapter 25

Blacker than any midnight, the tunnel wound its way through the upper foothills of the Aracadian Mountains. In fear of pursuit, the troop stumbled through the inky dark, running into walls and bashing elbows, foreheads, and toes on protruding stone.

It took only ten minutes for tempers to melt. To Anna's great frustration, Murgen had begun to moan and weep like a lost child almost the minute they'd left the bodacha's home, and now she began scrabbling and clutching at her with the ferocity of one drowning. Her patience finally broke under the constant pawing, and she burst.

"Grief! This isn't any picnic for me either, you know."

This brought out the chivalrous in Augie, who started yelling at Anna. Eli, too, began shouting hysterically for them all to shut up, but in the utter dark her words took on the strained tone of someone about to burst into mad laughter. Sounds of shoving, slapping, and cursing ensued, and from the ground Rose, knocked down, dissolved into tears.

They were all suddenly silenced by a burst of light. A tiny flame shot upward from Romul's hand. It was hardly bigger than a match light, but in that murk, it filled the passage like a bonfire. Romul saw the whites of ten eyes staring back at him.

"That's enough." He spoke quietly but with as much authority as he could muster. "Now, we're far enough away from there to be safe for one minute. Let's just see what good the old hag's done by us." He shot a finger toward the sack Augie had thrown down during his defense of Murgen. Then he nodded to Eli, who looked most like she needed something to do.

With shaky hands she knelt and gently poured out the bag's contents. Out rolled a small round of cheese, a skin of something that sloshed—probably water or wine—a few apples, a length of rope, and a smaller sealed slick skin from which Eli pulled two short sticks with a lump of cloth on the end. They smelled faintly of glycerin.

Eli held up one of the torches with a look of relief. Then her eyes fell back to the small pile of goods and began scanning frantically. "But," she began in a tremulous whisper, "she didn't give us anything to light it with."

"Oh, for the love of Jiminy freaking Christmas," cried Anna, whose temper was barely under control. With her free hand she yanked the torch away from her sister and held it over Romul's flame. It sputtered and burst into a cheery blaze.

"Doofus," muttered Anna, thrusting the burning stick toward Eli.

Eli jumped back, tripped over Rose, and fell on the ground next to her.

"Now you see," Augie flared again, snatching the torch. "That's exactly what I'm talking about. Young lady, you need to show a little—"`

"Don't *young lady* me. Ugh!" Anna whirled on him, but forgetting that one arm was still pinioned to Murgen's side, she lost her footing and slumped onto the ground by her sisters. She looked like a downed marionette, one arm still held aloft by her puppeteer.

"Hey!" shouted Romul, trying to regain control. "We don't need this. The hag said—"

"Stop calling her that," Augie shouted. "She's probably a Thesian priestess and deserves to be—"

"She's a hag," Romul snapped, feeling his temper slip. This was no good. He had to keep his head. He closed his hand, and the firebrand's little flame puffed out. "Fine." He sighed. "The bodacha said this would lead us out if we just—"

"But look." Now Rose interrupted, pointing in a wide arc with her finger. By the light of the torch they looked around and realized this was not a single tunnel. Romul saw at least two other passages branching off within a few feet. By the odd shadows further up the passage, it looked like the tunnel was nearly a honeycomb of tunnels. He could imagine the way before them was the central tunnel, but with almost no effort, that same imagination could also make any of the other passages the primary one.

"Great." They'd already been stumbling blindly through and around these branch tunnels for more than ten minutes.

"How do we know we're still going right?" said Eli in a small voice.

Augie's sense of circumstance was returning to him. "We don't. We just have to take our best guess and hope. This one looks like it's going up, which she said it would, so our best bet is to just go forward."

"I agree," said Anna and Romul almost at the same time.

Then there was silence for a moment.

"All right, then. Off we go." Augie was holding the torch, so he stepped to the fore.

Now that the crisis of temper had passed and heads were deflating, Romul felt his gut sag in relief. He gladly took up his place at the end of the column. Somehow the back of a line always moves more slowly than the front, so he had time to think about what had just happened.

He didn't like being in charge. He hated the heavy feeling that came with it. He didn't want other people depending on him. Yet in the crisis, he often found himself stepping up and taking the lead. As he thought about that and then how easily he'd handed it all back to Augie, he realized that, in fact, the only thing he hated more than being in charge was having no one in charge. When that happened, his mind just took over, and he became a different person. He didn't know why.

Maybe 'cause I hate trusting my life to nobody in particular. He trusted Augie as far as he could trust any adult, and he knew Eli was smart and Anna, though really annoying, was strong. He was fine if any one of them took charge, but sometimes weird things happened, and they all canceled one another out. Then nobody was in control, and it got scary.

He thought about the coach that had taken them to Umbra. The driver had said he didn't need to do much; the horses knew the road well enough. But what if none of them wanted to pull the same way? Then the driver had to be stronger than the horses— not stronger in his muscles but stronger in his mind, in his will. That was Romul—happy to let anyone else run the show so long as *someone* was running it.

He'd spent so much of his life concerned with basic survival that he'd never spent much time thinking about his own mental life, what sort of person he was. It was a new thought—no, a new way of thinking—to have thoughts about his own thoughts, to hate something and love the fact he hated it. His mind suddenly felt like a deep well into which he was looking for the first time but couldn't see a bottom. His mind wasn't just full of things he hid from other people, but many things also lived in there hidden from even himself. It frightened him and excited him at the same time.

They traveled in silence for some time through the passage that went more or less straight ahead. Twice they came to branch tunnels that were close enough to the angle of the main tunnel that debate broke out as to which was the trunk and which the branch. Both times one appeared to be headed more uphill than the other, so the decision was made with relative ease. But the third was so nearly a perfect fork that the debate lasted awhile. Finally the decision was made on the basis of Augie taking twenty paces into each and determining that one most certainly had a more generally upward slant than the other. All this continued to lower their confidence that they were getting anywhere useful.

They'd been trudging through this tunnel for an unknown time when Eli said in an uncertain voice, "Do you feel that?"

"What?" said several others.

"Doesn't the ground feel like it's going down now? Instead of up, I mean."

There was a moment of heavy silence before Augie said, "I think she's right." And Romul was forced to agree that it did *seem* like they were headed downhill, but it was hard to tell since he had only the indistinct feeling underfoot to go by.

"Well, what do we do?" asked Anna. "Go back?"

"That's no good," said Romul. "It could just be a dip in the tunnel. We'd never know if we go back."

"Yeah, but if we're not sure, what's the point of going on . . ." began Anna. Then Augie and Eli began to weigh in, and a full debate ensued. Even Murgen began gesturing wildly, although Augie was too busy making his own case to translate any of it.

They had lit the other torch sometime earlier, and while Augie held the lead torch, the other had been periodically passed around to each of the others. Right now Rose held it. And she took this moment to explore an intersecting passage a bit further on.

She stood looking down the side passage for a moment, then took several steps down it. The result was that the light that had surrounded the arguing faces was instantly reduced by half. It was such a shock to the debaters that they were stunned into silence.

Into that moment like a rock into a dry bucket dropped Rose's clear voice. "Um, what's this?"

Before anyone could react, her light returned to the main artery, and she approached, dragging something behind her with great effort. When she reached them, panting, she heaved the thing forward onto the ground before them.

"Look what I found." She smiled victoriously, like a cat presenting a dead mouse.

"It's a . . ." began Eli, and indeed it was—a small pickaxe, only about the length of her arm. When Augie bent to pick it up with one hand, he "oomphed." He looked around in surprise; he could hardly lift it. It took both hands and a good deal of his strength to wield the thing. It had obviously been made for someone half his height but twice his strength. Everyone knew immediately what this meant.

"It's dwarf-made or I'm a fairy," grunted Augie.

"More importantly, it was made *for* a dwarf," said Eli, getting excited, "and that means we're near dwarves, and that means we'll be able to—"

"No, it doesn't," said Anna, arms crossed. "You remember last time? There was only one dwarf, and he was so freaking crazy that he tried to kill us in our sleep. That thing could've been lying there for a hundred years. It only means there *were* dwarves around here sometime, long ago."

"Sad to say, she's probably right," said Augie. The layer of rust on the metal seemed to confirm this.

Eli was not detoured. "But shouldn't we at least look around? I mean, we've got this mission to—"

Anna groaned. "Yeah, I got a mission all right—get back to the surface so I can have my arm back." She was struggling not to be annoyed by Murgen, who, though having grown more docile out of sheer necessity, would still not let go of Anna's arm.

Romul could feel things going sour again. "Look, as I see it, we got only three things we can do—stand here arguing, go back, or go on. And stumbling around looking for dwarves that probably ain't there is as good as going on. So I say we just keep walking."

No one could argue against this, for even Eli wasn't really serious about just wandering down cross tunnels in the hope of running into a dwarf.

"And don't forget," said Anna with a shudder, "dwarves aren't the only things that live underground. Sooner we get out into the light, the happier I'll be."

With that settled, they stumbled onward even after it became apparent that the path they were on was indeed gradually descending. Despair would have quickly accompanied this reality had not stranger things begun happening as well. They began hearing faint sounds—or thinking they did. Sounds that didn't fit with their own movements. First, Eli thought she heard extra footfalls behind them, but when they stopped to listen, all was silent. Then Augie swore he heard whispering from a side tunnel as they passed.

When Romul was positive he'd heard the clink of metal somewhere near, Anna lost it. "Geez o' freaking whillikers! It's like Gollum's back there." She turned and started screaming back up the tunnel. "Well, you can keep your stupid *precious*. I just want out!" Murgen, in a shocking reversal of roles, yanked her into an embrace and began whispering calming sounds in her ear.

Romul had no idea what a Gollum was or why it was so precious, but he, too, was feeling strange and jittery. The edges of the torchlight danced and played on his eyes, and his imagination began throwing up awful images of what sorts of things might be lurking just beyond its protective glow.

"Look!" said Rose with a calm that was itself disturbing. She pointed down a passage that descended steeply to their right. "Oops, it's gone."

"What?" said Augie in a voice that betrayed that he, too, was succumbing to the paranoia.

"A light, but it's gone now."

"You saw a light?"

"Yeah, but it's gone now," she replied, as if that fact made everything all right.

"It's just the dark. You know? How it tricks your eyes?" Eli clearly had no confidence in her own idea.

Suddenly Murgen began to wave her arms frantically at Augie, who was busy peering down Rose's tunnel of tranquility.

"Um, Augie," said Anna, "you want to turn around. Your girlfriend's having a conniption fit."

"What . . ." began Augie, but before Murgen could lift another finger, a tempest of torrential wind came billowing up out of the passage, throwing them all off their feet and against the far wall of the tunnel. They crumpled to the floor in a pile of bodies. The torchlight was extinguished, and the darkness poured over them like floodwaters. Romul still saw light dancing before his eyes from the blow of his head upon the wall. Somewhere near them a drum boomed out a hollow and horrible sound, and another answered from somewhere far off.

"Oh crap!" said Anna, her muffled voice coming from the bottom of the pile. "Now it's Orcs!"

Chapter 26

The swirling lights in Romul's aching head resolved themselves into a hazy amber glow. He was being jostled every which way as everyone tried to disentangle themselves from the heap. He was forcibly rolled from the top of the stack by Augie. From his new position on the ground, Romul at first thought he was looking at a host of children, then shriveled old men. But a deeper sense than sight knew they were surrounded by dwarves, a more-than-countable number of them. He had never before seen a dwarf, but he'd grown up hearing stories, and knew it meant no good for them.

As his eyes grew accustomed to the golden light, he began to make out the details of strange hairy faces that squinted and gawked at them, and more importantly, the star-like shimmer of light cascading off a constellation of arrowheads and spear tips.

A voice thick and shaggy spoke. "Lookie here, me brothers, what Sweet Berducca has laid low at our very doorstep."

Another voice spoke. "Tain't nothing but a collection of wee'uns. How under earth did they come to—"

"Nar' this one," said the first voice, and a hairy thick hand grabbed Augie by the arm and dragged him forward into the mass of bushy heads.

"See here! It's not what you—" The same hand, now in the form of a fist, closed Augie's mouth for him with enough violence to knock him to the ground. Augie moaned, "Oh, my tongue . . ." and his hand came away from his mouth covered in blood. His lower lip was split and swelling. It now matched the fat upper lip he'd received from the Garlandish soldier the previous day, and he must have also taken a hard bite on the tongue.

Love, however, is apparently stronger than the elemental forces, for at this mistreatment Murgen rushed forward, yanking Anna off her feet and dragging her to Augie's side. She knelt next to the fallen inventor. Romul drew back from the mermaid, for the look of absolute loathing she laid upon the dwarf leader was toxic enough to peel paint. And for a moment he thought she possessed some great power, for the host of dwarves all drew back with a collection of gasps and groans—and not from surprise, wonder, or anything so useful as that. It was disgust. Like someone drawing back from a leper or a corpse.

He heard a whisper from the back. "'Bomination." The word broke the spell that held them, and they began pushing forward with shouts of what should be done to the 'bomination and all who were with her.

It was only through sheer force of lungs that the leader managed to prevent the horde from running them through then and there. "Back! Back, I say! I say back, you jumpy lot of filthy sylphi! This ain't the way, curse your stones. I said back!" This reduced the uproar to a mere rumble, allowing him to continue by shouting, "This is a wonder, to be sure. And I'm sure she's a danger to every living dwarf, no doubt, but we weren't sent here to prick them like hogs. This . . . this horror here, this unnatural *fish* do only make the point. They must go to the Gaderung. We must let all the ga-mol look at them. We take 'em all, we does."

From next to the chief, a dimwitted voice, that in other times would have made Romul laugh, sang out in genuine wonder and confusion "What, chief? We's taking the tots, too?"

The chief gave an exasperated sigh, like a small explosion. "Now, I told you, Ylfig, to keep your mouth shut, I did! Yes, the whole lot goes, every manjack of 'em."

Despite some tittering from the back of the crowd, the simple voice sounded out again. "But what about that one?" And a hairy finger was thrust out at Murgen. "I mean, chief, she ain't even a man, and I'm sure her name ain't Jack."

At this several broke into loud guffaws. Whatever sort of fearful spell the chief had been trying to cast over the prisoners crumbled under the idiocy of Ylfig, and the chief knew it. "Blast you, Ylfig! Don't be so simple! Of course she's got to go, you bleeding jackanapes! Ain't that the whole point, ain't it?"

Now that the whole troop was laughing, Romul dared to believe that perhaps they may just survive a few more hours underground. The dwarves seemed a bit moronic, especially the one called Ylfig, but there were still two or more dozen of them, all heavily armed. It was clear even Ylfig's idiocy wouldn't prevent them from going to the Gaderung, whatever that was—a sort of torture, he had no doubt.

They were marched downward through tunnel after tunnel, for what felt like miles. It was all dark and gloomy and indistinct— sameness upon sameness. The only light came from several large topaz-colored stones carried by a number of dwarves on chains around their necks. These jewels glowed with a strange but powerful golden light and illuminated everything in the direction they faced.

Their captors were a confusing lot. They were companionable and vicious in alternating breaths. The leader, a terse red-haired pudge of a dwarf in leather jerkin and skull cap, could go in a heartbeat from cheerful chattiness to putting a knife to Augie's throat with threats of violence. He would then burst out in great belly laughter as if only kidding, then follow this with a sober face of malevolent hatred. It would have been comical to watch happening to someone else, but it lacked humor at the moment.

Augie could not even respond to the mistreatment. His mangled tongue and two great swollen masses that had been his upper and lower lips left him as mute as Murgen for the time being. A few times early on, he mumbled things none of them could understand, and when this met with only great guffaws of derision from the dwarves, he lapsed into a brooding silence.

Augie's gloom stood in contrast with Murgen's newfound mettle. She remained as affixed to the miserable Anna as a barnacle to a hull but was no longer simpering. Now she walked proud and erect and lovely. Having resigned herself to death at the hands of her elemental foes, she seemed determined to endure it with the dignity of a martyr and the grace of a queen. And she managed both with an effortless finesse that widened even Anna's blurry eyes.

The dwarves sensed it, too, and were unwilling to even approach the undine. This left them to mainly ignore her, except in their black and bushy stares, which peered at her with a hatred as thick and solid as her own.

Of all the prisoners, only Eli was able to make any headway with the dwarves. She had her biggest success as they passed through an old mining cavern. It wasn't in use at present, but the intricacy of the dwarves' work on the rock face was stunning. It looked rather like a honeycomb with carved pillars standing before each entrance. When Eli asked about the pillars, she was informed this wasn't actually a mine but rather a sort of staging area or entrance to the real mines.

"Each of the orifices is marked by the clan that holds the claim to that orifice." The chief pointed a stubby arm at the various pillars. "We have to mark them like that, see, since we have so many orifices, some larger than this!"

Anna and Rose both burst into fits of giggles.

Eli attempted to salvage the dignity of the conversation with a quelling look that only partly succeeded. "We also have orifi . . . um . . . Where we come from, we have mines too. Some of them are very deep, almost two and a half miles, I think."

From nowhere Ylfig was at her side, his face right in front of hers, threatening to bump noses. "Them ain't mines, chief, are they? They is just farms, they is." Eli jumped back from the eyes, which were unusually large, glassy, and somehow golden. They turned for a moment on Romul, and he, too, paused in step. They seemed to look through him and into the rock as if he wasn't even there.

"A farm, Ylfig? Don't be such a fool," cried the chief, chuckling over his shoulder. "A farm indeed. What would make you say such a damn fool thing?"

"'Tis but a farm, chief, it is," said Ylfig, prancing up to the chief like a retriever to its master. "Shallow little scrape like that tain't a real mine at all. 'Tis like making wee furrows in the dirt to grow things in, you know—like a farmer do, right, chief?"

With this the chief burst into a great belly laugh and most of the troop with him. "You do say it for true, Ylfig. You is a fool and cur, but you speak the very words of Berducca, you do, bless ye!"

Next to him, Rose muttered, "I don't like the way they laugh at him. I think he's quite clever. More than they think."

She was going to say more, but Ylfig had prepared an encore performance. He pranced back to Eli and thrust his face into hers again, but when he spoke, it was to the rest of the troop. "Me thinks, I does, that if she wanted to impress us, she might've told us that her mines was deeper. Deeper than ours. Deep enough to reach . . ." He paused for great dramatic effect and finished in a hoarse and awe-filled whisper that carried throughout the cavern. "To reach the Glaem."

All at once a great clatter fell around Romul and the other travelers. Every dwarf had immediately dropped whatever he was holding—a spear, a bow, a canteen of water—and bent to one knee. They all covered their eyes with their hands for a moment and then spread them wide in a manner of supplication and all grunted *"Leoht!"* It happened almost in unison, and then with the same immediacy, each gathered up his dropped possessions and resumed his march as if the whole obeisance had not even occurred.

So, too, with the chief, who continued right on. "You're right as rock again, Ylfig. That would be a story to hear! But would be a lie, it would, and of the nastiest sort, to be sure."

"No doubt," mumbled Ylfig, who, losing interest in Eli, melted back into the troop.

They passed out of the cavern now, and Romul began to notice a difference in their surroundings. For one thing, it no longer felt like a tunnel but a wide passage, more like a road. And the ground ceased to be earth and became stone, fit so tightly together that he could hardly see the seams. The sounds also changed. The dwarf boots now slapped the pavement with a decidedly military sound, and they knew it and took pride in it. Lights now twinkled from the walls and ceiling in blues or ambers or greens, all with the same brightness and qualities as the light stones borne by the dwarves. Thus the close feeling that usually comes with being underground could be almost forgotten for long periods of time.

The road widened as it descended, and doors began appearing in the walls of the tunnel. From these, additional small and puckered faces occasionally emerged, and without fail, as soon as one of the troop explained what was afoot, they joined in the procession. So within the space of a half-hour, the troop had swelled to a crowd, and the mood changed from militaristic to festive. Romul could hear Ylfig's strident voice from somewhere in the mob behind them, singing out his own version of the story. From the catches he got of it, it sounded as though Ylfig was taking credit for single-handedly subduing the whole Therran race and dragging the lot of them underground. This version of events, known by all to be absurdly false, was met with much cheering, laughter, and shouts of encouragement. He must have been the town fool or something like it.

As the jovial spirit arose behind them, the prisoners were forced farther forward till they were walking cheek by jowl with the chief and his immediate crew.

At this point, Rose left Romul's side, sidled up next to the chief, and said in a voice that everyone could hear, "Why do they treat him like that?"

"Who you mean?" grunted the chief. His demeanor had not

loosened up with the rest. He'd become serious, as if he disliked all the attention they were drawing.

"Ylfig," she replied. "Why do they laugh at him?"

The chief cast a sidelong glance of disbelief. "How you mean? He's raving, he is. What else are they to do with him? You don't expect they ought to believe him, do you?"

Rose looked thoughtful. "But what's wrong with him?"

"As I said, he's raving. Mad as a fairy."

"Has he always been like that?"

Romul could see the chief was becoming annoyed at her line of questioning.

"For near a century. Ever since he came among us. Was born that way, I s'pose. Some say he had a traumer in the deep mines or sommat. But he's harmless, I tell you. You probably shan't even see him again. He'll slink off somewhere for a week or two, liken he always does, before popping up again. But don't fret. You got greater problems afore you than a young'un what's off his sauce."

"But what kind of—"

"Lookie here, see." The chief's patience was ended. "I don't care if he saw the very Glaem . . ." Right in mid-sentence, he dropped his weapons, genuflected, spread his hands, and grunted "Leoht!" As he did this, so did the dwarves around him, and as Romul looked over his shoulder, he saw wave after wave of dwarves falling to one knee and repeating the act, even those who could not possibly have heard the chief say the word. As quickly as it started, it was over, and the chief was continuing as if he'd only taken a breath. "Itself. Now get yourself back in line, tot, or I'll forget that dwarves don't do harm to women and cubs."

"And fools, chief!" came Ylfig's voice from somewhere behind. "We don't hurts fools neither!"

"True enough, Ylfig, me merry lad. You're the safest one here, to be sure!"

Rose shrank back before this exhortation, but it strangely emboldened Eli. She took the place of her sister beside the chief.

"Um . . . can you tell me what the . . . uh—" she looked over her shoulder at the growing mass of dwarves—"that word . . . that makes you all . . . uh, bow like that . . . um . . . is?"

"You mean the Lemerrian Glaem?" said the chief reverently. Predictably, the whole ritual reoccurred. Romul had begun to wonder if this might be a useful thing—all the dwarves dropping their weapons at once like they did. It might provide some room for escape. But even as he had the thought, he cast about the cavernous highway and realized he had nowhere to go. He was by now a mile or more under the heavy earth. Even if they let him go free that very moment, it would be no good. He would have to ask them for directions.

Once again, Eli had coaxed the dwarf into talking freely by taking him to a topic he cared about. He spoke softly and adoringly now. "It's the utter bottom. The great fire that burns at the base of the world. Upholds all this." He gestured about him. "Melts the living rock, stokes the fires of Errus, and delivers every manner of precious things into Berducca's hand."

"Have you ever been there?"

The dwarf pulled up so sharply that his boots made a squeal on the paving stones. He stared at her in dismay. "Sweet Berducca! 'Course I ain't been there. There's no going to *there*, I tells you. Filled with cursed salamanders, it is. It's their home. And the habitation of ole Lemerrus himself, some say. It ain't our place at all to be *going* there, even if we knew how."

"But I thought dwarves were . . . um . . . earthborn, uh . . . gnomi, which is Berduccan."

"That we are."

. Unfortunately Anna decided to enter the conversation at this point, and her question bore the slightest tinge of sarcasm. "But why do you worship the fire, then?"

A collective gasp went up from the whole assembly, and in the time it took Romul's heart to skip a beat, the chief had bared his knife and gone for Anna. But Murgen also had the instincts of the longaevi, and in the space of that same heartbeat she'd interposed herself between them. With a thrust of her arm, which had a decidedly fishy look to it, her stiff fingertips met the flat of the blade and sent it flying from the chief's hand. The confounded silence that followed was punctuated only by the clatter of the knife as it skidded across the paving stones, coming to rest at Ylfig's feet. The half-wit uttered a soft, "Cool!"

Romul's mouth was open in surprise, but his expression must have been nothing compared to the look of shock the chief wore. He ground his teeth and spluttered, "If I didn't have me orders, you bleeding fish . . ."

Murgen met his gaze unmoved, and his words ricocheted off her like a pebble off a brick wall. So he turned his vehemence back to Anna, who cowered behind Murgen, a child in her mother's skirts. "We worship the One, the Holy Maker, the Unnamable—"

Rose spoke, her voice rich with epiphany. "Do you mean *The*—" But Eli clapped her hand over her sister's mouth before she got the final *s* out and began whispering furiously in her ear.

The chief bawled on without hearing her. "And we are gnomi. We revere Sweet Mother Berducca, Heavenly Servant of the One. But we ain't such fools as to lack respect for fire—*the* fire. Now don't be blaspheming, or ye won't live to see the Gaderung, orders or none. In fact, I doesn't want to hear so much as a chick's peep from the lot of you." His accompanying gesture here included Eli. "Or by Sweet Berducca's horns I'll skewer the one I hears!"

Then they marched again, with the chief's final word on the matter being, "Ylfig! Pick up me knife!"

Chapter 27

Nothing in Romul's travels had prepared him for what awaited them at their destination—not the wealth of the Ternion nor the withered glory of Halighyll. Not even his best dreams possessed a glimmer of the awe that fell upon him when they reached the end of the underground road.

He'd realized the tunnel's end was coming but had assumed that the road, now wider than the main city street in Farwell, was merely coming into another cavern. While he was right that it was a cavern, it was of such immense size and height that the whole of Farwell—Ternion and Ward combined—could have fit comfortably into it with room to sprawl.

He looked down onto a great city of stone spires, colonnades, and broad, flat rooftops. The ceiling stretched away to a height that could have hosted low-flying clouds. Great gem lights glistened from that distant ceiling, casting the whole place into, if not quite daylight, at least something like a brightly lit room. Thousands of gems down below filled streets and buildings with lights of every possible hue. He couldn't be sure, but he thought he even saw something like fields or farms along the edges of the city, lit by huge gem lights.

"It's like Jules Verne," whispered Eli in the throes of a similar wonder.

"More like *City of Ember*," muttered Anna.

"How do they do . . . that?" Rose cast a vague gesture toward the ceiling.

"The *gimmbeorht*?" The chief had stopped the assembly as if to enjoy the traveler's awe at the dwarf city. "They glow like that when we find them. Well, they're brighter after we cut them to shape, but they burn with the fires of the deep earth. Only the Holy knows how." Then, as if that were enough awe for one sitting, "Well, down we go!" And the whole assembly began descending the slope.

It looked like the entire city had turned out for their arrival, a spirit of jubilation filling the air, but Romul couldn't figure out what they were celebrating. Perhaps it was mere novelty to have human prisoners, but in any event, the conscientious chief did not allow the revelers, now numbering several hundred, to slow his pace. He cried out in continual agitation, "Get out the way, you filthy blatherskites. They go to the Gaderung! To the Gaderung, I say. Now move yourselves!"

Here Eli managed to extract from the leader the fact that the Gaderung was the high counsel of the city, and a gamol was any shrunken old dwarf. Only the oldest and wisest gamol were allowed to sit upon the Gaderung. And indeed, when they'd been herded into a great coliseum, Romul beheld a collection of gamol so old and desiccated that he wondered that any could think or speak. All the merry-making dwarves scurried in behind them like cats getting out of the cold and filled the seats of the hall, which was really more of an open amphitheater.

Somehow the Gaderung was expecting them, for they were all seated at a semi-circular dais at the front of the arena, looking down upon them with beady eyes—bright like shiny black marbles. When all was ready, the chief gamol stood (although doing so did not change his height) and removed his left boot. This he used as a gavel on the podium to bang the room into silence.

He raised his hands in a gesture of benediction to the whole congregation and spoke in a withered voice that somehow carried to every corner of the room. "May you, the chosen of Sweet Berducca, be sheltered within the glory of the Glaem." Predictably every dwarf in the place fell to one knee and uttered the "Leoht!" He lowered his hands. "We the chosen have assembled."

Then turning to the chief, who alone remained in the center with the prisoners, he spoke. "Well, Gram, you appear to have brought with you more than you was sent for." His eyes scanned Murgen malevolently. For her part, she, if possible, stood a little taller and smiled an imperious smile.

Chief Gram replied, "Yes, Gamol Fehro, I have returned with the trespassers as ordered. But among them we discovered—" his voice fell hushed—"a 'bomination."

"Yes, indeed. This will require careful consideration, it will. But for now, let us have the story from the rest of the rabble." Here Fehro began to scan the collection of prisoners, and Romul was sure his face wore a look of disappointment till his eyes came to rest upon Augie. "That one is, I presume, in charge?"

"Aye, Gamol Fehro, near as we can make it, he is." Gram grabbed Augie by the arm and dragged him forward.

The chief gamol eyed Augie for several minutes before folding his hands across the podium and speaking. "Pray tell this counsel, oh man, what it is you was doing trespassing in the Sarkonish Kingdom."

The look on Augie's face was very legible. It read *The what kingdom?* But he composed himself for a respectful answer. "Sirs, we meant no trespass upon your land. We were forced underground by . . . uh, unfortunate circumstances and lost our way." Augie's response was loud and confident, but his swollen lips and wounded tongue added an absurd quality to his words, robbing them of their intended effect.

"Ah-hum." Fehro cast sidelong glances of affirmation to his colleagues left and right, who nodded in return. "And where, pray, was you headed when you was intercepted?"

"We were seeking a passage over the mountains into Rokan. We have urgent business there." Few heard the last sentence, for as soon as he had said their destination, a great furor of surprise and disbelief ran through the room. Dwarves all around were sneering, catcalling, and waving their hands dismissively at Augie.

Even the members of the Gaderung whispered to one another and shook their heads. Fehro answered for them all. "That is hardly to be believed, human. The snowy Wastes have spread out of the south so far that 'tis nigh impossible to make the pass but for a week or two each year. And only the hardiest of humans would dare it then. In short, we doesn't believe you."

So deep seemed their trouble that the implications of this weather report for their journey hardly registered in Romul's mind. At the moment he wasn't worried about getting to Rokan; he just wanted out of this fix with his skin intact.

Augie tried to speak again but could not be heard for the shouting and jeering that reverberated from every quarter. Fehro called out a single word, "Bargheist!" Romul saw that the portcullis was going up on a great arch that stood opposite the doors by which they'd entered. It revealed the gaping mouth of a tunnel whose floor fell away into dark nothingness. But as the gate creaked upward, the cries of the crowd turned to cheers—very disquieting cheers—as every eye turned to that black void. Romul was quite sure something was going to come out of it, and that this *something* was a thing the dwarves would like and the prisoners would not.

Nothing happened immediately. This anticipation made it worse for Romul. He had expected something slimy and horrid to come slithering out and set up a great screeching or roaring. But this silence? Far worse! And he was relieved when eventually he heard a loud snuffling noise in the passage, like a dog nosing about a garden for moles.

What emerged was dog-like but larger. More like a bear. Except a bear would have seemed only a dog next to it. The raised hair on its back, black as the darkness that preceded it, brushed against the rails of the lifted gate as it passed under, and it was restrained by a great studded metal collar from which hung taut chains as several dwarves tried to hold its pace in check. It was a great monstrous thing with a bear-like muzzle and long squirrel-like claws that furrowed the stone as it scrabbled forward.

Then Romul saw the whites of its ghostly eyes—white, without a trace of color. It was blind and making its way silently forward by scenting the ground with its nose. Then it winded them, and its head came up. It did not roar or shriek or make any sound at all. It only opened and closed its jaws in a smacking, hungry sort of way. Its silent response was more terrifying than if it had bellowed. Here was a creature with no bravado. Bred for the caves, it hunted and killed with efficiency and stealth.

"Now, human," continued Fehro in a voice of irritating calm, "do you have anything else to say before sentence is passed?"

Augie swallowed hard, his oversized epiglottis bobbing up and down like a fish on a line. He opened his mouth to say something, but it ended only in a hoarse gurgle. Many dwarves found this mildly humorous, and some guffawing commenced.

Then Eli stepped up beside Augie. "Let me try. I learned something about this last time I was here." She faced the Gaderung with that same strange confidence she'd exercised already, like someone finally in her element. "*Monsieurs*, I know that—" she began, but cries went up around the room, drowning her out.

Fehro banged his boot on the podium for silence. When the clamor had mostly receded, he spoke gravely to her. "Young miss, this is not the Alappundas. It'd do you better service and lengthen your life if you would remember who you're speaking at."

Eli's head leaned a little to one side in confusion. "But I was taught that was the proper way to address a dwarf."

"Who was the simpleton what taught you that?" Fehro folded his arms and smiled.

Eli was a bit incensed. "He was a very noble captain of the Azhwana. That's how he addressed the dwarf we met in the north." This caused a great stir as every dwarf turned to his neighbor and began whispering. So many heads were bobbing up and down with understanding that the whole looked like a collection of child's toys all set in motion at once.

"Ah!" said Fehro slowly. "That 'splains it, it does. You, missy, have been laboring under a delusion. We of the Sarkonish clan do not take kindly to being addressed as if we was mere Narmonds."

"Mere what?" said Eli, but Fehro took no notice.

"Were you not a young'un and a woman besides, you'd pay dearly for mistaking the difference. As it is, it sounds as though you know sommat that we should like for to be enlightened on."

"I don't understand."

Fehro stood and shouted at her as if at an idiot. "Tell us what you know of the Narmond clan!"

"Do you . . ." Her head was bent in thought. "Do you mean the other dwarf, the one in Azhwana?"

"'Course I does! We've had no tidings from our old foe for many a year. And if you've seen them, then we'd be very keen to know of their condition . . . as well as any plans of treachery you may have beheld."

Romul could almost see the gears in Eli's head turning. He didn't understand anything of what was going on, but he was quite certain that whatever Eli said next would mean either their death or . . . well, their not-death.

"So you," said Eli, thinking out loud, "need information on the dwarves in the north—the Narmonds, as you call them. How badly do you want to know?"

Romul was shocked, as was the rest of the room. This wasn't the time to play games!

"Of course we want to know, girl!" cried Fehro in exasperation. "Else we wouldn't of asked! And it's no concern of yours how badly we wants it. Now tell us what you know, and be quick, or we'll—"

Eli cut him off. "See, I did learn something about dwarves in the Alappunda Mountains."

Her confidence had returned, and Romul could see she was working out some plan. He prayed it was a good one.

"For example," Eli continued, "I know that if you promise me something, you have to keep your promise."

Fehro eyed her cautiously, his fingers fluttering together as if reviewing his words for some accidental promise he'd uttered. But Eli plowed on.

"I also learned that a dwarf won't make a promise unless you can give him something he wants badly." Now Fehro had caught up with her, and his face wore the obvious question. "So before I tell you anything about our experiences with the . . . um, Narmonds, I want a specific promise from you."

The room was silent now except for the scrabbling claws of the bargheist. Romul was feeling a grudging admiration for Eli's pluck. Fehro had left his podium and was consulting with the other gamol. When he returned, he said only, "What do you want?"

"Freedom."

Fehro did not consult with the others, nor was there any outburst from the room. Romul supposed that's what everyone expected her to demand.

"'S'at all?" he asked.

"That will be enough," she said with confidence.

"Think so, eh?" Fehro muttered and then responded in a loud, officious voice, "Very well. We promise that if you tell about the Narmond clan, you may go free."

Something about this didn't sit well with Romul, but he couldn't think it through, because Eli had launched into her story of how they'd ended up under the Alappunda Mountains with its single mad inhabitant, leaving out the significant details of Rose's compass and Anna's amulet. The whole room sat mesmerized and silent. Even the bargheist settled down onto its haunches and turned its head slowly left and right as if trying to see Eli out of its frosty eyes. Romul wondered if it understood what was going on or was dumb like the sheep.

Romul had heard all this before, but seeing a host of dwarves respond to it brought the details to life for him. And respond they did! They expressed admiration at her description of the great halls and passages, they were shocked at the emptiness of those same halls, they laughed sympathetically at the dwarf's trickery, and they leapt to their feet outraged at the dwarf's death at the hands of the sylph. Apparently death-by-fairy was a fate the Sarkonish dwarves would not wish upon their greatest enemy. But the dwarves were clearly fond of a good show, because when Eli finished her account, there was even a smattering of applause from the gallery.

Fehro and several other members of the Gaderung were nodding with satisfaction. "Merry brothers," he finally said to the whole congregation, "it would seem that the long conflict with the Narmond clan has ended after all. Yet such a tragic end it was. Even more since *our* numbers have begun to grow again."

"They have?" burst out Eli in eager surprise.

Now Fehro was downright cheery with Eli after her tale. "Yes, young miss. After the long dark tunnel, we sees the light. We have begun to grow again. Our halls are filling at a rate that 'as not been seen for a millennium."

"Then I have some other questions I need to ask."

"Tsk, tsk. I'm afraid that was not part of the promise."

"But I need to—"

"You may go." The dwarf pointed a finger at the door of the hall.

"But—"

"Now."

Eli stood staring at the gamol for a long moment, then turned dejectedly and shuffled back to the group. "I guess we have to go, but I really needed to—"

"Who cares?" cut in Romul. "Let's just get out of here before they change their minds!"

"Romul's right," said Augie.

The whole group of prisoners took a few steps toward the door when from the dais came a soft, "Ahem." They turned and saw

Fehro shaking his old white head. "That was not part of the promise either."

"What do you mean?" said Eli, panic rising in her voice.

"The promise was that *you* could go. Not them."

"But you said—"

"I said *you.*"

The promise had been in the singular, but they had heard it in the plural. That was the rub, the problem that had gnawed at Romul's mind. Eli could leave; they would have to stay.

"But I can't leave without them!" she cried.

"It is all we promised," said Fehro pointedly.

"But what happens to them?" Eli asked, but the authority had gone out of her voice. She was just a child again.

"That one—" he pointed at Murgen—"we must consider. This is new to us and seems related to your queer story somehow. For there are things you didn't say, to be sure—important things, too, I shouldn't wonder."

"But—"

"And that one," he bowled on, pointing at Augie. "He has an appointment to keep." He inclined his head to the blind monster, who was growing restless again.

So for all that, Eli's scheme had gained them nothing. They were still prisoners with nowhere to go. And as if that weren't enough, Augie was about to be fed to the bargheist.

Chapter 28

"But you haven't even told us what we're guilty of," cried Eli.

"You ain't guilty of nothing, missy," said Fehro benignly, "nor any of your wee friends there. Just him." And his finger thrust like a spear at Augie. "Gram, your knife for the prisoner."

The chief stepped forward and brought his hand to his belt, fumbled a bit, and looked down in surprise. His knife wasn't there. He looked stunned for a moment. Then his face cleared, and he yelled up into the stands, "Ylfig, you better still got me knife, you better."

"Sure does, chief," came a voice from somewhere. And Romul was aware of a vague movement in the crowd off to his right.

"But what's he done?" said Eli again.

"He's a man. Ain't that enough?"

"No, of course it isn't. We're all men," said Eli, pointing at Romul and her sisters. "Well, except her, maybe." This last part was directed at Murgen and drew more laughter from the crowd.

Fehro leaned back and folded his arms as if educating an ignorant child. "I don't mean *man* like that. He's a man in the two more important senses. He's male—that is, the gender thingamee. And second, he's growed up and is all responsible-like. You're just one of the small things, plus you is that other gender thingamee too. Of course, dwarves don't know nothing about growing up, since Sweet Berducca makes us as we are, and we don't understand genders, since we ain't got none."

At this, Romul looked around at the crowd. He knew there

couldn't be dwarf children. Anyone who knew anything about the world at all knew that the longaevi did not reproduce but were born of their elemental caretaker fully grown, as Murgen had been. But he was surprised by the gender comment. He scanned the crowd, and sure enough, every face was distinctly male—which isn't exactly the same as "no gender," but that was too much to think about right now. The gamol was still speaking.

"So 'tis our general policy not to hurt things we don't understand none. That is, we don't hurts women nor children."

Ylfig emerged from the crowd, bearing the chief's knife. He was in a fervor to please Gram, and his golden eyes were fixated on the twinkling blade. Predictably, he tripped over a rock and went sprawling on his face in front of the whole assembly. The knife, now free, flew through the air for the second time that day. With astounding reflexes, Gram deftly shot out a hand and swatted the blade to the earth as it passed his head.

The chief looked sardonically at Fehro and said in a voice to match, "And fools! We don't hurt fools neither." The whole crowd burst into belly laughter as Gram shook his head and picked up his knife.

"Quite right, to be sure," added Fehro with a reproving look at Ylfig, who was sitting up and staring round with a stupefied grin.

Eli was not deterred by any amount of farce. "But I don't understand. Why do you hate men? I mean men like him, who never did you any harm?" This comment sobered the whole assembly, and angry shouts recommenced, which were quieted only when Fehro vigorously reapplied his boot to the podium.

When he spoke, it was with a kind of cold fury that gave Romul gooseflesh. "Never did harm? Never did harm! Now tell me, merry brothers, if a more batty and asinine thing were ever said in this here assembly. Need I remind you, sons of Berducca, how we have suffered because of the infestation of Man? How he has fouled the waters that come down to us with his scratchin's in the crust he calls mines? How he has hunted and killed us where e'er he finds us? How the ancient Ebontarn below lies bereft of every fish and plant 'cause of the filth they pour down into it? Who here has had even so much as a mussel from that fetid water in a dwarf's age?"

He went on like this for several minutes, but as if to underscore the inevitable conclusion of the rant, Chief Gram stepped up to Augie and held out his knife. The inventor's eyes slid from the tiny blade to the bargheist, and he began to tremble.

Gram rolled his own eyes at Augie's paralysis, dropped the knife in the dirt at the condemned man's feet, and marched back to the stands. Augie turned to Romul and the girls, a hopeless look in his eyes. Then he saw Murgen. Still standing erect and resolute like a fated queen, she looked at him and made a few gentle but firm gestures.

Whatever she said, it emboldened him. He stood up straight, his face grave. He took in the whole Gaderung with new eyes, and the timing of his redemption was good, for the gamol was just finishing up his harangue with "Why, indeed! The harder question would be why on the horns of Berducca ought we *not* to feed him to the bargheist!"

Augie's answer came not a breath after Fehro finished, cutting off the applause that had begun to leak out. He squared his shoulders. "I am not a woman or a child, but I've been called a fool before, as recently as yesterday. Perhaps I am just a fool among fools, and although I have committed none of the crimes of which you accuse me, perhaps my role is but to stand for the crimes of my people. This I will do, but . . ."

His voice was confident and clear now. But the odd quality imparted by his fat lip remained. This caused titters and giggles from several around the room. Even after "crimes of my people" came out "cribbums of my peeboble," he plowed on valiantly, but the laughter only grew. Romul was no longer listening to his speech. Something was crystalizing in his mind. He was thinking hard, trying to remember exactly what the bodacha had said. *You must be a fool.*

Then it hit him like lightning. *The bodacha weren't insulting Augie. That was his fortune from his beads. She was telling him what he was* going *to do.*

He turned to the others and hurriedly explained what had happened between Augie and the old woman.

Augie's testimony was becoming weaker and more unsure as his bum lips and wounded tongue betrayed him at every word. Several of the spectators were now catcalling and jeering at him. The bargheist handler was looking at the Gaderung eagerly, his hairy hands itching to loose the reins.

"Don't you see?" Romul said loudly to the girls, trying to speak over the growing merriment of the dwarves. "He's not a fool, but he's gotta make them think he is—like that idiot Ylfig."

Eli and Anna both nodded in understanding, and fell to discussing their options. Rose said nothing, but walked over to Augie, where he stood sweating, hands outstretched in impassioned plea. She tugged on his pant leg. He ignored her and continued his garbled argument, which was reaching its bumbling zenith. The resourceful Rose was not to be denied. She stomped as hard as she could on his foot, and as he howled and bent to grab his crunched toes, she nabbed him by the ear, forcefully bent his head to hers, and began whispering into it vigorously.

This had all the look of a very overgrown child being disciplined by his diminutive mother. The heroic image of a small person besting a big one could not possibly be lost on a gathering of dwarves, and that was all it took to push the whole crowd into a state of mass hilarity. So successful was Rose's diversion and so robust the dwarves' amusement, that the head gamol began banging the podium with his boot in an attempt to restore some sense of dignity to the proceedings.

Rose had Augie's full attention now and continued whispering madly. Soon Augie's head was bobbing up and down with understanding. Rose gave a final exhortation, released his ear, and walked calmly back to the others.

Augie's mind was now working hard. His eyes darted oddly to-and-fro across the ground as if searching for something. He saw the knife and darted for it. This focused the dwarves' attention.

Whatever the dwarves expected Augie to do with the knife, he didn't do it. Instead, he put it to his own throat and gave a cry of alarm. It was a bizarre thing to do, but even odder was that the hand that held the knife was cocked out beside him, with his elbow up in the air as if someone else's arm was holding it.

Then, with the blade still at his own throat, Augie's face changed to one of malice and hatred, and he yelled out in a crazed voice, "Don't anybody move. I'll kill 'im. I swear I'll kill 'im!"

Then his face changed again—to a look of mortal terror, his eyes darting down to the blade then up at his imagined attacker, then out to the crowd of dwarves pleadingly. He cried out in a high-pitched voice, "Oh, please, don't let him. He'll do it! I know he will!"

Then the face switched back. "Shut up, you! Or I'll cut you here and now, see?"

Romul had no idea what Augie was doing. Had he *really* lost his mind? The dwarves were likewise mystified but greatly intrigued.

Eli's arms were folded, and she wore a somewhat disbelieving smile. "Is . . . is he doing the thing from *Blazing Saddles*?"

"Yup," Rose replied with satisfaction. She turned to Romul. "It's from Dad's favorite Western. He showed me this scene on YouTube." If this was supposed to be an explanation, it wasn't.

"No . . . freaking . . . way," breathed Anna in a husky voice. "It can't work. It's just too . . ." But no one was listening to her. Every eye was watching the circus unfold.

Suddenly, Augie gave an agonized cry. The blade had drawn back an inch from his neck, and a small line of red began to trickle down.

"See?" cried the captor. "Now we're both walking out of here. And we're not to be followed, you understand?" Augie began to edge the victim toward the door.

"Oh please," cried the hostage. "Don't let him take me! He's wicked, he is. There's no telling what he'll—"

Out of the crowd of dwarves a figure shot into the center ring. It was Ylfig. He had his hands up in a pacifying motion and a horrified look on his face. He ran out, stopping ten feet from Augie. "It's okay, it's okay. Now, don't fret none. He's not going to hurt you, not while Ylfig's here."

Augie was so surprised that, for a moment, both abductor and captive disappeared, and his eyes turned wonderingly toward Rose.

"What the . . ." whispered Anna. Then turning to Rose she said, "How did you . . ." But even the placid Rose was looking surprised and pleased. She only nodded encouragingly to Augie and waved the backs of her hands at him as if shooing a child out of doors.

Augie pulled himself together, and the hostage cried out with great sincerity, "Oh thank you, thank you, kind sir—"

"That's enough out of you," said the hooligan, and the knife went back to the victim's throat.

"Now, now," pleaded Ylfig. "It's ain't so bad as that. Let's not be hasty, let's not." He looked so sincerely worried that Romul couldn't help but give a great guffaw. But the host of dwarves were so utterly stupefied by what they were seeing that no one paid any attention to him. Even the bargheist seemed mesmerized by the drama it could only hear.

"Now, I'm walking out of here, see?" cried the desperado, and he edged another step closer to the door, keeping the blade close enough to carry out his threat if needed.

Ylfig, too, was edging closer in little mincing steps, speaking soothing words of hope and comfort. Romul could see on Augie's face that he had no idea where to take the charade from here, but at that moment, Ylfig charged with a speed unbecoming his size. In a crouching move only a dwarf could have accomplished, he came up under the thug's arm, and before Augie could even gasp, Ylfig had swatted the arm away from the hostage's throat with such force that the knife found itself flying free for the third time that day.

The blade twirled and twinkled as it flew, and every eye in the hall watched in hypnotic silence as it traveled through a terrifying arc, impaling itself smack in the center of Fehro's podium. The *thunk* of the blade broke the spell, and the room erupted into thunderous shouts and cheers.

Ylfig released the captured arm, took Augie's other hand, wrung it warmly, clapped him on the back, and stepped forward to accept the applause of the whole room.

Romul couldn't tell if they were applauding the dwarf's performance, like a freak show, or if they really thought he'd accomplished a harrowing rescue. What's more, he couldn't tell if Ylfig himself knew the difference. Either way, the whole thing was too preposterous to be believed, and yet...

Augie had collapsed in a heap where the dwarf had left him. His shoulder and hand were clearly hurting from being so roughly apprehended, but the threat of his situation still gripped him. He staggered back to his feet, stepped up behind the bowing dwarf, and took a little bow of his own. The ovation redoubled.

The chief gamol was conferring with the rest of the Gaderung. A few minutes later, he banged his boot for silence. When he spoke, there was both pity and disappointment in his voice. "It is clear to the whole counsel that you are at least as big a fool as Ylfig! Not for love of humans, but out of compassion for the wretched and childlike state of your mind, we do not feel it just to feed you to the bargheist . . . at this time." This remission was met with a mixed response. Many were disappointed at not getting to see the bargheist tear Augie's limbs off; others were glad to see him spared in hopes of an encore.

Fehro wasn't finished. "And upon further consideration of your general youth, we see no value in keeping you imprisoned at great cost and inconvenience to ourselves. You're likely to live a long time, and we doesn't fancy the responsibility of nursemaiding."

"So then we can leave?" asked Eli.

The reply consisted of a stubby index finger pointing toward Murgen. "All but that one."

"But we can't leave without her."

"Then we seems right back where we started, now don't we? Well, chief . . ." Fehro turned to Gram. "Instead of just the one, you'll needs to find a hole big enough for all of them."

And with that the whole Gaderung stood and began to file out, the bargheist was dragged back down its hole, and the stands began to clear.

"But . . . but . . ." cried Eli.

"Forget it," said Anna. "We're stuck. Face it."

Eli was still saying "but" as Gram led them out of the hall. He took them right out of the city and up a path onto the rocky heights, where he deposited them at the mouth of a large cave.

As he walked away, Augie called out to him, "What happens now?"

Gram never broke his stride. "You wait to find out what happens to the 'bomination."

"No, I mean, I thought we were prisoners."

"There's no mistaking that."

"But where are the guards?"

This brought Gram to a halt. He turned and threw his hands out in a wide gesture. "Where you going to go? You don't know the way out. Any dwarf finds you out that cave'll slit your throat. I can't come up with no better prison than that!"

He turned to go again, but paused and shouted as an afterthought, "Oh, and the bargheist? He don't live in no pen. He just roams about keeping the tunnels clean o' riff-raff. He don't hurt us, but he'd smell you out in a jiff. And that wee blade I gave you was just for show. It wouldn't of done you no good with him. But that thing you did with it, that two-people-in-one thingamee, that was sommat to remember for a long time. You is just as crazy as Ylfig, to be sure." He left, chuckling and muttering to himself.

They stood in stunned silence watching his small form fade into the darkness. Then they wandered over to the edge of the cliff, where they looked out over the underground city. Its beauty was now tarnished by the idea that it could be the last landscape they'd ever see.

Chapter 29

"No bars, no doors, no guards." Anna kicked a rock off the precipice in frustration. "It's a prison just the same. Geez! It's like *Holes!*"

"Except it's all one big hole," said Rose.

After Gram's departure, they'd stood in silence on the ledge for several numb minutes, pondering their options. When none materialized, they'd wandered into the cave and found it clean, dry, and big. Some minimal provisions had been provided them—several-days-old bread and some dried and unrecognizable salted meat. Augie, who claimed to have forgotten what food looked like, had fallen upon the pile with the energy of a bargheist, and Romul had needed to cuff him on the shoulder. "Shouldn't you let your girlfriend eat first . . . then me?"

The reprimand had cut Augie to an unexpected depth, and he immediately divided the provisions into six shares, giving himself the smallest.

Now they all sat on the edge of the cliff, their legs dangling in space, looking down on the dwarf city and eating their scanty meal. It was just far enough away that the urban sounds coming from it were a dull, indistinct commotion. Movement in the streets had diminished, and the whole city was growing quiet. Even the great lights on the fields were slowly dimming, though how one dimmed a gimmbeorht was a mystery. But it meant the dwarves kept a day-and-night cycle of sorts even down here. With the lights of the city gradually going out, those in the far-off ceiling of the cavern now looked like bright stars.

Romul felt a hand on his shoulder. It was Augie. "Rose told me about your deciphering the bodacha's fortune. That was good thinking. You probably saved my life—all of ours, maybe."

Romul blushed. "Yeah, well, your . . . uh, show was good too."

Augie laughed. "I still can't believe it worked. That poor idiot Ylfig!"

This raised Rose's ire. "I think he's really clever. And you shouldn't talk about him that way. He's as good an actor as you."

"Yeah, well, that's the difference. I was acting. He's just plain out of his head. Either way, we're fortunate that they don't hold with harming children and girls or our situation would've been worse."

"Yeah, what was that about?" Romul remembered Fehro's comments. "I know what he meant about no dwarf kids, but how can they have no genders?"

Augie sighed. "Well, that's complicated. It's a basic scientific principle to those who study such things, but it's no longer common knowledge. You can talk about dwarves two ways. Most people talk as if they're all males, and that's true if you mean there are no female dwarves. But that's not how dwarves think of it. They're all just . . . the same, so they don't even think about the idea of gender."

"But wait," said Anna. "This doesn't make sense. Mermaids have mermen. They've got two genders. Why don't the dwarves?"

"Like I said, scientists know these things, but most people don't. It's not just dwarves and mermaids. All undini have two genders, and all gnomi have only one . . . or none, however you want to say it. There's an old device I learned when I began studying the sciences . . .

> "Gnomi of one gender be.
> Two there are of undini.
> Vulcani, three in their own way.
> And of the sylphi, who can say?"

"Wait!" cried Anna. "Salamanders have three genders?"

"I've never worked with the vulcani, so I don't know the details, but it's pretty well documented that, yes, they have dimale, female, and urmale—a third sex, as biologically distinct as the other two. I've been told that if you turn a salamander over, you can actually tell whether—"

"But a real third sex?" spluttered Anna, "But how do they—I mean, if they want to get together to . . ." She nearly choked on her own awkwardness.

"Now you're talking like a foreigner. Everyone in Errus knows this one. Romul?"

Romul knew his cue. This was elementary knowledge even among the Rokan. He quoted the old axiom, "'*Where e'er there is disturbance in the earth, the elementals give longaevi birth.*'"

"Oh, that's right," said Anna. "They don't have babies. They just . . ." Her eyes wandered to Murgen, who seemed to be acclimating to her underground situation. She was sitting a few feet away, looking out over the city, unheeding and uninterested. Who could forget that, scarcely a week or so ago, they'd seen her born from the waves of a great squall?

"And the fairies?" asked Rose.

"Like the rhyme says, we don't exactly know. The sylphi have always been the most difficult to study. They're not communal. They tend to be smaller and harder to find, and they're so . . . mobile."

Romul looked again at the mermaid. He realized with new force just how human she seemed. He would never for a second mistake a dwarf or a salamander for a human . . . and, for sure, not a bargheist! But if he met Murgen walking down the road arm in arm with Augie, would he suspect he was seeing anything other than two lovers? Her skin was still slightly off in color, but in every other way . . . How had the dwarves so quickly realized what she was? It must be an elemental instinct—one longaevi to another sort of thing.

Murgen's mood had changed again. With her death sentence postponed till some undetermined time, the air of confident martyr had abandoned her. She'd wilted, not into her prior simper but into something more hopeless and hard—like a coral with the living part inside slowly dying. She even sighed, and Augie jumped to her side. Through him, she was able to express that she was beginning to despair of ever seeing the sky again, much less her beloved sea.

Romul wondered again how a creature technically less than two weeks old could have such longings. When he said this, Augie reminded him that humans have little instinct and no detectable racial memory, so he couldn't have any idea what it must be like to be a creature born in love with the open water.

"Her heart—her whole self—cries out for the sea. Her mind remembers things her body has never actually done. It's part of what make the longaevi different from us. They're tied to their elemental nature in ways we have no real analog for. Whether it's better to be the way we are or the way they are, I don't know, but she longs for water the way you would feel homesickness."

This struck a chord in Romul. He knew little of actual homesickness, but he knew what it meant not to belong. He knew what it was like to have his world overturned. For everything he thought he knew to be overthrown in a moment. To be without place or purpose, so cut off from anything like family that you can hardly believe others actually have them. So alone that you can't think or hope or . . . Oh yes, he knew that feeling well, and he pitied her for it.

His rumination was cut off by Anna whispering, "Shh. Do you hear that?"

The fields were black now, and the city lights had been going out one by one this whole time. Only a few pinpricks here and there were still visible from windows. They listened. Something was coming up the path to the cave. Something that huffed and puffed and staggered with an arrhythmic step. They all scrambled back from the edge, save for Murgen, who remained rooted and unmoved.

Then Anna hissed into Augie's ear, "Don't forget you're supposed to be crazy." To which Augie leapt up and began singing a child's rhyme at the top of his lungs, slightly out of tune, and dancing a jig.

> *"Merris danced across the sky,*
> *To her children waved bye-bye.*
> *On a journey she must go;*
> *Where she's going, they don't know.*
> *Vercandrus longs for her return;*
> *His children weep; their love he spurns.*
> *But she'll come back, and then they'll be*
> *One big happy fam—"*

"You can knock it off." Romul was disgusted at the display. "It's only Ylfig, and you'll just encourage him."

So it was. Romul could make out his strange golden eyes coming toward them like a cat's. As the dwarf approached, he unveiled a small blue light, which illuminated his hairy face and bulbous nose. He looked them all over in the ghostly glow. He said not a word but went to the edge and sat, some distance from Murgen, and looked up at the star-vaulted ceiling. The prisoners continued to watch, wondering what sort of lunacy was to come. They said nothing, nor did he. He only stared at the far-off lights, and Romul thought he wore a rather wistful, even longing expression. Many silent minutes passed, then Romul felt Rose brush past him. She went to the edge and sat down next to the dwarf and looked skyward with him.

"It's pretty," she offered in a soft and reverent whisper.

He didn't turn to look at her but said in a voice choked with some deep emotion, "Yes, it is. It is said that the star stones are set in the vault in the exact pattern of the sky on the night the world was made."

"Ohhh," Rose moaned softly, enchanted by the thought.

Then the dwarf sniffed, and his shoulders quivered. Romul was nearly sure he'd loosed a small sob. This was confirmed as Eli now rushed to the edge and sat on the other side of him. Both girls raised their arms at the same moment to embrace his shoulders, but it was to Eli the dwarf turned. He buried his face in her shoulder and wept. Eli turned and stared at them, eyes wide as if to say, *What do I do now?*

A moment later the dwarf had collected himself and was wiping his eyes and clearing his throat in the way people do when they don't want anyone to know they've been crying. Then he leapt up from the edge with an angry air and stood with his hands on his hips, surveying them.

"All right, that's enough. Where is she?" He looked them all over and came to rest on Anna. "It's gotta be you, it does. All right, stop stalling and out with it."

Anna stood frozen somewhere between shock and panic.

Augie, forgetting for a moment to be insane, said, "What are you talking about?"

To which the dwarf shot back, "Oh, shut your noise, you big faker! If I hadn't come to your pathetic rescue back there, you'd be bargheist dung right now! Kidnapping yourself! Of all the stupid, brainless, fool . . ." He then added a full ten seconds of colorful adjectives.

The whole group stared in stunned dismay at the dwarf, who was now stamping his foot impatiently and holding his hand out toward Anna. "Now I come to see Therra, and I ain't leaving till I does."

Romul heard Anna's sharp intake of breath and Augie's defeated exhalation at the same moment. It seemed that Augustus Lambient wasn't the only one with a gift for feigning madness.

Chapter 30

"Here, y'old faker." Ylfig threw Augie a tiny metal dish with a sort of cream or salve in it. "Rub that on your lips. It'll take the swelling down." Augie sniffed at the stuff and made a face. He then dabbed a hesitant finger into it.

"You're not crazy at all." Rose clapped her hands together. "I knew it!"

"I'm crazy enough to have passed a knife through all your throats iffin I hadn't gotten some satisfaction on the point." The dwarf turned Anna's amulet over slowly in his hands.

As there had seemed no alternative, Anna had produced the Therran amulet for the dwarf's inspection. He hadn't snatched at it in crazed ecstasy as they'd feared. He'd received it gingerly with the hands of an artist appraising a delicate specimen.

After a long moment, he handed it back to her. "All right. Enough loafing. Let's get a going." No one moved.

"Go where?" whispered Rose.

"Yeah," echoed Romul, "They told us we—"

"Fiddle-scotch and scrumble-drum!" cried the dwarf. "What do they know anything about anything! Iffin it was up to them . . ." He puffed out his cheeks and held his breath till he turned a little blue, then slammed his hands against his cheeks so the air came out in a great *pop*. Romul had expected a crazy Ylfig, but this one was angry and crazy—a far more disturbing combination.

His exhibition had winded him, so he panted for a few minutes before adding, "Well, you can either sit here and grow mold, or you can come and make yourself useful."

"But why should we come with you?" asked Augie, who sounded ready to concede his sanity.

"Not you, you big faker," sneered the dwarf. "Nor the rest of you. Just her." And he thrust a grimy finger at Anna.

"I'm not going with you," said Anna.

"And we're not letting her," said Augie.

"Blibble-fabble rabble-scat!" cried the dwarf, stamping the ground with impatience. "Don't you sees you gots to come? Don't you understand?"

"No, we don't see or understand," said Eli in a soothing voice. "But perhaps if you tell us what you want us . . . uh, her for, we might reach an agreement."

"Ha, ho! Going to try that again, are you? Going to try dealing with old Ylfig the way you did that nursling Fehro? What makes you think you'll get along any better with me than with him?"

Eli shrugged, stood, and started to walk away into the cave. The rest took the cue and followed her, leaving the dwarf standing alone and openmouthed.

"You . . . But . . . You can't just . . ." he squawked in disbelief.

Eli looked back over her shoulder. "Do we talk or do we walk?"

Whatever the dwarf wanted, he wanted very badly, for he crumbled in an instant. "Okay, okay, you win, you little . . ." The rest of his words trailed off in a long, indistinct mumble. "If you sit for a bit, I'll tell you a wee nighttime story."

Eli paused, waiting.

The dwarf sighed. "I'll . . . *humph* . . . I'll tell why the Gaderung hates men so much."

Eli's eyebrow went up.

"It's—" he groaned—"about why I need the little girl."

"Very well. We'll listen, but we promise no more than that," said Eli, returning and sitting down on the ground in front of him. The others joined her.

The dwarf sighed several long sighs, displaying an inner conflict. Romul couldn't tell if his resistance was because he really didn't want to tell them or because he just wasn't used to being taken seriously. He eventually began in a stumbling but matter-of-fact way.

"You'll . . . uh . . . remember Fehro complaining about the Ebontarn. Well—"

"Yeah, what the heck's a—" began Anna, but Eli gave her such a stony look that even Anna was cowed. "Geez, just asking."

The distraction was still enough to throw the dwarf, and he had to start over. "The Ebontarn . . . well, yes, uh, see, it's the great lake down below. For thousands of years it was part of our prosperity. 'Course, the mines are our glory and source of wealth, but the lake gave us most of our food. And we pumped the water into the city and the mines for every sort of use. But in the last century or two it's become . . . well, you'll just gotta see it."

"What's that got to do with Anna?" pressed Eli gently.

The dwarf looked around at each of them and nodded suggestively—as if this should make the whole thing clear. Finding nothing but questions on their faces, his own went as blank as a stone, and he said in a voice of awe and disbelief, "Are you really so dumb as all that? Do you not know? None of you?"

This brought out a defensive streak in Eli mixed with some candor. "We know many things. But we don't . . . well, we don't know who we can trust. And so we—"

"Well, don't trust me, that's for sure! I ain't earned it. And some things are too important to just bandy round to every silly sylph what crosses one's path."

This did not exactly encourage them to disclose any secrets, and so for a minute no one said anything.

Ylfig smacked his lips. "Well, I guess I might as well out with it. I need her to fix the Ebontarn."

"Why her?" It jumped out of Romul's mouth before he could stop it. He really didn't mean the scorn that colored it.

"Why not me?" Anna shot back, resenting the implication that she wasn't good enough to do something she didn't want to do anyway.

"Hey!" barked Eli at them both.

The dwarf had reassumed his mask of incredulity. "Surely you know at least that? If anyone can heal the Ebontarn, it must be Sweet Berducca's sister, who rules over all the waters of the world."

"But how did you know about Anna's Therran relic?" asked Eli.

He rolled his eyes in exasperation and thrust his stubby finger out toward the mermaid, who had not moved from her place on the edge but whose attention had been drawn gradually by the discussion of the underground lake.

"But surely the other dwarves would have known that as well," said Augie suspiciously.

To this the dwarf said nothing, only looked at his feet and shrugged his shoulders. To Romul it wasn't the gesture of one who doesn't know but of one who doesn't want to reveal too much. Clearly the dwarf wasn't yet willing to have the secrets buried in him mined.

"If she tries," said Eli after several minutes of hard thinking, "we're going to want two things."

"Don't barter with him! I'm not a mail-order bride—" began Anna, but Eli cut her off.

"First, we want you to answer truthfully any question we ask, and second, we want you to lead us back to the surface. Promise those two things, and she'll try."

The would-be bride muttered something to herself and crossed her arms.

The dwarf grinned a sly grin. "Confident we got all the kinks worked out of our promises, are we? I will promise. I will promise to do both things . . . if she *succeeds*."

Eli looked around at the rest for confirmation. A series of shruggings and grimacings commenced as everyone expressed their uncertainty of the proposal. Eli lost her patience. "Well, does anyone else have a better idea?"

No one did, so Augie conceded. "I suppose we'll have to go with him and see. Sitting here isn't going to get us anywhere." He went to Murgen and helped her up.

The dwarf cried out, "Oh no, not her! I'm not taking her anywhere, the filthy—"

Now it was Augie's turn to flare up. "Look, you obviously figured out that she can only be here because of the Therran relic. You can't very well deny it to her now! It would kill her as certainly as . . . well, as her dragging you into the Ebontarn would kill you."

The dwarf went pale and shuddered at the thought of being underwater, but after a minute he said, "Oh, very well. But if some bargheist or mollusk or worse sniffs us out 'cause of her, be it on your head!"

A few minutes later they were trooping down the rocky path behind the dwarf. Twenty minutes later they were crossing one of the fields, and Augie was commenting on the variety of crops that grew there. "Potatoes, carrots, beans . . . How do you manage all this?"

"You saw the lights," was all the dwarf would say.

The field was immense and a bit soggy from recent irrigation. At Eli's query, the dwarf added that water for the fields had to be transported down from the surface as snow, then melted.

"Why don't you just use water from your wonderful lake?" asked a slightly embittered Anna. The dwarf rolled his eyes as if the comment deserved no response. This time, Romul didn't begrudge her sarcasm. They had been very badly treated by the dwarves in general, and now the craziest of them all was demanding a service none of them understood for a promise he probably would find a way out of.

Yet madness didn't explain it. He seemed malevolent, calculating, and shrewd, but mad? Romul sidled up to Augie. "So you think he's crazy?"

Augie didn't take his eyes off the dwarf. "No, I think he's absolutely sane. And that makes him far more dangerous."

"What do you mean?" Romul thought a dwarf in his right mind would be infinitely preferable to one who was barking.

Augie's reply sobered him. "He's managed to deceive every dwarf in this kingdom. He's arranged it so we would be left alone, and he's manipulated events so that we have no choice but do as he demands. We're almost worse off than we were with the merqueen. At least we could expect her to do what was in her people's best interest. But he's a rogue—far more dangerous and unpredictable. We have no idea what his real game is. And no matter what horrible thing he does with us, the rest will write it off as foolishness. He'll abandon us in some black hole without so much as a match, I shouldn't wonder."

"No, you shouldn't," mumbled Romul.

From the fields, they entered a large tunnel like the one by which they'd come into the city. This was still illuminated by gem lights and intersected by numerous tunnels at every angle. Romul was pondering again how impossible it would be for them to leave the dwarf kingdom if Ylfig was as unreliable as Augie predicted. He began to hope very much that Anna would be able to do something for the dwarf's lake.

The passage began to wind left and right and descend steeply. Before long they all began to sniff with apprehension. An unpleasant odor hung on the air—tangy and sulfurous, deeply rust-colored—a rotten-egg smell. Not constant, just every few breaths. Romul recognized it from the foundry in Farwell, though he didn't know what it was. In the foundry it had been only an indistinct feature of the total industrial setting. Here it quickly crowded out all the damp earthy underground smells they'd grown used to in the past few hours.

It continued to grow steadily stronger and more constant till it was so pungent that Romul's eyes watered, Rose had a coughing fit, and Anna was plugging her nose and gulping air through her mouth.

The passage now leveled out into a broad, straight tunnel, and he could see a dark-orange glow ahead of him that appeared to be the end. As they approached, he began to feel a prickly warmth on his skin. The heat, the glow, and the smell all grew as they walked.

Romul had thought the dwarf city cavern was huge, but the cavern they now entered could have contained the whole city as if it were a mere anthill.

They stood on the shore, not of a mere lake, but of a vast underground sea. Romul couldn't see the other side in any direction, nor could he see the cavern's ceiling. Beaches stretched away both left and right. From its size and feeling, it could have been the Crescent Sea itself, only underground. But the size of it wasn't what drew him up short. The light, heat, and stench all had the same source—the lake itself. He stared, for a moment unable to understand what he was seeing.

The surface of the water was on fire! As far as the eye could see, orange flames danced on the waters, giving off black, acrid smoke. Pockets of flame would swirl, go out, and reignite a dozen feet from their original site. As his mind adjusted to the impossibility of what he was seeing, he began to notice other things as well.

The water lapping on the beach looked dark and oily. And stretching out into the lake before them stood a large system of buildings, docks, and derricks. Clearly, it had once been a place of great activity and work. But now everything was rotted and abandoned—many of the buildings little more than ruins.

"By all the emissaries of heaven . . ." said Augie in a hoarse whisper.

The dwarf did not pause but made straight for the ruins. They straggled behind, casting horrified eyes in every direction. As they entered the complex of buildings and made their way out onto a long pier, Romul realized he didn't see anything growing—not anywhere. Not on the beach or on the piers or in the shallows.

Not so much as a mold or a barnacle or a strand of seaweed. And before they'd gone five feet out over the water, the bottom was lost from view in a dark, murky black even though it couldn't have been more than a few feet deep.

A hot wind blew through the cavern, chasing the dancing flames across the water. Romul heard weeping, and he turned to see Murgen had covered her face with her hands and was sobbing uncontrollably. Augie put his arms around her, and the group came to a halt, instinctively drawing together into a little knot. The dwarf alone continued out toward the most distant dock.

"Ylfig," said Augie in a hollow voice. "Tell me again what caused all this?"

The dwarf paused, turned, and stared at the scientist. "Men."

"But it seems hard to believe that *just* one foundry could—"

At this Ylfig threw himself down on his belly at the edge of the pier. He plunged his hand into the fetid water and fished about for a second before producing a dark mass. He then stormed back up the pier toward Augie, carrying the whatever-it-was and shouting, "Just? Just, you say? If you doesn't believe the word of a dwarf, ask one of the vulcani. Do you think salamanders are not born in these fires too?"

He heaved the small oily mass onto the planks at Augie's feet without losing a beat in his rant. "And the undini? Ask your tart there if any merfolk would survive five minutes in that murk, newborn though they be? Just ask that abortion there at your feet iffin our lot in Errus is the better for the coming of men."

He now stood toe to toe with the scientist, his head upturned and shouting into his face. "What do men know of the longaevi? Do they care about the languishing of our peoples over the centuries? No, they merely takes over our ruins for themselves. Who do you suppose built the first mines in that wretched city overhead? Don't let me hear you speak of *just* again, or crazy old Ylfig'll give you what's *just*, to be sure! I only saved you from the bargheist 'cause of that little girl there. But for her, I'd a let your circus act go to the lions what it deserved."

Then he put the thumb of his dripping hand under the tip of his nose, and with a quick upward stroke, made a sign of disdain toward Augie, splattering his shirt with the dark excrement of the lake. Then he spun on his feet and marched away down the pier.

"Excuse us for living," muttered Anna.

As they gathered around the black lump, Augie sighed. "No, Anna, he may be right. I've read some of the old manuscripts in the temple. There are occasional references to such things happening. I always assumed the Great Change was just legend. But it seems there's something to it." And he turned the mass over with his foot.

Romul's breath caught in his throat. At their feet lay the bloated and decaying body of a small salamander. Born amid the fires of the lake, it had drowned at the very moment of its birth, its life snuffed by the dark waters.

"What *is* the Great Change?" asked Eli with a despondent sniff.

"Well, it's a . . . a nothing, really." Augie groped for words. "It's just a label scientists give to the great decline of the longaevi that's been going on for centuries. Strong evidence suggests that it was caused by a natural phenomenon of some kind or some cataclysmic event."

"Like a comet or something?" asked Eli. "Because in our world, some think the dinosaurs were wiped out because of something like that."

"What kind of sores?" asked Augie.

"Never mind her," said Anna. "She has a flair for the irrelevant. Go on."

"Well, the problem with the theory is simply that we can't find any cause—no natural phenomena we know of would cause longaevi to just . . . stop being born. So of course the other explanation, which most scientists wish to discount, is, well, human intervention."

"Human what?" asked Rose.

"It's a nice way of saying that the Garlandish hunted them down and wiped them out," said Romul, growing hot as he stared at the remains before him. "And I wouldn't be surprised. You been to Farwell. You tell me what they'd do if given the chance."

"Now, that's not quite fair," Augie began but was cut off by a loud banging sound.

The dwarf was standing at the far end of the pier, holding a long pole in his hands, hammering the butt of it on the dock to get their attention. He cleared his throat and held up his hands as if to ask what the delay was.

They toddled forward, further out over the water. The pier extended at least a quarter mile into the lake, and they passed the rotting stubs of an uncountable number of berths and smaller docks branching out at right angles to the main pier. When they'd traversed it all and met up with Ylfig, it felt like they were standing in the middle of the lake with the shore far behind.

Suddenly Eli shrieked and put her hand over her mouth.

"What is wrong with you?" asked Anna.

Eli pointed down at the water at the end of the pier. Romul looked and saw a large wooden raft moored there. The dwarf was staring at them with a feverish expression, and an intimidating finger pointed down at the raft. His intention was unmistakable.

"You mean we're going out into *that*?" cried Anna, gesturing wildly from the whole of the burning seascape to the raft. "On *that*?"

At that moment a tower of flame erupted on the surface of the water about ten yards away. Like a giant's pyre, it billowed up, sending such a wave of heat rolling over them that Romul thought it may have taken his eyebrows with it.

The dwarf made no reply but stepped down onto the raft and turned a sooty face toward them, his eyes glowing even more strangely in the dancing light. "Don't fret, missy. Men have nothing to fear from the work of their own hands, do they?"

Chapter 31

Sweat poured from Romul's forehead into his eyes. The land with its decrepit docks was almost out of sight behind them, and yet the lake was still shallow enough for the dwarf to push them forward with his pole. The fires were not so numerous or deadly out here as they were near shore, where the oozy contaminants sludged together. But they did have several close calls. Even with nothing blazing in the immediate vicinity, the temperature out on the lake was higher than the hottest day Romul had ever experienced, and the steamy humidity made him want to jump into the water—almost.

The dwarf had lit torches on poles at each corner of the raft. Their flames now bobbed and smoked as if hailing the more destructive fires that burned on the lake.

"Just what we needed—more fire," mumbled Anna from the back of the raft.

After a long while the dwarf drove his pole into the lake floor and held the raft still. "There." He pointed out into the dark water. "That's where the real sea begins. This has been but the shelf. Another few feet and the bottom drops away into the utter depths."

"How deep is it?" asked Anna.

The dwarf shrugged. "Deep enough. But in those depths lies the source, and from my study, I believe that if Therra is to aid her sister, it'll be from here or not at all."

"Your study?" Augie's voice rose in curiosity.

Ylfig turned a humorless smile on him, then turned to Anna.

"Now then, missy, up here to the bows with you. Let's see if Sweet Berducca's little sister can show her family qualities."

Anna approached the dwarf and stood, looking into the inky water with unsure eyes. "Um, what now?" she asked in a smaller voice than Romul was used to hearing from her.

The dwarf was momentarily peeved. "What you mean, *What now?* I be wanting you to heal these waters. Now out with the elemental and work your wonders."

"The what?"

The dwarf's eyes went toward the ceiling again. "Your pretty ickle necklace, if you don't mind."

Her hands went to her throat, but she still didn't take out the amulet.

The dwarf's patience was waning, and he spoke now as if to an idiot child. "Take out your wee toy, girl, and use it to fix these here waters."

Anna produced the amulet and looked down at it as if she was surprised it was still there. "With this?" she muttered. Then she thought hard for a moment. "Well, it found that water in the desert, and there's been all those strange dreams, but I don't know about this..."

Ylfig marched away to the other side of the raft, where he lifted his hands toward the vaulted ceiling and began cursing in some language Romul was glad he couldn't understand.

Romul hadn't given much thought to Anna's amulet during their journey. He now realized that he'd sort of been repressing his thoughts about it—as if by ignoring its existence, he could pretend once again that his firebrand was unique. Now he wondered. He knew he could make fire with his firebrand, so he supposed she might be able to "make" water with her amulet. But he wasn't exactly sure what good that would do them here.

Anna stood at the edge of the raft, holding the amulet out over the water in tentative fingers. Her eyes roamed the lake for several minutes. "Look, I'm sorry, but I really don't know what I'm doing."

The dwarf began to curse again, but Romul had already discerned that Anna knew less about her amulet than he knew about his firebrand. While he'd seen the firebrand do some dramatic things all on its own, he knew he could reliably summon small fires on command. He'd just never thought about *how* he did it.

Now he did.

He put his hand into his pocket and squeezed the metal lump. He closed his eyes and thought about a flame, heat, burning sticks, an orange tongue of fire licking at tinder, a kindled blaze. The firebrand grew hot in his hand, and he broke off concentration. It wouldn't help anyone to set his pants on fire.

"Anna." He stepped up to her and spoke softly. "Look, I don't know how your, uh, thing works, but you know I can start fires with mine, so maybe they're kinda alike."

She looked at him, eyebrow cocked. "Yeah, and so . . ."

"See, if I hold mine, and I think real hard about fire and heat and stuff, it gets real hot and makes a fire. So, uh, if you hold yours and think real hard about, uh, water, I guess, maybe something'll happen."

"That's it?" she replied through narrowed eyes. "Just think about water, huh? Gee, that's helpful, Romul. Thanks a bunch." She rolled her eyes.

Romul was stung and backed away, his cheeks pink with irritation. He flopped down by the others.

"What'd you say to her?" whispered Eli.

"I told her we're all going to die because of her."

The dwarf was now sitting crosslegged on the raft, his head in his hands, moaning something about how useless humans were for any worthwhile thing. It felt like they had come to that point in their adventure where they would simply go on sitting on that raft forever—because there was nowhere for any new information to come from. He shook his head and mumbled, "How do we go from where?" And indeed, it did feel like a small piece of eternity passed before anything else happened.

Without warning, Murgen stood and walked to Anna. It shocked the whole group. From the moment they'd stepped onto the raft, she had melted again into a morose and mournful pile at the edge. Romul had thought she looked seasick after the human fashion, but he realized now that, truly, she was seasick in a deeper and more dreadful way. The dead lake had affected her even more than it had the dwarf. He was only angry and resentful, but she looked as though she'd experienced a family death.

Her sudden movement had attracted Ylfig's attention too. He leapt to his feet and yelled, "Leave her alone, you 'bomination!" But a harrowing look from Murgen left him speechless and rooted to his spot.

She turned the fuddled Anna toward her and looked steadfastly into her eyes. When Anna's gaze was transfixed, the mermaid made a few short fluid signs with her hands. Anna's eyes went wide, and she nodded slowly. Romul turned to Augie, who was answering Romul's unasked question. "I don't know what she said. I didn't understand."

The mermaid took Anna's hands with the amulet into her own. She closed her eyes, and Anna did as well. Their brows furrowed in concentration. Their knuckles whitened as they gripped the amulet harder and harder. Anna's lips parted to show clenched teeth, and she began to shake slightly.

Romul thought he felt a cool breeze across his face—the first since they'd lost their way underground. Then he was sure his nose detected a salty tang in the air. He even imagined that he heard a hiss of steam, like when water is poured on a campfire. He looked around and felt deep within him a resistance within the fires. Somehow he knew they did not want to go out. They were fighting, resisting. He understood their point. What right did she have to kill the fires? They didn't belong to her!

He felt an inexplicable anger surge inside him. He was drawn to his feet. His purpose was clear now. He had to protect the fires. He must defend them. They were . . . they were . . . *his* children, not hers. He didn't know why he knew this or how. A power greater than himself knew it, and yet he himself was the power that knew. He felt a burning heat upon his leg, and his hand went reflexively to his pocket and drew forth the firebrand. It glowed with a white phosphorescence, but he was not burned. No, rather, the heat overwhelmed him with burning joy.

He looked down at himself and saw that his skin was a brilliant red. Fine silver streaks like veins wove about his arms, and he felt the white-hot fiery brilliance welling up within him from some deep and ancient depth. He felt his weightless feet dance quickly left and right, like tongues of fire bursting and retreating in an inferno. The fires of the earth burned within him, longing to break forth in great volcanic gusts and torrents of fire—to burn, to melt, to purify.

Then he looked up and saw her as if in a vision—a watery apparition staring back in a murderous rage. Her eyes were a dark and hideous green, crushing with the weight of an ocean's depth. Her skin had the green hew of the mermaid, and her weedy hair streamed out and floated about her head as if underwater. She held a hand out before her as he did. Where his held the burning infernos of the earth's belly, in hers were all the oceans of the world. A disgust of all things cool, wet, and watery—of swamps and rivers, of seas and falling rains—overwhelmed him. This wretched siren must be killed, and he knew he was the one to do it.

He took a step toward her and she toward him. Then somehow they were running at each other, covering some vast and impossible distance between them. Then they were upon each other—writhing and rolling together in a mortal conflict wherein each burned with longing to vanquish the other. With fiery hands he sought to boil the very blood in her veins, and she to pour her smothering self into his lungs with suffocating weight. They were both in utter abandon with nothing to hold them back—hunger without restraint, malice without mercy, locked in a crushing contest that threatened to burn the whole of creation to dust or plunge it into the infinite watery abyss.

Yet in the throes of this travail, something in him hesitated. Something that was also Romul floated above the tumult. It was his reason, his imagination, his humanity rising above and over the elemental chaos below. He saw it for what it was—the very elements of the world unchained, furious and ungoverned. The image of the dead salamander pressed upward from out of the torrent, and the mind that was Romul seized upon it and understood.

Yes, all fires were his, and he was theirs—he their champion and they his vassals, but *these* fires were wrong. They were lawless vagabonds inhabiting a place not made for them, unsuitable and unsustainable, for all their heated labor producing nothing but death. His own authority and the very nature of his raging charges demanded that they be quenched. Justice required it. The fires below bellowed rebelliously up at him, and he pitied them. But it was wrong. This fire must die so that order might be preserved. Sorrowful though it be, he must concede this battle to the watery witch.

He felt himself withdraw from the fray, drawing back with his hand the rogue fires, bringing them into himself, gathering them back home. The waters redoubled their assault and pounded upon him. But he sheltered his erring children till they had returned to the safety of his breast, and then and only then did he lower his protective hand and allow the odious cataract to thunder down upon him. The weight of deep, dark, wet suffocating death constricted him—crushing, quelling, smothering, drowning. He was fire, then but smoke, then but steam.

Then, in a final hissing gasp, he was no more.

Chapter 32

From an infinite depth, Romul heard muffled shouting. His mind, sluggish and waterlogged, shouted a single imperative—*Breathe!* He did and found with a shock that air actually entered his body. Several voices were yelling his name right above his face. A bit further off he heard someone wailing, "I killed him! Oh God, oh God! I killed him."

His eyelids shed the last of the water that covered them and slowly opened. He was looking into Augie's anxious face. With effort, he lolled his head toward the noise and saw Eli bending over Anna, shouting very nearly into her face. "Anna, Anna, he's not dead! You didn't—"

Anna was beyond all hearing, blind and inconsolable. "I knew I shouldn't. Something in me or maybe just me knew it wasn't right. He had no right to . . . But, oh, I wanted the fire out, and . . . and I did it. Oh . . . oh . . . oh . . ." She moaned with her face in her hands. Her whole body shook with sobs.

Romul began to cough as if to expel water but none came. Anna's head snapped up to stare at him. He was surprised to find in her eyes no happiness or even relief but rather fear—no, absolute horror. She stared at him, frozen as if confronted with her greatest nightmare come to life. He discovered that he, too, was consumed with terror and loathing, as if some horrific presence had followed them out of the vision and was trying to renew violence between the real Romul and Anna.

A moment later it was gone. His eyes cleared, and he was

sitting up and blinking all about. The light had changed. It was darker. It took him a full minute to realize why. The raft was bobbing softly in a pitchy blackness. The only fire he saw anywhere was from one torch beneath which stood Ylfig, flint still in hand, staring at him with as much fear as Anna had.

Augie helped Romul to his feet, where he stood shaky and wobbling like a landlubber in a gale. Suddenly he was smothered by two arms. Anna had very nearly tackled him again and was sobbing hysterically into his ear. "Oh, I'm so sorry. I didn't mean to. I don't even like you, but I never meant to . . . to . . ."

Romul had no idea what to say to her, but Augie was already peeling Anna away, handing her off to Murgen for further comfort. Then he was down on one knee, looking Romul in the eye.

"Romul," he said with a mixture of concern and professional interest. "What happened?"

Romul didn't know. He looked down at the cool metal lump in his hand and shook his head. Knowing he couldn't really explain anything that happened, he instead worked his mouth till he produced a garbled, "Wad'jyoo see?"

Augie seemed to understand. "Well, um, nothing much, really. You pulled out your firebrand and held it out toward Anna. She looked at you, let go of Murgen's hand and did the same with her amulet."

Here Rose joined in. "Then both your eyes went all, like, way weird. Like you were far away and only your body was still here."

Augie looked at Rose in surprise. "Yes. Well said, Rose. That's exactly what it looked like. And then you both started trembling and shaking—"

"Like you were having seizures."

"And then you cried out something horrible," said Augie.

Rose shuddered in affirmation. "And fell down as if you were . . . well . . ."

"Dead," said Anna from Murgen's arms in a much calmer voice.

"And he was—or almost. If I'd pushed any harder, even just the tiniest bit . . ." Her eyes went all liquid again.

Then with Anna's help, Romul stuttered his way through what he'd seen . . . or been . . . or done. Anna confessed the same sensation of being both part of the melee and yet being above it, like a puppet master working the strings.

"Some puppet," said Romul with a sigh.

Then he felt a tug at his sleeve and found himself staring into the wide golden eyes of Ylfig, whose face was still drawn in surprise and fear. His hairy lips moved noiselessly for a moment, and Romul started to back away, but the dwarf's grip on his shirtsleeve tightened. Then came the words in a hoarse croak. "I didn't know that you was here, oh Lemerrus. How could I? I'd have never asked her, iffin I'd known."

It was almost an apology—almost. The next minute the dwarf was standing at the edge of the raft with his hands on his hips surveying the dark water. When he spoke, he sounded a bit disappointed. "Well, I suppose that's as good a day's work as I have a right to expect."

Given his brush with death, Romul was a bit peeved by the comment. "Holy Angish! What more do you want?"

The dwarf exhibited a strange combination of apology and aggression. "Yes, uh, well, it is a marvelous fact, to be sure, that the fires are out. But you must admit—" he bent to scoop a palm full of the dark and oily-looking water out of the lake—"the waters aren't exactly . . . well, pristine."

Now it was Anna's turn to be vexed. "But I haven't done anything to the water yet!" Breaking from Murgen's arms, she stormed toward the dwarf.

Ylfig looked genuinely amazed. "But I thought—"

"No," she said defiantly and pointed at Romul. "All I did was almost kill him, and that's not the same thing."

"But Anna," said Eli soothingly, "just five minutes ago you said you didn't know what to—"

"Well, now I do!" Anna rounded on Eli, and Romul thought he caught just a glimpse of the Therran shade in her eyes.

The dwarf just backed away with a gesture that said *Be my guest.*

She pulled out the amulet again and held it out over the water, shutting her eyes in concentration. Murgen took a step to join her. Without even opening her eyes, Anna said, "No, I don't need you now." The mermaid retreated into Augie's arms with a crestfallen look.

"Now see here," began Augie, but Murgen put her hand to his lips, and he subsided.

Anna's teeth were gritted tightly together again, and perspiration was heavy on her brow. Almost as if she couldn't help it, she gave off small reports like "I can almost see it" and "It's so dark." Once again Romul detected the soft sea breeze on his nose. He tensed, wondering if he was in for a repeat performance, but he felt no pressure inside this time. The firebrand lay inert in his pocket.

After nearly five minutes of exertion, Anna opened her eyes. She was huffing from the effort. "It's . . . it's no good. It's too far down. I . . . just can't get at it."

No one understood what she meant till she explained in the tone of someone clarifying the painfully obvious to a group of nincompoops. "Look." She took a breath. "The only way to bring back these waters is from their source, right? Down there." She thrust a finger at the dark water. "But even in my mind I can't quite get there. I think I have to actually get closer, but . . . I don't know how."

Murgen broke from Augie's embrace and approached tentatively till she stood before Anna. She made a gesture, but Anna had lost the power of understanding it. She looked helplessly to Augie.

"She says, 'May I help you now?'" said Augie flatly.

Anna's eyes went wide. "Oh, I'm so sorry! I didn't even think about what I was saying. It just all felt so powerful that I was sure I could . . ." and her voice trailed away.

Murgen ignored the apology and gestured. Augie translated. "We must go down together."

Anna's head cocked to one side for a confused moment. "But how can I? We don't have any of that jelly stuff. I can't breathe in *that*. I don't think you can either, not like *that*." She pointed at Murgen's legs.

Having caught up with the implications, Augie stopped translating, darted forward, and grabbed Murgen's arm. "No! You can't. I won't let you. It's too—"

Again, the mermaid put her hand gently, lovingly, over his lips. "I must do this," she signed. Romul almost missed it, because it took Augie several hard swallows to translate. "We cannot leave unless I do this. And these waters . . ." A profound and withering sadness wilted her face. Then like fog on a mirror, it cleared, and she looked at the dwarf. Ylfig had resumed his dour station in the corner and was glaring at Murgen with his malignant frown.

Murgen squared her shoulders and continued. "And even for him I must." And again Romul almost missed it because Augie stumbled over the words in amazement. She cut off his surprised outburst by adding, "I do not love the gnomi, and I perceive that they have done great wrongs against my people in the ancient past. But I cannot rejoice in their sorrowful state. For I know what men have done to my people as well. So for Berducca's sake—my dear mother's sister—I will do this thing."

"But hold on," cut in Anna. "This is pointless! I still don't have the breathing stuff."

The mermaid looked at her. "Have you not guessed yet?" She waited but received only blank silence. "As I have pondered my impossible presence here in Berducca's realm, something never before heard of, I have come to understand even my own mother's power. Just as fire will obey him—" she pointed at Romul—"so the waters will obey you." Her hand extended, and the outstretched fingers came to rest reverently upon Anna's amulet. "The waters will not harm you, nor I if I am with you."

"But you'll still have to . . . the stegnoma!" moaned Augie in a despairing voice. For the third time Murgen silenced him with her gentle touch. Then she took Anna's hand and stood on the brink. She looked at Anna, and Romul saw that her queenly and majestic manner had returned. Anna stared at Murgen, then down at the amulet, then again at her. Her shoulders rose and fell in a great sigh. A small nod. A short intake of breath. Then the raft rocked violently with the force of their plunge.

All was silent. They were gone.

The next moment threatened to capsize the raft as four humans and a dwarf rushed to the side to look after them. It was useless, of course. After the ripples dispersed, there was no evidence to be seen. It was as if they'd never been there at all.

Augie stood looking after them for a minute, then reached down into the water and fished a dripping pile of cloth out of the water—Murgen's garment. He sighed, shook his head despondently, and collapsed in a heap, caressing the sodden clothing—an infant with his blanket. Even his Adam's apple hung lower in his throat than usual, and his stomach growled in sympathy.

Only then did Romul realize how long it had been since they'd really eaten . . . or slept, for that matter. He wasn't even sure how long they'd been lost underground. A few hours, a day, maybe two? With nothing to do but wait, fatigue began to creep over him steadily and uncontrollably, and he sat down. Eli and Rose, although alive with fear for their sister, also seemed unable to prevent themselves from fading.

After fighting to keep his eyes open for many minutes, he lost the battle and fell asleep.

Chapter 33

When Romul awoke, nothing had changed. Eli and Rose dozed on. The dwarf sat on the far edge of the raft staring at them, his golden eyes shifting left to right as if expecting someone to strike him. But Augie was the one who looked stricken. He sat with chin resting on knees hunched unnaturally tight to his chest, rocking slightly back-and-forth without regard for the gentle movement of the raft. Periodically he would cast a longing glance out over the water like a fisherman hoping to catch a glimpse of the one that got away.

All in a moment, it occurred to Romul that this was exactly what Augie feared—that if Anna succeeded in healing the waters, Murgen might just remain in the vast underground lake. Over the last week he'd seen Augie first terrified by Murgen's affections and later responding to them. He was under the impression that the scientist loved the mermaid, but he also knew that men used the word *love* in a bunch of different ways. Augie loved food, too, but Romul was sure that was different.

His mind wandered through all the different things the word *love* could mean. The sisters *loved* one another . . . after a fashion. The old Rokan carriage driver seemed to *love* his Rokan heritage and the old priest to *love* his god.

Who . . . or what did he love? He had never *been in* love. In fact, he found that whole idea a little silly. What about all those other kinds of love, though? He didn't *love* food like Augie did. He didn't *love* his Rokan heritage. He had no family to love. Here his mind got stuck.

He'd been wandering all over creation looking for his mother. But why? Because he *loved* her? He didn't have a good answer. It had seemed so important to find her. Yet he wasn't any closer to finding her now than at the start, and every step he'd taken had only made his life more complicated. He began to suspect that his search for his mother was just a way of searching for himself, just trying to figure out if he really mattered to anyone.

Till this point in his life, the question of his identity had sort of surged below the surface—making him do things without really thinking about the why. Now this need to know who he was became a full-blown crisis. He was a boy without mother, father, family, friend, or country. Even his traveling companions were his only by chance and only for the moment. With a kind of despair, he finally grasped that he had nothing but a false past, a dismal present, and an empty future—and not a soul in the world who really cared.

His mind, not used to such destructive thoughts, drew back, but he knew he couldn't escape this one any longer. Once he'd had the thought, he couldn't un-think it. He began to shake with a kind of terror that was new to him. Not a fear of any one thing but a haunting kind of fear that had no name. Maybe he wasn't *destined* to find his mom. Maybe the world really was meaningless, and maybe it was really possible he could wander his whole life away and die alone somewhere . . . forgotten.

He was finding it hard to breathe and was struggling to cut off this line of thought before despair took him when Augie cried out. Romul's mind, used to self-preservation, sobered up instantly at the possibility of new dangers. He leapt to his feet. *What now?*

Augie was nearly jumping up and down, pointing across the water and shouting, "Look there! Do you see it? Look!"

Romul did and was awed to see a blue-green glow under the surface a good way off. It seemed to be growing larger and brighter by the second as it rose from the depths. A few moments later a thunderous blister of air burst from the water. Then the scene was lost from sight in the wake of a series of huge rollers that pulled the raft down into deep troughs. For one panicked second Romul thought the first wave was going to crush them, but then they were tossed up to the top of it and over. In quick succession, several more tossed them about with great force. The light continued to spread through the water, rippling outward from the epicenter. Romul couldn't tell what was causing the light till the outgoing surge brought it past them. He saw the water filled with small glowing weeds that gave off a blue-green glow.

Reaching down, he pulled one from the water, but its subtle phosphorescence faded almost instantly. It looked like normal seaweed. He threw it back into the water, where the glow returned, and it floated away from them with the rest of the current.

The dwarf began to prance about the raft, shouting excitedly. But the humans all stared expectantly outward, scanning the surface of the water. There was, however, no sign of Anna or Murgen. Many long minutes passed. A cauldron of percolating water and glowing vegetation continued to bubble up out of the water, but otherwise the lake began to settle. No more great rollers rocked the raft.

From experience, Romul knew waiting comes in several stages. First is the conviction that the thing one is waiting for could happen at any moment, and attention is fully absorbed in the waiting. Soon the novelty wears away, and one is left with the mere habit of waiting but no longer with the expectation of fulfillment. If prolonged, however, the mind wanders, and eventually part of it may even forget it's waiting. This, of course, is when the thing will happen. The shock of that moment is almost the same as if one hadn't known it was coming at all.

This is precisely how the return of Anna and Murgen came.

In the very moment of Romul's eyes growing heavy again with boredom and sleep, he heard a splash off to his left, unexplained by the rolling bloom that continued to churn luminous vegetation out onto the surface. Then a voice was calling out broken words from the water, but he couldn't make out any of the gargled speech. Yet it was enough to draw the whole crew to that side of the raft.

There, not a hundred yards away, a black blob moved rapidly toward them through the green glow. In less than a minute he could tell it was indeed the mermaid swimming gracefully toward them with Anna hanging on somewhat clumsily like a child on a piggyback ride.

As they approached the raft, they suddenly disappeared below the surface for a moment. Then in a fountain of spray that drenched the whole raft, Anna burst from the depths. Her feet were on the mermaid's shoulders, and Romul was reminded of plantation reaping in Farwell, where often one Rokan worker would stand on another's shoulders to reach the fruit hanging from higher branches. Powerful strokes from Murgen's tail pushed Anna higher and higher till she quite literally stepped off the mermaid's shoulders and onto the raft. Murgen grabbed the side of the raft, and Anna collapsed in a sopping heap on the deck.

Eli and Rose rushed to their sister and pulled her closer to the center, where there was more room. Her face looked drawn and haggard yet triumphant. As she spoke, her weary panting subsided and was replaced by the effusive energy of victory. In staccato bursts, she told how she had plunged into the depths on Murgen's back, how inexplicably she'd experienced no want for air or discomfort to her open eyes, how she could resist the urge to rise if she wanted and sink like a stone, how absolute the darkness had been.

"Somehow Murgen knew when we reached the bottom. It all looked like the same glassful of muddy water to me, but somehow she knew. And then we had to find the source. Again, I couldn't have found it without her. She could feel the slightest movements in the water, and in a couple of hours, I guess, she pushed my hand into the mud."

A corner of Romul's rapt attention was distracted by Augie's raised voice behind him. He had rushed to Murgen as the girls had to Anna and was now exchanging words with her in exaggerated signs, punctuated by his own verbal outbursts.

Anna plowed on. "I could feel the smallest current bubbling up out of the mire, but it was . . . well, clogged. You know, like how the gutters used to get in the fall, and Dad had to go up and pull all the junk out of them." Romul didn't but encouraged her with a bobbing head anyway. "Well, I pulled out the amulet and held it there in the dark over the spot, and I thought about it . . ." She paused and looked at Romul with wide eyes. "I'm . . . I'm sorry, Romul, I didn't listen to you. I know what you meant now."

Romul, glorying in his vindication, paid little attention to the scuffling that had commenced behind him, where Augie and Murgen continued their discussion.

Anna drove on with fevered excitement. "I just knew what had to happen. It needed pressure—lots of pressure, like a hose. So I forced the water to stay still."

"You forced it?" asked Eli. "How?"

"With my mind, you know. No, you don't. You can't." But Romul did. "Just like putting your finger over the end of a hose. The water didn't like it and started building pressure."

"You put your finger in the—" began Rose.

"No, not my real finger, doofus. Just like, in my mind. Well, it took all my concentration, but I kept my finger . . . well, you know what I mean, my, uh, *mind* finger in the hole. It hurt like anything. But I held it as long as I could, then a little longer . . ."

The raft rocked as Murgen dragged her great fishy bulk up out of the water. Augie was protesting vigorously, but the others remained transfixed by Anna's story.

"And when I let it go—" Anna banged her hands together concussively—"Boom! Murgen and I were shot back through the water as the thing let go! Remember that time, Rose, when you shoved that whole wad of Silly Putty up the tub faucet and then turned it on? Well, no, it was nothing like that. It was just like . . . like . . . an explosion, a volcano made of water. And it was so bright that I couldn't see anything for a while. It took me, like, five minutes just to find Murgen. She'd been blown the other way by the pressure. And . . . and . . . and—" she threw her hands out to encompass the whole of the underground lake—"and, like, wow!"

Her frenzied anecdote was cut short by a blood-chilling cry. Murgen was in the travails of a great agony. Augie was kneeling next to her, holding her hand, and crying like a toddler.

"Oh crap!" Anna whispered. "She's doing it again!"

Chapter 34

Romul never asked whether the transformation from legs back into tail had been painful, but the reverse left no doubt. All the familiar, agonized writhing was repeated as Murgen "dried." Her face contorted like a woman giving birth. Anna turn away, unable to watch. Romul tried to turn away but could not. He felt dizzy and nauseated by the cries but was also rooted in place by them.

He also felt the presence of the dwarf next to him. Ylfig had slowly sidled up to the group and was watching the travail in a stiffened state of horror Romul could feel without looking. The dwarf was unable to avert his eyes as well, and Romul understood why. As Murgen contorted in agony, she had fixed the dwarf in an unwavering gaze. Her sea-green eyes bored into his bloodshot ones with a look of . . . of . . . Romul couldn't place it. It wasn't anger or blame. It wasn't hatred or recrimination. It wasn't even complaint.

Then he remembered where he'd seen it. It was at the hanging of Old Barnabas. The Rokan weaver had been hung for the murder of a Garlandish woman, which Romul knew he had not committed. Every Rokan in Farwell had known Old Barnabas didn't do it. Her death had been the accidental consequence of an act by a wealthy Garlandish merchant, who had been smuggling food and money into the Ward. Everyone knew the suffering of all the Rokan would only increase if the true identity of the smuggler was discovered and the shipments stopped.

Old Barnabas had inserted himself into the inquest as the

guilty one, knowing it would mean his death. As he stood upon the gallows, he'd stared out at someone in the crowd with just this look. Romul had no word for it, but he'd known what that look meant. Every line of the old man's face, every bead of sweat on his forehead had heralded it—*I have chosen this for the greater good . . . for your good.* Romul had not understood what could bring a person to do such a thing. He still didn't. Nothing in the world was worth that sort of sacrifice.

Now here was a mermaid preaching the same sermon to a dwarf—two creatures whose differences made those between the Rokan and the Garlandish look small and meaningless. Romul found his head turning without his consent to look at the dwarf. His face had gone so pale that even his beard looked gray. The smoky anger that had smoldered in his eye was gone. His eyebrows reached toward the rock ceiling, pushing even deeper furrows into his fertile forehead as a bead of sweat, then another and another, sprouted. Every other muscle in his face had gone limp, lengthening the whole of it into brooding wonder. A single involuntary tear clung to an eyelash for a moment and fell like rain into the tangled forest of his beard. Thus between sweat and tears, he grew damp even as the mermaid dried.

Murgen's cries crescendoed, climaxed, and then died away in a slur of tears as she buried her head in Augie's shirt. In the terrible silence that followed, the dwarf collapsed to his knees as if he, too, had just endured the sundering of something within himself.

Now that the change was complete, Anna helped Murgen into her garments, and Augie lifted her to her feet.

As she was raised, Ylfig rose as well. They stood looking at each other for a moment before the dwarf whispered, "Truly, I am a great fool." He took a tottering step toward her, then stopped. He held out his hands, and his head wandered from side to side with the confused look of a person who wants to ask why but cannot find the words.

Murgen, twice his height, looked down upon him, her regal and gracious bearing now returning to her, and made a sign.

"In time these waters will purify themselves," translated Augie.

The dwarf's hands went to his heart in what Romul took as a sign of gratitude, and his eyes became moist again. He turned to Eli and croaked, "Ask your questions. I'll hold nothing back."

Eli opened her mouth, but Anna broke in. "Half a min! Some of us haven't eaten in a while. I need some calories and maybe a nap before we start all that."

The dwarf was in the grip of a full metamorphosis now, and he practically gibbered about "knowing the perfect place" and "You're in for a treat, to be sure" and "Just needs to get this wee dingy back to the shore." He immediately took up his pole and began to push for all he was worth. Within a few minutes the distant shore was in view. The upwelling of fresh water had been pushing them gently toward it this whole time. But even so, the dwarf's energetic gondoliering quickly outpaced the current, and they plowed the remainder of the journey through sludgy waters not yet touched by the glowing fountainhead.

So great was the dwarf's elation that, rather than stopping at the end of the pier, he thrust forward aggressively and beached the raft on the sand like a whale without a compass. He leapt to the shore and began moving, not toward the passage but along the beach. He broke into a run, which in a dwarf looks rather like a gallop.

"Hey! Whoa there!" cried Anna. "Some of us have short legs, you know!" The dwarf actually guffawed and waited for them to disembark and catch up.

"Just where are we going?" asked Augie.

The dwarf was all smiles and bubbles now. "Oh, oh, someplace special. You'll see! Just follow old Ylfig, and he'll show you a wonder, to be sure."

Romul heard Anna mumble to Eli, "Geez, why does every dwarf eventually sound like Gollum?"

Eli shrugged, but Rose added, "Maybe they're all bipolar."

Anna pulled up short. "Rose! You can't just go around call-ing . . . that's not what that word . . . ugh, I give up."

Romul didn't understand any of that, but he thought the dwarf was certainly acting more like the crazy Ylfig of earlier—and he didn't necessarily consider that a good thing. He could not for the life of him figure out the dwarf's mood swings. First he was happy crazy, then mad crazy, now happy crazy again. Romul could only guess that when he got them to where he was going, he'd switch crazies and try to murder them all. But they'd been half murdered so many times already that the whole idea of dying felt like the threat of being bitten by a toothless man.

They followed the dwarf for a quarter of an hour along the shore of the lake. As they walked, the beach got wider till they'd actually left the sand at the water's edge and were walking over rough gravel and dirt. Some complication in the wall of the cav-ern appeared ahead of them and grew larger as they approached, till the whole troop stood before a set of huge wooden doors—huge at least for a dwarf. In actuality, the doors were only a few inches taller than a very tall man. They were lightly illuminated by the glow of the water behind them, which grew steadily brighter every minute.

The doors were set with iron bars and hinges and a great key-hole in each. The dwarf dug under his tunic with both hands, and by means of a few curses produced a ring bearing two skeletal keys. He thrust one into the left-hand lock and the other into the right. Then with a grunt twisted them opposite directions at the same time. The mechanism gave with a loud click, and the dwarf began pushing at the doors, employing the same verbal encour-agement by which he'd coaxed the keys from under his jerkin. In a moment they were looking into a black hole in the rock.

"Now let us see." The dwarf produced a match, which he struck on one of the metal door hinges. The flame illuminated nothing, but the sound of his voice did. It went out into a great void, and not the slightest echo returned. From this Romul was prepared to enter a good-sized cavern, but he could not have prepared himself for what the cavern contained.

They cautiously followed Ylfig into the twilight edges. The dwarf fumbled a bit with the match on the interior wall a moment, and with a whoosh, a small trail of fire raced away from them up a small track set in the wall. Thirty feet above them it leveled off and sped away into the dark. It divided in two, then divided again, racing this way and that, presumably through tracts suspended from the ceiling. Then all at once the room burst into a blaze of depth and color as the tiny hurdling flames reached torches and candles set in candelabras high overhead.

The team stood gawking in surprise. The cavern was as big as a good-sized warehouse and covered floor to ceiling with shelves. And upon nearly every shelf stood piles of papers, scrolls, and books—hundreds and thousands of volumes written on every medium from animal skin to bark to papyrus.

"Whoa," said Eli and Augie together, and both took hesitant steps forward. Their faces shone like children at a fair.

"That's right." The dwarf nodded. "You sees what I mean? Look your fill, but can't tell what all you'll see. The years have been hard on many of them." Ylfig scurried forward and began pulling chairs and stools out from under stacks of books and papers. He shoved piles of folios into corners to make a clearing in the middle.

When he had an assortment of seats clumped together, he pulled down several small boxes and waxy sacks from shelves and dumped them onto a stool in the middle. A few pieces of what looked like dried meat or fruit fell out of one of them. Last, he unburied a padded armchair, the perfect size for a dwarf who wanted to sit up late reading. The high back and carved legs indicated that it had once been very plush, but the upholstery was now faded to an indistinct gray, and the fabric was torn in places. Into this chair the dwarf plopped and gestured vigorously for them to sit and eat.

Anna led the way, grabbing the first bag that presented itself.

Pulling out a laden fist, she sniffed. "Raisins . . . I think," she said, and began stuffing them into her mouth with a gusto that would have done credit to Augie, who was already reaching for a second bag. It contained a collection of root vegetables.

The dwarf only peered at them with his weird glassy eyes and waited silently for whatever was to come. Eli opened her mouth to ask her first question, but Romul cut her off.

"Just a minute," he said in what he hoped was a sobering tone. "Afore we get into all that, I want to know just how crazy this dwarf is." Ylfig merely stared back impassively. "Just what's your game, acting crazy one minute and all crafty and wily the next? I'm not sure I can trust you till I know something about all that."

The dwarf stared at him a moment longer, then gestured at the trove of books surrounding them. "So what you think of me collection?"

Romul was taken aback by the evasion. "Uh . . . I like it just fine, but that's not what I'm asking—"

"It is, however, your answer."

Whatever this meant, Romul missed it. It must have showed on his face, though, for the dwarf sighed. "Here's sommat I'll bet you don't know. But for a handful of symbols, dwarves have no written language."

Augie now leaned forward with great interest. "Yes, I've read that, but I was never sure it was true."

"'Tis. Dwarves prefer to 'member. It's more reliable-like. But—" he raised a stubby digit—"'membering ain't the same as knowing." He nodded in a knowing sort of way. But apparently he didn't get the affirmation he was looking for from his bewildered audience, so he continued. "I have taken it upon myself to gather together a few books in hopes of finding some clues to what is about to happen."

Eli opened her mouth again and again lost to Romul. "Yeah, but what's this got to do with you being crazy?"

"Ylfig is not crazy."

"Then why do you act like—"

"Do you have any idea what that horde up there would do to me iffin they found out old Ylfig had a collection of five thousand man-books and knew from them more about what's going on in the world than the whole Gaderung put together?"

Augie's head was bobbing with a singular clarity. "So you pretend to be simple so they'll leave you alone. Of course. I've played the same game."

"Well, I hope you're better at it with your own kind than with dwarves. Now, iffin that gaggle of gamol up yonder ever suspected the truth about what old Ylfig's been up to, or how long he's been doing it, they'd have me strung up by me thumbs and fed to the bargheist afore breakfast."

Finally Eli managed to break in with an attempt to segue the dwarf to topics she wanted to talk about. "And what *have* you been up to . . . and for how long?"

He smiled and laid one finger next to his nose and tapped it in a mischievous way Romul had seen people do when imparting a secret. "Your little story in front of the Gaderung about the Narmonds confirmed sommat I been thinking for a long time. You, missy, is probably looking at the oldest dwarf alive."

Anna laughed out loud. "No way. You *are* crazy. That guy up front was way older than you."

"Nope." He brushed off her skepticism. "I'm twice or more times Fehro's age, though he don't know it. Nor'll I be the one to tell him."

"But how?" Eli pressed. "You don't look it."

"Oh for that," sighed the dwarf, as he leaned back in his chair with a dramatic air and shining eyes. "It's a bit of a story, that. But it's what comes from seeing the Glaem with your own eyes."

Chapter 35

The whole troop cried out in wonder. The dwarf was pleased to have gotten a strong reaction out of them at last.

"Oh yes. Long afore Fehro was born, I was already an old dwarf. I alone remain who saw the very first war with the Narmonds with me own eyes." He paused, and when he was sure he held their whole attention, he continued with the refinement of a storyteller.

"I was old, as I said. I had delved every mine we'd ever opened to its very depths. Had a passion in those days, as all dwarves have, for going deeper and deeper, you understand. But I had it worse than most. I'd pack myself away at the bottom of a burrow for weeks on end, looking for a way through the nidernes—"

"The what?" said Anna.

"The nidernes, the nidernes," repeated the dwarf as if repetition was the key to meaning. "The . . . well, the bottom. The rock of the world. You know, on which the world sits. Dwarves have hit upon it now and again, and there isn't the tool devised by dwarf nor man that's able to wheedle through it. But I weren't trying to go through it—no, of course not. No, sir, Ylfig were too smart to break his pick on the nidernes.

"So when one deep dark day I hits it, I says to myself, *'Ylfig, what you needs do is turn an' go along it.'* 'Cause I had an idea, see, that while there was no going *through* the nidernes, it might well have gaps in it. I thought there had to be, in order to let the fires of the world get through. I'd never knew anyone to do what I was

– 259 –

thinking. Months I worked along the floor of the nidernes, following its curves, its rises, and its falls. 'Til one day . . ."

The group was so intent on the story that even Augie had stopped chewing with a full mouth to listen.

"One day I broke through a wall of rock and found myself looking into a great fissure. It was only a dozen feet across, but it went up into darkness to Berducca knows where, and it went straight down, too, 'til it was nearly out of sight. And yet at the wee bottom of it I could see a dim light, like at the end of a tunnel."

"What did you do?" asked Rose in a breathless voice.

"What did I do?" The dwarf was offended by the question. "What *could* I do? I'd come all that away to find the very bottom of the world, and here I was a-looking at it. I couldn't ne're well turn back, now could I? So I started to climb down, I did." He shook his head at the memory. "Took near a whole day of climbing too. My poor digits were worn to nubs, but that light grew and grew on me. Put me in a kinda frenzy, it did. It pulled at me, like the rope of a bell, and set my brain ringing so's I could hardly think straight. And do you know what happened when I was just a score of fathoms from the bottom of that shaft?"

"What?" came the whispered response of five humans. Even Murgen mouthed the word.

"A wind!" cried the dwarf. "A wind like no kin of longaevi has ever felt afore came a rushing up that fissure fit to tear my limbs from me. I clung to that rock face like a barnacle to a hull." He said this with a gesture of sympathy to the mermaid.

"But just as I thought that wind was about to quit, it gave a final puff what tore me loose off the rocks. It carried me up a bit and then gave out. And then, I fell like a stone."

Rose squealed in sympathetic fright, and Eli hugged her close. The dwarf was warm to his work now and throwing in vocal flourishes and gestures fit to grace the royal stage.

"But just as I reached the bottom of the shaft, I stopped falling—right in midair. I was floating—being pushed backward up the shaft, except I weren't moving. I was just looking out, looking down at . . . at . . ."

The dwarf's rhetoric had finally caught up with him. He was now so into his own story that he was staring upward with unfocused eyes at something only he was able to see. Romul thought the golden tint in them had gotten deeper or was perhaps moving slightly within his eyes like smoke in a glass. The hand with which he'd been describing his flotation was frozen in front of him as immobile as he was. He was not merely retelling but reliving the story.

"The Glaem?" whispered Eli into the silence. "Was it the Glaem?"

Her voice brought the dwarf back, and he mumbled in a voice heavy with awe, "What? Yes. I've always assumed it was." Then he fell into a meditative silence, his eyes cast down to the floor.

"But . . . but then what happened?" demanded Anna, losing patience.

The dwarf's eyes shot heavenward again in a reverie of memory, but he added no more. So Eli pushed him. "The Glaem? You saw it? You saw the fire your people worship?"

This successfully roused the dwarf, but not in the way Eli had hoped. His eyes instantly regained their penetrating clarity, and he coldly transfixed her with them. "I do not worship the Glaem."

"But I thought . . ." began Eli, then started again. "But you all kneel when you say the word, and so I—"

"The fools!" cried Ylfig, scattering books as he leapt from his chair. "The fools! The heretics! The stupid, idiotic, cowardly . . ." His rant descended into his incomprehensible old language, which actually sounded uglier than when he cursed in the common tongue. He stamped around the room, kicking stacks of books. And with every swing of the boot, Eli winced. Augie was already on his feet, trying to move old tomes out of the path of the tirade. A full minute of ranting found Ylfig leaning against the wall, panting and exhausted.

"Sweet Berducca is our mother," he finally said in a barely audible voice. Romul saw tears gathering on his beard. "But they has forgotten. They is so overtight about a thing they knows nothing about. They *say* Berducca but think only of the Glaem. They keep the holy words but have lost the holy meaning. Their hearts be given over to the folly of Lemerrian dreams, and they don't even know it. They is so lost . . . so lost . . ." Here he gave up all pretense and shrank to the floor in great sobs.

Romul and Augie exchanged uncomfortable looks, Anna stared awkwardly at the ceiling, Rose was choking back a sympathetic sob of her own, and Eli was simply frozen in her place. Then in a great and regal motion, Murgen swept to her feet, crossed the room in three strides, and knelt by the dwarf. He looked up at her in surprise and wonder.

She began to make motions, and when Augie failed to translate, she clapped her hands and looked at him in consternation. He babbled to catch up as she resumed her signs. "Oh . . . uh . . . I see that you truly love your people as I do mine. You fear for them, as I do for mine. The days are uncertain, and they are changing. Come, friend dwarf. Among all men, these are our friends. The best way to help your people is to keep to your word and tell them all you know. We must help them so they can help both our people. Therra has descended. Lemerrus too. Who knows but that your mother may not be next if you will but aid her." She extended her hand in an offer of assistance.

He continued to stare at her in an astonished awe. Rather than take her hand, however, he reached out to take a leather-bound book from the shelf against which he'd fallen. He opened the book and held it out to her. She looked at it, then took it. The dwarf, eyes still locked on the mermaid, whispered, "That is how I knew Therra was come. I knew from this book that only in the very presence of a heavenly emissary could a longaevi endure to pass beyond their own realm. When I saw you . . . here . . ." His eyes were still overlarge, and the light reflected off them. They seemed deep like a well—deep enough to hold an eternity of years. And in that moment, Romul knew the dwarf was telling no lie about his age.

Murgen was engrossed in the book, which was filled with brightly colored illuminations. She flipped from page to page as the dwarf got slowly to his feet and brushed himself off, as if trying to rid himself of the memory of his breakdown. When he spoke again, however, it was still in a searching and uncertain voice.

"The, uh, man who wrote this book was, I think, a Therran priest. And he makes a statement in there that I never understood 'til tonight. He says, 'Surely the burden borne by Therra's children is greatest of all.' I thought it only a man's pride in his work, but then on the raft tonight, when you came out of the water and . . . and . . ." He lost the thread of his thoughts in the awkwardness of trying to refer to Murgen's sufferings without actually mentioning them. "I think now I understand."

With this he took a deep breath, squared his shoulders, and marched back to his seat. Kicking the stack of papers next to the chair for good measure, he planted himself amid his cushions and gazed at Eli with a look that suggested she should get on with her questions.

She opened her mouth, but Romul burst in ahead of her again. "Oh no you don't. We're not changing the subject till I get the end of the last story. I want to know what the fire looked like." He'd been so keenly drawn to the idea of the fiery Glaem that he wasn't going to let the story get sidetracked again.

The dwarf very nearly relapsed, but with a supportive look from Murgen over the top of her book, he pulled himself together. "That's just what the fools up there don't understand. 'Tisn't even a fire under the nidernes—least not in the proper sense. It's actually a great gulf of smothering wind."

"It's what?" Romul wasn't sure he heard rightly.

"Just what I said. I looked down upon a vast chasm of air that stretched on and on. Great misty clouds there was floating in it. It felt like I was looking up into the sky . . . but a sky that went down toward the center."

"But what about the light?" Romul was unable to hide his disappointment. "You said there were a light."

"That's just it. In the sky above there is the sun. And there, as far below me as the sun is over me, it seems, I seen it." He had regained his following now, and even Murgen had lowered her book and was listening intently. "A great fire *did* burn there, like the sun, but darker and redder. I don't know how long I hung there—could've been days or years. I had no way of moving. But in all that time of staring at it, the fire never moved. Not like the sun does, anyway. It was like it was fixed there—the center of the world, maybe."

"How did you get away then?" whispered Rose.

Now the dwarf shuddered and said in a low voice to himself, "I said I'd say it all, so now I got to." He took another deep breath. "So there I was, hanging at the mouth of that shaft, looking out into the sky under the world, when one day I think I see sommat happening down below. There was a kind of explosion way down in the Glaem. A great burst of fire spins off it. But it took hours to grow large enough for me to see it clear, which is why I knows it were so very far away. Well, this great plume of fire goes slowly up like a volcano. I watches it for ever-so-long a time, but eventually it drops back down into itself like it never happened.

"But then after an even longer while, I thinks I see a little spot way down there—a little red dot of a thing. But after another while, it was bigger, like it was closer, and it was leaving a little black line behind it as it swirled higher. Well, I starts to get a real sickly scared feeling, I'm not ashamed to say. Sommat inside me was telling me that whatever was coming up meant no good for little me, I tell you."

"What was it?" said several voices.

The dwarf was trembling now, again in the grip of his own narrative. He was struggling to keep his composure, so real before his eyes were the things he was describing. "Understand, it took a terrible long time for that little dot to grow big enough for me to see it proper-like."

"What was it?" came the refrain.

"It got bigger, and as it got bigger, it got redder. And then I realized that all the redness was actually fire. It was letting off great billowing jets of fire and leaving a great black trail of smoke behind it as it came on."

"What was it?" The voices now sounded as frantic as the dwarf's.

"It came on till I was sure it was close enough to see me. And then it did see me. And it came right up to me and looked me in the eye."

The question was not repeated this time, so spellbound were the listeners. The dwarf wasn't paying any attention to them anyhow. He was reliving an event as beyond his control now as it was when it happened.

"There he was. What no living dwarf ever believed even existed. Falak!"

"Falak?" said Eli without comprehension.

The dwarf gripped the arms of his chair in terror and frustration, "Don't you understand? Have you not heard the ancient songs in Mulek of him? Of what he did? Of the great purge of Embola what changed the world?" His pleading looks and gestures gained no glimmer of recognition. "Damn it all! I tell you I've seen with these here eyes of mine, him what was called Jormangand in Garlandium, whom the Rokan call Uroborus and the Azhwana Oshumare—no less than the infernal dragon himself."

Chapter 36

All the dwarf's labors were now paid off in the reaction he earned from this final detail. The girls let out a series of cries, Augie wore a face of blank wonder, and Murgen dropped her book and put her hands over her mouth. Only Romul gave no reaction at all, because he had no idea what any of it meant. He had completely forgotten that the subject of the dragon stood at the very center of their quest. All his traipsing hither and yon since being ejected from Halighyll by the surly priest had all been for the sake of this revelation. Since he'd cared little for that mission, the dragon had gradually receded from his mind, and even now it took a bit of digging before he could recover the memory. But he dug quickly, motivated by a desire to not look stupid.

Augie was the first to speak, edging Eli out as she inhaled. "Really, dwarf? A dragon? I mean, that's . . . No one's ever . . ."

No telling how long he would have blathered had Eli not had enough of the backseat and erupted in a frenzy. "Oh, Augie, will you just shut up a minute! Look, this is important. This is my whole question—what is this dragon about, Ylfig? We've got to know. Do you know what happened to it? Did it really mean to start the Ever-War?"

At this final question, the dwarf started and looked at her with surprise. "Falak? The Ever-War?" Then his eyes narrowed maliciously. "I bet my oldest book he did. That vile, cursed, wretched, old—" And surely another fit of cursing and book-booting would have been the result had not Eli leaned forward and put both hands on the arms of his chair.

"Ylfig!" she pleaded, but Romul thought it sounded more like a command. "We need to know what you know."

The dwarf, unaccustomed to being interrupted mid-connip-tion, was startled back to the present and deflated in his chair.

"I . . . uh . . . well, I'll tell you what I know, but you're certain to be disappointed."

Eli, finally in control of the interrogation, responded in a small hard voice. "I'll risk it."

"All righty, then. Well, see, the reason I don't know too much about it is that when the old worm looked me in the eyes, I closed mine tight. His eyes were deep and red and knew things, I could tell. I couldn't bear to look at them. I didn't know what was to happen, but I figured it was the end of old Ylfig for sure. But when nothing did happen, I opened my eyes. And there he still was just looking at me. And I think he was smiling."

"Smiling." Augie was still in a bit of shock over the revelation.

"Well, I was looking at a whole lot of teeth, so what's one to do but put a best face on it, so, yes, he was smiling. And then he spoke."

"What did he say?" asked Eli.

"Well, see, he asked me questions, all gentle-like. Wanted to know what was going on in the world above. Hadn't been there in a while, I supposed. So I told him all I knew about things."

"What things?" Eli pressed. "Did he say anything about Halighyll or about the prophecies?"

The dwarf looked at her curiously. "Not about the prophecies, although I'd like to know just what you know of them."

"Will you just—"

"Okay, okay. Yes, he did ask me where Halighyll was in relation to where we was at the moment. And, of course, a dwarf always knows where he is even underground, so I tells him."

"And then . . ."

"Well, here's the part that gets . . . strange. I thought for sure that when he got what he wanted, he'd be sending me off to Sweet Berducca. But rather, he said—and it's been at least a thousand years, so I ain't sure I got all the details right no more—he said a sort of thanks. A 'You served me well, and I'll be 'membering it' or sommat like that but more grand and terrible-like. And then he turns round and sucks in a whomping load of air from that dark sky he was swimming in, looks back at me with those garnet eyes, and blows a gust of air what made the other one look like the breeze of spring. And up that shaft I went like a bird falling to the ground."

Then he fell into a silent reverie.

"And . . ." Eli prodded.

"And . . . well, like I says, here it gets complicated. I don't know what happened at that point."

"You blacked out?" asked Eli, trying to draw clarity out of him.

"Well, if I did, it was a blackening out like this world ain't never seen afore! When I opened my eyes, I was back in my own little trench wherein I'd started like it had all been a dream. But it was all dark and old now, you know? How a shaft gets when it's been abandoned a long time?"

He nodded encouragingly, but when no one affirmed they knew what that was like, he shrugged and continued. "Well, it did feel abandoned, which meant I had been gone a while. And I felt all funny inside, like the world had turned a bunch without me— left me behind, so to speak . . . but I had no idea . . ."

He lapsed again.

Into this silence Augie decided to drop a little scientific skepticism. "Okay, Eli, this is a remarkable tale if true. But sooner or later we've got to apply a little healthy suspicion. Scientific consensus is that dragons are only myths, and we know the world can't possibly sit atop a cushion of air like he's describing. It doesn't work. So either he was dreaming about the dragon, or he's deceived, or else—"

"No!" said Eli. "We've seen it . . . and so has your father."

Augie's mouth fell open, and so did the dwarf's. But only the latter spoke. "You've seen the beast?" A hint of fear had crept into his voice.

"Well, we saw his skeleton on the same trip we met the other dwarf." And she rehearsed the discovery of the ancient Therran well deep in the Alappunda Mountains, and what's more, how the creature had managed in its death to stop up the well by plunging its fang into the aperture. Rose added additional irrelevancies, like the fact that the opposing fang was missing and the detail of its one withered claw. Eli explained how it had all been a great mystery to Professor Lambient, Augie's father, and how the Therran knight Dashonae, who had accompanied them, had concluded that the dragon's final act was the first cause of the Ever-War.

By the end of the story, the dwarf was nodding his head in understanding, but the hole in Augie's face remained wide open as if inviting someone to shove a cake into it.

"Now, that fits," said the dwarf with a chuckle and not a small measure of relief. "I never knew what became of the old stinker. For when I dug my way back up to the tunnels—and it took a while, for parts had come down—I found the whole world was changed. There was war among the nations above, and here in the Sarkonish Kingdom, there weren't a single dwarf I knew."

"Why not?" asked Rose, making a shy debut. "Did you hit your head or something?"

The dwarf laughed. "No, missy. All my kin had passed on, the way all longaevi do eventually. We don't die, but we can be killed. Everything was changed, I tell you. There was only about half as many dwarves, the wars with the Narmonds had fallen off after taking all my kin, and all the tunnels and dwarf cities had changed. And apparently I'd been gone for . . . I still don't know. Hundreds of years, it seemed."

"So no one knew you?" asked Eli.

"How could they? They got excited when they saw me, because

they thought I was a new birth, and they hadn't seen any in a long time."

"But couldn't they tell you were really old?"

"There, friends, is the queerest part of my tale. When I looked in a glass, I found that sommat—the Glaem or Falak or some even stranger force—had made me look like a newborn. I looked brand-new again, even though I was older by double than every dwarf in the world."

"Didn't you try to explain what happened?" asked Eli.

"No, ma'am, I did not!" He shook his head vigorously. "I'm not so much a fool as that! I knew they'd never believe me. But that's about when I decided it was time for old Ylfig to go a little crazy in the head, so's to give himself a little room to figure out what was on the up-and-up. Asides, no one had heard of the dragon in years. Appears he did his work of turning the world upside down, then left . . . or died, as it seems."

Eli's head was down in thought, and Augie was still reeling from learning that dragons did exist.

"This is all very interesting, but—" Anna began in a tone that meant the exact opposite, but then Eli fixed her with an angry look. "No, I mean it really is interesting, but it's not exactly what we needed to know . . . or at least not all of it." The dwarf raised an eyebrow and watched her mildly. "What we need to know is how the dragon is related to the prophecies in the temple. Can you tell us that?"

He got up and drew another book from a shelf, flipped through it, and held it out toward Anna. "I assume you mean the lines about the legate?"

Anna looked over the page, nodding vaguely. Eli had slid up beside her and was reading over her shoulder. "It's the prophecy," she whispered.

Both girls read down.

Anna finished first, as Eli bent to study the lines. "Ugh. Cholerish was right. I don't understand hardly any of it. It's just like random lines of text. But I do see the line Cholerish mentioned—'*In death, he takes the water from the earth.*'"

Ylfig shifted in his chair. "Well, if you want to know whether I think Falak was the Legate of Hamayune, then I think he must'a been. It seems to fit mostly."

"What about the legate who's still coming?" asked Anna.

The dwarf shrugged. "Of that, I can tell you nothing."

"Wait, the final lines of the prophecy are missing in this book too—just like in the temple!" cried Eli, grabbing the book away from Anna. "We need to know what the last lines say."

"There again I cannot help," said Ylfig. "Most of the libraries in Garlandium were burned near the beginning of the Ever-War. These books nearly all come from after those days. And the Ravagement happened long afore that, even."

"And that's all you know?" If Eli was trying not to sound disappointed, she was failing.

"'Tis all," said the dwarf before cocking an eyebrow toward Anna. "But I is a bit surprised that Therra and her big brother there don't know more about it themselves."

Anna cast a haughty look at Romul and laughed. "Big brother. Yeah, right! Baby cousin, maybe."

This had the predictable effect, and Augie had to step in to prevent fisticuffs. "I think," he grunted, holding a windmilling Romul at arm's length while Anna stuck her tongue out at him from her chair, "it's time for the dwarf to keep the other half of his promise."

Ten minutes later they stood again upon the shore of the underground lake. The glowing water was visible from the shore, and the first tiny piece of luminescent weed had already washed up at their feet. The dwarf stood with his hand on his hips, laughing at the sight.

"No one comes down this way anymore. Although I imagine that's about to change. I'll have to find a new home for my books, farther down to keep prying eyes away." He inhaled deeply, like a man on a spring morning. A fresh breeze blew gently over them, and Romul noticed how greatly the acrid smell had already decreased.

The dwarf rubbed his hands together like a farmhand at the end of his labor. "Well, that's a work near done. Come, all you big-guns. It's time I lead you to a place of your own." Then he marched off down the shore, opposite the way they had come.

Anna trotted up next to him. "But what are you going to tell the others?'

"About what?"

Anna blew out her lips in disbelief. "About all this. Don't you think they'll notice that the lake has changed just a tiny bit?"

The dwarf pursed his lips. "That's another reason to get you out. You shouldn't be here when it's discovered. Once you're out the way, won't matter how it was done."

"You're not going to tell them?"

The dwarf sneered. "Why? They'd just chalk it up to my insan-ity. No, no, sweetie. With any luck they'll praise Sweet Berducca for her gift, but more likely they'll find a way of saying the Glaem did it, the poor fools."

This was too much for Romul. "So you would let them think Berducca did a miracle rather than take the credit yourself? I mean, that could change everything for you. They'd have to re-spect you, then. You could be on the Gaderung or even take that stinker Fehro's place."

The dwarf came to such an abrupt halt that Anna ran into him. He turned and fixed Romul with his weird golden eyes. "Don't you understand, my wee latecomer? Yes, credit would be my just desert, but it would not be so good for my people. More than I want to be free from the charade of my life, I want them to return to Sweet Berducca. This may be the only way."

"But isn't it kind of a lie to let them think—"

"Just 'cause Berducca is credited with a miracle she didn't do ain't a proof against her authority. To have the Ebontarn healed at only the cost of my pride of place . . . What is that? They're my people, they is. Ain't it right for me to bear a little suffering in order to call them back to her? I'd endure greater than this, if needs be. Sure is you'd do the same for your own people."

"Whoever they may be," mumbled Romul. But his eyes were cast down to the dirt. He again knew himself to be a fraud. He would never be Garlandish, but he felt as though he'd forfeited his share among the Rokan. His hand wandered to his stringy locks of hair from which he'd so carefully removed every trace of white. He felt like a traitor, he felt alone, and again the awful certainty of having no people to call his own settled down upon him with the crushing weight of a mountain.

Murgen approached the dwarf and made signs. "I see, then, that we are alike after all, friend dwarf."

The dwarf shied from her gaze but mumbled, "I cannot say I would yet do for your people what you have done for mine, but I think I understand many things better than I did afore."

"Um," said Anna, "this is all very touching, but I'm kind of itching to get out of this hole."

"Anna!" cried Rose in dismay. "That's mean. Can't you tell they like each other?"

If Ylfig and Murgen had indeed shared a moment, it was eclipsed by a new one as both turned wide-eyed to stare at Rose in disbelieving horror.

Rose burst into giggles. "Just kidding. I know you've no choice but hate each other."

The dwarf and mermaid exchanged a searching look, and Romul wondered if that were really so.

Chapter 37

While Romul was itching to see the land of sunshine again, he was not enthusiastic about the long underground march required to get there. Ylfig had led them along the shore of the Ebontarn for several miles—or more. Romul couldn't be sure. He'd then led them into a tunnel that had obviously been a main road long ago. Now, however, the paving stones were so cracked and crumbled that it was little different from the rocky coast they'd just left. The tunnel led gradually upward but contained no lights, so Ylfig had lit a couple of torches.

The passage zigged and zagged, featured innumerable cross tunnels, and was in every way indistinguishable from the tunnel that had brought them into the dwarf kingdom. The maze-like complexity of the whole thing made Romul's head swim. Were Ylfig not leading them, they'd have been lost in ten minutes.

His claustrophobic fear increased when Ylfig led them down a narrow side burrow, explaining, "We used to have a bit of trouble with trolls what lived in these parts. Don't know if they're still about, but mayhaps they've been multiplying, too, so let's not take chances. I promised to get you out into the shine, and I'll be jiggered if anything's going to stop me now. Asides, you'll want to get down into Rokehaven to be sure, afore full winter sets in."

Augie pulled up short. "Wait, we're coming out on the western side of the mountains? I was hoping we'd—"

Rose put her hand on his arm. "It's okay, Augie. Remember what the old lady said. Rommie has to go there to find his mom."

Augie nodded resignedly, and Romul realized this was further from home than Augie had really meant to go.

Romul, too, was now forced to think about exactly where they were headed. He realized with a sour sickening in his stomach that he was of two minds about the journey. Every Rokan at some time or other romanticized about making the journey back to the homeland, but he'd never heard of anyone actually doing it. The dwarves had said the pass was actually impassable with snow these days, and he realized that the only stories he'd heard about the Rokan homeland came from the oldest and generally least reliable people—superstitious cronies and hoary drunkards.

And even by these accounts, Rokan was not a very nice place. He'd always understood that the final Garlandish atrocity had been to push the Rokan back across the mountains to subsist on the snowy high plains, where life would be too hard for them to grow numerous enough to be a threat. Romul's mind was filled with images of a weatherworn and generally toothless tribe of hunter-gatherers, living literally hand-to-mouth on scrub grass like cattle. Underfed and underclothed women and children huddling around fires while fur-draped men staggered in from a day of hunting inedible shadows, desiring nothing more than to get drunk, fall down, and do the same thing tomorrow.

Of course, much of this imagery really came from his own experiences among the Rokan of Farwell, whose lives were almost as desperate as his imagined Rokan homeland. His recent remorse over rejecting his Rokan identity was undermined, and he felt a hardening in his innards toward what awaited him at the end of this black tunnel. He found himself thinking, *I won't go, I just won't*, but then having the smothering realization that "going back" and "going forward" meant the same for him. If he was Rokan, he would be Rokan on either side of the mountain. He could see no way of escape from the deprivation and shame that awaited him no matter where his tired feet took him.

He realized he'd stopped moving. Had he been last in the

queue, he might actually have let them all troop away—left to despair in the dark, maybe as a gift for a nice troll. But he was not last in line.

"What's wrong, Rommie?" came a soft voice next to him. Rose had sidled up to him. "Are you sad about going home?" The depth of her perception disturbed him and made him defensive.

"What? No, I was just thinking about . . . uh, trolls."

"It's okay. I don't really want to go home either."

He was so surprised that all that came out was a vague, "Huh?"

"No." Her voice mirrored his own melancholy. "There's not really much for us there. Oh, it's an awesome house, but it's not really home. And there's Dad, but he's not really there. And even when he is . . ." Another big sigh. "And Naggie's kind of a pain . . . most of the time. Ever since Mom died . . ."

What she said after that never made it into Romul's brain, for a great thunderclap of clarity rumbled around every corner of it. He spoke, heedless of whether he was interrupting or not. "You don't got a mom either?"

"No. I thought you knew that."

"Uh, no."

"Yeah, some kind of accident at her work . . . in Europe somewhere, I think. Dad won't talk about it."

"How old were you?"

"Don't know. Really young, I guess. I don't remember any of it."

"Me neither."

"I hope you find your mom, Romul."

Romul didn't say anything, because he knew his voice would crack. So he just nodded in the dark. Rose said nothing more either. They walked in silence for a long time.

Finally, some commotion further on brought them both out of their private reflections. A cry echoed back down the tunnel to them. "Oh, thank the gods!" They both knew what this meant and quickened their pace.

At first Romul couldn't figure out what was going on. He'd

been expecting to be dazzled by sunlight, but he was actually out of the cave and into the open air before he realized it. It was just as dark as the moment before, but his skin responded instantly to the chilly breeze. He shivered and looked up in confusion, knowing Merris was not there to greet him and yet hoping this was not a deception. His eyes were bathed instead by the light of a thousand stars, and nearly straight overhead the bright glow of Vercandrus assured him he was not mistaken. They were out of the maze and had come out into the glory of a clear winter's night.

Their expulsion from the earth gave birth to such a spirit of gaiety that they ignored the cold. Rose inhaled the frosty air deeply and with such vigor that she became light-headed and stumbled. He was obliged to catch her and prop her up. Anna was thumping her chest and whooping like a madman, while Eli babbled on about someplace called Tahoe. Augie stood with his head thrown back and his arms wide, laughing a bit maniacally. Murgen, however, put all their celebrations to shame. The regal empress had been reduced to a little girl, and she cavorted and danced like a nymph amid the dusting of white powder.

The only one unmoved was Ylfig, who stood looking out westward into the darkness. It was clearly the west because the sky in that direction wore that first smudge of color that portends the coming morning. He turned with an amused patience to watch the festivities. "Well, now old Ylfig has kept his word, he has. Here you is on the western slopes of the Aracadians. And down there about a half day's walk is Rokehaven. When Merris rises, you'll see her there in the distance. I trust you can make it there your own selves?"

"We'll manage, thank you," said Augie. "But what'll you do now?"

"Oh, me? I'll head back to watch over my little flock of gnomi. Sooner or later someone'll venture down to the Ebontarn and discover that Sweet Berducca still cares for her children. Till then, every city needs a nutter. Might as well be me."

Rose ran forward and embraced the dwarf, encouraging the

others to follow suit. When the group hug had dissolved, the two longaevi stood looking at each other in the starlight.

"Well, ma'am," began the dwarf awkwardly, glancing up into the mermaid's face briefly before dropping his eyes, "can't say as I expect to see you down my ways again."

"Nor could I persuade you to visit my home waters," came the reply.

"Too true, too true." He chuckled. "But if on some impossible topsy-turvy day I should see you again, I'll consider the honor to be wholly mine." Then he bowed so low that his beard brushed the tops of his boots.

"No, the honor will be shared." The mermaid's head likewise descended in a regal nod.

"Well, that's enough starshine for me for one day," said the dwarf with a wink, and turned toward the hole. "Oh, for love of Sweet Berducca! I almost forgot." He produced a small volume from under his jerkin and held it out to Eli. "This is for you, since you seemed so interested in that dragon."

"What is it?" Romul could hear the excitement in her voice.

"Well, as I was working through my books o'er the years, I'd gotten in the habit of whenever I comes across a tidbit about old Falak, I'd tear out the page and—" Eli and Augie let out a collective gasp of anguish, but the dwarf continued unheeding—"stick it on a stack. When I had a goodly number of pages, I stitched them all together and made a new book. And there it is. Be warned, though. It's none too reliable nor clear." With that, he waved a cheery farewell and disappeared down the tunnel. Eli stood holding the book gently, reverently, as if it were of spun glass.

"Well," said Augie, smacking his lips and pointing westward toward the glowing horizon. "I'm guessing the only hope of any breakfast lies that way."

Romul blew out his cheeks. "Only if you're going to kill it yourself." The chipper mood that had descended upon the rest was driving Romul more deeply into himself. Of them all, he had some sense of the hunger that probably lay ahead of them on the cold highlands of the Rokan homeland. But he had no wish to be left behind, so as they all trooped off after Augie, he shuffled along behind with his hands jammed into his pockets.

"Merris will be up anytime now," came Augie's buoyant voice from the head of the procession. And it was so. The horizon was growing brighter by the minute. Stars were winking out overhead. Even Vercandrus was winding his way slowly eastward over the mountain, taking on a slightly yellowed and sleepy look as if he, weary from his task of defending the night sky, was preparing for bed.

They were making their way down what felt like a path amid the boulders and hillocks of rock that made up the western side of the Aracadians. The great mountains loomed up behind them. The dwarf had brought them out in the foothills, but Romul knew they were already higher than some of the lower peaks on the Garlandish side of the range. At any minute he expected to round a corner and see the Rokan high plain stretched out before them in all its bleakness.

Romul was lagging behind now, shuffling his feet through the thin white rime that covered the ground, when he was pulled up short. He stared down in amazement. There in one of the footprints of the others, a spot of color caught his eye. He bent and found it to be a small blue wildflower. Its long stem had been laid low by the frost and was now bent by the trampling. He picked it and held it up in the growing light. It was the most vivid shade of ripe blue one could imagine.

Wild azule. It was a rare flower—the rarest. He'd seen them in shop windows in the Ternion. They were used to produce blue dyes and paints and other things but very hard to find. Even a handful of crushed petals would earn a Rokan more than a day's field wages. He took a step, then stopped again. There between two rocks, he saw another. He snatched at it. No, it was actually three flowers crammed into the dense soil between the boulders.

He was about to yell for the others when the light changed. He looked up, then behind him, and gasped. The highest summits of the mountains were golden with new sunlight. The bright line of morning light fell toward him like a shining wave more quickly than he could have imagined.

Then he heard yelling ahead of him. He couldn't make out words, but it sounded as if Augie was really excited about something. He tore his gaze away from the descending curtain of radiance and ran down the path. He rounded several boulders and came out finally into an open place where the others were shouting and pointing. It was the breaking point of the hills. A flat plain fell gently away from them as far as they could see.

Merris chose this moment to crown the horizon. Her first shimmering ray caught Romul full in the face with a breath of warmth so forceful that he dropped his precious bale of flowers. Perhaps it was not only the morning sun that so affected him. Before him stretched a wide field dressed thickly in wild azule. Acres of brilliant sapphire flowers were shaking off the frost to greet the new day.

Romul's gaze stretched outward to take in the more distant landscape, where the blue of the precious spray gave way to the lush green of grass, speckled with the white and brown dots of sheep and cattle. Further on, the green was abandoned for the gold of ripening wheat. And beyond all this, like an isle of wakefulness in a sea of dreams, lay a small hill. And upon the hill, a city with wide streets and spires of smoky marble ascending from the plain like a prayer.

In a moment of staggering epiphany, Romul knew he'd been deceived. Everything he'd ever been told about being Rokan—everything he thought he knew about himself—had been a lie. Here was a land for waking sleepers from their dark terrors. Here, he thought for the first time in his life, was a place he could willingly call . . . home.

BOOK 5

Rokan Birth Pangs

Poets like my vaunted brother write incessantly of how the Great Change affected the longaevi. But I now believe the Rokan were victims of it as well. So much of the suffering endured by the Garlandian Rokan resulted from being almost completely cut off from their western homeland by the expansion of the snowy southern Wastes. Within a few generations, the Rokan in the east knew almost nothing of their ancient homeland. But I have read many testimonies by Rokan expatriates returning to the old high country. In every case, the event was radicalizing to their sense of Rokan-selfhood. A hypothesis suggests itself at this point: if a people can understand where they have come from, it will produce a vision of what they might yet become.

> DR. SONJI RAZHAMANÌAH, *An Attempted History of the Halighyllian Prophecies and Their Fulfillment*, Vol 3: *The Saga of the Great Change and the Diminution of the Natural Longaevi*, 87v.

Chapter 38

The cries of delight were lost on Romul's muddled mind. The only words that penetrated were Augie's, for they echoed his own thoughts. "This isn't right," he'd said with head cocked sideways in confusion.

No, thought Romul, *it ain't*. Yet it was so right in a more important and unlooked-for way. This was not the barren wilderland he'd always been told about. The Garlandish Rokan always considered themselves the fortunate ones despite their oppression. It was always said that the weather was milder and the land richer east of the mountains. Their subordinate status was a small price to pay for the increased comforts they enjoyed.

Yet here was proof that this dreary vision of the Rokan homeland was completely wrong. If something so basic as the weather could be wrong, how deep might the deception go?

Augie continued to speak Romul's thoughts for him even as they waded forward into the blue meadow. "This can't be right. The Rokan highlands are desolate. Every map I've ever seen shows Rokan as really . . . well, austere. Rokan is the end of the world. Everyone knows it!"

"Here there be dragons," mumbled Eli, bending to pick a blue flower.

Romul then realized Anna and Rose were not with them. He turned and saw them standing with heads together, looking at something in Rose's hand. Anna was shaking her head in disbelief.

"What's up?" called Eli.

"It's the compass," said Anna. "It's pointing right at the city."

They all gathered to peer at the little ball Rose held up proudly.

"See? Right at that city there." It was so. One arrow of the strange compass was pointing downhill, and the other pointed right toward the city.

"What's wrong with that?" Romul had somewhat forgotten what the compass was for. "We're going that way anyway."

"That's the point." Anna shook her head again. "I just can't understand why it would point exactly to the place we need to go anyway—again!"

Eli mused for a minute. "Well, Cholerish did say something about the whole thing being governed by something bigger, didn't he? So did the bodacha. I guess we should just be thankful and get on with it." She suddenly began counting on her fingers. "Oh, crap! We've already been here longer than we should. We're going to have some explaining to do if Naggie's already back when we get there."

"Maybe she'll get stuck in traffic," offered Rose with a hopeful smile.

"Or they'll send her luggage to Egypt," mumbled Anna.

"Anna! That's not nice," cried Eli. "No, we'll just have to get back as fast as we can."

They meandered down through the wildflowers. As Merris continued her dramatic ascent, they heard a great baying from behind them, which Romul understood roughly to mean, *Hey there, wait you up for me!* They turned to see a huge dog bounding down the slopes toward them. Romul had barely understood the animal. Apparently dogs had accents just like people did, and this one had a sort of . . . well, it was just different from the dogs' in Garlandium. It was wilder, woolier, as if the dog were chewing on something as it barked.

As it waded into the wild azule, the dog began to leap unnaturally, as if trying to minimize stepping on the flowers. It was a beautiful animal, heavily built, with a coat of brown, black, and white. When it reached them, Romul realized it was even bigger than he'd thought—its head came to his shoulders.

"How you come here to be?" it barked, panting through its gaping mouth.

It took Augie a minute to think about the answer. "We're travelers. We've just come . . . uh, through the mountains."

"How the pass you came to find? The snows have come." Even with its bizarre accent, Romul heard the wonder in the dog's question.

"We, uh . . ." began Augie, and then he looked around at the others helplessly. Eli shook her head ever so slightly from side to side. "We were lucky, I guess."

The dog tilted its head in a way Romul interpreted as disbelief. Then it sniffed at Romul's pant leg. "Strange. Your smell not of the outside of the mountain is but of the inside."

Romul didn't know how the Rokan felt about dwarves and didn't feel like trying to explain. The others must have felt the same, for no one responded. The dog sniffed at them for a minute, then its shoulders went up and down in the canine version of a shrug. "My name Lebenjager is, of clan Sennenhund. For lost and injured in the mountains we patrol." Had the dog stood upon its hind legs and thumped its chest with its paws, it could not have given off a stronger air of pride.

"Well, then," said Augie, "we're very glad to meet you, uh, Libinsjugger. Perhaps you can help us get to . . . Well, we don't know where we're going. We're new in Rokan. This is Rokan, isn't it?" He passed a tentative finger over the landscape.

"It is, it is! But all new ones to the Primus must go."

"The Primus?" asked Eli, who, like Romul, was getting used to the accent.

"Yes, the second one."

"Why isn't he the first?" said Rose.

The dog burst into yelps, its own way of laughing. "How he

first be? First the Queen always is. The Primus only second can ever be."

"Do you mean like a prime minister?" asked Eli.

Now it was the dog's turn to cock its head in Augie-like confusion. Then it loped off through the field toward the city, calling, "You come! You see!"

"Do we go?" Anna softly asked the others.

"I say, yes," said Augie. "It's not like we have a better option." Everyone agreed and started after the dog, who had stopped like a statue and was sniffing the air. It turned back to the group and nosed its way in among them till it came to Murgen.

"What you be?" it barked suspiciously. "Not like the man-pups or the big one."

Rather than make a bunch of gestures, which Augie would have had to translate anyway, Murgen bent to the ground, stroked the dog's head, and whispered for a moment into its ears. At first Romul saw the hair on its neck rise up, but after a moment the hair went down as the tail went up. It began wagging furiously with excitement, then broke away from the mermaid and began to run in great circles around the group, woofing in its doggy voice, "And so! And so! And so! To the Primus! To the Primus! Of all, you to the Primus must go! He must see!"

"Well, I guess that settles it," said Augie with a coy smile. "The mermaid trumps us all . . . again."

They set off after the dog, who had already bounded into the distance.

A half-hour's diligent walking brought them into the fields of livestock. The city loomed large before them now, with tower piled upon tower so that Romul had to lift his head to see the tops of them. The dog now walked at their side, shadowing them like a sheepdog. If any of them stepped out of the group, it would nudge at their knees till they rejoined the "flock." This annoyed Romul to the point of complaining, whereupon the dog apologized and explained that he hadn't even realized he was doing it.

Rose suddenly asked the dog, "Do many people come over the mountains?"

"Few, and all the time fewer."

"When was the last?" said Rose, glancing at Romul.

"But one this year, and just last week. A most remarkable one she was."

Romul stopped in his tracks, sensing something of immense importance. "Who was she?"

The dog looked at him curiously. "Old woman she was. Should not have survived but did. Very sick she is now, much injured. For sure will not live long."

Suspicion was clouding Romul's mind, but he still could not pull it into conscious thought. "Did she say why she came?" The others had stopped now and were staring back-and-forth from Romul to the dog.

"For someone she looks, she said, but he not here. We search already."

A thought was growing small and firm in Romul's mind—like a mist condensing into a pool and then hardening into a block of ice. He felt cold in his limbs. He was afraid to ask the next question. "Who was she looking for?" he asked quietly.

Lebenjager looked at him curiously. Something was dawning on the dog too. "She described him. And gave a name."

Romul tried to ask the obvious question, but his mouth had gone very dry. After a few seconds of awkward silence, Anna burst out with it. "Well, geez! What was it? What was the freaking name?"

The dog took a step toward him and sniffed his hand. "She looks for him she calls . . . Romul."

Chapter 39

Romul felt surly and impatient. He sat apart from the others, his legs dangling down from a chair too big for him, feeling smaller than his . . . however many years he had. The dog had absolutely refused to take them to the sick woman till he'd herded them into the city to meet the Primus. Romul had tried to explain his need to see her immediately, especially if she was dying, but the dog had its orders. It passed them off to the guards at the city gate with a quick summary of the situation that left out all the important details except the one the dog cared about—that they'd come over the mountains. The guards had stared in wonder at the troop, before marching them to the House of Assembly.

Now as they sat in an anteroom of the House, Eli prattled on about the contents of Ylfig's book. Romul paid little attention. It sounded like she was more impressed by the age of the book than by anything it said, partly because she didn't actually understand much of it.

"This has just *got* to go back to Whinsom and Cholerish," she was saying. "I mean, listen to this. '*There are powers in the world that rival even those of the emissaries. The time comes when all must choose their side.*' And this one . . ." She flipped a couple of pages. "'*And so the great worm mocked even the elementals themselves, coveting their power and attempting to subdue them. But he paid the price of his arrogance in the withering of his flesh.*' I can't make any sense of it, but it just sounds so important. And I'm sure if anybody can figure it out, they can."

"Oh marvie!" groused Anna, who had not been having a good time. "How are we going to get it to them? We have to get home as soon as we can find the stupid window."

Before Eli or anyone else could say more, there was a clatter at the door, and two soldiers appeared.

"You will come with us, please," one said and gestured toward the doorway.

Romul was weary of making appearances. It felt like everywhere he'd gone, he'd been dragged in front of someone—priests, salamanders, dwarves. It was no different here. He was preparing for a confrontation with some undersecretary and was trying to figure out how to get through it quickly and unseen. So when the doors of the assembly room swung open, he shuffled in at the end of the procession with his head down. He didn't care what happened here. So far as he was concerned, every minute spent in this place potentially cost him answers from the sick woman.

One casual glance up, and his attention was caught and held. This was nothing like the arena of the dwarves. It was a large but simple room, filled with light from windows high overhead that let in the sun. He also saw many alcoves along the walls, each with a door. He gawked with wonder at a long table with chairs at the far end, spread with food in abundance beyond his dreams—platters of steaming omelets and warm breads, bowls of fruit, cold ham and chicken, and crystal flasks sparkling with fruit juices. Beautiful place settings with silver utensils winked at him under the morning sun.

Figures were rising at the table—perhaps a dozen of them in great furry robes with a regal look. Like kings or gods, they stood tall and proud. And—here Romul's breath caught in his chest—every one of them had hair as white as snow.

The central figure raised his hands in greeting. "Hail, weary travelers from the lowlands! Welcome to the humble city of Rokehaven, you who have braved many dangers. Sit and be welcome."

Then the whole of the assembly spoke words that rang in

Romul's ears like a clarion call: *"Semper Eadem!"*—the words of the eregina, which he now saw hung above the table on the front wall in huge, ornate letters.

The man in the center was speaking again. "We took liberties, as we did not believe you had breakfasted. My name is Lord Burleigh. I hold the position of Primus of Rokehaven. Please come, eat, and be at peace."

Augie was already seated, stabbing with his fork at a plate of ham while the others were still finding chairs opposite the robed figures. The travelers each tucked in with relish, all except Murgen, who took only a piece of fruit and ate it in small, delicate bites. It was a full minute before Romul realized that none of the robed men were eating, and he paused, feeling awkward. This occurred to the girls at the same moment, and they all stopped mid-bite to look uncomfortably at their hosts. Only Augie munched on with occasional groans of pleasure till Murgen applied her elbow to his ribs. Then he sat upright, looking chastened.

Lord Burleigh spoke. "Please, continue eating, by all means. Do not let our ways disturb you. We shall not join you until proper thanks has been given, but clearly none of you are Rokan, and we do not expect outsiders to follow our traditions."

Here Rose, who was sitting next to Romul, decided to be helpful. She thrust out a thumb toward him. "He is!"

All eyes turned to Romul, whose stomach suddenly decided food was not on the menu. A fierce and frustrated anger welled up in him. It was too much. Just as he'd begun to maybe . . . perhaps . . . consider not being so opposed to possibly being Rokan, was he now to be publicly shamed in front of the leaders of the whole deal? He had no idea what tradition they were talking about, but clearly by eating he hadn't followed it. What a homecoming! He sat dumbly, his gaze fixed on his full plate, feeling the pressure of the eyes on him.

"Peace, my child. There is no shame. It is not unusual for our countrymen from the lowlands to be ignorant of our ways. But wait, if you *are* Rokan, you will understand what follows." He clapped his hands together loudly, and from the alcoves along the edges of the room, eight men stepped forward. Each bore the uilleanus into which they were blowing vigorously. As if by long practice, each musician ceased blowing at the same moment and set the instruments to moaning. With raised heads they sang, "*Come, hear the voice of the wooly pipes that groan and weep and wail . . .*"

At the first sigh from those pipes, each of the robed men stood.

Romul was stunned to the very core of his being. Of course he knew this song.

"*Oh sore the weight, the Garlandish yoke . . .*"

He'd heard it his whole life—played in dark hostels, by vagabonds on roadsides and hangdog servants in fields, but always as a solitary and lamenting solo—a man and his moth-eaten pipes, groaning out his sorrow and his hopelessness. But here in this place, eight men with eight pipes belted it out, not as a dirge of despair but like an anthem—the anthem of a nation. They smiled as they sang, their heads uplifted to the morning sun. The men at the table lent their voices till the air rang with it.

"*Yet strong were they in the face of death . . .*"

Suddenly Romul found himself rising to his feet. His mouth opened, and he sang. He realized that he'd never sung a note in his life, and he had no idea how to sing, but it didn't matter. Here, in this place, they sang of the wooly pipes with the pride of a full heart, and he knew he must join them. His young voice cut in above all the men's deep ones as he gave himself over to the passion of the moment. This *was* his song . . .

> *So long we wait for appointed days*
> *When our Queen's own heir will awake.*
> *In fire he'll rise and we with him,*
> *Garlandish bonds to break.*

The final notes hung in the air like the smoke of a fire, and like a fire it burned inside Romul's breast. He stood very still, feeling the heat of it coursing through him. So curved inward was his vision that he didn't realize the robed men had all sat down. When he opened his eyes, he saw everyone staring at him.

"It would seem," said Burleigh, "that our young friend knows something of our ways after all." He gave Romul a warm smile.

Romul couldn't think of anything to say, so he just sat down. But the strange warmth had worked its way into the pit of his stomach and awakened his appetite. He began to eat with relish. The robed men likewise began to eat.

"So . . ." Augie had begun eating again with the final chord of the song, and Romul could see that he was struggling between being a well-mannered guest and appeasing his ungovernable appetite. "I've heard that song a few times, or parts of it, anyway. I don't understand it, especially that last part." Romul couldn't tell if he was really interested or just using conversation as a way to slow his eating to an acceptable pace. If the latter, it wasn't working.

"You are a Garlandish gentleman, I can see," said Burleigh, directing a thin smile at the slovenly inventor, who now had bits of egg and breadcrumbs clinging to his face and clothing. "So I shall speak graciously of these matters. But the anthem expresses the hope that our Rokan brethren in the east shall not always be at the mercy of . . . well-fed Garlandish gentlemen." There was the slightest touch of hostility in the man's voice.

Augie was at that moment in the act of dragging half a cold chicken from a nearby platter onto his plate. That was nothing in itself; Burleigh's own plate held a lightly nibbled chicken. But Romul saw the older man's jaws clench tightly together. When he spoke, however, his tone was still gracious. "It also records a prophecy of one who is to come—the very son of the Queen of Angish. He will come and liberate his people from, as it says, 'Garlandish bonds.'"

"Well, I sure hope he does." Romul knew Augie well enough to know that the comment was sincerely meant, but as it was spoken through his mouthful of poultry, it did little to soften the look on Burleigh's face.

Poor Augie. He was not a Garlandish gentleman. He was just a silly inventor with a huge appetite and poor table manners. But even Romul could see he was bumbling down this road in the wrong direction. If he would just shut up . . .

Romul found himself jumping in. "Um . . . thanks so much for all this. We haven't really eaten well in a long time." This succeeded in diverting all the attention to Romul for the moment, but now that he'd done it, he realized he had absolutely nothing else to say to these men. "And he's not a gentleman. He's just an inventor and . . . uh . . ."

"So this queen . . ." said Augie between bites. Romul groaned inside. The man was unwilling to be saved. As the oldest member of the troop, he was used to taking the lead, even if he had no idea where he was leading them. The room went still again. "I know a little about the Rokan workers I've helped in Umbra. Nice people, all of them, and they all talk about her, but she's, like, only a mythical figure, right? This queen? Like our own emissaries, right?" Even Murgen and the girls stopped eating and stared at Augie in disbelief.

"There are occasional Rokan who will break under the yoke and lose faith in the Good Queen," Burleigh replied. "But I have never heard of one who, disbelieving in his own gods, would on that basis assume those of others were false as well. It would here not be considered . . . well-mannered."

This final word broke through Augie's social density. He glanced up in surprise, his face covered in chicken grease, and actually managed to look offended at Lord Burleigh's suggestion his manners were wanting.

The sight was so absurd that Romul laughed out loud. Burleigh's eyes shot to him and remained there for a moment before a smile broke across his own lips. He then laughed as well, and several of his robed companions joined him. In a moment the whole table was rolling with laughter at the poor scientist. Even Augie, who was not quite sure why everyone was laughing at him, had the grace to at least blush and look contrite.

"I was clearly wrong about you, my dear fellow," said Burleigh to the inventor. "You certainly are no gentleman nor man of influence among the Garlandish. You are clearly what we would call an artisan of some sort. It is obvious to all of us that genteel manners should not be expected of you. Very well. Ask as you will. We will not hold it against you."

"Uh . . . thank you, I think," said Augie a bit sheepishly. "Well, I . . . uh . . . was really just trying to figure out what it means for this queen to have a son and for him to . . . uh . . . show up."

"You heard the anthem," said Burleigh patiently. "He will arise and lead our brothers in the east to liberty and establish the whole of Rokan as a land of promise to all Rokan everywhere. What more is there to tell?"

"But that's just it. What does it really *mean?* You don't really mean this queen has an actual son. You just mean a hero will grow up somewhere, right? It'll be as *if* he were a son but not really, right?"

"No," said Burleigh with the finality of a drumbeat. "He shall be her kindred son, of her blood, and heir to the throne of Rokan."

"But after all this time, how would you even . . . even . . ." Augie stumbled to a halt.

"We shall know him with certainty, for he shall know the Queen's true name."

Augie sat mouth open but at least with no food in it. He was at a loss. So was Romul.

"The Queen's true name is the most closely guarded secret of the Rokan," Burleigh went on. "Only I and the members of this council know it. And we are bound by many oaths never to repeat it. He shall know the Queen's true name, and by it we shall know the heir of Angish when he arises."

"So you want him to set you free from Garlandium, but you

all wear the albsignum." Augie gestured at the Primus's white hair. He'd eaten all he could now, and his attention was catching up with his inquisitive nature.

Burleigh shook his head. "A common myth. The albsignum was not the invention of the Garlandish. They only taught the Rokan to feel shame for it. It is a tradition our forefathers brought with them from Angish. All the nobility of Rokehaven wear it proudly. Likewise, many commoners and tradesmen also choose the albsignum as a statement of Rokan pride. Only in the east have they been deceived by the Garlandish lie."

Augie was clearly warming up for some sort of debate when a small voice cut in. It was Rose. "Excuse me, sir. Are we prisoners? Or can we leave when we want?"

Burleigh looked surprised. "Young lady, we have only brought you here as a display of courtesy, a welcome to our fair city. It is our custom to embrace all who brave the pass and survive. We wish you to know that you are free to remain with us as long as you wish."

But Eli wanted clarification. "So we're free to go?"

"Of course." Burleigh still wore a look of shocked consternation as if the idea of preventing her had never occurred to him.

"*All* of us?" Eli asked like someone debating a dwarf over the details of a promise.

"Yes."

"Even her?" Eli pointed at Murgen.

"Of course," said Burleigh with a laugh. "The longaevi are not unknown to us. Although it has been awhile since we have been in the presence of an undini, they are as welcome here as the dwarves, who used to trade goods with us in our grandcestors' days. They are not common or well-known among us now, but they are welcome so long as they come in peace."

"Better than the Azhwana," mumbled Anna.

"We are not often compared to our northern neighbors. But

yes, you would find us more accommodating than those with whom the Garlandish are at perpetual war."

"Thank you," said Eli tentatively, more to the travelers than to the Rokan lords, "'cause we do need to be moving along if we're going to . . ." She made a tapping gesture on her wrist to her sisters but then paused and addressed Burleigh again. "Oh, um, can you tell us what the White Rocks of Rokehaven are? Because we were, uh, told to make sure we saw them."

The Primus's eyebrows rose. "Well, strange must be the person who spoke to you of those. I am surprised to hear that an easterling knew of them."

"Yeah, strange is a good word for—" began Romul, but the vicious look Eli turned on him took the words out of him.

The Primus waited, but realizing she was not going to reveal any more, he continued. "Yes, well. The White Rocks mark the place where the Rokan entered Errus from the Queen's own country. They stand as a reminder to us all that Errus is not our first home. We are still Angish in our hearts. We are not of this world but merely sojourners."

"Can we see them?" asked Eli.

"By all means. In fact, even if you had not asked, it would have been the first place I would have recommended my young brother visit." He cast a sidelong glance at Romul. "Homecomers often find it a stirring way to reconnect with their true selves."

This comment about "true selves" reignited within Romul his previous fire. "Wait!" he cried. "Before that, there's someone I got to see! The dog told us about the sick woman who came over the mountain. I have to see her right away!"

At this, all the robed persons set their utensils down in surprise and looked hard at Romul. He could feel the single unspoken question boring into him. But again, it was Lord Burleigh who voiced it. "And what pray might you have to do with her?"

"Well, I think . . . she's . . . uh . . . my stepmom."

Chapter 40

The others stood silent behind Romul. Through the open door before him was a room shrouded in darkness, like the mouth of a cave. Beyond the frame lay the woman who'd been found near death in the snows of the lower foothills of the Aracadian Mountains. They'd been told she'd made her way over the mountains on foot without help of pack, beast, or guide. This alone was remarkable, but it was her story, given in delirious and broken syllables, that had captured the imagination of the city. She sought the boy who was both her son and not her son—the boy named Romul. With Romul's confession, the council had immediately put two guards at their disposal to escort them to the sick house.

Now Romul stood on the threshold with a nauseating mixture of fear and anticipation. From everything he'd been told, there was only one person this could be—Leaserae, his stepmom. He stared at this shadow, stretching passively out in front of him, merging with the gloom of the odious room.

"Do you . . . uh . . . want us to come in with you?" said Augie softly in his ear. Romul's head moved only an inch in response, but his meaning was clear. "Well, then, we'll wait here for you. Just call if you need us." Romul felt rather than heard them withdraw to a respectful distance.

He was alone now—alone to face his past. Everything had come back to this woman. It seemed ridiculous to him now that he'd traipsed all over creation seeking answers, only to end up back at this woman's bedside full of the same questions that had made him leave.

He took a deep breath and stepped into the room.

He stopped and sniffed. The dimness blinded him, and a strange and astringent odor assaulted his nostrils. A little way off in the gloomy dark, he heard a moan and a sob. Something in his throat went very hard as something in his gut went very soft. He took another step.

A flash of white like a diving gull sprang at him out of the darkness.

"What do you think you're doing in here!" came the—well, not a question. It was an implicit order to leave. A rotund nurse halted right in front of him like a wall, her hands spread out upon the wideness of her hips.

"I'm . . . I'm . . ."

"I don't care if you're the Koning of Azhwana himself. This is not the place for a little boy, and by Angish, it is not the time. That poor wight hasn't but a hair's hold on life, and I'll not have her disturbed under—"

"I'm Romul." It was all he could muster, but it was enough.

The corpulent nurse threw her hands over her mouth and uttered a muffled scream as if meeting one newly returned from the dead. She began muttering and rocking from side to side.

"Oh, oh, oh, the poor dear. It'll be the end of her to be sure, it will. Oh, oh, oh." But after a moment of furious wringing of her meaty hands on her white apron, she subsided, and her training took control once again. "Well, it can't be helped, I suppose. It's what drove the poor thing to do it. It'd be worse for her soul to die not knowing. Very well."

She grabbed Romul's hand, dragged him into the gloom, and stood him at the foot of a bed in which lay, so far as Romul could tell, only a pile of blankets and bandages.

"Dearie," cooed the nurse in a voice meant to be gentle but was actually shrill enough to make a dog yelp. "Dearie, you need to wake this last time for you to see what I've found."

The bedsheets stirred, and a hand rose up from the pile, accompanied by another groan. Romul nearly cried out. The hand was a mass of white bandages, but clearly several fingers were missing.

The creature moaned, returning to miserable consciousness. "Oh, the wretched agony!" She coughed. "Dead, he's dead. Born still, I told her . . ."

"Now, now, dearie," soothed the abundant nurse. "No need to start all that up again. It's good news this time. Here, let me help you up, and you'll see the nice surprise we have for you."

The only response was another sob, another cough, and an indistinct tearful muttering, but the ponderous nurse heaved the bird-like figure to a sitting position and stuffed several pillows behind it. Even in the semidarkness, Romul could see the bloated cheeks, the blackened nose.

The creature was now fully awake, mumbling something about pain in her feet, to which the nurse babbled on distractedly as she arranged the pillows. "Now, now. Explained that already, dear. Your feet can't hurt, remember, as they're not there no more. The frost got 'em. It's just the ghost-pain, and so you just decide to not feel it anymore, and see if it don't—" But suddenly the patient gave a great start and a cry.

Romul's eyes shot up. He'd been staring at the bedclothes where her feet should have been. He locked eyes with the woman.

"It's . . . it's you," she croaked in a voice he both knew and hardly recognized.

"Yes, yes, you see him now," crooned the oblivious nurse. "Now I'll just step into the other room and let you have a nice chat. It'll do you a world of good. And I suppose someone ought to be told something about it." She flounced away.

The wreckage of Leaserae fell back into the pillows and stared unblinking at Romul. "So I was right. You did come here."

Romul dropped his eyes and said nothing. He hadn't the heart to tell her he'd actually gone in the opposite direction and that her suffering had been without purpose. What drew his eyes back to the shattered form was the sound of weeping.

Great tears rolled down the puffy cheeks, and the mouth was moving awkwardly as she tried to speak. "I . . . I hoped to die in peace here in Rokan, my eyes now opened to the truth of it. How's come no one ever told us how beautiful it were here? If I'd knowed, I'd have never—" Her voice broke, and she lifted a bandaged hand to wipe the tears. "But one thing was left to me—I had to find you. I had to say . . . to tell you—" Here a coughing fit took her, and she could not continue.

The hard thing in Romul's throat, which had begun to subside, now reformed. He couldn't speak, but he felt he had to say something. His mouth worked awkwardly, trying to form sounds. He eventually got out two short words. "My . . . mom?"

The woman had been gradually recovering from the hacking, but the two words produced an immediate effect. She began to wail and moan and beat the bandaged stumps of her hands against the bedclothes. "Oh, the loss! Oh, the separation. I wish I'd never set eyes upon the poor creature for what I done to her. Oh, sweet Merris! Forgive me! Oh, sweet Merris, preserve a miserable wretch."

Romul was taken by a flood of diverse thoughts and emotions. Part of his mind was enraged by the confession that this broken thing had done *something* to his mother. But just as shocking was her plea for forgiveness made to the Garlandish goddess, rather than the Queen of Angish. It felt a little blasphemous to hear a Rokan woman using her final breaths to beg forgiveness of the foreign deity.

The idiotic wailing was enough to bring her bulging caregiver waddling back with cries of "Oh, oh, oh, you've upset the dear, you have!" She shoved Romul back out of the way—or perhaps she was merely making room for her large frame to pass by. She grabbed at her patient's shoulders, cooing and shushing her, but without effect. Leaserae continued to wail in ever-increasing volume and incoherence.

"Dead, I told her! Born still, I said. I was the midwife, I was. Let go of me, you great lump!" This last was aimed at the burly nurse, whose calming words were at odds with her increasingly forceful attempts to hold the woman still. "I must confess, I must . . . You must let me confess!" the patient screamed. "I took 'im, I did! Stole 'im, I did. To sell, but the wicked man wouldn't take them both. 'Twas the first time he wouldn't take a child off my hands! Curse him. Curse the Garlandish devil that he were!"

Suddenly, at the very peak of her rant, she burst into another coughing fit, and red fluid bubbled from her mouth. Romul's breath caught in his throat as she collapsed back onto the pillows, straining to look at him out of watery eyes.

The nurse continued to prattle on in this final calm, but she was only background noise now. Romul and Leaserae held each other's gaze as she whispered, "So I raised you, I did. I raised you . . . as me own . . . me dear, dear Romul, me . . . me own son." The lids closed over the filmy eyes, the hands fell to the sheets, and she was still.

"Well," said the nurse heavily, "that is the end of it, it is. May the good Queen carry her soul to Angish in peace. Amen."

In that moment Romul discovered the awful absurdity of life. He had run away in search of his real mother. Though he still hadn't found her, now, with a terrible clarity, he saw that here in this deathbed lay the only mother he'd ever known. But this time, it was she who had left him.

It was the most alone he'd ever felt in his short life.

Chapter 41

"She could've been wrong about your mom," said Eli sympathetically. "I mean, the bodacha said she wasn't dead."

"What would she know, the batty old—" began Romul before Augie cut him off.

"I can't speak to the hows of it all, but plenty of what she said did happen. I mean, I'm no fool, but . . ." He smiled broadly at Romul.

Romul's brief summary of the event had actually taken awhile to get out because he was determined not to break down in front of the others. He'd kept getting choked up and having to collect himself. Merris was shining almost straight down on them now as they sat on the steps of the sick house. The city was wide awake around them, but the street on which they were camped was close and not well trafficked, so they felt more privacy than they actually had.

"What did she mean she stole you *both*?" asked Anna. "Didn't the bodacha say something like that, too, which I guess would mean . . . you have a brother or sister?" She said these last words in the tone of one horrified by the possibility.

Romul was about to be offended by this when the real gravity of it settled onto him. Was it possible that he was not only looking for his mother but a sibling as well? Once again his world inverted. Some part of him had envied the relationship between the three girls, how they belonged to one another, even when they fought. Could it be that he, too, had someone with whom he could share such things?

One of their escorting soldiers approached tentatively. "Excuse me, friends, but we're under orders to see you to the White Rocks and then return to our posts. Are you ready to go?" He was perfectly polite, but the subtext was clear—the soldiers wanted to leave.

"Yeah, we can go." Romul thumbed in the direction of the sick room. "Nothing left for me in there."

The soldiers led them through the streets. The others pointed and talked excitedly about the public fountains, the street musicians, the stunning blues and purples that adorned all the people and the buildings. Rokehaven seemed to be a haven to all sorts of beauty, but Romul was only half paying attention to the splendors around him. His mind chewed relentlessly on what he'd just learned. The realization that he had not just a lone relative but potentially a "family" had caused him to reevaluate his identity . . . again.

He'd thought of being Rokan as only an idea—being part of a "race"—but might it be something closer? Something he actually shared with people as immediate as a family? His mother would be Rokan; his brother or sister would be Rokan. This was something they would share. This notion, combined with what he now knew of his Rokan heritage, was working a final change in him. He was still troubled by what the Old One had said about his *not* being Rokan, but even the bodacha had admitted the salamander could be wrong, and almost everyone else had seen his Rokan identity immediately.

He hardly noticed that the group had come to a stop till Eli's elevated voice began yammering. He looked up to discover that they were standing at the gates of a city garden. A high stone wall extended away to right and left, and before them stood large iron gates, standing open and giving access to green acres of grass and fruit trees. Through the trees came glimpses of some hazy white-opaque something towering over them. Romul assumed this was the White Rocks, but he couldn't see anything clearly through the thick branches.

Eli, however, was gesturing wildly at the arched sign that extended over the gates and nearly shouting at the two soldiers. "What does it mean? Where does it come from? How did it get here?" Romul could see iron letters set in the sign, but not being able to read, they meant nothing to him.

The soldiers were looking at each other in confusion, and Eli would have continued to repeat her babbling questions had Anna not cut her off with a "Will you shut up and let them answer!"

"Well," said the first soldier in a slow drawl that had Eli biting her tongue and dancing on her tiptoes with impatience. "It's just an old word for farewell. I don't know where it comes from."

"Ancient Angish, I think," said the other. "Just a formal way of saying goodbye, usually used before a long trip or a great change of circumstance."

"But I recognize the word!" Eli was unreasonably bugged by it. "I just can't think where from!" She pointed at the sign again and said slowly, "*Croatoan*. I've seen it before."

Romul now made his own sound of impatient disgust. "Oh, that? Geez, only old people say that!" He'd heard it used many times, but the soldier was right. It was just an old-fashioned word. No young person would use it now. Eli had probably heard someone use it in Farwell.

"Well," drawled the soldier again, "we must be away to the council chambers. Just follow the path straight in, and you'll meet the White Rocks, sure enough."

"Can't miss them," said the other as they turned to leave.

Now it was Eli's turn to be sullen as they took the stone path into the garden. She lagged behind with her head in her hands, muttering. Romul ignored her. What was coming into view was far more interesting. The trees had suddenly ended to reveal a wide green lawn. The stone walk also ended here.

There in the middle of the field stood two huge white columns of rocks. Gigantic rocks, they were—like great, white eyeteeth jutting up out of the world as tall as a giant.

Anna was reading a small placard erected at the edge of the path. *"Here our forefathers first set foot in Errus, coming at the Queen's bidding from their own place, bearing into this new world the testimony of her gracious majesty. Semper Eadem."*

Rose was holding up her little compass ball toward the stones. "Yup, that's the place. Should be right over there."

Romul now saw that cut into each of the two great stones were letters a foot high and were the same ones on the sign at the gates. Suddenly they heard Eli wail behind them.

"O . . . M . . . G!" She had fallen to her knees. "That's it! *Croatoan.* I know where it's from. It's . . . it's . . . just impossible!" The group all looked at her as if she'd lost her mind. For her part, she was staring back at them, nodding her head and waving her hands as if to say, *Don't you see? It's so obvious!*

No one saw. No one thought it obvious.

"I know where you came from," she said to Romul.

Now she had his full attention. "Me?"

"No, all of you. The whole Rokan people . . . you . . . you latecomers!" This was actually less interesting to Romul, but still important enough to hold his attention.

Eli was on her feet again, rushing forward, pointing at the words carved into the rocks.

"*Cro-a-toan.* It's not a farewell, or not originally. It's the name of an American Indian tribe." She turned to her sisters for support. They stared blankly at her. "Come on! Don't either of you pay attention? Remember the field trip? Geez, it's so obvious." Then she went rigid herself with another epiphany. "Rokan? Rokan? Doesn't that sound a little like . . . Roanoke?"

Suddenly Anna went pale. "You don't mean . . ."

Eli was nodding in ecstatic satisfaction. "Yeah. After hundreds of years of forgetting what it meant, it gets corrupted or garbled into *Rokan*! And *Croatoan*—"

Anna, now fully on the same page, cut her off. "*Croatoan* was the word carved into the tree at the settlement!"

"Okay, okay, enough!" cried Augie. "I can't take it. Start making some sense, or I'm going to die of impatience!"

Eli went into lecture mode. "See, in our world, we live at a place called Roanoke Island, where hundreds of years ago the English set up this colony . . . like one of the first on the New Wor—" She stalled again and gawked at Anna.

This time Anna was with her before she said it. "Angish . . . English! Do you think . . ."

Eli put her finger on her nose like a dwarf imparting a secret. "It was an *English* colony, and they all vanished without a trace. Except for one word carved into a tree, *Croatoan*, which was the name of a local Indian tribe."

"It was the name of that island, too," added Anna. "You remember? It's Hatteras Island now."

"That's right!" Eli plowed on. "Some say the word was carved into the tree because the Indians attacked the colony. Or maybe they all relocated to the other island. But nobody knows to this day what happened to them."

"Except us." It was just a whisper, but Rose's two words caused Eli and Anna to go mute with wonder.

The moment of silence brought Augie into the fray. "Hold on a minute. Are you saying the Rokan originally came from your world?"

"Well, yeah! But then, all you Garlandians did, too, just like a zillion years before they did," said Anna dismissively.

"What? What do you mean?"

Romul was having trouble following it all, and when Eli launched into another story about some guy named Stemmathus leading a host of people on a sea voyage from which they never returned, he totally lost the thread of the conversation. But it meant something to Augie, for he had to sit down on the grass and rub his temples. He was muttering something that sounded like "*Opsiercom* . . . latecomers . . . of course. And we're just early comers, but both from the same world. It makes sense out of so much..."

Murgen knelt next to Augie and took his hand. All were quiet as they watched the only Garlandian in the group come to grips with the facts of his own ancestral origins. Even the sounds of the city were muted there in the garden.

After several minutes, Augie looked up at Romul with a face filled with many conflicting thoughts. He rose to his knees before Romul so he could look him in the eye. It was such a penetrating look that it made Romul really uncomfortable, but he couldn't pull his gaze away.

"Romul, I've always thought the treatment of the Rokan back home was wrong. You know that, right?" He waited for Romul to nod vaguely before continuing. "But I have only just begun to realize that, in my heart, I did always think of the Rokan as less . . . well . . . relevant. That is, when I thought about them at all. I didn't realize till this minute how, deep inside me, I just assumed that even though Garlandians were wrong to do what they did, they were still . . . um . . . better somehow. Even though I never really thought it consciously, I guess I assumed that the Rokan were just less well adapted or intelligent or hard working than we were. And that was the reason they were treated so poorly . . . like it was their own fault somehow."

Romul was starting to be annoyed by the speech and would've pulled away, but Augie grabbed his arms and held him as he continued. "But being here . . . I mean, looking around me and seeing this city that could rival Garlandvale itself . . . It's like I was lied to also, by my own people. And if what Eli said is truth, that my people come from the same place, then in the end, we're like cousins . . . estranged brothers, even. I should have seen it sooner, but I was wrong to just go about my life assuming the way we all treated you was someone else's problem. Well, no more!" He grabbed Romul and hugged him.

Romul stood paralyzed in the embrace. After all they'd been through—shipwreck, fire, prison, hunger, and weariness—this was to him the strangest thing he'd yet encountered: a Garlandian, who'd never actually done him any personal wrong, saying he was sorry for *not* doing something for him or his people. And in this moment, he could almost see Augie's point. Distant cousins? Estranged brothers? Maybe his idea of family was still too small.

Chapter 42

They stood between the White Rocks staring at a vision of another world—a very dull world by the looks of it. It featured a dim view of a set of shelves stacked with canned goods. The girls said the window must be showing the pantry of the kitchen—meaning, this is where they would find themselves when they stepped through it. Romul thought it must be a shop or something because he'd never seen that much food on the shelves of anybody's home.

This "window," as the girls called it, was how they'd come into Errus and the way they intended to leave. Now a heated argument was taking place between Eli and Anna about the nature of their mission.

"And if we don't leave now, we're going to have some serious explaining to do to Naggie or even Dad. We're already later than we—"

"Baloney!" cried Anna. "I don't care how late we're going to be. We haven't finished the mission. Cholerish said we had to find out about the legate, and the emissaries, and . . . and we haven't seen a single fairy or anything else from . . . uh . . ." Her eyes rolled upward in frustrated concentration.

"Avonia," said Rose.

"Whoever! And we hardly got any answers out of the ones we did talk to."

"Plus," added Augie, "you would have very little luck finding a sylph anyway. They're not very communal like the dwarves and mermaids. So you'd almost have to just happen across one. Even then, I don't think sylphs have quite the same racial memory as other longaevi, so I don't know how much one could tell you."

"I think Finch knew things," offered Rose in a quiet voice that everyone ignored.

"But Ylfig has made up for all that." Eli held up the tattered collection of pages the dwarf had given her. "The answers to the dragon and the prophecies have got to be in here."

"That's my point! Whinsom and Cholerish are the only ones who'll know what all that means. You're not expecting them to just trot over the mountains to read it, are you? *We* have to take it back to them."

"*We* can't! We're out of time."

"Well, somebody's got to!"

Romul, who'd been ignoring the argument in his contemplation of a world filled with canned goods on pantry shelves, realized everyone had gone silent. He turned—and they were all looking at him. Augie had fixed upon him a penetrating look, nodding slightly as if he was agreeing to something Romul was supposed to understand. Romul was trying not to think about what that nod might mean, but his mind already knew and shouted at him. *You went all the way to Halighyll, and then they made you march all the way back to Farwell. Now you've come all the way to Rokehaven, and they want you to . . . No, no, for love of Angish, no!*

He already knew how it would end. He looked up at the shining spires of Rokehaven and felt them slipping through his fingers. He had, in a sense he didn't even understand, finally come home, and before he'd been there even a single day, he was being asked to leave.

He looked at the others, hoping for some support for his refusal. He found none. Rose was looking at him with sad blue eyes as if she alone understood what he was thinking. She probably did. The revelation that she, too, had lost her mother and her home was still searching for its final meaning within him. He saw Murgen, hanging devotedly on Augie's arm, a mermaid who'd left her own people for love of a crazy, gangly, hungry scientist. Was he really being asked to do anything the others hadn't already done?

It was unfair, sure, but he was also realizing something he hadn't before. Life was unfair, not just to him but to everyone. Maybe sooner or later everybody was asked to give themselves up for the sake of something else? Maybe that sort of unfairness just came with being alive.

The weight of these thoughts became oppressive. He shuffled his feet. That familiar hard sour lump had formed in his throat, and despite the late morning chill, he felt moisture on his forehead.

"Romul?" said Eli softly.

Here it came. Whatever came next—whatever plea Eli made at this point—Romul never heard it. For his mind was filled with the words of that wretched bodacha about his mother. *"Ye must cross the mountains three times to find her."* His mind roared with the implications. He'd crossed the mountains once to get to Roke-haven. Now he was being asked to go back to Halighyll. That would be twice. Would he then have to cross them a third time? Did that mean he would indeed come back to this place? Perhaps to discover his mother was here after all? He realized too late that he was nodding and that the girls were beaming at him.

Augie clapped him on the back. "That's it, little brother! Of course you'll take the book back to Halighyll. But don't fret—I'm going with you. Maybe not all the way to Halighyll, but at least so far as Umbra." He looked at Murgen, who nodded and smiled as radiantly as Merris herself.

Romul sighed. "Well, I suppose I have to just enjoy what's right in front of me. No telling what's coming tomorrow."

"But for us it's goodbye," said Rose after a moment's silence. This brought everyone's attention back to the window before them.

"Ugh," mumbled Anna. "I'm never ready for it when it comes. It's like last time. It just gets interesting, and then it's time to leave."

"Well, at least it's not for good." Rose held up the compass.

"Yeah, I hope not," Romul heard himself say as he looked at the sisters. He was surprised to realize he really meant it. He hoped they would come back.

"I just wish I had time to make a copy of this," moaned Eli, clutching Ylfig's book.

Anna gently pried the volume from her hands. "No reason to delay the inevitable. Here you go, messenger boy." She handed the tattered collection of pages to Romul. He took it, realizing that it might be the first book he'd ever actually held, and a sudden longing to be able to read it—to read anything—came over him. He determined to ask Augie to teach him.

Augie put hands on Romul's shoulders. "Don't worry, ladies. We'll see it safely to Halighyll. I promise."

With that and a final round of hugs, the girls turned their backs to Romul, Augie, and Murgen, joined hands, and stepped over the threshold of the window, which faded the moment they were through.

The three left behind stood looking at the empty space in silence for several minutes before Murgen took Romul's and Augie's hands and led them away.

As they passed back into the city, Augie observed, "Well, look at us. A Rokan, a Garlandian, and a longaevi all holding hands. If this is possible, then anything is."

Romul thought that sounded just about right.

Epilogue

Arise now, you who've traveled far,
Fought e're long for your survival.
Come, discover who you are.
We've waited long for your arrival.

Learn the story of your race,
Not from moldy books on shelves,
But through our kiss and our embrace.
For when we're loved, we become ourselves.

> FRANKO RAZHAMANÌAH,
> from "Homecoming" in *Songs from
> the Rokan Highlands.*

∽

"You know," said Romul, grunting as he tied off the rucksack, "that old salamander in Farwell wasn't sure I was even Rokan."

Augie looked at him with new interest. "What did he think you were?"

Romul didn't answer right away. This was the first moment he'd had to really appreciate the beauty of Rokehaven, even as they were packing up to go. The council had expressed some surprise at their decision to head back east. Few Rokan who "came home" ever wanted to leave again. But Augie's story of scientific interests among longaevi, of which Murgen was a potent testimonial, was sufficient explanation for their departure.

Because their fellow Rokan Romul would be going along, the council had offered to fund and equip their expedition. So they now had a hired pair of willing horses, clothes, blankets, maps, and loads of food—an incredible quantity of food. Had the council not actually seen Augie's appetite in action, they might have thought it over-prepared. Even so, it would be a long journey for a young boy, a crazy inventor, and a mermaid. They could not take the mountain pass and would need to travel far north to Whitshire, to the lower pass where the Aracadians descended to meet the Flats of Kavue. Romul hoped that would still qualify as "crossing the mountains."

They now sat in the street, packing supplies, chatting with the horses, and enjoying the sun. Romul thought about all the revelations he'd had on the journey. Despite them, he didn't know much more than when he'd set out. In fact, he knew less. He wasn't sure whether his mother was alive or long dead. He didn't know whether he did or did not have a brother or sister. He wasn't even sure whether he was Rokan. Topping all, he understood just enough about the strange relics he and Anna carried to know how little he knew about them.

Yet in the face of all these questions, he felt like he knew himself better than he ever had. He felt a sort of inner peace that defied explanation. He knew little of what he was, but he knew what he wasn't. He was no longer a lost, scared, and angry little boy. He fingered the firebrand in his pocket. It warmed to his touch, in sympathy with his newfound resolution. He looked at the Aracadian peaks that, for the first time in his life, filled the eastern instead of the western horizon.

"It doesn't matter what the lizard thinks. I don't know what I was born, but I *am* Rokan . . . in here, where it counts." He tapped his chest as he stood up, shouldering the pack.

Now it was Augie's turn to reflect. "I believe you are. And good for you." He patted Romul on the shoulder as Murgen gave him a hug.

Romul looked about the wide street of the city, at its prosperity and beauty, and sighed. "Yeah, it's what *I* choose to be." His eye fell on a shop across the street. "Augie, what's that sign say?" He thought he more or less knew but wanted to be sure. Another resolution was forming in his heart.

Augie squinted. "It says, *Jakob Finigan, Best Hair-Whiter in Town.*"

Yup, that settled it. "Before we go, I got something I need to do." Romul passed his hand through his ragged brown hair as he walked to the door of the whiter's shop and went in.

Cast of Characters

Romul: *The Lost Guide*

Homeless, parentless, hopeless, the eight year old orphan Romul is looking for the mother he's never known. Stolen at birth and raised callously, he's pragmatic and street-wise. He resists at every turn being responsible for the Hoover sisters in their quest, at least till he realizes that, in the end, everyone's looking for the same thing—a place called home.

The Hoover Sisters: *The Perplexing Trio*

Eli (EL-ee), Anna, and Rose—three sisters from another world—become Romul's charges on their mission to speak to the Old One in Farwell. Bookish, self-reliant, and clueless respectively, they are a mystery to Romul, but swiftly become the closest thing he's ever had to family, whether he wants them to be or not.

Brother Cholerish: *The Irascible Ascetic*

One of the last priests of the old monotheism, Cholerish is cantankerous but wise. He has spent his years contemplating the ancient prophecy carved into the walls under the temple in Halighyll. He now knows enough to know they'll need help with what's coming—lots of it.

Augustus Lambient: *The Insatiable Genius*

Son of his more illustrious father Ambrosius Lambient of the famous SkyCricket expedition, Augie struggles to find his place as an inventor, scientist, and man in his own right. Used to playing the craven idiot for his own safety, he struggles to grow into the responsibilities of being a friend, a leader, and even a suitor.

Murgen the Mermaid: *The Helpless Heroine*
Sharing a strange bond with the screwball scientist Augie, she leaves her people's waters to join the girls' quest and remain near the inventor's side. She is a helpless figure literally out of her element, till things get tough. Then she may show herself strongest of them all.

The Old One: *The Rapacious Savant*
The Old One is an ancient fire salamander, who dwells in the foundry fires of Farwell, the industrial center of Garlandium. Wise, cunning, and predatory, he'll tell you the truth so far as he's willing, but it may not matter as his next intention is to make a meal of you.

Ylfig: *The Mad Poser*
Crazy old Ylfig, the dwarf. He's shown no respect by the rest of his community, nor does he seem to care. After all, he's raving. Yet there's more to the addlepated dwarf than he's willing to let on.

Sonji and Franko Razhamaniah: *The Sibling Narrators*
A sister and brother—historian and poet respectively—who each take their turn at interpreting these events from some future point. They often trade barbs in their writing because they disagree over the best way to understand what is for them a mysterious past.

About the Author

Gordon Greenhill was a university professor for many years before accidently writing his first piece of fiction. He was surprised to discover that people enjoyed it, so he kept going. Now he's a professional audiobook narrator in addition to his real day job—husband and father of four wonderful kids, who inspired him to create the Relics of Errus series. He still speaks and writes in the academic world, but as fantasy readers know, it's just not the same.

gordongreenhill.com
relicsoferrus.com
relicoferrus@gmail.com
facebook.com/relicsoferrus

The Hoover Sisters return to Errus.

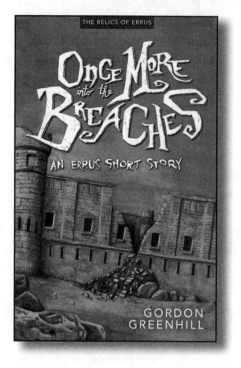

Once More into the Breaches presents an alternate opening to
The Relics of Errus, volume 2: *Plight of the Rokan Boy.*

Eli, Anna, and Rose again step through the portal in their North
Carolina mansion home and find themselves in Errus. This time
they arrive in the desert. Can they find their way to civilization
before heat, thirst, and ravening desert longaevi find them?

EBOOK 978-0-9996795-5-5

*Available now as ebook and audiobook
only at Amazon and Audible.*